"Touch me," Idess whispered.
"No holding back anymore."

For a long, desperate moment, Lore did nothing. And then he cupped her cheek, the pressure so feather-light she barely felt it.

"I've never—" His voice cracked, and he cleared his throat. "I've never felt a woman like this."

"I've never been touched like this." It was an admission she shouldn't have made, but right now she couldn't care.

His heated gaze snapped up to capture hers, and that fast, the smolder was over and the flames burst out of control. In a mighty surge, he gripped her shoulders and backed her up against the side of the building.

He nuzzled her throat, nipping and kissing. "Now," he said against her skin. "I'm going to have you now."

"Ione knows how to make your heart race."
—CHEYENNE MCCRAY, *New York Times* **best-selling author of *Dark Magic***

Please turn this page for more praise for Larissa Ione . . .

MORE PRAISE FOR LARISSA IONE

PASSION UNLEASHED

"4½ Stars! The third book in Ione's supercharged Demonica series ignites on the first page and never looks back. . . . Adventure, action, and danger leap off every page. The best of the series to date!"
—*Romantic Times BOOKreviews Magazine*

"Fast-paced from the onset and never slows down until the exhilarating climax. . . . Readers will be enthralled by the action and the charmed lead couple."
—*Midwest Book Reviews*

"Larissa Ione pulls no punches. . . . The love scenes are scorching hot and grab at your heart with their emotional intensity. Dark moments are written with just the right touch of hope that leaves the reader begging for a happy ending. I couldn't have loved *Passion Unleashed* more and hated for it to end. Raw, gritty, and tremendously passionate. . . . It was awesome!"
—**RomanceJunkies.com**

"Serena and Wraith are good characters, layered and multi-faceted . . . Ms. Ione has created a world unique to the genre. Huge kudos for accomplishing with style what few authors can do. Bring on book four."
—**LikesBooks.com**

"5 Stars! Larissa has outdone herself with the story of Wraith. I was pulled into this story from the first page. The action is intense and nonstop. I was engrossed and enthralled . . . and highly recommend adding this series to your library."
—**BittenByBooks.com**

"Each book has gotten better . . . *Passion Unleashed* is the best book in the series." —**TheBookBinge.com**

"Awesome. . . . Everyone loves a bad boy and Wraith is *so* the poster bad boy. Another great novel . . . Ione gives us a great spin on the relationship between her 'Buffys' and the demons of the world, along with a good apocalypse."
  —**LiteraryEscapism.com**

"Heart-pounding . . . outstandingly superb . . . an adventure-filled romance where passion and danger continuously mount. . . . A paranormal story by Larissa Ione never disappoints readers, as the plot and characters are truly unforgettable. Her Demonica series only becomes more engrossing with each book. With genuine feelings being intensely depicted by the well-portrayed characters on every page of *Passion Unleashed*, there is never an instant when I was not held spellbound. . . . The sexual relationship between Wraith and Serena is particularly sensual and overflowing with tension." —**SingleTitles.com**

"A delightful paranormal romance with strong world-building and a suspenseful plot. *Passion Unleashed* will captivate readers. . . . The seducer is about to be seduced, and fans won't be disappointed."
  —**DarqueReviews.com**

"Plenty of steamy love scenes . . . nicely balanced with a high-octane plot . . . Larissa Ione is fast becoming a master at telling dark, edgy, and highly complex paranormal tales."
  —**BookLoons.com**

more . . .

"Absolutely fabulous! I have thoroughly enjoyed all three Demonica novels, but this one is by far my favorite. Wraith is the ultimate bad boy who is just begging for salvation and Serena is his perfect complement. Ms. Ione will have paranormal fans begging for more."

—TheRomanceReadersConnection.com

DESIRE UNCHAINED

"4 Stars! Rising star Ione is back in this latest Demonica novel . . . Ione has a true gift for imbuing her characters with dark-edged passion . . . thrilling action and treacherous vengeance . . . a top-notch read."

—*Romantic Times BOOKreviews Magazine*

"A fabulous tale. . . . The story line is fast-paced from the opening sequence . . . fans will relish a visit to the Ione realm."

—*Midwest Book Review*

"Warning! Read at your own risk. Highly addictive. . . . Rising star Larissa Ione takes her already well-crafted and unique demon world to new heights. The sex is darker, hotter, wickeder, and wonderfully erotic; the vengeful enemy is diabolical, and the story line is unparalleled. Ione is a master at creating tortured, sexy bad boys who are full of flaws and make you melt . . . *Desire Unchained* may only be book two in her Demonica series, but I'm completely head-over-heels in love. I have never been so enthralled with a series before. With the end of each book, I'm left desperately wanting more."

—FreshFiction.com

"Imaginatively riveting. . . . Emotional intensity is the driving force behind every Larissa Ione book. Scenes may be packed with suspenseful peril or steamy passions or even quick humor and clever banter, yet it is the emotions behind the reactions of the characters that really grab the reader. There are a myriad of potent feelings displayed all throughout *Desire Unchained*, and each one is shown with believable realism . . . [and] will cause the reader to be profoundly affected, often on numerous levels at once." **—SingleTitles.com**

"Everything a paranormal romance lover could want . . . a raw, edgy, and enthralling read—Sure to scorch every inch of you. . . . Credit to Larissa Ione for an imaginative, dark world that haunts you as much as it intrigues you. "

—-BookPleasures.com

"I was completely captivated. . . . From the first moment I picked *Desire Unchained* up, I was glued to its pages. Ione gives us a unique twist . . . something a little different and fresh (and involving hot Demons)." **—LiteraryEscapism.com**

"Fascinating. . . . This book started fast and didn't slow down. I really enjoyed how Larissa continued to build the Demonica world." **—TheBookBinge.com**

"Five Stars! Recommended read. I have to say that I absolutely love this book. Larissa Ione has become one of my favorite authors, and I crave more of her books. The first book in her Demonica series was fantastic, and this one is even better . . . [Shade] is the perfect romance hero. . . . The whole world and all the other characters have taken a place in my heart . . . I wish I could go back and read *Desire Unchained* again for the first time. It was just that good."

—FallenAngelReviews.com

more . . .

PLEASURE UNBOUND

"Fast-paced . . . never slows down. . . . Romantic fantasy fans will appreciate the first Demonica tale."
—*Midwest Book Review*

"Intense, engrossing, and titillating, *Pleasure Unbound* is a story not to be missed. I can't wait for the next story."
—RRTErotic.com

"Ione has . . . created a very imaginative demonic tapestry as well as rich, multilayered characterizations . . . a heady blend that I look forward to revisiting in her next installment."
—BookLoons.com

"Ione writes a passionate tale. She is able to blend two different worlds together seamlessly."
—NightOwlRomance.com

"What a great read! Very sexy . . . Tayla is an incredible heroine and the conflict and sexual attraction between her and Eidolon just burns on the page."
—JOELY SUE BURKHART, author of *Beautiful Death*

"4½ Stars! Wow, wow, wow! This is one hot demon love story! The pages are riddled with action, sex, and danger. The intensity is palpable. I was moved by this love story and will think about it for some time."
—TheRomanceReadersConnection.com

"Sexy, dark, and emotion-filled. . . . Took me on a rip-roaring ride through every emotion I have. . . . Go out and buy a copy today." **—JoyfullyReviewed.com**

ALSO BY LARISSA IONE

Passion Unleashed
Desire Unchained
Pleasure Unbound

ECSTASY UNVEILED

A *Demonica* NOVEL

LARISSA IONE

FOREVER

NEW YORK   BOSTON

This book is a work of fiction. Names, characters, places, and incidents are the product of the author's imagination or are used fictitiously. Any resemblance to actual events, locales, or persons, living or dead, is coincidental.

Cover design by Claire Brown
Book design by TexTech

Forever
Hachette Book Group
237 Park Avenue
New York, NY 10017
Visit our website at www.HachetteBookGroup.com.

Forever is an imprint of Grand Central Publishing. The Forever name and logo is a trademark of Hachette Book Group, Inc.

Printed in the United States of America

First Printing: February 2010

10 9 8 7 6 5 4 3 2 1

For my mom, who taught me to be strong, to believe I could be anything I want to be. I love you.

And for all my fellow military spouses out there—you handle so much while your other half is away, you deal with the moves, the functions, and the constant changes that put pressure on your families. Your sacrifices deserve recognition and thanks.

For all the members of LIST—you LISTEEZ are fabulous, and huge thanks especially to the women who made it happen—Lo, Cin, Ada, Olivia, Natasja, and Luna. You ladies rock!

Big nods go to Ayla and Ilona Fenton, Fatin Soufan, Valerie Tibbs, Kristin Manter, Charlotte Johnson, Maureen Klatte, Lea Franczak, Ing Cruz, Greta Wheeler, Joy Harris, Melissa Bradley, Hilda Oquendo, Lillie Applegarth…your support and friendship have been beyond amazing.

And for Mho, the demon sheep, because you just crack me up…

Acknowledgments

Writing this series has been a dream come true for me, and it didn't happen alone. Thank you to my agent, Irene Goodman, the entire staff at Hachette Book Group, and huge, special, mushy thanks to my editor, Amy Pierpont. You're a saint, Amy!

Glossary

The Aegis—Society of human warriors dedicated to protecting the world from evil. See: Guardians, Regent, Sigil.

Carceris—The jailers of the underworld. All demon species send representatives to serve terms in the Carceris. Carceris members are responsible for apprehending demons accused of violating demon law, and for acting as guards in the Carceris prisons.

Council—All demon species and breeds are governed by a Council that makes laws and metes out punishment for individual members of their species or breed.

Dresdiin—The demon equivalent of angels. See: Memitim.

Fakires—Derogatory term used by vampires to describe humans who either believe themselves to be real vampires or pretend to be vampires.

Guardians—Warriors for The Aegis, trained in combat techniques, weapons, magic. Upon induction into The

Aegis, all Guardians are presented with an enchanted piece of jewelry bearing the Aegis shield, which, among other things, allows for night vision and the ability to see through demon invisibility enchantment.

Harrowgate—Vertical portals, invisible to humans, which demons use to travel between locations on Earth and Sheoul.

Infadre—A female of any demon species who has been impregnated by a Seminus demon.

Maleconcieo—Highest level of ruling demon boards, served by a representative from each species Council. The U.N. of the demon world.

Marked Sentinel—Humans charmed by angels and tasked with protecting a vital artifact. Sentinels are immortal and immune to harm. Only angels (fallen included) can injure or kill a Sentinel. Their existence is a closely guarded secret.

Memitim—Earthbound angels assigned to protect Primori. Memitim remain earthbound until they complete their duties, at which time they Ascend, earning their wings and entry into Heaven. Also known to demons as dresdiin. See: Dresdiin, Primori.

Orgesu—A demon sex slave, often taken from breeds bred specifically for the purpose of providing sex.

Primori—Humans and demons whose lives are fated to affect the world in some crucial way.

Regent—Head(s) of local Aegis cells.

Renfield—Fictional character in Bram Stoker's *Dracula*. Also, derogatory term for any human who serves a vampire. A vampire groupie.

S'genesis—Final maturation cycle for Seminus demons. Occurs at one hundred years of age. A post-*s'genesis* male is capable of procreation and possesses the ability to shape-shift into the male of any demon species.

Sheoul—Demon realm. Located deep in the bowels of the earth, accessible only by Harrowgates.

Sheoul-gra—A holding tank for demon souls. The place where demon souls go until they can be reborn or kept in torturous limbo.

Sheoulic—Universal demon language spoken by all, though many species speak their own language.

Sigil—Board of twelve humans known as Elders, who serve as the supreme leaders of The Aegis. Based in Berlin, they oversee all Aegis cells worldwide.

Swans—Humans who act as blood or energy donors for vampires, either actual undead or *fakires*.

Ter'taceo—Demons who can pass as human, either because their species is naturally human in appearance, or because they can shapeshift into human form.

Therionidryo—Term a were-beast uses for a person he or she bit and turned into another were-beast.

Therionidrysi—Any survivor of a were-beast attack. Term used to clarify the relationship between the sire and his therionidryo.

Ufelskala—A scoring system for demons, based on their degree of evil. All supernatural creatures and evil humans can be categorized into the five Tiers, with the Fifth Tier composed of the worst of the wicked.

Classification of Demons, as listed by Baradoc, Umber demon, using the demon breed, Seminus, as an example:

Kingdom: Animalia
Class: Demon
Family: Sexual Demon
Genus: Terrestrial
Species: Incubus
Breed: Seminus

One

⌒

He who does not see the angels and devils in the beauty and malice of life will be far removed from knowledge, and his spirit will be empty of affection.

—Kahlil Gibran

Lore had always believed that when it came to sex, the more the merrier. Too bad for him that when "more" meant more than just himself, people tended to die.

So what the hell was he doing in bed with a curvy liquor store clerk he'd picked up while on his third tequila run in as many days?

Sure, technically, he wasn't in bed. He was standing at the foot of the human-looking demon's California King, pounding into her from behind as she kneeled on the mattress, moaning through her fourth orgasm.

Pressure built in his balls and his shaft throbbed with the need to blow, but no matter what he did, he couldn't ignite. He gripped her hips harder, thrust deeper. Faster.

Nothing.

He lifted her so her knees came off the bed, giving him absolute control as he ground against her with feverish gyrations.

Still nothing.

Sweat streamed down his face, and his lungs burned with the force of his panting breaths.

"Come on, baby," the female—he thought her name was April...or May...maybe June—cried. She bucked, consumed by yet another climax, and then dropped her head in exhaustion, her flaxen hair pooling on the black satin sheets.

She was pretty—not as pretty as Gem, but then, no one was. Lore shook the image of the Goth half-Soulshredder doctor out of his head, because she was in love with a human jerk named Kynan, and Lore hadn't truly had a shot with her anyway.

That he couldn't climax because he was worried about snuffing this mystery species demon chick was really fucking funny considering that he killed for money, with no qualms, no regrets, and there were definitely worse ways to go than death-by-orgasm.

But Gem seemed to have opened up a vein in him, one that ran with pansy-ass feelings instead of blood. And in truth, there was a reason he hadn't had sex in decades, even though his Seminus breeding gave him the overwhelming need to screw every female who crossed his path. Fortunately for him, his human side allowed him to handle those urges himself, unlike purebred Sems who had to have a female partner or die.

When Lore had female partners, *they* died.

With a frustrated roar, he tore himself away from AprilMayJune and fisted his cock in his gloved hand. His release was hard and fast...and, as expected, no more satisfying than if he'd been by himself. And now, with nothing to distract him, he couldn't ignore the handprint-shaped welt that burned on his chest.

Lore had to go. No more stalling. After three weeks of avoidance—mainly to piss off his boss—it was time to take his punishment like a man. Well, a half-man, half-incubus.

The female rolled over, watched him with drowsy eyes. He still wasn't sure why he'd fallen off the celibacy wagon for her, except maybe for the fact that she'd been in the right place, right time when he'd gotten yet another text from *Eidolon, M.D.* Christ, the guy just *had* to include the M.D. in his signature, as if the entire underworld didn't know what he was.

The reminder that his brother was a respected doctor who saved lives, while Lore was nothing but a low-life half-breed killer, had sent him into a destructive, downward spiral that involved a lot of alcohol and a proposition for AprilMayJune.

Still, he was eventually going to have to face Eidolon and his other brothers again, no matter what Lore had promised his sister, because he had a feeling that if his newfound brothers wanted to find him, they would. And they didn't seem like the types to respect space and privacy.

"I told you I'm not in season," AprilMayJune said, her voice sleepy with sexual satiation. "I can't get pregnant."

"Doesn't matter." He tucked himself back into his leather pants. "I'm sterile." At least, that was what one of the other brothers, Shade, had told him. Lore wasn't sure how he felt about that, but it was definitely for the best.

She sighed and fell back against the pillows. "Then why did you just cream all over my floor? And why are you still wearing that glove?"

"To reduce the chances that I'll kill you." Anyone who touched the bare skin of his right arm and hand, marked by the color-diluted glyphs called a *dermoire* that snaked from shoulder to fingernail, dropped dead on contact. He'd worn a jacket and gloves around everyone except his sister for decades, but if he orgasmed or summoned his "gift," he could kill right through the protective leather, which was why, during sex, he tried not to touch his partners as he neared climax. Tried, because with very few exceptions, something had always gone wrong.

The female bared her teeth, which, in the last couple of seconds, had grown sharper. And longer. "You think you can take me?"

I just did, honey. "I know I can." He patted his pocket to make sure she hadn't lifted his wallet, then checked his weapons harness for the same reason. He'd have to kill her if she'd swiped his Gargantua-bone dagger.

Gracefully, she came to her feet, which were now tipped by curved claws, just like her hands. What the hell kind of demon was she? "Arrogant prick." Her pronunciation was mushy now, the words spoken through an extra row of teeth that hadn't been there before.

"You're messing with the wrong arrogant prick, little girl." Lore moved toward the door. "Thanks for the laughs. See ya."

"Little girl?" She launched at him, catching him in the back and knocking him into the wall. As he spun away, she raked her claws across his chest, tearing open his T-shirt and leaving a bloody trail of scratches behind.

Hunger glimmered in her black eyes as she crept toward him like a cat preparing to pounce. "I'm going to eat your brains raw."

Lore clapped a hand over his stinging cuts. "Jesus. You're a fucking Dire Mantis." Figured that after sixty years of celibacy, the first partner he picked would be one that ate the heads of demon males.

"If it's any consolation," she purred, "that was the best sex any of my mates have given me."

"Well, duh." He watched her lick her lips as though she was already tasting his brain. Disgusting. "I can't believe I was worried about killing you."

She lunged. He dodged. He could kill her with a snap of the neck, but Dire Mantis bites were paralyzing, and he didn't want to risk getting anywhere near that mouth.

She came at him again, teeth gnashing. As she reached for him, he twisted aside and seized her forearm. Killing power sizzled like lightning from his shoulder to his fingers, and she fell to the floor, her lifeless body making a soft thud. It twitched a few times before falling still.

Most purebred demons who died aboveground disintegrated within seconds, but he didn't stick around to watch. Or to care. He strode out of the bedroom and out of the house without looking back. He was, after all, a killer. In the three weeks since witnessing the near end of the world, meeting his brothers, and bringing back to life a human he would rather have left dead, he'd done nothing but drown himself in liquor bottles. But no more. Losing himself and his edge had almost cost him his life in AprilMayJune's bedroom.

He wouldn't make that mistake ever again.

"Give me one reason why I shouldn't kill you."

Tapping his tongue piercing against his teeth, Lore

considered his answer as he stood before his master-slash-asshole boss. The tag of pimp could also apply to the demon, seeing how Deth allowed his assassins to take freelance work...as long as he received a 60 percent cut of the money earned. And none of the kills made on outside contracts counted toward Lore's obligation to Deth, even though the demon required his assassins to accept three outside jobs a year. Asshole.

Lore kept his gaze level with Deth's, more to keep himself grounded than to show that he wasn't nervous. He'd come straight from the mantis's place, but that had been yesterday. For twelve hours he'd been imprisoned below the main chamber, in stocks and kneeling on shards of glass.

Which meant he hadn't been able to fulfill his body's sexual needs, and he could feel the resulting tension, the growing rage that threatened to turn him into a beast clawing at the inside of his skin. The rest of his body didn't feel much better. His joints ached, his balls were tender, and every inch of his skin burned.

But all of that pain was minor compared to the torture he'd endured while in the stocks, a punishment he'd earned when he'd used his gift of resurrection. Before Lore had handed his soul over to Deth, Lore would spend a good twenty-four hours in bloody agony after bringing someone back from the dead. But now, because of his slave bond, it was his master, Detharu, who instead experienced the agonizing price Lore paid for bringing a being back to life. And Deth made damned sure Lore paid hugely for his suffering.

Funny how his two special abilities—taking and giving life—were so opposite, but only the "good" one came with pain. He supposed it made sense; life fucking hurt.

"Well," he drawled finally, with a calm he didn't feel, "I'm your best-looking assassin, and without me, you'd have to stare at the likes of Hadrian Maggotface all day."

Detharu, a demon whose species Lore had never determined, mainly because he appeared different to everyone who saw him, smiled. At least, the upturn of his black, crusted lips was the closest thing to a smile Lore had ever seen from the guy. Whatever it was, it didn't do anything to quell the unease churning in Lore's gut, an unease that was even more crushing than usual.

"You make a good point. But not good enough." Shifting in his throne constructed of the bones of several demon species and at least one human, Detharu gestured with his steel-gauntleted fist.

Two of his sentries, huge Ramreel demons with curled horns and an unholy love of machetes, peeled away from the jagged stone walls. Their small, piggish eyes glowed with murderous anticipation as they came at Lore from both sides.

Four more Ramreels watched from their positions at the chamber entrance, drool dripping from their snouts as though Pavlov had rung the dinner bell. And in the shadows behind Detharu, another male stood, the expression on his face unreadable, but Lore sensed a certain...anticipation. Weird. Lore had seen the dude before, hanging out with his insane brother, Roag, and Byzamoth, an equally insane fallen angel who had tried to start Armageddon.

But both nutcases were gone now, and there was no point in wondering why the demon was there, because at the moment, the biggest mystery facing him was whether he was keeping his head.

Lore rolled his shoulders, doing his best impression of

a guy who wasn't at all worried that his next breath might be the last. "Look, Deth, no need to get your knickers in a twist. I'll make it up to you—"

"You gave someone life so I would spend two sunsets in agony!"

Only Deth would think that Kynan's resurrection was all about him. "Yeah, but—"

"We're assassins, you imbecile! We don't *give life*! You make me a laughingstock." Detharu came to his feet with a snarl, the fire from the huge hearth in the center of the room casting flickering shadows into the valleys between his ribs—which were on the outside of his body. "Worse, you and Zaw failed to kill the Seminus demons as you were contracted to do!"

Lore clenched his hands into fists at his sides to keep from doing something stupid, like strangle his boss. "I can get you the money."

That was a big, fat lie. There was no way in Hades he could come up with the twenty million he would have gotten from the executor of Roag's estate upon proof of Wraith, Eidolon, and Shade's deaths. Half of that, maybe, but not the full amount.

"But you can't get back the respect I lost in the eyes of the Assassins' Guild," Deth roared.

"There has to be a way."

"There is." Detharu sank back down as if his display of temper never happened. "Your head on a pike, displayed in the Guild hall."

"Yeah, that doesn't work for me." Lore shoved his gloved hand through his hair, but that didn't massage the tension out of his skull. "Cut me some slack, will ya? They were my brothers."

Fortunately, Lore had failed to kill them. After the attempt and consequent revelations of blood ties, Lore had only stuck around his brothers long enough to get a little history of the Seminus breed and see what happened with Wraith's female, and then he'd gotten out of the demon hospital as if it was burning down.

Hadn't seen or spoken with his brothers since, though Eidolon's constant text messages had been as irritating as claws on a chalkboard.

"Family?" Detharu leaned forward in his seat. "Then why did you agree to kill them?"

"I didn't know they were my brothers at the time the job was offered." No, that little secret had been as twisted as Roag.

The chair creaked as Detharu sat back and rubbed his pointed chin. "I have siblings. I killed two of them. Liked doing it."

This wasn't looking good. "No doubt they deserved it." Yep, Lore could kiss ass with the best of them.

Detharu shrugged. For a long moment, the only sound in the room was the crackle of the fire and the occasional drip of Ramreel drool. Lore eyed the exit, hastily piecing together an escape plan. He could take out the demon closest to him, snag his machete, and then hope to God he could mow down the others before Detharu caught up to him. If he made it to the outer chamber, Detharu's other slave-assassins would help him escape.

Not that he'd be free for long. The slave-bond, the hand imprint burned into the flesh above his heart, would eventually compel him to return here or face unimaginable suffering as the bond first seared his skin, and then worked its way to his muscles and organs. You either returned to the den, or you cooked to death. Slowly.

Finally, Detharu shook his head. "I won't execute you for not killing your brothers."

"Big of you," Lore muttered.

A serrated growl rumbled in Deth's skeletal chest. "What did you say?"

"I said thank you." Lore scowled at the Ramreels. "You heard him. Beat it. No murder for you today." The Ramreel minions acted more as guards than executioners, but they pretty much did whatever Deth wanted them to do, and the bloodier the task, the happier they were.

Detharu's glowing orange eyes narrowed. "There is a price, of course."

"Naturally."

"I have a job for you."

Which meant that despite the threats and posturing, Deth hadn't intended to impale Lore's head on a pointy stick at all. "What do I have to do?" Lore asked through gritted teeth. "Collect another debt? Deliver a bloody warning to someone? Want me to fetch a pizza? Because you know how I love playing delivery boy."

He *hated* playing pizza minion.

"You can bring me an all-meat topped with a certain human's head. I'm giving you your hundredth kill."

Lore stopped breathing even as his pulse revved. He'd been waiting thirty years for this. After he completed his hundredth kill, Deth would no longer have any hold on him. He'd be a free man. But wait...something wasn't right. Detharu had avoided giving him an assassin job for years, unwilling to hand out that last assignment that would free both Lore and his sister, Sin, forever.

Lore studied Deth's impassive face, seeking, but not finding, any clues to what he was thinking. "What's the catch?"

Deth's bony fingers made irritating clicking noises as he tapped on the arm of his chair. "You violated the terms of our bargain by breaking the subcontract with Roag and not killing the Seminus brothers. I missed out on my share and look like a fool. Therefore, I'm amending our agreement."

Fuck. He knew it. "And what are your new terms?" he ground out.

"In the past, you have been allowed to refuse assignments."

"And I paid the price in blood." A lot of blood.

"You will not refuse this one."

Uh-oh. A chill skittered up Lore's spine. Deth was expecting him to refuse, which meant the mark would be a child or pregnant woman or something. "And if I do?"

"If you refuse or don't succeed, then I'll have Sin's head in place of yours for your failure to kill your brothers."

A red curtain came down over his vision. *Stay calm. Stay... calm.* Didn't work. The rage inside Lore screamed to the surface, completely missing the usual transition period, and he lunged at the demon. "You fuck!"

The sentries caught him, one on each arm. Instinct and anger merged, and without thinking, he charged up his gift. The Ramreel clutching Lore's right biceps didn't even have time to scream. He fell to the floor, eyes wider in death than they'd ever been in life.

Instantly, the other one wheeled away, drawing his machete, which he jabbed into Lore's ribs.

Detharu came to his feet, and the next thing Lore

knew, Deth's steel-gauntleted fist was in his face. Lore's head snapped back and pain exploded in his skull. Fury contorted Detharu's expression, peeling his lips from his sharp, blackened teeth.

"That was stupid, Lore. Even after all this time, you have not learned to control your temper."

It chafed to admit it, but Detharu was right on both counts. Lore's rages had been a problem since he was twenty, when he'd gone through the weird transformation that had given him an arm covered with tattoos. But that was just for starters. He also gained the "gift" to kill everything he touched with the tattooed arm, the ability to resurrect the dead or "feel" how a person had died, and a rampant libido that had to be addressed several times daily lest he go into rages that didn't end until he either killed or had sex—sex that ended in the death of his partner.

But being sexually sated wasn't a guarantee against the rages. Pain and anger could still set him off no matter how many times or how recently he'd relieved himself.

Breathing deeply, he willed himself to come down before the rage took him to the point of no return or before he did something stupid again. The move he'd made against Detharu carried with it a penalty of death.

Thing was, Lore couldn't have hurt Detharu anyway. The bond's magic prevented violence against one's master. Lore couldn't so much as touch Detharu unless the demon wanted to be touched.

And thank God Deth had long ago decided Lore wasn't allowed to touch. Few of Deth's assassins were so lucky.

Lore clenched his teeth, determined to keep from smarting off, but refusing to apologize. Instead, he gritted out, "Who's the target? Who is my hundredth kill?"

Lore had forgotten all about the male in the shadows, but now he shifted slightly, his black, waist-length hair seeming to absorb all the light in the room. It was as if the dude wore his shadow like a cloak. That was seriously fucked up.

A sinister smile split Deth's face wide open. "The target," he said, "is Kynan Morgan. The very human you brought back to life."

The ground shifted beneath Lore's feet. *Oh, holy hell.* Though Lore had saved Kynan's life, he hated him and really wouldn't mind putting him in the ground. But Jesus . . . if he killed the human, Lore would spend the rest of his sorry life looking over his shoulder. He'd have every Aegis Guardian on the planet aiming to gut him with a stang, which would be pleasant compared to what Gem and his brothers would do to him.

Deth leaned in close, so close Lore could feel the ugly demon's heat on his face. "You have your assignment. You will kill Morgan—using your death touch—and retrieve his amulet within ninety-six hours. And if you refuse or fail, Sin will die."

Sin, whose favorite saying was now becoming ironic reality.

No good deed shall go unpunished.

No fucking shit.

By sparing his brothers, Lore might have condemned his sister to death.

Rariel couldn't contain a smile as he watched Lore exit Detharu's chamber. He'd waited so long to put his plan into motion, and now that the ball was rolling, nothing could stop it.

"Why did you specifically request Lore for this job?" Detharu stood at the hearth's edge, his normally white skin taking on the orange of the flames like a chameleon's. Unlike most, Rariel could see the Molegra demon's true form, though he wished he couldn't. The eyeless man-shaped creature was one of the most repulsive demons Rariel had ever come across.

"He has a reputation as being one of the best," Rariel lied.

Lore *did* have a reputation for excellence at his job, but that wasn't why Rariel had chosen him. Rariel had chosen him because by giving Kynan, a Marked Sentinel, life, Lore had become the only being other than an angel who could take it away.

Detharu nodded, still facing the fire. "I'll be sorry to lose him. And Sin."

Yes, Rariel had been curious about this Sin person Detharu had dangled over Lore's head. "Is she his mate?"

"Sister."

Rariel's breath caught. *Sister*... "Is she an assassin?"

Detharu turned around, his sausage-body undulating grotesquely. "She is. Ruthless and cunning, like her brother."

Oh, this was perfect. Poetic, even. "Then I want Sin for the other target."

"Same time frame?" Deth asked.

"Yes."

The assassin master shuffled to his throne. "The rush job will cost you quadruple, as it did with Lore."

"I'm paying quadruple because my insistence on using Lore is depriving you of him as a slave."

"Double then. Take it or leave it."

Rariel could leave it and go with another assassin, but the brother-sister thing gave him shivers of pleasure. "Done."

Detharu smiled, his pale, shapeless lips forming a deep fissure that revealed tiny, pointed teeth. "Tell me, why is this amulet of Morgan's important to you?"

"It's a bauble. Worthless except as a trophy." The truth, that it was a priceless bargaining chip that would get Rariel everything he wanted, was not something he would share with anyone, let alone assassin scum.

The demon seemed to buy the lie. "Come then," he said, gesturing toward the door. "We'll feast on the sweet flesh of a newly hatched huldrefox while we draw up the contracts."

Furry little huldrefox hatchlings weren't cheap, and with what Rariel was paying, the bastard could afford to eat them—or the young of any species—every day if he wanted to. Still, Rariel couldn't scrounge up much in the way of bitterness. Not when centuries of planning was about to yield results.

Oh, yes. He could almost hear Idess's screams of misery already.

The icy whisper of a hand caressed his arm, reminding him of the debt Rariel had yet to pay. Because Rariel wasn't the only being in the room who was after revenge.

And after what Roag's brothers had done to him, Rariel couldn't blame the demon at all.

Two

Idess was close to the end. She could feel it. Could practically taste it, and as she stood at the top of Mount Everest and gazed up at the heavens, she could picture it.

An icy gale whipped up the snow around her, but she didn't notice despite the fact that she was wearing low-waisted, cropped cammy pants, a tummy-revealing tank top, and hiking boots. As a Memitim, the only class of angel that was born, not made by the direct hand of God, she was impervious to the elements. Was impervious to most things that could harm others. Soon, even those few things that could hurt or kill her would no longer be a threat. Soon, she would Ascend, would earn her wings and join her fully transitioned angel mother, brothers, and sisters in Heaven.

Not that she cared about seeing many of them. With the exception of her brother Rami, she knew few of her siblings very well, most not at all. But she couldn't wait to see Rami, had spent the last five hundred years since he Ascended in solitude and loneliness.

The only contact she had with people was when she shopped, a favorite pastime, and when she fed, a necessary evil she despised. "Feeding is the curse of our father," Rami had said. "It reminds us that no one is perfect, and that we must all resist temptations of the flesh, lest we allow corruption to blacken our souls."

Rami had feared that she would enjoy the physical contact feeding on Primori required, and that she'd gradually succumb to sin.

He was right to worry. Drinking blood did more than deliver the brief infusion of power Memitim needed to maintain their ability to flash. It also temporarily connected them psychically to their host, forcing Memitim to, for hours, feel what the Primori felt, whether it be anger, sadness, lust...

Oh, Idess couldn't wait until the day she Ascended and didn't need to engage in such intimacies anymore. As it was, she despised feeding so much that she had a tendency to walk a fine line with it, holding off until the last possible moment.

"It's almost over," she shouted to the sky. The wind ate her words, but she knew she'd been heard. In Heaven, they heard everything.

The thought brought an instant twinge of fear to her gut, because in truth, she hoped that wasn't the case. She hadn't exactly been...an angel.

Still, she was close to being one. She now had only two Primori to watch over, and one of them was the jewel in her crown.

Kynan Morgan was a Marked Sentinel, a human who

had been charmed by an angel. Sentinels couldn't be hurt or killed except by a being of angelic origin, which usually meant that they didn't rate Memitim watchers. But for some reason he did, and she had been chosen to protect him from the infinitesimal chance that someone could get past his charm. On the other hand, he was immortal, which meant that she could have to guard him for hundreds of years. Thousands, even.

But she didn't think so. Her other Primori, a werewolf, was long-lived but not immortal, so once he died or had fulfilled whatever destiny made him critical to the fate of the world, she would be left with only Kynan... and everyone knew that Memitim never guarded only one Primori.

Surely the honor of keeping Kynan safe would fall to one of her brethren, and she'd earn her wings for a job well done.

She couldn't wait.

Earth sucked, as humans these days liked to say.

Sighing, she visualized the living room of her Italian villa and flashed from the mountain to her house. She'd been born nearby, and even after thousands of years, she still felt the pull that brought her home every day.

The soles of her boots clacked on the beige and gold stone tiles as she moved toward the kitchen. Usually she'd turn on the stereo, get some Mozart going, but excitement still stirred her blood, and hunger rumbled her stomach.

She eyed the fruit bowl on her dining room table and the dish of fine Italian chocolate on her kitchen counter, waffled... and then reached for a pomegranate.

Fruit is nature's blessing, Rami used to say. *We shouldn't defile the bodies God gave us with spirits and unhealthful sweets.*

Sure, none of that could hurt her, but Rami had been devout and pure, even before he'd been plucked out of his human life at the customary age of nineteen to become a Memitim, and as her teacher in all things holy, he'd been a strict taskmaster. Which, she thought, as she palmed a candy, was all the more reason to indulge now and then. She actually looked forward to his giving her a stern lecture when she finally saw him again.

A faint twinge streaked across her right wrist. Odd. She twisted her arm to view the two quarter-sized Primori marks on the underside. Chase's *heraldi* had been there for eight years, was the same color as her skin, the thin lines raised like a brand or the outline of a fresh tattoo. But Kynan's was new, only three weeks old, and she still hadn't gotten used to seeing it. Frowning, she looked closer. The edges were pink... swelling rapidly... it began to burn, glow, and she dropped the candy with a gasp.

Kynan, one of the few untouchable people on the planet, was in danger.

Lore stood at the entrance to an upstate New York mansion, fists clenched and watching Kynan search the huge-ass sitting room, S-shaped stang in one hand and holy water in the other. Apparently, Croucher demons had set up shop in the dwelling, and Kynan intended to take them out before the wealthy family who lived there got too talky about what was going on. And before someone got hurt.

The Aegis to the rescue.

Bunch of do-gooder, holier-than-thou hypocrites. Lore had never liked Guardians all that much, but the dislike had turned to downright hatred two decades ago, when one of his contracted hits had been a Guardian who'd pissed off the wrong demon. The Guardian had been good enough at his job that he'd nearly taken Lore out.

Almost getting whacked wasn't what had annoyed Lore—he'd deserved it for letting his guard down. What had gotten Lore all worked up was the fact that the Guardian had used some seriously underhanded, sleazy methods for catching and killing demons, including keeping cages full of baby demons to torture until adults came to save the little ones.

Lore didn't harbor a whole lot of love for demons, but there were some things you just didn't do. *Er... yeah.* Lore's hypocrite switch flipped at that, because some of those things you just didn't do had been done by him during his hell years as an assassin. He shot Kynan a glance, and okay, Lore had no qualms about putting that guy down. They'd been enemies since they first identified each other as competition for the same woman. Back then, Lore had hoped for an opportunity to take the guy's head off, which made the fact that Lore had brought Kynan back to life after he'd been bled out so ironic. Then again, he'd only resurrected Kynan because he'd hated seeing Gem in pain.

This time, he wouldn't have to see it.

The slave-bond on Lore's chest pulsed, marking time in the countdown to his deadline, and there was no sense in waiting. Lore strode inside, his boots striking the black-veined red marble and announcing his presence with no subtlety whatsoever. Lore never had been subtle.

Instantly, Kynan swung around. "What the hell are you doing here?" His voice was a knot of suspicion and snarl, and yeah, there was no love lost between them.

Lore didn't remove his glove; too obvious. He'd power-punch his death special through the leather. "I want to call a truce."

Kynan snorted. "I hadn't heard that hell froze over."

Funny guy. Lore almost regretted having to kill him. Almost. "True story. I figure the more I get to know my brothers, the more you and I will have to see each other, and I'm thinking brawls at family picnics are frowned upon."

"Clearly you don't know your brothers," Kynan said wryly, and Lore experienced a weird sensation... as if maybe he could like the human under the right circumstances.

Ruthlessly, he shoved aside the candy-ass sentiments and grew a set. His sister's life was at stake, here. "Well, that's sort of the point of hanging around with them." Not that that was going to happen. He'd made Sin a promise, and this time, he wouldn't fail her. "So what do you say?"

Skepticism put shadows in Kynan's denim-blue eyes, and Lore's palms dampened with sweat. "I haven't thanked you for saving my life."

"No need." Actually, some serious sucking up would be cool, considering how much pain Deth had put Lore through for using his power of resurrection.

"Bullshit." Kynan jammed his stang into the weapons harness criss-crossing his chest, the sound of metal sliding home into its leather housing ringing out in the cavernous space. "No way am I letting you hold *that* over my head for eternity. I'll thank you, and somehow, I'll make us even."

They'd be even when Kynan was the guest of honor at his own wake. And wait...eternity? What the hell did he mean by eternity? Lore eyed the gold chain hanging around Kynan's neck, the one Lore was supposed to grab after killing him. Wraith had given him the crystal amulet...did it bestow magical protection or longevity?

Well, there was only one way to find out. "Fine. I accept your thanks. Truce?" Lore offered his hand, let his gift fire up with so much power that his arm burned from the top symbol at the crook of his neck to his fingertips. If he took off his jacket, he knew every glyph would be glowing like a brand.

For a long time, Kynan just stood there. *Take it, take it*...Lore made a come-on gesture with his fingers, hoping the guy would get with the program. Finally, Kynan nodded.

And held out his hand. "Truce."

Idess materialized inside a house—an expensive one, judging by the decor. Instantly, an intense itch flared up between her shoulder blades along the twin marks where her wings would someday sprout. They were like twin demon sensors, and right now, they were screaming warnings.

In the center of a richly decorated but spacious room, Kynan was facing off with a huge male clad in black leather. The male must be a demon, and somehow the source of the danger vibes that buzzed through her as though she was gripping an electric wire. But how could he be a threat to Kynan? The male wasn't a fallen angel; she'd sense that.

Still, Kynan's *heraldi* was searing her arm, so the impossibility of the situation didn't matter. She flashed between the two men, using the element of surprise and her superior strength to slam her palms into the stranger's massive chest and heave him across the room.

"What the—" He hit the wall with a resounding crack, the impact so forceful that plaster and dust came down around him. He shook his head, flinging white wall particles from his short, nearly black hair.

Idess summoned a scythe, the Memitim's signature weapon and very handy for separating a head from a body. She hated to kill—as the daughter of an angel, she was a giver and protector of life, by nature—but she would do anything to ensure the safety of her Primori. *Anything*, thanks to the more violent genes passed down by her father.

She swung the weapon in a graceful arc—Kynan hit her from behind, and her aim went awry as he slammed her to the floor.

"Idiot!" she spat. Kynan clearly didn't realize that she was there to protect him, and didn't it just figure that he'd come to the aid of the very man who was there to kill him. She rolled, saw the flash of a stang as it plunged downward, felt the whisper of metal as it grazed her shoulder.

Then the demon was there, his gloved fist coming at her so fast she barely had time to twist away. Blocking his next punch, she leaped to her feet and swept her leg out, catching him in the shin, and though he grunted, he didn't go down.

Kynan attacked from her flank, landing what would, on a human, have been a knee-breaking strike, and darn it, she didn't need to be fighting both of these guys. Spinning, she nailed Kynan in the jaw with a powerful, but measured punch. Shock flickered in his eyes before they rolled up in his head and he crumpled to the ground.

Pivoting, she faced the remaining male. He swung at her. She blocked. Slashed with the scythe. Caught him

with an ax kick that knocked him backward, but only for
a moment. He was big, but he moved like a panther, dancing lightly on his feet, every blow controlled and more
often than not landing on her body.

Surprised by his skill, she lost momentum, and in a
series of impressive moves, he made her spine intimate
with the wall and was on her, his forearm jammed into
her throat and his six-foot-six body pinning her. His fingers circled her wrist and held it at her hip, rendering the
weapon useless. For the moment.

"Who the fuck are you?" The male's ebony eyes,
framed by long, lush lashes any female would kill for,
glittered with anger and little gold flecks.

"Seeing as how you're a murderer, I'd say you don't
have the right to be indignant."

"Seeing as how I could kill you with one more pound
of pressure on your larynx, I'd say that your being a smart-
ass is pretty damned stupid." He leaned into her a little
more, so they were chest to chest and his lips were brushing her cheek. "But you're hot, and I'll bet you fuck like
you fight, so I can forgive your lack of brains."

This cretin was—what was the popular saying in this
decade—toast? Yes, this cretin was toast. "I'm going to
enjoy killing you."

He tightened his grip on her wrist. "Who sent you?"

"*God.*" She jerked up her knee. He shifted, and she
struck only a glancing blow to his groin. Still, he sucked
air. Nice.

"Bad girl," he snarled, taking her to the floor with a
hook to the back of her leg and a firm shove to her neck.

He dropped, coming down on top of her. With a quick
thought and a flick of her hand, the scythe morphed into a

dagger. She struck out, catching him in the shoulder. He hissed and yanked sideways as the blade cut through his leather jacket and into his flesh.

Score one for the bad girl. She rolled out from under him, stabbing him in the thigh on her way. The metallic tang of blood filled her nostrils, a tantalizing scent for the part of her that must feed once a month, but more important, it told her that this male was of both human and demon descent.

The species of demon was still unknown, but given how impossibly handsome he was, she'd guess he was a breed of incubus.

Lunging, she sliced at him again, but in a cat-quick move, he flattened himself on the ground. He'd saved himself from a nasty cut, but his position gave her the opportunity to leap to her feet and smash one heel into his rib cage. Bone gave way beneath her boot, and he grunted as he grabbed her ankle with both hands.

"What *is* it with females trying to kill me lately?"

"Says a lot about you, don't you think?" Feeling a twinge of regret for having to destroy such a fine male specimen, she thrust the dagger down.

A sense of foreboding prickled her skin a split second before the distinct click of a firing crossbow pierced the air. Idess jerked under the force of what felt like a cannonball punching into her spine. Blood exploded in a puff of fine mist from her chest, and steam hissed from the hole just below her breastbone where the bolt had gone through.

Agony lanced her, rending and unique in its intensity. She tasted bile. Blood. What could have done this? Gasping for breath, Idess staggered around to the female holding the crossbow. Dressed in blood-red leather that clashed with her merlot hair, she stood protectively over Kynan's prone form. Another Guardian.

Realization and horror cut through the fog of pain. The bolt had been coated in *qeres,* an ancient Egyptian mummification perfume used by The Aegis to combat fallen angels. It wouldn't kill them, but the poison could cripple and incapacitate for years.

It *could,* however, kill pre-Ascension Memitim.

The demon male rolled away from Idess and crawled toward Kynan.

Idess's muscles turned rubbery, but spurred by a desperate need to keep the demon away from Kynan, she gathered the last of her strength and yanked the male to his feet. She flashed them to the most remote place she could think of—a forest deep in the Ukraine. A lot of demons died in the cold. She hoped he'd be one of them.

As they materialized in two feet of snow, it became obvious that he wasn't one of them, and if he was surprised by their sudden wilderness adventure, he didn't show it. But then, her vision had begun to blur, and even the pristine white landscape took on a fuzzy, gray cast. Her fingers went numb, and the dagger disappeared as her ability to maintain the conjured weapon failed. A tremor of dread ran through her soul. This was it. The end. She'd survived the fall of Rome. The Inquisition. World War II. And some little slayer who played for the same side, Team Good and Holy, had just killed her.

Blackness swirled in her vision, overtaking her senses, and she went down. A voice rang in her ears, muted and distant, and then she was being lifted, yet somehow she doubted that the arms around her were those of a savior.

Three

What. The. Fuck.

Lore stood like a dope, knee-deep in snow in the middle of some godforsaken forest, cradling his would-be killer to his chest and wondering how everything had gone to hell so fast. He'd been a heartbeat away from completing his assignment, and now he was in the middle of nowhere, confused, and in a shitload of pain.

Agony screamed through his chest with every breath. Damned ribs were broken. A raspy moan reminded him that the female in his arms was far worse off. Whatever Tayla had shot her with had done some serious damage. Obviously, his Guardian sister-in-law had believed the female to be the threat to Kynan, rather than Lore.

He still wasn't sure why he was holding the little troublemaker instead of killing her. The bitch was mouthy, she'd tried to kill him, and her heavy ass was hell on his ribs.

Though to be fair, she wasn't that heavy. Just…tall. And curvy. And athletically solid. Hell, she looked like she worked out with some serious weights.

As far as mouthy…damn, she had a nice one. Wide, with full lips made to make a male beg. Her features were perfect—finely wrought, delicate, feminine in a way that was utterly out of sync with the dangerous power she wielded. And she smelled as if she'd bathed in cinnamon sugar. Exotic. Sexy. Edible.

But what the hell was she, why was she after him, and why the fuck did he suddenly crave cookies in bed?

The need to get the answers to his questions had him putting out feelers for the nearest Harrowgate. His demon senses picked up on one nearby, which was good, because carrying her was going to hurt. As much as he hated to do it, he'd have to get her to Underworld General so his brothers could patch her up well enough for interrogation. If someone had put out a hit on him, he needed to know.

Who sent you?

God.

Yeah, right. How many assassin masters did he know who insisted upon being called God? This chick could be working for any of a dozen assholes.

He weaved through the trees, leaving a trail of blood—both his and hers—in the snow as he limped toward the gate. Twice he had to stop to gather her waist-length pony-tail so he didn't step on it. At least it was tightly bound, the thick brown rope secured every six inches or so by elaborately jeweled gold bands. The effect, combined with her smooth, porcelain skin and honey-colored, almond eyes, made her one of the most striking females he'd ever seen.

But hey, if someone was going to try to kill him, he'd

rather it be a hot, bloodthirsty chick than some ugly-ass dude. He hefted her higher to avoid impaling her on a tree branch, and yep, definitely better that his would-be killer was a feather-light female.

The Harrowgate loomed ahead, a vertical, shimmering curtain of light, visible only to demons. God, he hated those things. Every time he stepped into one, he felt as if his humanity was being leached out. He was always a little more raw, a little more on edge when he came out on the other side, and he wondered when the day would come that he arrived at his destination as nothing but a monster.

He hoped it wouldn't be this day.

He limped inside and was immediately swallowed by almost complete darkness as the gate closed. Obsidian walls etched with crude maps that represented Earth and Sheoul surrounded him on all sides, the thin lines that made up the maps glowing in a painter's palette of colors.

In his arms, the female spasmed, the force of her seizure knocking him hard into the wall. Pain tore through his upper body and his arm went limp, and motherfuck, his left shoulder had wrenched from the socket. Sucking air between his teeth, he gently lowered the female to the floor and used his good hand to tap out the map—North America, the United States, New York state, New York City—until he found the medical emblem that would take him to Underworld General Hospital, which existed beneath the streets of the Big Apple, right under unsuspecting human noses.

The gate opened into an emergency room illuminated by red bulbs caged in rows on the ceiling. A tremor of unease tripped through him, which wasn't a surprise, given that the last time he was here, he'd come to kill his brothers.

Talk about awkward.

Cookie was still lying motionless on the floor of the Harrowgate, and she was going to stay there unless Lore got his act together. He cradled his useless arm and eyeballed one of the stone columns supporting the Harrowgate entrance. Shit. This was gonna hurt like a mother.

Bracing himself, he jammed his shoulder into the pillar. Pain cluster-bombed his arm as it popped back into the socket. A wave of nausea rolled over him, but he gathered up the female and limped toward the triage desk.

The nurse manning the station, a dark-skinned, humanoid Bedim demon, looked up from a stack of paperwork. An extremely sensual species whose females were usually kept in a harem, the Bedim rarely ventured into the world outside whatever Sheoulin palace they lived in. Lore might have appreciated her bid for independence, had he not been bleeding to death.

"You are both injured," she said.

"You think?"

She jabbed her pen at him. "An attitude like that will get you nothing but an ass-kicking, mister."

Jesus. Bedim were usually a peaceful, friendly people, but give demons some power, and they turned into . . . well, demons. "Whatever. Just get us some help."

The Bedim sniffed haughtily, but already medical staff were surrounding them. A guy in scrubs gestured for Lore to follow. Lore did, to a trauma room where he laid out Cookie on the examination table. A female Trillah nurse put her fingers to the female's wrist.

"What are you doing?" Scrubs Guy shouted at the Trillah, startling Lore. "ABCs, you idiot! Airway, breathing, circulation...in that order. You've been a nurse for how long?"

Snarling, whiskers twitching, the nurse bit out some choice curses, and Lore swore Scrubs Guy was going to go right over the exam table at her.

"Hey," Lore snapped. "Is this a hospital or not?"

Scrubs Guy and the Trillah uttered more obscenities, but at least they got back to the crisis at hand.

"What happened?" Scrubs Guy had a star-shaped mole behind his ear, which meant he was some sort of shape-shifter. He cut Cookie's shirt up the middle with shears and peeled the flaps of fabric away from her skin.

"Shot with a crossbow." *Ooh, black bra.* "I don't know what kind of bolt."

"What species is she?"

Satin, not lace. "No clue." *And front closure. Nice.*

Eidolon, dressed in green scrubs and black boots, stalked into the room with the authority of a king entering his castle. "She's a fallen angel."

At once, in a move so coordinated it seemed rehearsed and almost comical, everyone backed away from her, hands up.

Lore turned to Eidolon. "How do you know?"

"Tayla called. Is this the female who injured you and Kynan?"

"The very cookie."

Eidolon lowered his voice so no one but Lore could hear. "Ky can only be injured by angels, and only fallen ones would *want* to harm him."

What? Eidolon had better be wrong about that, or Lore's job just took a turn down the Royally Fucked Highway, and there were no exits on *that* road to hell. "Are you sure?"

"There's a way to confirm it."

Eidolon went to the female's side and touched her arm. His *dermoire* lit up, and she moaned. "Female? What's your name?"

She moaned again, and Eidolon leaned close. She whispered something, and Eidolon nodded as he straightened to his full height. Concentration put lines in his brow as he channeled power into her through his hand. Eidolon's Seminus gift allowed him to probe deep inside a body for injury and heal wounds, but when his mouth tightened into a grim slash, Lore knew the news was not good.

"What's wrong with her?"

"Poisoned. Spine's broken and she's got massive internal injuries." Eidolon barked some orders to the nearby staff, and when no one moved, Eidolon snapped, "Now! It's safe to touch her. You never had a problem with Reaver."

Reaver...right. The fallen angel who had helped in the big battle last month. Except, apparently, he was no longer fallen. Still, what did any of this have to do with Kynan?

Carefully, the medical team turned the angel chick onto her stomach. Eidolon's fingertips feathered over two scarlike slashes between her shoulder blades. "Definitely angel." He glanced over at Lore. "These are wing anchors." He continued, smoothing his long fingers down her spine to probe the bolt's entrance wound. Before Lore's eyes, flesh and bone began to mend. "Page Doctor Shakvhan. We need to get her into a healing bath."

A healing bath sounded great to Lore, what with the way his gut was doing gymnastics and the room was spinning. "Hey, uh...could I get a little help here? Snickerdoodle isn't the only one bleeding to death."

Eidolon caught Lore by the arm and guided him into the room next to the female's. "What happened?"

"Stabbed. My arm and leg." Lore tugged off his jacket. "Pretty sure I've got some broken ribs, too."

"Gods, you're as bad as Wraith." Eidolon jerked his chin toward the bed as he washed his hands in the sink. "Sit. And if you can take off your clothes, do."

While E gloved up, Lore stripped, wincing at the tug of his muscles against his ribs and around the stab wounds. Eidolon arched an eyebrow at the pile of weapons Lore had placed next to his clothes, but he didn't say anything.

Naked except for his boxer briefs, Lore eased onto the bed and killed time by studying a crack that snaked several feet along one gray wall, bisecting the protective symbols and letters written in blood. "Thought you guys fixed the place after all that shit last month."

"We did," Eidolon said, as he grabbed a towel. "But we're still having a few issues. I've got contractors looking into it. The integrity of the building might have been compromised."

Lore eyed the ceiling. "So you're saying the building could come down on top of us?"

"Do you really think I'd keep the hospital operating if it wasn't safe?" Eidolon wrapped the towel around Lore's right arm, covering the tattoo that, with the exception of the lack of a personal symbol, was nearly identical to his brothers'. They'd discovered that Lore's death touch didn't affect Eidolon, Shade, or Wraith, but all other staff would be exposed. And since the exposure would be accidental, the Haven spell, which prevented violence and intentional injury inside the hospital, wouldn't offer any protection.

"I dunno," Lore said, which earned him a dirty look.

Touchy. "So, aren't angels, even fallen ones, sort of immortal?"

"Yes."

"Why did you bother fixing her, then? She'll heal on her own."

"I want answers, and I don't want to wait. The weapon Tayla used could put an angel on her ass for years."

Lore frowned. "Why did Tayla just happen to be in possession of something that can take down a fallen angel?"

"Because she's one of Kynan's bodyguards."

Bodyguards? What a pussy. "And Kynan needs protection, why?"

"Because The Aegis are a bunch of paranoid drama queens." Eidolon tore open a packet of gauze. "Except in this case, it looks like their paranoia was justified."

"Why would fallen angels be a threat to him?" When Eidolon said nothing, Lore cursed. "Can you at least tell me why it is that only angels can harm him?"

"And fallen angels," Eidolon said, which wasn't the answer to his question, but Lore had a feeling it was all he was going to get from his brother. Eidolon wheeled a tray containing various medical tools to the side of the bed. "So what were you doing with Kynan, anyway?"

"Just trying to make amends."

Eidolon let out a dubious snort, and inside, Lore tensed. He needed his brother to buy his innocence.

"I'm serious."

"So you're saying this has nothing to do with Gem." Eidolon pinched Lore's flesh near his shoulder blade. "Hold still. This is going to hurt."

Relieved that Eidolon's suspicions were misplaced, Lore relaxed. "Yeah, I'm saying—ouch! Fuck!"

"I warned you."

"You're an asshole."

"Do you want me to patch you up, or not?"

"Are you this rude to all your patients? Or just long-lost brothers?"

Eidolon cleared his throat. "Who called who an asshole?"

If the shoe fits . . . "Whatever. Do I need surgery?"

"Nope. The lacerations are shallow, and nothing was hit that I can't fix right here." He picked up an evil-looking instrument off the tray. "A little sting. . . ."

Lore nearly came off the damned table. Little sting, his ass. "Why aren't you just doing the heal thing with your gift?"

"I used a lot of power on the fallen angel. Had a busy day and I was already nearly tapped before I worked on her. I don't want to waste too much of what's left on non-life-threatening injuries like this. Hold still."

Lore gnashed his teeth as Eidolon went to work, mending his flesh with a combination of manual tools and, toward the end, a little of his gift, a process that burned and was almost as painful as the initial injuries. When he was done, Lore had to admit—grudgingly—that the guy had done a good job, and his efficiency and professionalism had been downright surprising.

He was still an asshole.

"Thanks," Lore muttered, and Eidolon gave a brief nod before calling in a nurse to clean Lore up.

The nurse lumbered in, and didn't it just figure that it would be male. And Slogthu, which meant furry and *fugly*.

Lore waited to do any more probing until the nurse

had finished sponging blood off him and left. When he
and Eidolon were alone, Lore played casual. "So...how's
Kynan?" With any luck, dead.

A low growl rumbled up from Eidolon's chest. "I don't
know. Shade and Tay are bringing him in. They should be
here any second. What happened with Idess?"

"Idess? That's the angel's name?" Pretty. Idess. Eye-
dess. Idess, Idess, Idess. He liked the way it rolled off his
tongue. "Idess."

Eidolon looked at Lore as if he was nuts. "Ah, yeah.
Idess. What happened?"

"She popped out of thin air and attacked us."

Eidolon frowned. "Why did she disappear from the
mansion with you? Where did she take you?"

The scent of cinnamon sugar came back to Lore, hitch-
hiking on the memory of Idess's tall, slinky body clad in
low-riding cammy pants and a matching olive-drab and
pink tank top that had revealed a long expanse of toned,
flat belly.

"She took me to some bumfuck forest, and I have no
idea why she did it," Lore said, now more confused than
ever. He'd figured she was after him, but if what E had
said about angels being the only creatures who could hurt
Kynan was true, then maybe Lore was merely collateral
damage. "I thought I was the target. She said she was
going to kill me. That's why I brought her here instead of
finishing her off. I need to know if some ass-wipe put out
a hit on me." Eidolon laughed, which was pretty damned
rude. "What's so fucking funny?"

"You're an assassin, but you're indignant about the fact
that someone might be trying to assassinate *you*?"

"Double standards get a bad rap." An eerie chill whispered across Lore's skin, but Eidolon didn't seem to notice as he rummaged through a drawer. "Look, why don't you give me the skinny on Kynan. If I know what you're keeping from me, we might be able to piece together what's up with this Idess chick."

Eidolon tossed him a set of scrubs. "It's not that I want to keep anything from you, but it's Kynan's story to tell. Not mine."

Man, Lore hated demons with ethics. He tugged on the oh-so-manly mint-green pants while his brother dumped the bloodied tools into a biohazard bin. He was pulling the shirt over his head when that weird buzz of unease he'd gotten when he first arrived swamped him again.

"Do you feel that, E? It's like I'm being watched." *Or hunted.*

Eidolon's head whipped around. "Like sandpaper on nerve endings?"

Lore couldn't have said it better. Shrugging into his jacket, he nodded.

"Everyone's feeling it. Shade, Wraith, the staff. We've all been on edge."

Which explained the snippy triage nurse and the pissy folks who examined Idess when Lore first brought her in. Then again, so could the fact that they were demons.

Raised voices outside the room snapped Lore's gaze to the doorway, where Tayla stood, green eyes blazing. "Where is that bitch?"

"Recovery," Eidolon said, and when Tayla opened her mouth, he held up a hand. "I know what you're going to say, but I had to fix her so we can find out what she's up to." He glanced at Lore. "And who she's actually after. Where's Ky?"

Shade brushed past Tayla. "He's in exam three. He lost consciousness for a few minutes, but I did a quick probe inside his head and aside from a mild concussion, he's fine. You might want to give him a tune-up with a healing wave, though." He swung around to Lore. "What the fuck were you doing there?"

Okaaay. Lore hadn't expected a hug or anything, but last time he'd seen Shade, the guy had at least been conversational. Sort of.

"Hello to you, too, bro."

"Answer the question."

Already on edge from the malevolent vibe and everything else that had gone down today, Lore shoved to his feet, through with Shade's bullshit. "None of your fucking business."

Shadows writhed in Shade's eyes. "I told you to stay away from Gem."

Like Lore needed the reminder. The warning had been the very last thing Shade had said to him as Lore left the hospital three weeks ago. *Don't be a stranger, Lore. Oh, and stay the hell away from Gem.*

"Last time I checked," Lore gritted out, "you weren't my boss."

Shade's fists clenched at his sides as he took a menacing step forward, and good goddamn, if the boy wanted to throw down, Lore was more than ready. The weird venomous vibe tangled with his temper, and he met Shade head-on. The first throw was his. Seminus brother-on-brother violence wasn't covered by the Haven spell.

Eidolon stepped between them, and Tayla flanked him. Too bad. "Shade...." The warning in Eidolon's voice was gentle but unmistakable. "Back off. This isn't about Gem."

"You seriously believe that?" Shade demanded.

"What I think doesn't matter, but yeah, I do. Lore fought the angel, which may have saved Kynan's life. So let it go."

There was a long, tense silence, during which a tiny stab of guilt pricked Lore's conscience. Lore cleared his throat, more to make noise in his mind than to end the silence. "Ah, hey, can someone finally tell me what's up with Kynan and the angel thing?"

"It's none of your fucking business," Shade said, throwing Lore's words back at him.

Lore shot Eidolon a glare. "If you're wondering why I haven't answered any of your texts, there's your answer. You've all been so welcoming." Of course, the fact that he'd tried to kill them might have something to do with that.

"I only wanted to run some tests, find out why your gift was mutated," Eidolon said.

"I thought everything was fucked up because I'm half human, and Seminus and human don't mix."

"I'm sure that's why, but if I can ascertain exactly what went wrong, I might be able to fix it."

Lore's heart gave an excited thump. His *gift* had caused him a lifetime of misery and loneliness, and he'd give his left nut to be rid of the damned thing.

But a lifetime of disappointment had also taught him to be skeptical, so he brought himself down with a bitter laugh. "And then I'll be grateful, and we'll bond and be one big, happy family?"

"You have a lot of other options, then?" Eidolon drawled.

"I manage fine on my own."

Eidolon cocked an eyebrow at the bloody pile of clothes on the floor. "Obviously."

Sarcastic ass. Then again, Eidolon might have a tweaked sense of humor, but at least he had one. As far as Lore could tell, Shade barely knew what a smile was, and Wraith hadn't been a bundle of laughs, either.

None of it mattered, though, because even if Lore hadn't promised his sister he'd stay away from them, they wouldn't ever forgive him for killing Kynan.

Assuming he could. The fact that Kynan had demon-slayer bodyguards watching out for him was a complication he didn't need. Lore could handle it—he'd trounced Buffies before. But once he got past them, he had a much bigger issue to deal with if only angels could waste Kynan.

Suffocating under the crush of so many hostile glares, Lore moved toward the door. "I'm outta here."

"In a hurry to kill someone?" Shade asked.

The question hit a little too close to home, but Lore rolled with it, happy to needle Shade. "Yep."

Eidolon crossed his arms over his broad chest. "You're not going to wait for our injured angel to wake up? It isn't like whoever you have to kill is going to get any more alive. Kill him later. Maybe while you're waiting, he'll get struck by lightning or something. Save you some work." Yep, Eidolon was a comedian.

"Let him go," Shade said. "Obviously, he has work to do."

Shade's false niceness made Lore want to stay out of spite. "What do you guys plan to do with Idess?"

"As soon as she's awake, we'll get some answers out of her." Eidolon leveled Lore a cold look, made all the more chilling by the fact that there was no emotion in it. "One way or another."

Lore hoofed it toward UGH's Harrowgate, away from his brothers, and away from Kynan. But he wasn't heading home. Not yet.

Casting a covert glance over his shoulder to make sure his nosy siblings weren't watching, he slipped past the triage desk and down a hall, knowing exactly where he was going. He'd interrogated staff and memorized the hospital blueprints when he'd plotted out the hits on Shade and Eidolon. The recovery rooms, three suites outfitted with various types of baths, chairs, and heated and chilled beds, were at the end of the wing, just past the seawater pool that was big enough for a killer whale to do laps in.

He found Idess in the first recovery room.

Everything but her head had been immersed in a vat of what was probably water infused with magical herbs. A spicy, medicinal fragrance permeated the air and made him want to sneeze as he closed the door behind him and moved toward her. The water bubbled around Idess, and steam swirled over the surface, but none of that hid the fact that she was naked. Shadows thrown by the dim light accented full breasts and slim hips, but left details tantalizingly to the imagination.

Lore had always had a great imagination.

Someone had taken the gold rings out of her hair, and now her chestnut mane fanned out across an inflatable pillow and the tiled floor behind her head, and he had the strangest urge to touch it and see if it was as silky as it looked.

Instead, he went down on his heels at the edge of the pool and studied her profile, so feminine and peaceful, as if she were lounging in a Jacuzzi instead of recovering from an injury that would have killed anyone else. Her long, sable lashes cast shadows across the delicate ivory skin beneath her eyes, and her cheeks had pinked up, maybe from the heat of the water—or a sexy dream.

"Don't suppose you can hear me?"

Her eyelids fluttered, but didn't open.

"What's your deal?" he asked quietly. "You after Kynan, or me?" This time, her eyes opened and fixed on him. There was no recognition there, no sign that she even knew where she was.

"Rami?" There was hope and desperation in her voice, both of which made a person vulnerable. Exploitable.

He could use that. "Yes," he said, running with the exploitation thing. "It's Rami."

Her lush lips curved into a smile that punched him right in the gut. That was a mouth any man would kill to taste—or to have taste *him*.

"You've come for me?"

He couldn't help it; he let his gaze slide down the long, lean length of her. *Freaking gorgeous.* "Yeah," he rasped. "I've come for you." I'd come *with* you.

"Good," she sighed. "Take me to heaven."

His dick jerked, all, *Sure, we'll take you up on that offer*, and Lore had to admit, if circumstances were different—meaning, she hadn't tried to kill him—he'd be all over that. "First, why don't you tell me what your mission is?"

She frowned. "Did I fail?"

"Fail to kill Kynan?"

"Kill?" She shifted, and a lock of hair slipped into the water, spreading like blood over her chest. "Protect."

Acid bubbled up in Lore's throat. She was Kynan's *protector*?

"Take me, brother," she said, and whoa, *that* cooled his jets. "Take me to Heaven so I can get my wings."

Lore rocked backward, remembering what she'd told him at the mansion.

Who sent you?

God.

Oh, Jesus, she was really talking about Heaven. *The* Heaven. Not a fallen angel. An *angel*.

Not that it mattered. She was a threat to him if she was truly protecting Kynan.

Numbly, he peeled off his glove. The hospital was safe-guarded by the Haven spell, but he was willing to risk a skull-splitting headache if it meant saving his sister's life. He'd suffered worse, for sure.

He reached for Idess. All he needed to do was to brush a knuckle over her cheek...a lover's caress that would send her to Heaven, just as she'd asked. She closed her eyes, as if anticipating his touch, and his hand began to shake.

What the hell? He was an assassin. A cold-blooded killer. And she was dangerous, someone who not only stood between him and his goal, but who had tried to whack him.

But right now, she didn't look dangerous. She looked sweet and angelic. Fragile. Helpless.

Lore might be a killer, but he had standards, and he'd never, ever taken the coward's way out. He gave every one of his victims the courtesy of a wide-awake, face-to-face

assassination. Murdering a female while she recovered
from injuries was low, even for him.

The door opened. Lore leaped to his feet to face Wraith,
who stood there, blond hair falling around a severe jawline
and fangs bared in a silent snarl. "What are you doing?"

"Just thought I'd check on her. Why are you here?"

Wraith's gaze dropped to Lore's exposed hand, and
when he looked back up, the glint of awareness in his blue
eyes told Lore his brother knew exactly what had been
about to happen. "Your revenge will have to wait."

Lore exhaled, a futile attempt to release some tension.
"Why?"

"Because," Wraith said, his voice thick with anger,
"I'm going to get into her head. I want to know who wants
Kynan dead. And then I'm going to make them wish
they'd never been born."

Four

⌒

"I need your help. Please, Idess." Clutching his forearm, Rami doubled over at the Nile River edge. Idess kneeled beside him.

"What's wrong?" But even as she spoke, she knew. Two of his four *heraldi* were glowing angrily. Two? That was beyond rare—so much so that she'd never heard of it happening. When a single Primori was in trouble, the pain was excruciating. She couldn't imagine having two in danger at the same time. "What can I do?"

"Help...the Viking."

"Of course." She feathered her finger over a *heraldi* on Rami's arm, and instantly, she was transported to some sort of battle.

The stench of death was as thick as the fog around her. The ground was soaked with blood, strewn with body parts and bowels. The victims...oh, sweet Lord, the victims...women. Children. This wasn't a battle. It was a *slaughter. And in the center of it all, hacking up a dying man with an ax, was Rami's Primori, a Viking whose evil aura wrapped around him like a shroud, nearly snuffing the blue glow that gave away his Primori status. Though humans could be as evil as any underworld creature, this one made her wing marks itch and sent chills slithering up her spine. Demon blood flowed through this Primori's veins.*

A woman in tattered rags was crawling toward the Viking, murder burning in her eyes and a dagger clutched tightly in her fist. She was the threat to the Primori. Should the woman kill him, whatever fate he was supposed to bring about in the world, be it good or evil, would not happen.

Should she kill him, Rami would have a black mark on his record, would be forced to make amends by remaining earthbound even longer.

Which meant he could stay with Idess. Maybe even long enough that they could Ascend together.

The thought flickered through Idess as excitement, followed immediately by shame. She wanted Rami to earn his wings and find eternal happiness in Heaven. But once he was gone, Idess would be left on Earth, lonely and miserable without the brother she'd relied on for centuries.

The woman crept through the blood and gore, revenge and pain etched in her face as she eased up behind the Viking and raised her knife . . .

Stop her. The compulsion to do her job lashed at Idess, but so did the knowledge that if she saved the Primori's life, he'd slaughter the woman, probably after raping and torturing her. A tremor rattled Idess's very soul. The half of her that was her mother's daughter demanded mercy for this woman even though Idess's duty required her to do what was right for the world, not an individual.

But she'd seen the horrors men inflicted on women. The evidence lay strewn all around her.

Idess closed her eyes.

And did nothing.

The woman sank the blade deep into the Viking's back. His roar of fury and pain carried through the veil of fog, silencing the sounds of battle in the distance. The woman stabbed again, striking the Viking in his neck, and he crumpled to his knees. Idess didn't wait around to see more. She flashed to her brother, who was standing outside an Asian temple near the body of a male whose head lay several feet away. Nearby, the female Primori sat propped against a tree, stunned, but alive.

Rami turned to Idess, panting, clutching his forearm. "Thank you, God," he whispered. "You are uninjured. When I felt my Primori die I worried that you had been hurt—"

"I'm sorry," she rasped. "I...failed."

"You tried. That is all I can ask." Rami slipped his arms around her and held her close. "I'm so proud of you, sister. You've come to my aid how many times now? You are a credit to all Memitim, and I know our Lord will reward you well."

Guilt settled over her like a two-ton shroud, and her knees buckled under the weight of the enormous, loathsome mistake she'd made. She'd betrayed her brother. Her race. Her God...

Idess sat up with a scream. Her lungs burned with the force of her panting breaths, and her pulse hammered in her veins. She hated that dream. That nightmare. She couldn't believe that even after twelve hundred years it still had the power to reduce her to a quivering mess.

Couldn't believe that even now the searing, twisting guilt was gripping her in a vise of sorrow once again. Especially since she'd long ago convinced herself that Rami would forgive her once she explained what she'd done. He'd always been a forgiving soul, gentle and caring. More important, he'd operated on the same wavelength as she did. He'd understood her like no one else, and he'd been reluctant to leave her alone when he Ascended. So reluctant that he'd avoided stepping into the beacon of light for months, even at the risk of incurring the Memitim Council's wrath.

That had been five hundred years ago, and still, the pangs of betrayal coursed through her. Clutching her stomach with one hand and rubbing her eyes with the other, she willed herself out of the past. The present was better. Much, much better. Humans had coffee now. And gelato. She could use a gallon of both...

Mouth watering, she opened her eyes, wincing at the sandpaper texture of the inside of her eyelids, and at the reddish light that filled her vision. Where was she? Squinting, she made out the hospital-equipment-lined gray walls, which were splashed with what appeared to be protective spells written in blood. Skulls and creepy things in jars sat in perfect rows on high shelves. She looked down at herself, at the thin cotton hospital gown covering her bandaged body.

She was a patient at Underworld General. This had to be the infamous demon hospital. How had she gotten here?

Something blew by her in a blur. Startled, she rolled

her head to the side. Two ghosts hovered near the far wall, as clear to her as solid beings.

He's back. Back! Hurry! The male's voice was tinny, high-pitched, and dripping with panic.

The female launched into an attack against the wall, a flurry of fists against the long crack that ran horizontally from one corner to the other. Idess watched covertly, because as soon as they realized she could see and hear them, they'd mob her, either with pleas to help them cross over or with messages to deliver to surviving loved ones.

Hurrrrrrry! The crack widened into a deep fissure beneath their fists. The terror emanating from the ghosts was a low-level buzz of electricity over Idess's skin. What could frighten the dead like that? And even more mysterious was the fact that they were humans. How had they gotten here? Were they trapped because *the light* couldn't penetrate a demon-built facility?

Shuddering at that thought, she tried to swing her legs off the bed...and was jerked short. She'd been chained down. Fools. Restraints couldn't hold her. With a snarl, she drew on two of her innate Memitim powers; super strength and speed.

Nothing happened. She couldn't break the chains. She tried again. Still nothing. Well, damnation. Frowning, she tried to flash out of the hospital. Again, failure. She renewed her efforts with a sense of urgency, yanking on the chains that connected her wrists to what appeared to be huge bolts in the floor. She even tried morphing into her alternate form, but she couldn't grow a single claw.

"Fighting is futile, female. Those are Bracken Cuffs, used by demon jailers and Justice Dealers to negate any powers you might have."

A dark-haired Seminus demon in scrubs strode into the room, everything about him exuding confidence, from his rolling gait to the shrewd intelligence in his gaze. He bore a striking resemblance to the demon who had tried to kill Kynan, and she wondered if they were kin. She didn't know much about the rare breed of incubus, but she did know that those related within a few generations tended to bear family traits, and brothers could often be mistaken for twins.

"And," he continued, "you should know that in the demon legal system, you're guilty until proven innocent. Burden of proof is on the one wearing the cuffs, not the victim." An arch smile turned up one corner of his mouth. "It's a great system. Very few repeat offenders."

"Release me," she snapped. "You have no right to detain me, no matter what your idiotic demon laws state."

"This is my hospital. I have the right to do whatever I want."

"Who are you?"

"I'm your doctor. Name's Eidolon. I know your name is Idess, but who are you?"

"I'm not telling you anything." The ghosts beating against the wall slipped through it and disappeared. Another popped inside from the opposite wall. "Why would you have human ghosts?"

"Excuse me?"

"Ghosts. You know, dead people. Your hospital is infested with humans. Why?"

He gaze was maddeningly calm, his tone condescending. "Some species, like shifters and vamps, have human souls."

Of course. If they'd died here, they'd be trapped. How awful.

The door opened, and two more Seminus demons stalked in, one with dark hair and wearing a black paramedic uniform, and the other a big blond in jeans and a Jack Daniel's T-shirt. Both had longish hair that fell to their shoulders, and all had glyphs running from the tips of their right fingers to their throats, where two linked, tattooed rings circled their necks.

"The only way you're getting released is if we take you outside and separate your head from your body," the blond said in a ho-hum voice, as if he was the hospital's resident decapitation specialist who was prepping for yet another routine job.

And decapitation would definitely be one of the sure-fire ways to kill her. She opened her mouth to respond...and left it hanging open when Kynan entered. Following him was the Guardian who had nailed her with the crossbow bolt, and Kynan's wife, Gem, whom Idess had seen only once, when she'd gone to acquaint herself with—basically, spy on—her new Primori. Gem was dressed much as she'd been then, in midnight Goth pants, buckled boots, a skull-patterned corset, and a dog collar. Only her hair was different; instead of black and pink, her braided pigtails were black and electric violet.

What were Kynan and Gem doing in a demon hospital? What was a *Guardian* doing here? They were supposed to kill demons, not hang out with them. Idess knuckled her eyes, wondering if she was asleep. But when she looked again, they were all still there, surrounding her like hyenas going in for the kill.

She tugged futilely at her chains. "What's going on?"

Gem shouldered Eidolon aside to get in Idess's face. She more than anyone looked as if she wanted to cause

Idess some serious pain, and as her black-painted lips curled away from her teeth, it seemed maybe she wanted to take a few bites out of Idess, as well. "Why did you try to kill Kynan?"

Idess gaped. "Kill him? I was trying to save his life."

"And that's why you knocked me out?" Kynan's voice was gravelly, and though Idess hadn't learned much about Kynan's background yet, she suspected the mass of scars on his throat had something to do with that.

"*You* attacked *me*. I only hit you to get you out of the way so I could protect you."

"I don't need protection."

The paramedic crossed his arms over his chest and looked pointedly at her. "Except from fallen angels."

"Fallen angel? That's what you think I am?" She snorted. "Please. Those scum wouldn't lift a finger to protect their own mothers. If they had them."

"Then what are you, and why do you claim to watch over Kynan?" Gem gestured to the blond demon. "Wraith couldn't get into your head to get any information, so we know you're some kind of powerful evil."

"I'm not evil," she gritted out, but that was all she was saying, because there was no way she was letting demons know about Kynan's Marked Sentinel status.

"Then you'd better start talking," Kynan said. "You know I'm charmed. And you know only angels and fallen angels can harm me. So I want to know why and how you learned about me. And I hope for your sake you aren't planning some sort of apocalypse, because we're still recovering from the last one."

Idess's blood froze in her veins at the word "charmed," because the only reason he'd feel comfortable admitting such a huge secret was if the demons already knew, and if he didn't feel that Idess's knowing such a thing was a risk.

Which meant that they planned to kill her. "I'm not looking to start an apocalypse, I assure you."

"So you thought you'd pop into a demon-infested mansion and punch me? If not for Tayla and Lore, who knows what would have happened?"

Tayla must be the crossbow-happy Guardian next to Eidolon, but... "Lore?"

"The demon who was with me. The one who brought you in."

The demon she'd tried to kill had saved her? "Fools," she muttered. "You halfwits! I'm assigned to protect you. I'm a Memitim, a Primori guardian."

Eidolon repeated the word, "Memitim," under his breath.

Gem turned to the doctor, her braids slapping softly against the bare skin of her shoulders. "What's a Memitim?"

The room fell silent as Eidolon ran his hands through his hair a few times. "According to some religious scholars, Memitim are angels who preside over dying humans who are no longer being watched over by guardian angels."

He was right, in a way. But what he described was a Memitim's duties *after* Ascension. Right now she was earthbound, and little more than a glorified bodyguard. She locked gazes with Kynan. "May I speak with you alone?"

"No." Kynan gestured to the demons surrounding him. "They're my friends and in-laws, and they know everything about me."

Oh, *so* not good. Kynan was not only an Elder, the very top of the Guardian tier, but as a Marked Sentinel, he was in possession of something so important to the survival of the human race that he'd been charmed by angels with immortality in order to protect the item—an item that demons could use against humans to enslave them, destroy them, or worse.

"There are things I cannot discuss in front of demons."

"These *demons* made me what I am. I'm even married to one. So get over it."

The paramedic rapped his knuckles on her chains. "It's not like you have a choice."

She scowled at him. "What's your name?"

"Shade."

"Well, Shade, I might not have a choice, but neither do you. Kynan is in great danger, and if you don't release me, he could die."

Kynan slid her a look edged with doubt. "Who is after me? A fallen angel? As you saw, I'm prepared."

"Not a fallen angel. The demon you call Lore."

Eidolon arched a brow. "That's impossible."

"I'd have thought so, too, but I wouldn't have been summoned to Kynan if he hadn't been in true danger."

The entire lot of them exchanged glances, and then Kynan unclipped her chains from the stakes in the floor. "Only one way to find out."

"Reaver?" Shade asked.

"Yup."

They dragged her unceremoniously through the sliding ER doors into an underground parking lot, the Bracken Cuffs still circling her wrists, which meant there'd be no flashing out of there. Not that she would. She needed Kynan to understand the seriousness of his situation. But why the parking lot?

"There's a spell shielding the hospital from entry and exit via any means other than the Harrowgate and the parking garage," Eidolon said, obviously anticipating her question. "Since Reaver can't use Harrowgates anymore, he has to materialize someplace unprotected."

Kynan stood at the back of a black ambulance in the middle of the lot and shouted for Reaver.

"Who *is* Reaver?" she asked.

"An angel."

An angel? Surely he meant a fallen angel...

A bright light flooded the lot, blinding in its intensity. Idess winced, shielded her eyes until it faded away. And there, standing in front of Kynan, was a beautiful male angel, his golden hair flowing in an impossibly perfect curtain around his broad shoulders. His clothes were modern, business casual...black slacks and a dark blue shirt that matched his eyes, and no way was this a fallen angel.

Idess gaped like an idiot. Since true, full angels tended to hang out in Heaven, she'd seen very few, and those had been only in passing and from a distance.

"Hey, man," Kynan said with a smile. "Good to see you."

Reaver shoved his hands in his pockets and gave them all a once-over, his gaze lingering for an extra second on Idess. "Wish I could say the same," he said gruffly, though a slight tilt of his mouth gave away the fact that he wasn't completely annoyed at having been summoned. "It's not really cool for me to be hanging out with demons at a demon hospital."

"Oh, sure," Wraith drawled. "Now that you're all angel-fied, you're too good for us, huh?"

Reaver appeared to consider that. Then he nodded. "Pretty much."

Wraith snorted, revealing fangs. He was part vampire?

"Lemme see your wings," he said, and when Reaver leveled a flat stare at him, Wraith rolled his eyes. "Oh, come on. I saved the world. I should at least get to see your wings."

He'd saved the world? Surely this insolent sex demon was not the one rumored to have prevented Armageddon. Over the last few weeks, the story had spread like hellfire through the earthbound Memitim ranks, but the information she'd gleaned from her brethren had been all speculation. And the demon supposedly fighting on the side of good against the fallen angel, Byzamoth, was said to be twenty feet tall, humble, and a servant of God.

"I'll show you mine if you show me yours," the demon cajoled, with a waggle of brows, and this definitely could not be the unholy champion who was already a legend. "Show the savior of the human race some feathers."

"We'll never hear the end of that, will we?" Reaver asked, and Eidolon shook his head.

My God, it's true.

"We get to listen to it every day."

The blond Sem grinned. "The Vamp Council hung a portrait of me on their hero wall. How's that for ironic?"

"Especially since they showed it to you just before they tortured you for Serena's turning," Shade said.

Wraith snorted again. "Fuckers."

"We won't keep you," Eidolon interrupted. He gestured to Idess, who was still processing what she'd just learned. "But we need to know if what this...*person* told us is true."

"What did she tell you?"

Idess raised her chin and stepped forward. "I'm Memitim, and Kynan is my assigned Primori."

Reaver narrowed his eyes at her before nodding. "She is Memitim." He turned to Kynan, who had his arm around Gem's waist. "You are Primori."

"What's a Primori?" Kynan asked.

Reaver shrugged as if it was no big deal. Probably because he was a full angel and not a low-ranking, bottom-of-the-barrel pre-Ascension Memitim like she was.

"Primori are humans and, occasionally, demons, who have a destiny to fulfill. They might change the course of history or cause, by their actions, changes in law, etcetera. Once their destiny is realized, they either die or go back to being regular people. But until then, they have guardians assigned to keep anything from interfering with an untimely death."

"So what you're saying is that she's a good guy?" Kynan asked.

"Yes. An angel-wannabe, of sorts." Reaver shot Kynan a miffed look. "What have you gotten yourself into now?"

Idess resisted the childish urge to say, "I told you so," to all of them. Instead, she stepped forward. "He's in danger. But not from a fallen angel."

Reaver's head swiveled around to Idess, his eyes flashing. "Then who? No one but an angel—"

"Lore," Gem said abruptly. "Idess claims it's Lore."

Reaver turned back to Kynan. "The one who resurrected you?"

"I could have done without the reminder, but yeah."

Reaver's expression grew contemplative. "It's possible. He gave you life with mystical powers that shouldn't exist. It's the order of the universe that he can take that life away." Reaver's eyes locked on Idess's so intently the air whooshed from her lungs. "You know Kynan is a Sentinel, and that the amulet he wears is the most important object in the universe, but do you understand that *he* is just as important?" Of course she did—sort of—but when she opened her mouth to say so, the angel cut her off. "If you fail to keep him safe, Memitim, you will fail humankind, and you will *never* Ascend."

"Dude." Wraith looked at her. "No pressure, right?"

Eidolon swore softly. "I'll talk to Lore."

"Kynan must be protected at all costs," Reaver said. "*Talking* isn't enough." Reaver's face turned to stone, but his eyes burned with celestial fire as he narrowed his gaze on the doctor. "*You must kill him.*"

Lore used the Harrowgate to get to his North Carolina home, which was really nothing but a one-bedroom shack in the middle of the woods. He had money—lots of it—but he didn't see the point in buying a big, fancy house when this one did him just fine and had for a hundred years.

He walked past his ancient pickup and new Hummer, neither of which saw much drive time, but he liked the reminders of his humanity. He sensed his twin sister's presence before he entered through the back door and saw her lounging on his couch in her usual leather pants and black, short-sleeved hoodie, tipping back shots of his homemade moonshine. Before Detharu had enslaved him, the illegal alcohol had provided his primary income for over half a century. Prohibition had been a great thing for Lore.

As he stepped into the living room, Sin slammed her glass down on the coffee table, sloshing liquid all over the oak top. "What the hell happened to you?"

"Got into a little scuffle."

Coal-black eyes narrowed into fierce slits as she shot to her feet and fingered his scrub top. "You went to that...that *hospital*, didn't you?" She spat out the word "hospital" as though she'd bitten into something bitter and vile.

He tugged off his jacket and shirt and dropped them on the floor, eager to shed the foreign-feeling garment. "Can't get anything by you."

"Did you see...*them*?"

"Yes."

Her expression tightened. "You didn't say anything about me, did you?"

"I promised I wouldn't." He headed toward the bathroom, but Sin didn't take the hint and Velcroed herself to his heels. At the door, he spun around, and she nearly collided with him. "Do you mind?"

"They can't know about me."

"I don't think it would be a big deal—"

"Really? A sister who shouldn't exist? Who is an aberration? A freak?" She jammed her fists on her hips. The muscles in her biceps twitched, making the *dermoire* on her right arm writhe, and making the scars intertwined with the marks ripple. "Come on. Even humans kill their own kind when someone 'isn't right.' You think demons won't? We've seen it happen."

Yeah, they'd seen it happen. In fact, there were species of demons that dedicated themselves entirely to the destruction of human-demon hybrids and mixed-breed demons. Seminus demons were one of a handful of breeds that bred with other species, mainly using the females as incubators, but the offspring were always male, and always purebred no matter what the mother's species.

Unless the mother was human.

But as funky as Lore's breeding had gone with a Sem father and human mother, it couldn't compare to what had happened with Sin. As far as he knew, there had never been a female Seminus, and yet, they'd shared a womb, a birthday, and arm markings.

"You're not a freak. And I doubt you have anything to worry about with them." He held up his hands when she opened her mouth to argue. "But don't spaz. I promised."

"Spaz?" She huffed. "I'm going for a walk. Have a nice shower."

She stalked away, her blue-black hair slapping against the small of her back. With one last noise of disgust, she slammed out of the house. She was overreacting. A lot. But she had a tendency to fly off the handle first and think later, and she used her long walks as a way to work off the initial burn of whatever had set her off.

Lore just shook his head and stepped into the shower. His sister was the most closed-off person he'd ever met, but then, with her past, he could understand that. He just wished he'd been able to help her long before she came back into his life. Like, maybe before he'd abandoned her to decades of abuse. Yeah, that would have been good.

He washed, but no matter how hard he scrubbed, his past wouldn't come clean. Too much had happened, too many people had died, and too many mistakes had been made. A shower wasn't going to send it all down the drain.

Still, he savored the feel of hot water and soap suds sluicing down his body, washing away the blood and dirt the Slogthu nurse missed when he'd sponged Lore down. At least the wounds were healed. The lacerations had been closed internally with dissolving stitches, and though Eidolon had barely used his healing gift, it had been enough to seal the outer layer of skin and leave only the thinnest of shiny white scars. It had also knitted his ribs back together, and his shoulder felt good as new.

All in all, Lore was back in top form and ready to take out Kynan. With any luck, there wouldn't be some crazy-hot female who smelled like sugar and spice around to get in his way this time.

Idess's interference had been unfortunate, annoying, and...arousing. And how fucked up was that? She'd tried to snuff him, yet some twisted part of him found that to be one hell of a turn-on. Enough of one that she became the image in his mind as he fisted his cock and began to stroke. Usually his sessions were a matter of keeping his rage at bay, but for the first time in a long time, he was in need of a release for himself, not for his rage. Even AprilMayJune, like all the females before her, had been about the rage, and ultimately, she'd been nothing more than a means to an end.

But Idess...she was different, and in this hot fantasy, she was the sexy female on her knees in front of him. He could picture her gazing up at him, her eyes drowsy, lips swollen, the little hoop earring at the top of her right ear glinting in the light. He bit back a moan as he pumped his palm up and down his shaft, imagined it was Idess's wet mouth doing the work. Fuck, yeah, she was good...so freaking good he couldn't hold on, and when he came it was the best damned orgasm he'd had in decades.

When his legs stopped shaking, he finished with the shower, slung a towel around his hips, and went to his bedroom. He dressed in sweat shorts and a tee, and made a mental note to go shopping soon—he was down to his last leather jacket.

He padded barefoot into the living room, where the morning sun was just peeking through the window. Sin had come back, was sitting on the couch watching the *Today Show,* the bottle of moonshine and her glass balanced on the cushion next to her. Overhead, the ceiling fan spun in lazy circles that did nothing to ease the spring humidity.

Sin didn't seem to notice the sticky breeze as she idly flipped one of her blades into the air and caught it with nimble fingers. She could hit a target in the eye from ten yards with those throwing knives. Not that she needed to kill that way; her *dermoire* gift was similar to his but more controlled, and she used it often.

She continued to toss the knife as he took a seat in the leather recliner at the end of the coffee table. "So, did you kick his ass?" Her words were slightly slurred. "The guy you got into the fight with?"

"It wasn't a guy."

"Well, I know you weren't out tomcatting, so what happened?"

"Hey," he said, offended. "I can tomcat. Did it just the other night."

She snatched the knife out of the air and tossed it again. "Uh-huh."

"Seriously."

"You kill her?"

"A little." He kicked his feet onto the coffee table. "But it wasn't my fault. She was a mantis. Tried to eat me."

Sin barked out a laugh. "Only you, bro. Only you." She turned back to the TV and flipped off a guest talking about love and marriage. "So? The chick who kicked your ass hard enough to land you in the hospital?"

"She was defending my target," Lore said carefully, because although the assignment was good news, he didn't want Sin to know that her life could end if he failed.

"Freelance job?"

"No."

She turned to him so fast he heard her neck crack. The blade in the air came down and embedded in the arm of the couch. "Are you serious? Lore? Are you fucking with me?" She hit the mute button on the remote, cutting off Ann Curry.

The rhythmic thump of his heartbeat in his ears filled the silence. "I'm dead serious."

She squealed. His sister *never* squealed. "Oh, my God! I thought you'd say no. This is your hundredth, Lore. We're almost free!" She splashed liquor into a shot glass with a shaky hand.

"Yup."

"Okaaaay." She put down her glass. "You don't seem very excited."

Shit. "I am. We've wanted this for decades, right?" Felt like centuries, though, since the day he'd agreed to a hundred kills in exchange for both his and Sin's freedom.

"It's the deadline, isn't it?"

He blinked. "How do you know?"

"It was a guess, because I have one, too. A job. With an impossibly short deadline."

Dread curdled the contents of Lore's stomach. They'd never had to complete an assignment in under two weeks before. "What happens if you don't make your deadline?"

Sin's gaze skipped away, and she retrieved her knife.

"Sin?" Lore's voice cracked. For the first time in a very long time, he was afraid. Not for himself, but for Sin, who had been through more than her fair share of misery in her life.

"He'll sell me," she said between clenched teeth. "He'll hack off my arm so I can't use it to kill, and sell me to the Neethuls."

Oh, Jesus. Neethuls were an incredibly cruel race who bred, trained, and traded slaves...particularly sex slaves. Before being sold to Detharu, Sin had suffered as a slave who had to do anything her master wanted, from selling drugs to killing enemies, but the Neethuls would make what she'd gone through seem like a day at the beach.

"That won't happen," he swore. "I'll help you take out your target. Who is it?"

"You have your own mark to deal with." She tested the edge of her blade with her thumb. "What happens if you miss your deadline?"

"Nothing."

Her gaze turned steely, silver shards against a black backdrop. "Bullshit. Tell me."

"If I miss the deadline, Deth gets to double my time of service," he lied.

She regarded him warily, as though trying to decide if he was telling the truth or not. She had a tendency to question everything, especially if it came from Lore, and he wondered if she'd ever fully trust him again.

"You won't miss your deadline," she said finally. "You never do. So what happened while you were trying to take out your mark? It's not like you to get caught out like that."

Outside the open window, the high-pitched warble of a bird sounded like laughter, which was fitting. "I got cocky."

"Now *that* I believe," she said wryly. "So who is it? Your mark?"

It was a question no assassin asked another—the risk of someone homing in on your kill and stealing it from under you was too great—but Lore and Sin had always shared deets. "Remember I told you about that human asshole I brought back to life? It's him. Should have left him dead, I guess."

Sin's grip on her knife tightened. "Ah... isn't that guy friends with..." She trailed off, because she refused to say it. *Our brothers.*

"Yeah. It's okay. I'll handle it so they never find out it was me." Doubt set her jaw in a stubborn line, so he steered the conversation away from Kynan and the potential trouble Lore was in. "What about you? Who's your mark?"

Sin stretched out on the couch and tucked an arm behind her head. Dark circles under her half-lidded eyes revealed her exhaustion. "Some werewolf. Loner. Should be a quick in and out."

Sounded like an easy enough hit for Sin, but still, the second Kynan was dead, Lore was going to help Sin with the werewolf, or warg, as they liked to be called. No way was she going to be sold to the Neethul.

A faint buzzing noise snagged his attention, and he heaved himself out of the chair to grab his cell phone from the scrub pants' pocket. Figured it would be Eidolon. Again. Sighing, he opened up the message... and promptly stopped breathing.

Come to my apartment. Now. We need to discuss Kynan.

Five

~

Lore stood outside Eidolon's door, unable to shake the feeling that he was walking into a trap. And yet, like a cat with a string dangling before it, he couldn't resist.

But that didn't mean he was a total chump. He'd play this to his advantage, would use this opportunity to learn anything he could about Kynan. Usually Lore had weeks to plan a hit, to educate himself about his marks' jobs, friends, families, vulnerabilities, and habits, but the expiration date on this assignment was bearing down on him too fast for comfort and with extra complications, and the whole thing was about to go sour.

As he raised his fist to knock on the door, a tingling sensation prickled the back of his neck.

"Well, well," a female voice purred. "Fancy seeing you here."

"Idess." He pivoted around. She stood a few feet away, her faded, ripped jeans revealing tantalizing slashes of skin from her slim thighs to her knees, where the denim disappeared into heeled leather boots. Lore entertained an image of lying on the ground with her straddling him, one sexy boot on each side of his chest as she lowered herself onto him, and shit, his hormones were out of control lately.

She cocked her head to the side, and her ponytail swung behind her, the curled tip brushing her hip and only adding to that straddle fantasy. "What are you doing?"

"I think you know."

Her sly smile made her eyes sparkle. "You want to see how much your brothers know about you trying to kill Kynan."

"I don't want to kill him," he said easily. "I have no idea what you're talking about."

Idess tsked. "I wasn't born yesterday, demon."

"Angels are born?" Breathing deeply to take in her rich, spicy scent, he took a step closer, testing his boundaries. Her chin came up a fraction of an inch, but she didn't budge. "So all the pure, holier-than-thou shit is bullshit? You guys are fucked into existence like everyone else? Like us lowly demons?"

That sinful, wicked mouth pursed. "You know what I meant. There's no need to be crude."

"There's always a need to be crude." He raked his gaze from her head to her toes, lingering on all the sweet spots. Mostly, he was just being obnoxious. Mostly. Her sweet spots really did deserve extra ogling. "Especially when you want to shock the shit out of some prissy little angel."

"Prissy?" She brought her ponytail over her shoulder and played with it idly, her fingers stroking the gold bands that secured the exotic length at evenly spaced intervals. "Stay away from Kynan, because next time you try to harm him, I'll spank you. And not in the fun way, either. How's that for prissy?" Winking, she waggled her fingers at him and poofed out of the hallway.

Man, he hated poofers. You couldn't ever nail them down. Not that he wouldn't *like* to nail her.

And what was that about spanking? Because *all* spankings were the good kind. If she was going to threaten him, she had a lot to learn.

He knocked on the door, and Eidolon must have been right there, because it swung open. Without so much as a hello, Eidolon turned and stalked down the hall, obviously expecting to be followed. As if a Ph.D. made him God.

Lore went after him, catching up to his brother in the huge living room, where a black and tan mutt lay on the leather couch, valiantly trying to ignore the ferret playing with his tail.

Eidolon rounded on Lore. "What's up with you and Kynan? And don't bullshit me. We know you want him dead. I want you to promise to leave him the fuck alone."

Idess, you little rat. "Look, whatever Cookie told you, it's a lie. I don't want anything to do with Kynan—"

Suddenly, his back was kissing the wall and Eidolon's fist was tangled in his shirt. Gold eyes glowed with fury. "I said, don't bullshit me," he snarled. "We *know*. You need to lay off this obsession with Gem. She's Kynan's, and that isn't going to change, even if he's dead."

Lore's own temper flared, and he dragged in a deep breath, fighting to stay calm. Raging out on his brother wasn't going to help anything, and really, the fact that E thought this was about Gem was a good thing. "Fine. Okay, I get it. Gem's taken." He *was* over her, and if his brothers believed it, they might leave him alone if he promised to let it go. "Now step off."

Muscles twitched in Eidolon's jaw, and Lore heard the grind of enamel as he worked his molars together. Finally, with a shove, he released Lore. "I'm dead serious. This isn't about protecting a friend. This is about saving a brother."

"Yeah, I know you're tight with Kynan—"

"No. It's about saving *you*." Eidolon jabbed his finger at Lore's chest. "You so much as breathe in Kynan's direction, and your life is going to mean jack shit. Do you understand?"

"I can handle Idess."

Eidolon's face was grim. "Just promise me, Lore. Promise me you'll stay away from Kynan. And while you're in avoidance mode, add Shade and Wraith to your list."

"That's not going to be easy," Wraith drawled from the entrance, where he, Shade, and Kynan stood, all glaring daggers at him. Perfect. Just perfect.

Shade pushed past Wraith and Kynan. "What the fuck, E? Nice that Idess had to clue us in on your little get-together."

"Maybe your invitation got lost in the mail," Lore offered.

Eidolon put himself between Lore and his other brothers. "Calm down. Lore has agreed to stay away from Kynan."

Wraith pegged Lore with a hard stare. "I don't believe him."

"I don't care what you believe," Lore shot back. "You guys can go fuck yourselves. I'm out of here." He fired up his gift and headed toward the hall. He could just brush by Ky—

A fist slammed into his jaw, spinning him into Eidolon.

Idess stood there, looking pretty proud of herself, and he supposed she should be—she had one hell of an uppercut.

Wraith came out of nowhere, making like a linebacker and taking Lore to the carpet. Lore snarled, bucking his brother hard enough to throw him, but Wraith moved like a phantom, somehow avoiding Lore's deadly accurate spin-kick. Shade drove his boot into Lore's side, and Lore grunted, but he leaped to his feet and got in his own well-placed kick to Shade's thigh. Now, he could rush Kynan—

"*Stop!*" Eidolon's roar froze everyone except the animals, who scampered out of the room. "Let him leave."

"He wasn't trying to leave," Idess said. "He was gunning for Kynan." She rubbed her forearm as though it hurt. "He's still planning to kill him."

Eidolon's eyes went from gold to red, and he shoved Wraith and Shade away, fisted Lore's shirt again, and brought them nose-to-nose, his entire body shaking. "You said you were done with Gem." There was so much rage in his voice that it was warped, hard to understand. "Why are you doing this? Answer me, damn you!"

"Because I don't have a choice," Lore shouted. "He's an assignment."

A flicker of uncertainty crossed Eidolon's face, and Lore used the moment to slam him into the wall and rush Kynan. He needed to be done with this, once and for all. If his brothers killed him afterward, who cared? Hell, bring it on. At least he'd die knowing Sin would be safe.

And free.

A fierce sting at the base of his skull made him stumble, and Idess's grip on his biceps brought him to a full stop.

"Take another step and I release the bore worm," she

said, and ice froze the marrow in his bones. Being eaten alive from the inside was not on his list of fun ways to die.

She pressed the length of her body against his left side, gluing herself to him so she could feel even the smallest twitch, the tiniest warning that he might fight back. Smart cookie.

Her fingers gouged his arm. "I can't allow Lore to harm Kynan. So either one of you kill him, or I will."

Shade, Wraith, and Kynan raised their hands to volunteer. How special. Brotherly love ran like syrup in the room.

Lore weighed his options. He could kill Idess...but once she was dead, he doubted he'd make it through the advancing wall of demon brothers to get to Kynan.

And if he failed to kill her, he had a bore worm attached to his spine. If she sent it into his body, one of the side-effects of being eaten alive was that it would render him susceptible to commands, and she could make Lore do anything she wanted, from clucking like a chicken, to stepping in front of a bus.

The upside was that she'd be reluctant to use it. As long as the creature was inside its host, the summoner suffered nearly debilitating pain. Bore worms were temporary measures, at best.

As his brothers and Kynan closed in on him like rabid wolves, the first stirrings of apprehension that he might not make it out of this scrape alive rippled through him. He didn't fear death; he feared dying before he could make sure Sin was safe.

The very real possibility that he was going to die right now brought a veil of lava-red cascading down over his vision. He breathed deeply, willing it to recede as he glared at his brothers. "Back the hell off—"

Idess spun him into the wall so he was eating plaster, her pelvis hugging his ass—in a great fit, he couldn't help but notice, even through his growing anger. Her plump breasts rubbed on his back, and he popped an erection as the sexual side-effect of his rage took hold.

"It's a little late for backing off," she murmured against his ear, and his blood thickened with both fury and desire. "The only reason I haven't killed you yet is that I want to know who wants Kynan dead. Plus, I thought I'd allow your brothers that honor."

"Aren't you the vicious one," he growled. "That's hot." *I'm going to kill these guys and then fuck you hard.* The thought blasted into his brain, pumped in on the rage that was poisoning his system. He panted, desperate to come down from this, because he was only one insult, or one prick of pain away from no-return.

And then he could guarantee that males were going to die. The female . . .

Idess jammed her knee into a pressure point in his thigh and tripped his land mine. Lore exploded out of her grip, knocking her into Shade. They both went down. *Kynan. Kill the human first—*

Idess leaped to her feet, spitting commands in the universal demon language, Sheoulic.

Lore checked up hard as pain shot from his brain stem to his tailbone. His lungs vapor-locked and his muscles cemented in place. He was a dead man now.

His last semicoherent thought as his brain function shut down like a computer's blue screen of death was that he should have negotiated with Detharu for ninety-nine kills instead of a hundred.

Idess doubled over as the full body migraine struck, squeezing her brain, her spinal fluid, and even the marrow in her bones. She hated using bore worms, but she liked to win, and she'd take the tradeoff any day.

Wincing, eyes slitted against the light that stabbed her nerve endings, she lifted her head—and gasped. Lore was standing there, surrounded by his baffled brothers, gaze vacant thanks to the worm's influence. That was to be expected. What was unexpected—and a whole lot of trouble—was the fact that he was surrounded by a faint azure glow.

In the span of time it took for an angel to flap her wings, he'd become a Primori, important to the very fabric of the world. Which meant she couldn't kill him. And worse, her arm burned anew as a circular symbol set into her wrist...

Impossible. *No, no, no!* Nausea swirled in her stomach, but from the agony wrenching her brain and bones or from the growing fear that the *heraldi* forming in her skin was bad news, she didn't know.

But as the mark embedded firmly into her arm above the other two to form a triangle of circles, she couldn't deny the new link that stretched like an invisible string from her to the new charge.

Lore was not just Primori; he was *her* Primori.

Oh, this was a sick joke.

His symbol began to throb harder, a screaming warning that Lore was in danger. She looked in time to see Kynan draw a pistol from his chest holster, murderous intent turning the blue in his eyes to glacial arctic ice.

Weakly, because the bore worm was sapping her energy, she grasped Lore's wrist and flashed him to her house.

She had to restrain him, and fast, before the worm caused permanent damage to him, and before her own pain became so overwhelming that she lost control over the creature.

Quickly, she led Lore to the bedroom and ordered him to strip off his gloves and jacket—and his leather chest harness that was loaded with weapons...and the wrist housing...and the ankle holster with the pistol, and the other ankle sheath with the blade...and the throwing stars in his pants pockets...

She eyed one weapon in particular as it fell to the floor, an exquisite, rare Gargantua-bone dagger. Those priceless beauties were practically indestructible, and once wetted with the blood of an intended victim, the dagger would virtually guide the wielder's hand to unerringly accurate strikes against that victim. Wow—Lore was one well-equipped assassin.

When he lifted his shirt to remove a ceramic blade taped to his ribs, she sucked in a harsh breath at the sight of his muscular abs and hard-cut chest. Yes, *very* well-equipped. He was massive, a mountain of power she wanted to touch, if only to see if she'd feel the shock of it through her fingertips.

She scowled, eyes locked on the odd, handprint-shaped mark over his heart. An assassin bond?

Speaking of bonds, Lore's *heraldi* had settled down, but another one had started to tingle. The werewolf's. The buzz was mild, which meant the threat was real but not immediate, and it could even pass. Still, this was truly unbelievable. Even at her busiest, when she'd been in charge of a dozen Primori, she'd rarely responded to more than one incident a month. Now she'd had three Primori in trouble in a matter of hours.

Not good. "Get on the bed," she told Lore. "Back against the headboard."

He obeyed like a good little zombie, though she swore she heard the faintest rumble of a growl. Amazing. Few could maintain any kind of awareness while under the spell of a bore worm.

A particularly sharp burst of worm-hurt stabbed her brain and, wincing, she flashed to the garage, where she'd dropped the Bracken Cuffs she'd stolen from Eidolon when she left the demon hospital. What handy devices. Everyone should have a set.

The sting of the warg's *heraldi* intensified. *Hurry, hurry…*

Urgency kicked her into high gear as she dug through the neat stacks of her brother's belongings until she found what she was looking for; a twenty-foot length of finely wrought but strong chain. Gathering it and the Bracken Cuffs, she hurried back to Lore and ordered him to snap his own wrists into the cuffs while she looped the chain over the top of her canopy bed and attached the ends to each cuff. The result left him sitting with his arms stretched up and out, with little give in the chain to allow him leverage. He was strong, no doubt, but he was no match for the bed she'd had specially made to buffer her nightmares.

"Estalila enalt."

The bore worm spell broke, and instantly, her body migraine disappeared, but so did her strength. She'd need to feed very soon. Lore's snarl followed her as she grabbed the Gargantua-bone dagger, touched her warg's *heraldi*, and materialized in the wooded backyard of a tiny mobile home.

Praying she wasn't too late, she burst through the open back door. She found Chase Barnstead in the living room, naked and doubled over, arms wrapped tightly around his abdomen. A woman wearing only underwear and a bra was clutching his shoulder, almost as if she were concerned, trying to help him…but the markings on her right arm were writhing fiercely.

Those were Seminus markings. A Sem mate? So many coincidences, and none of them good. Whatever she was doing to Chase was killing him, and the damage had already been done. The warg's brand on Idess's arm was fading, and a sickly gray light pulsed around him, marking him as one who was fated to die. Her healing powers wouldn't help him. His death was locked into the web of life now.

Fury and the need for vengeance roared to all-consuming life inside Idess. She launched herself, nailing the female in the chest—dead center in the middle of a handprint-shaped scar—with a roundhouse kick.

The female flew backward into a duct-taped recliner, smashing a beer bottle, but to Idess the kick felt sloppy, with not nearly enough power behind it. The black-haired harlot should have gone right through the wall.

That's what I get for not feeding. And all these fights were only draining her faster. She rushed the other female, preparing to drive the Gargantua-bone dagger right into her heart. "I'm going to laugh when the *griminions* come for your soul."

Idess raised the blade…and a hot poker of pain shot through her arm. *Lore.* In danger. How? She staggered, dropping the dagger. The raven-haired devil tore a bloody shard of bottle glass out of her thigh and, with a snarl, she came at Idess, a whirlwind of arms and legs.

Off-balance from pain and surprise, Idess fell back under the rain of blows, dodging and blocking and unable to land a blow of her own. Knuckles smashed into Idess's mouth, splitting her lip. Her head snapped back on her spine and *ow*, she was going to feel that one for a month.

Idess dropped and rolled away from the other female, who had somehow gotten hold of the dagger. The Sem struck out, and Idess hissed at the bite of metal in the flesh of her left biceps. Now that her blood had wetted the blade, the dagger would not miss if swung at Idess again.

She flung herself backward, out of the range of the other female's reach. This was a lost battle. Chase was as good as dead, anyway.

In fact... he was gone. While she'd been fighting with this assassin, he'd fled.

Slapping a palm over the cut made by the Gargantua dagger, Idess flashed out of there, sickened by her failure to save Chase, and by the knowledge that his death had just cost her several more centuries on earth.

The tension inside Eidolon's apartment could have been measured by a barometer, even several minutes after Idess had disappeared with Lore. What the hell had she done with him?

Kynan finally headed for the front door. "I'm going to Aegis HQ. There's got to be a way to neutralize Lore's ability." He paused before he got too far, and when he spoke, there was resolve in his voice, but not unkindness. "I know he's your brother. But I'll do what I have to do to protect myself. Gem's pregnant, and I won't leave her alone or my child fatherless."

Eidolon's breath caught at the unexpected news, and Shade let out a juicy curse.

"That's not going to happen," Wraith swore.

Kynan inclined his head and swept out of the apartment, leaving E alone with Shade and Wraith, both of whom radiated anger in sharp bursts Eidolon could feel like tiny whips against his skin.

"Well?" Shade prompted, and if he expected an apology for cutting him and Wraith out of the talk with Lore, he'd be waiting a long time. Eidolon had done what he needed to do to keep his family intact. "You want to explain why Idess had to tell us about your little meeting?"

"It doesn't matter. We've got to find her," E said. "Before she kills Lore."

"Fuck that," Shade growled. "I say we let her."

"He's our brother, Shade."

"So is Ky," Shade pointed out. "He's not blood or even the right damned species, but he gave his life to save us, our families, and this entire fucking planet. We don't know shit about Lore except that he tried to kill us."

Eidolon stared, unable to believe what his brother had just said. "I agree with you about Kynan, but seriously? You don't care if Lore dies?"

"Better him than Ky," Wraith ground out.

"We'll handle this." Eidolon's gaze flicked back and forth between Wraith and Shade. "We've got to give him a chance."

Shade made a sound of disgust. "Like you did with Roag? Over and over?"

Gods, he was so sick of the Roag conversation. Yeah, Eidolon had fucked up. But he could only beg for forgiveness so many times. "You're never going to let that go, are you?"

"*Let it go?*" Shade asked incredulously. "I lost Skulk because you kept giving Roag chances. Kept saying, 'He's our brother.' Well, fuck that, E. If we'd taken care of him when we should have, Skulk wouldn't be dead."

Skulk had been Shade's Umber demon sister, and they'd been close. So close that she'd worked as a paramedic at UG just so Shade could keep an eye on her. Eidolon missed her, and every day his heart squeezed with guilt at his unintentional role in her death.

"And you wouldn't have a mate and kids if not for Roag." It was the wrong thing to say, and Eidolon knew it. Knew it even as Shade's fist slammed into his jaw.

Eidolon's head rocked back and pain shot through his face, sparking his own anger. He returned fire with the power of his entire body behind the cross-punch. A crack rang out as Shade's nose sprayed blood. Crimson swallowed the black in Shade's eyes, no doubt matching E's, and it was on.

They came together with the force of two bulls. Distantly, Eidolon heard furniture breaking and pictures coming off the walls, and then the crash of the television.

They went to the floor, pummeling the unholy hell out of each other in a no-holds-barred, who-can-hurt-who-the-most fight, something E and Shade had never done.

This was what Wraith and Shade did.

A particularly hard hammer-fist to the side of the head made Eidolon see stars and hear bells. Snarling, he jammed his knee up and into Shade's gut. Shade slammed Eidolon's skull into the floor, putting Eidolon's fury onto a whole new tier of pissed.

"Stop it!" Tayla tore them apart, shoving Shade so hard

he wheeled backward and tumbled over the back of the couch. Then she rounded on Wraith, who was propped against the doorway, arms crossed over his chest and ankles locked casually together.

"Thanks for the help, jerk. You couldn't have stopped this before I had to?"

"Stop it?" Wraith cocked his thumb toward the kitchen. "Hell, I was about to go make popcorn to go with the Jerry Springer."

Shade came around the couch, ready to go at it again. Once more, Tayla put herself between them, crouching in a defensive position, and E had to bite back a smile at her fierceness.

He was so going to make love to her the second he got his brothers out the door. Right now, though, he wasn't going to let her fight his battles. Gently, he squeezed her shoulder and pulled her back. "Hey, it's okay."

"*No, Eidolon, it's not.* It's far from okay." Blood ran in multiple streams from Shade's nose and a nasty gash in his brow, and his bared teeth were streaked with crimson. Powering up his gift, Eidolon reached out to heal him, but Shade reared back. "Don't fucking touch me."

Shade had never been so pissed that he wouldn't let Eidolon tend to his wounds.

"Shade, listen to me—"

Eidolon's beeper went off. He ignored it, though he knew his plan to get Tayla naked would have to be put on hold. "We can't let Lore die," he finished.

Wraith pushed away from the wall. "We can't let Kynan die either."

"This isn't an either-or," Eidolon said, suddenly weary despite the adrenaline that was still rushing through his system. "No one dies. We'll talk sense into Lore, and if that doesn't work, we'll contain him."

Shade's eyes flashed violently. "Do what you have to do. But know that if it comes down to a choice, I choose Kynan."

"But if—"

Shade cut him off with a snarl. "You *really* don't want to go there."

With that, Shade stalked out of the apartment. Wraith shot E a don't-say-a-word look and followed their brother out.

Releasing a frustrated breath, Eidolon dabbed blood off his split lip with the back of his hand,

Tay wrapped herself around him. "You okay?"

"Yeah," he lied, even though she'd sense the truth through their mate-bond. And the truth was that when he'd told Lore that his staff had been on edge lately, that wasn't the half of it. Everyone at UG was at each others' throats, which had led to critical errors and slipshod patient care.

"You can't lie to me, Hellboy," Tay said.

"I know," he sighed. "I've just never seen Shade so worked up. I seriously think he would let this tear us all apart."

"That won't happen. You guys have survived worse than this. Shade's angry now, but the very thing he's angry about, your loyalty to your brothers and family, is why he loves you. Give him a chance to cool off."

Tayla was young—compared to Eidolon—but she'd been around the block, and she understood people. And demons...in part because she was half Soulshredder, and she could see scars most couldn't.

But in this case, Eidolon had his doubts about Tayla's

prediction. Where Roag had failed to tear them apart, Lore just might succeed.

⌒

The rage was like drowning in an ocean of boiling blood. It wrapped around Lore and squeezed so that every breath was an agonizing struggle.

He'd come to chained to a bed in a frilly bedroom, his head pounding and still engaged in fight mode. He didn't know where he was, who had taken him, and he burned with the need to kill.

Every second he fought against the chains made him angrier, and that, combined with the jackhammer in the brain and a lack of a recent release, was putting him on a tightrope where the slightest nudge would plunge him right into Noreturnsville Avenue's hard pavement.

No net in sight.

Adrenaline surged through him as if a dam had burst. He yanked on the restraints. No good. He yanked harder, until he felt the pop of his elbow and shoulder sockets. Pain exploded in a flash of light behind his eyes.

His groin throbbed, and fuck, if he could just reach his cock, he could end this before it went too far...

A warm trickle ran down his wrist. Blood. The feel, sight, the smell...it triggered his need to slaughter as if someone had flipped a switch and turned on his inner Jason Voorhees.

He roared as the only thread keeping his sanity in check snapped.

At least he was restrained, so he couldn't run rampant. Couldn't kill innocents.

No, this rage would kill *him*.

Six

⌒

The bloodcurdling snarl reached Idess's ears before she'd fully materialized in her living room. Exhausted but fueled by fear, she sprinted to the bedroom, skidding to a shocked halt at the doorway. Lore was alone. No one was trying to kill him.

But...he'd transformed. His eyes, burning like coal embers, bored into her, and his skin had darkened to a deep, dusky red shot through with dark veins on top of bulging muscle. He bared his teeth, as if he wanted to take a bite out of her. He was beautiful and terrifying, and a tremor ran through her as she stepped into the bedroom.

What in the world had happened to him? Whatever it was, it threatened his life. The *heraldi* on her arm still burned, hurting much more than the dagger wound. She'd heard that some species could become uncontrollably enraged to the point of permanence.

Or, apparently, death.

"Lore—"

His violent roar shook the house's very foundation. Blood dripped from his wrists, which he'd worn raw beneath the shackles. The soles of his boots had shredded the bedspread and sheets, all the way to the mattress.

"What can I do?"

"Release. Me." His words were distorted by rage and hatred.

Steeling herself, she said, "That's not possible."

A torrent of f-word-spiced curses ripped from his mouth. "Damn you and the bitch who whelped you!"

She inched toward him. "I can't release you. What else can ease you?"

He went mad, his flailings so violent that a crack rang out as her bed frame broke. Red flecks danced in eyes that had gone fully black, swallowing the whites, the demon behind the handsome face coming through like some sort of transparent overlay.

She halted beside his hip, a huge mistake, because although his wrists were bound above his head, his legs were free, and he kicked out at her, catching her in the ribs and slamming her into the door to the bathroom.

Rubbing her aching chest, she went back to him, this time easing next to his shoulders and out of range of those huge, booted feet. Still, he whipped his knees back and nearly brained her. The boy was remarkably flexible.

He was hurting himself, and it was only going to get worse. "Tell me what will make this better."

He clenched his teeth so hard his jaw popped. "Fuck."

She really hated demons and their foul mouths. "Tell me," she repeated.

"Fuck," he snarled. "Sex."

"Sex?" She laughed. "If you think I'm falling for that, you're beyond stupid."

Punching his head back with such force that he left a dent in the plaster, he let loose an agonized roar that rattled through her insides. A blast of heat rolled off him, a wave of need she felt as a loosening of her muscles and a sudden liquid rush between her legs. A dark, sinful scent wrapped around her, filling her lungs and making her sway toward him. She caught herself, took an awkward, stumbling step back. She'd been around long enough to know incubi could throw off pheromones to attract partners, but she'd never experienced it... until now.

Her gaze flickered involuntarily to his hips, where, sure enough, a massive erection was straining against the fly of his pants. No way. Nuh-uh. There had to be another way. *Any* way.

"Just...hold still." She took another lungful of that delicious scent into her. "I'll release you or something—"

"No!" His head snapped forward, and his eyes, glowing with an eerie luminosity, fastened on her. "I...can't...control...myself." Every word was delivered between clenched teeth. "Not safe...I'll attack. Or worse."

Idess let out a startled breath. He was worried about what he'd do to her, to others if he escaped in this condition. She hadn't known all that many demons, but those she had known wouldn't have cared. A thread of admiration crept up on her, and curse him, she had no business feeling anything for this male but hatred and disgust. She despised assassins, wasn't overly fond of demons, and he'd caused her a lot of trouble.

Then again, he'd also saved her life.

Of course, he wouldn't have had to save her life if he hadn't been trying to kill Kynan in the first place.

His moment of clarity passed quickly, and suddenly he was a mass of violence again, throwing himself against the chains, testing their strength, and the bed cracked some more.

Guilt pricked at her; she was the cause of his misery. She might not like demons, but it wasn't in her nature to cause suffering. Her mind worked frantically for a way to help him. First, she had to stop him from hurting himself worse. Hastily, she forced his legs down with a firm grip on his thighs.

He went into a renewed frenzy, trying to bite her, his arms jerking against the chains. His hips bucked, brushing that massive erection against her arm. The moment he made contact, he calmed a little. He did it again, this time with a controlled roll of his pelvis.

Interesting. All right, so maybe addressing his arousal was the only way to help him. She eyed the massive bulge in his pants. Oh, my. How long had it been since she'd touched a man intimately? The answer to that question was, *too long*. She'd lived the first nineteen years of her life believing she was human, and though she'd known sex for only the last two years of her human existence, she remembered exactly how good male flesh felt against hers.

Even after two thousand years of celibacy. And not one orgasm.

Be not tempted by the pleasures of the flesh, Idess. She'd heard that from Rami with annoying frequency whenever he caught her admiring men. It had been so easy for her brother to say, since he'd never had sex—he'd been celibate even during his human years. But she'd had a wild side as a human, and for centuries afterward, and he'd been ruthless in his quest to tame her.

It had taken her betrayal of him to finally bring her to heel.

She let out a long, slow breath. "Be not tempted by the pleasures of the flesh," she whispered. Telling herself she had no choice and that it was no big deal, she palmed the thick length that pressed so hard against the leather that she could make out the shape of his shaft. The thick head. He shouted and stiffened, but at least he'd stopped thrashing. The whites had returned to his eyes, and now they were wild, wide, like those of a spooked horse. He was panting, but he remained motionless, as though waiting to see what she was going to do next.

He was remarkable. Even in his fury, he was gorgeous. Her body responded once again, warming and tingling, growing achy in that most primal of instincts.

Instincts that must be ignored. It was forbidden for Memitim to have sex with humans, so she could only imagine how much trouble she'd be in for having sex with a *demon*.

She frowned. Was this some sort of final test? Rami had faced something similar, just before his Ascension, when he'd fallen in love with a human woman he'd nursed back to health after finding her injured by an archer's arrow. When, after a serious internal struggle, he'd resisted her invitation into her bed, he'd been offered his final reward.

What if this was Idess's test? Not that she'd ever be in danger of falling in love with a demon, but this was a sex demon, a species known to be irresistible to all females. Had he been given to her in order to determine her ability to resist? That would explain why he'd suddenly become a Primori. *Her* Primori.

And if so, it was a poor test of her willpower. Like all Memitim, she'd taken a vow of chastity, and no male, human or demon, could make her break it after thousands of years.

Satisfied that she could handle this without losing herself to lust, she ran her hand down his shaft, letting her palm mold to the firm length of him. His lips parted on a soft gasp, and crazily enough, she wanted to touch them. With her fingers, her mouth...

Cursing her response but encouraged by his, she rubbed harder, and his gasp became a long, tortured moan.

She took her hand away.

Instantly, he arched his back, yanked his chains, and howled...a sound of unimaginable pain.

"Okay," she said quickly, and palmed him again. Once more, he settled down, but his entire body trembled. "I'm sorry."

Maybe she could use this. Just a little...

"Tell me," she said, as she straddled his knees and plucked at the top button on his pants, "who hired you to kill Kynan?"

He shook his head, and she drew her hand away.

The sound of his teeth snapping together jarred the air. He shook so hard she was nearly dislodged from her seat.

"Bad idea," she muttered, as she tore open the remaining buttons and released him. He was enormous, a thick column of deep, blushing brown that disappeared into the V of his fly. Only a very light dusting of dark hair trailed from beneath the hem of his shirt across his abdomen, which was marked with all manner of scars, to his groin.

Forbidden need washed over her, and at the same time,

Lore pushed his hips upward, putting the blunt head of his penis in contact with her hand.

"Aren't we impatient?" *We* was right, because this was as close as she could get to a male, and she wanted this nearly as much as he did. Using only the tips of her fingers, she stroked the velvety cap until Lore's head fell back against the wall and his eyes closed with relief. "This feels good, doesn't it?" It certainly felt good to her. Oh, she remembered this. Except she didn't recall taking so much pleasure in touching a man.

"Mmm-hmm."

She squeezed his shaft, marveling at the satiny skin that stretched over a thick rod of iron. She didn't recall the men of her day being this big, either. "About Kynan..."

Baring his teeth, he shook his head. She drew her hand away once more.

He went crazy, and her heart clenched and that was enough testing him. Hastily, she gripped him again, the effect on him so dramatic she could hardly fathom how crucial sex must be to his very existence. The way he settled down so quickly, his expression reflecting both stark relief and misery...it was fascinating. For so long she'd avoided anything even remotely sensual or sexual, because while not bedding a man was simple enough, the vow of chastity also banned self-pleasure, and *that* hadn't been so easy. And now, as if her body had come out of a deep freeze, it flared hot and went liquid, and she couldn't wait to see Lore come, to watch pleasure take him in the most male of ecstasies.

"Good boy," she murmured. Adjusting her position, she made room for her other hand so she could reach below his shaft to his balls. They lay heavily in her hand,

and when she began to roll them gently, he cursed on a low, ragged breath.

She dragged her other hand up, from the thick base to the flared head. A crystal drop formed in the slit, and she swiped her thumb through it, spreading the silky moisture around the crown. Lore rocked his hips, his chest rising and falling in an uneven rhythm. His shaft pulsed and swelled, and she sensed he was close.

"Faster," he said hoarsely. "Harder."

She obeyed, pumping him the way he wanted her to, loving the friction building between her palm and his skin. She tore her gaze away from what her hand was doing so she could gauge every reaction.

And oh, what reactions he had. His eyes were open, hungry, and focused on her face. The tendons in his neck and the muscles in his arms stood out starkly as he strained against the chains, and she knew if he got free she'd be under him in a heartbeat.

Desire curled in her gut, and a heady sense of power shot right to her head with dizzying speed. She could change the intervals between his breaths by altering the speed of her strokes. She could make him moan by altering the tightness of her grip. And when she swiped her thumb against the area just under the head, his entire body arched.

Crazily, her body arched, too. Toward him. She was shockingly aroused by this, in a way she'd never been. Oh, she got antsy at times, but punishing exercise or dessert sprees never failed to rescue her from lust's clutches. This time, she had a feeling no amount of push-ups or tiramisu would ease the ache that throbbed through her. Her pulse beat erratically through her veins, her nipples hardened into sensitive pearls that rasped against her bra with every uneven breath, and somehow she had slid right up to the edge of orgasm.

Would it go against her vow to come even without touching herself? If it was an accident?

An accidental orgasm. She didn't know whether to laugh or cry, because her body was a pot about to boil over, and as much as she craved what she'd been denied for so long, she also couldn't risk it.

Angry and hurting, she took it out on Lore, since really, this was his fault. She squeezed him harder, pumped him faster, drawing a pleasured hiss out of him. He watched her as though trying to figure out a way to get to her, but when she looked back down at the erotic sight of his plum-ripe head thrusting through the ring of her fingers, he became lost in the rhythm, throwing his head back once more.

"Don't...stop." His guttural voice was at once a command and a plea, and he came suddenly, his body bucking with such violence that she had to grip his hip to keep from being thrown. A raw curse erupted from deep inside his chest, and semen shot onto her hand and in thick ropes over his six-pack abs.

He was beautiful, so big, his muscles straining and his body hard. He'd feel good on top of her, his weight holding her down as he thrust into her. He'd be naked, sweaty, and they'd be skin on hot skin, their bodies joined and their tongues tangling.

Pressure reached critical at her core, and she realized she was grinding herself against his thigh even as she finished him off with her hand. Her gaze flew up to his face, and she drew a startled, horrified breath at the way he was focused on her, eyes drowsy but glowing with knowledge.

Clearing her throat, she released his penis, which was still semihard. "How often do you need sex?" she asked casually, though she felt anything but, especially with the way her skin tingled where his seed had splashed over her hand, filling her with the oddest urge to smooth it over sensitive, private places.

"Few times a day." His voice was husky, a lovely post-coital growl.

More rattled than she cared to admit, she peeled her-self off him to visit the bathroom and slap a bandage over the cut on her arm. By the time she finished, she felt almost normal again, though she could definitely use a cold shower and two gallons of spumoni ice cream.

She found a tube of antibiotic ointment in her medicine cabinet, wetted a washcloth, and returned to Lore. "If you don't get sex, you go into rages?"

"Yes," he grunted, as though embarrassed. "How did you manage to truss me up? And what do you plan to do to me?"

"I made you truss your own self up." She sank down on the mattress beside him. "And I plan to keep you from killing Kynan."

"You're an angel, right? Like, Kynan's guardian angel?"

"Something like that." Gently, she wiped away the blood on his left arm, working her way from his thick shoulder to the cuff around his wrist. His skin was supple, smooth, the muscles beneath set with deep grooves between the mounds of steel. She lingered more than she should.

"So why not just kill me? Why hold me prisoner?"

Because I have to protect you, too, and your brothers seem ready to cut your heart out.

"Maybe I want to keep you chained to my bed as a sex

slave before I kill you." Stupid thing to say, because the possibilities started rolling through her head.

"If that were true," he drawled, "you'd have fucked me instead of jerking me off." His lopsided smile and mussed hair gave him a charming boyish appearance that was at odds with the crude words and the raw masculinity he threw off. "And I know you wanted to fuck me, but you didn't. So the sex slave thing? Not buying it."

"You are incredibly arrogant."

"Am I wrong?" His tone said he knew damned good and well that he wasn't wrong.

She ignored his question. "Tell me who hired you."

He rolled his eyes and sighed. "We're back to that again?"

"It's kind of important."

Lore shrugged, rattling the chains. "No one hired me. Kynan's a tool. Isn't that reason enough?"

"Even though you told Eidolon that Kynan was an assignment, I might believe you if I hadn't found another one of my charges being slaughtered by a female assassin."

Something flickered in his dark gaze. "Coincidence."

"Really?" She gently wiped his shredded wrist beneath the cuff. It must have hurt, but he didn't flinch. "Is it also coincidence that the assassin bore faded Seminus tattoos just like yours?"

This time, the change in his expression was an easy read: fear. He schooled it hastily, but still too late.

"Who is she?" Idess pressed. "And why have assassins been sent after my Primori?"

"No idea. What are Primori?"

"Primori are what I'm assigned to protect," she said vaguely. "And you're lying."

"You think assassin masters share anything with their slave-assassins? We're given a job to do and we don't care why."

"Lovely."

He snorted. "*You* are judging *me*? Hello, I didn't chain anyone to a bed to use as a sex slave. Not that I mind," he added. "But I could sex you up a lot better if I were free."

Impossible male. "Tell me about the female Seminus," she ground out.

"There are no female Sems," Lore said. "Male Sems use females of other species as hosts for their offspring, which are all born male."

"Then she's a mate." Again, some unknown emotion brought color into his cheeks, and a disturbing thought made her gut twist. "Yours? Is she yours?"

He just stared. *Now* he decided to clam up. But his silence was answer enough.

Lore kept a curious eye on Idess, noting how suddenly ill she seemed after asking if Sin was his mate. No way was she jealous. Maybe the idea that she might have gotten intimate with a taken male disturbed her goodie-two-shoes self.

Funny.

But it wasn't funny that she knew about Sin, and by the looks of it, their introduction hadn't involved handshakes. Idess's bottom lip was swollen and cut, there was a gash in her upper arm, and thick locks of hair had come free of her ponytail, giving her a Xena, Warrior Princess, look he shouldn't appreciate. But did. Or would have, if he wasn't worried about his sister.

He kept his voice level. Barely. "Where is the female?" She said nothing, and he snarled, sick of her game, whatever it was. "What did you do to her?"

Idess avoided eye contact, instead concentrating on smoothing ointment onto his wrist. He couldn't wait until she got to his right arm. She'd be so dead. She might have managed to escape contact with his *dermoire* earlier, but he'd get her to touch it now.

"If you tell me what I want to know, I'll tell you what you want to know."

"Answer me!" he roared, and she recoiled.

"Don't worry," she snapped. "She got away. But she did kill one of my Primori."

Good. Sounded like Sin had completed her mission. No slavery at the hands of the Neethul for her. But if he didn't take care of Kynan, doing vile things for the Neethul would be the least of her concerns. "That's too bad, Cookie."

Idess ignored his sarcasm and moved to his other side. Anticipation swelled as she prepared to wipe down his right arm. He rolled his head toward her and tried not to admire the long, lush lashes framing her big toffee eyes. Eyes that had watched him with stark hunger as she stroked him. They'd gone half-mast, darkened, and she'd rolled her bottom lip between sexy white teeth as though she'd wanted to use her mouth instead of her hand.

He'd have been all right with that. More than all right. Hell, he was getting hard again just thinking about it. Idess leaned in. Maybe she'd kiss him. If she got into it the way she had when she'd jerked him off, he'd enjoy every second of it. At least, until she got carried away and came into contact with his arm.

Closer. Closer...in a moment she'd be dead and he'd...what? He'd be chained up with no way to get free.

"Stop!"

She froze, the cloth mere millimeters from his arm. "What?"

"My arm...it's sensitive. Leave it alone."

"Oh, for Pete's sake. For a big, bad demon assassin, you're a baby." Glaring at him, she dropped the washcloth, and he breathed a sigh of relief. And then, to his horror, she put her palm gently on his forearm.

"Idess!"

She gasped, her eyes going wide. Her fingers dug into his skin and she groaned...but oddly, she didn't seem to be in pain. If anything, he'd say the expression on her face was as far from death as it could be.

Was she...? Nah. If she was coming, she'd be wild. And loud. Somehow he knew she'd be vocal in bed.

"Lore," she moaned. Her touch grew lighter, her fingers barely resting on his arm—but she *was* touching him.

Stunned, he stared at her hand. Her warmth seeped into his *dermoire* and radiated up his arm, the exact opposite of what should have happened. Why hadn't she keeled over? It didn't escape his notice that he'd called her by her name in his panic, and for some reason, doing so felt strangely...intimate. Finally, she pulled away, her eyes focused on the way his markings writhed on his skin. "What...what just happened?"

"Ah...I don't know. What *did* just happen?"

Tentatively, she touched him again. This time, the experimental swipe of her fingers seemed to have no effect. "I don't understand. When I touched you before, it was..."

"Orgasmic?"

She speared him a look of annoyance. "Hardly. It was as if I took energy from you. Do you feel drained?"

Winking, he rocked his hips. "Oh, yeah."

This time she just huffed. "I'm serious."

"So was I."

She muttered something about incubi that didn't sound complimentary. "Maybe it has something to do with the Bracken Cuffs."

Bracken Cuffs, the same demon jailer devices his brothers had used on him last month to negate his gift. He should have known. No wonder she hadn't fried when she touched him.

"Is it okay to wash it now?" she asked.

His cock jerked. "It?"

"Your *arm*," she ground out.

"Why do you care?"

She shrugged and reached for the wet cloth again. "I have to keep you from killing Kynan, but that doesn't mean I want you to suffer." She dabbed blood from his abraded wrists. "Does it hurt?"

Far from it. The swirling glyphs had always been sensitive; he hadn't lied about that. But they were sensitive in a highly erotic way, and now that it was clear she wasn't going to die from touching them, the nerve endings just beneath their surfaces sparked, each brush of her fingertips sending pleasant jolts straight to his groin. God, no female had ever touched his arm like that, and it shook him. Excited him. Threatened to drive him to heights he'd never known.

"No," he rasped. "I'm good."

"The glyphs are remarkable," she said. "They seem to move." She traced one with a fingernail, and he bit back a groan. "They're not tattoos, are they?"

"They're a history of our paternity."

"Were you born with them?"

"Most Sems are."

She rinsed the cloth and went back to wiping down his arm, even though it no longer seemed necessary, and a shiver stole through him. "But you weren't? Does this have anything to do with your human breeding?"

"How do you know I'm from human stock?"

"I can smell the human in your blood." She shifted on the bed.

He didn't see any reason to keep his background a secret, and besides, maybe if he could get her talking, she'd reveal information he could use. Like why she was guarding Kynan. And if it was true that only angels could harm him. And how Lore could get around that minor detail. "My mother was human. Apparently, that makes things go a little screwy."

"So when did you gain the symbols?"

"When I was twenty." They'd come with a side order of pain, followed by a dessert of lust and rage. Oh, yeah...good times.

She used a square fingernail to trace the outline of the arrowhead symbol in the crook of his elbow. His erection throbbed as though it hadn't just enjoyed the most intense orgasm of its life. "And how long ago was that?"

"If you want to know how old I am," he said, "you can just ask."

"Fine. How old are you?"

"I was born in 1880. You?"

Her grin transformed her face from beautiful to drop-dead gorgeous. "I'm considerably older than you are."

"Yeah?" He waggled his brows. "I've always had a thing for older women."

There was more muttering about incubi as she dropped the cloth into the laundry basket. "I was born the day Julius Caesar died. That's very old."

"So you really were born. And on the Ides of March," he mused. "Is that what you're named after?" When she nodded, he settled back and gave her a sleepy, seductive look. "It's a pretty name. Pretty, like you."

She snorted, totally calling him out. "I'm not going to fall for any of your tricks. Especially not when they're so obvious."

"Give me a break. I don't have a lot of experience seducing women."

"Yeah, right." She frowned when he didn't react. "You're serious. How can you be an incubus and not have that kind of experience?"

He shrugged, unwilling to tell her about his death touch. "Guess there are anomalies in every species."

"Seeing how you're a sex demon who kills, I'd say that's true."

"There *are* incubi that use sex to kill. But it's not like I *want* to kill anyone," he added, and though it was true that he was playing up to her soft side, it was also just...true. He wasn't a killer because he wanted to be.

No, you kill for money. That's so *much better.*

"Good," she said. "Then I need you to not kill Kynan."

"Yeah, okay. I won't."

Her eyelashes swept down, creating shadows under her eyes, and she suddenly looked tired. "I know how assassin masters work, Lore. You can't just ignore your orders."

"Then why are you asking me to not kill Kynan if you know I have to?"

"I just want your word that you won't kill him while I'm trying to find out who hired you, and why."

"So you think that if you take out whoever hired me, the hit will be called off and Kynan will be safe?"

"Yes."

It was a nice thought, but it wasn't going to happen. The Assassins' Guild had built its rep on its vow of discretion and silence, and no one learned the identity of any party who had hired an assassin. It had happened only once, several hundred years ago, when a client had been betrayed by an assassin master, and that master had been made an example of.

His wrecked body, preserved in wax, graced the entrance to the Guild Hall, his flesh peeled like a banana away from the bone. But the worst part was that somehow his soul had been trapped with the body, and his screams could be heard by every demon who entered.

But he wasn't going to tell Idess that. Nope. He'd play along.

"You'll need my help," he said.

She swiped at her brow, which glistened with a fine sheen of sweat. "I can manage on my own."

"Really? You know who my master is? You can contact him?"

Pink mottled Idess's cheeks, because he had her there. "Will you tell me?"

"Will you let me go?"

She wobbled on her feet, and a lightning strike of panic zinged through him. "Cookie? What's wrong?"

"Nothing." She lifted her chin and straightened her

back in a show of strength, but a trickle of perspiration ran down her temple.

"You want my help? You tell me what the fuck is wrong. Right. Now."

She hesitated, and he got that. Vulnerability was not easy, especially in front of an enemy. A whimper escaped her as she sagged, catching herself on the dresser.

"Idess? What is it?"

Her jerky gaze tracked to his, a little glassy and a whole lot desperate. "It seems," she whispered, "that I need to feed."

Seven

I need to feed.

Had she really said that? The words were still ringing in Idess's ears as an undying echo. It grew louder and louder, until she slapped her palms over her ears. She heard Lore calling her name, his deep voice a mere buzz.

Calm down...calm down...

Oh, this was bad. Her utter hatred of feeding had led her to ignore her body's needs for too long, and the battle with Lore and subsequent injury hadn't helped anything. As the nausea waned, she tentatively peeled her hands away from her head.

"Idess." Lore's hard tone finally penetrated the haze in her brain. "When you say *feed*, do you mean what I think you mean?"

"Yes." She sank down on the bed next to him, her legs too wobbly to support her for much longer, and the last thing she wanted was to do a face-plant right in front of her captive. *That* would certainly go a long way toward showing him who was in charge.

"But aren't you some sort of angel?"

"Consider me an angel in training." She rubbed her eyes even as she swiped her tongue over the tip of a canine that had started to descend.

"Do all angels drink blood?"

She was so tired she no longer cared about keeping things from Lore. So exhausted, in fact, that she swayed, her head spinning as if she'd had one too many glasses of wine—which was the only alcohol Memitim were supposed to drink. She'd indulged a *lot* during her wilder days. Now she avoided it—and anything that might chip away at her control and lead her away from the path of goodness she tried so hard to follow. "No. Only my kind."

"And what kind are you, exactly?"

"I'm Memitim." She skimmed her hand over the handmade royal blue and gold comforter she'd bought in the Italian countryside. Small things like this would be what she missed when she Ascended. "Unlike Cherubim and Thrones and all the other classes of angels you may have heard about, Memitim are born on Earth and we remain here until we Ascend. And because we're tied to the earth and this plane, we must feed if we've depleted our energy." Or maybe what Rami said was true; that they fed not because they were bound to this life, but because of who their father was and that Memitim were, in essence, paying for his sins. *The sins of the father they all shared,* as it were.

"Why are you depleted?"

"Fighting with you, for one," she said wryly. "Being shot and losing the Primori your mate killed took a lot out of me, too."

He was silent for a long time, leaving her alone with the throbbing in her head. "Feed from me."

Her gaze flew up to meet his. "Ah...excuse me?"

"Take my blood."

Already her teeth were pulsing inside her gums, eager to extend. "Why are you offering?"

"Because you look like you're going to keel over at any second. And if you starve to death, I'm never getting out of these chains."

Her belly was practically twisting in anticipation, her mouth was watering, and her fangs punched down. Lore noticed, his gaze going to her parted lips, and she swore she saw a flicker of hunger in his eyes, as well. She squirmed, unsure about this. She'd never taken from a demon before. In fact, she'd always sought out the gentlest, most decent human Primori she could.

When their emotions remained with you, you didn't want a psychopath's blood thrumming through your veins.

"I can't," she said. "I'll find someone else—"

"Take it," he said, and this time his voice was rough. Commanding. "Take whatever you need." His eyes dropped, and she followed his gaze to his erection. "Take whatever you *want*."

"Arrogant bastard," she muttered, but there was no power behind the words. She wanted his blood, and truth be told, her treasonous body ached for everything he was so boldly offering.

She had to get out of there.

She flashed. Tried to flash. Her body flickered like a dying lightbulb. Oh, sweet Lord, she was stuck. If Kynan were to be attacked right now...

She had to do it. She had to take from Lore, if only to

ensure Kynan's safety. But the thought of drinking from him, of taking lifeblood from his powerful body... it was dangerous. What kind of emotions would stay with her if she drank from an incubus? Already, the very idea had her warming up all over, her thighs clenching and wetness blooming between her legs.

He tilted his head to the side. His muscular neck was exposed, his jugular pulsing strong and steady beneath tan skin.

Just a small taste. A sip. Enough to give her the strength to hunt down a proper host. Decision made, she mounted him, straddling his thighs. She scooted backward in an attempt to avoid intimate contact, but his wicked grin said he wasn't going to play that way. He lifted his knees to shift her forward, and she nearly gasped at the feel of the hard ridge of his sex against hers.

Damn him. She refused to give him the satisfaction of a reaction, so she braced her hands on his shoulders and leaned in. His scent, earthy and bold, ignited a pleasurable hum inside her. Oh, how she needed this.

"It won't hurt," she whispered against his skin.

"Not worried about that," he whispered back.

She told herself that touching him was necessary, that it meant nothing, told herself all kinds of lies as she dragged her tongue up his neck, right along the jugular. His body went taut beneath her, but with anticipation or dread, she didn't know. She licked again, taking her time, even though she didn't need to; her first stroke numbed the bite site. No, this second taste was for her, not him, and there was no lying about that.

"I'm starting to feel like a Tootsie Pop, here," he rasped.

She couldn't contain a smile. "Yes... how did that old

commercial go?" She licked him. "One." She licked him
again, and he moaned. "Two." She licked him once more,
and his hips came off the bed.

"Three."

Idess's fangs slid into Lore's throat so smoothly he felt
only the slightest tingle, and then her mouth latched on.

Oh... *yeah*.

No one had ever bitten him before, but wow, this was
amazing. He still wasn't sure why he'd offered to play
juice box, but he definitely didn't regret it. Warmth flowed
from her mouth through his body, loosening his muscles
and his mind. He drifted in a happy place as she sucked
on his neck, her tongue and lips caressing his skin so gently he almost asked her to suck harder, to give him even
more to feel.

With the way the bed canopy bowed from his struggles,
the chains had enough give in them to allow him to touch
her if he strained. Stretching, he raked his fingers through
the loose strands of her hair, marveling at the silky texture and curling waves. At his touch, she gave a little start,
and then she sagged against him, putting them into full
body contact.

It shouldn't feel so good. She was his captor. If he didn't
get free, Sin would die. No amount of pleasure should be
able to sway him, but Idess was pleasure in the flesh, and
his incubus body could only respond.

And did it ever respond. Despite the earlier release, his
cock was aching inside its leather prison, his balls were
tight, and his skin burned all over.

God, he wished he could touch her, really touch her.

He wanted to rip off her clothes, roll her onto her back, and drive into her until she screamed. He'd show her what it was like to be held captive, helpless to feel anything but what your captor wanted you to feel.

He'd torture her, all right. He'd take her to the edge of passion and hold her there until she was insane with the need to come. Only after she begged for it long enough and good enough, would he give it to her.

She was panting, and so was he, his body out of control. Lost in his own head, he hadn't been aware that they were grinding against each other, having sex with their clothes on. "Touch me," he said roughly.

Her fingers tightened on his shoulders, digging in with such sweet pain. It was damn good, but he wanted her fingers to take a leisurely slide south. Far south.

"Like that. But lower."

Her fingers dug in even more, and he hissed. How was it possible to feel both relaxed and energized at the same time?

He cocked one leg up for leverage—and to put his erection more firmly against her. But even as she arched into him, a low moan dredged up from deep in her chest and her grip on his shoulders eased. Her teeth unplugged, and he felt the warm stroke of her tongue over the skin of his neck.

Strangely, she didn't move off him. Instead, she laid her head down on his shoulder.

"Ah…this can't be all there is to feeding, right? I mean, we got a little below the waist action going on…"

She didn't move. Shit.

"Angel Cake?" He rattled his chains. "Idess!" Worried that she was injured or ill or that his demon blood was poison to an angel, he tugged on her hair.

And was rewarded with a tiny squeak...followed by a series of soft snores.

She'd fallen asleep. She'd taken nourishment from him, and then, like a contented kitten, she'd nuzzled against him and fallen asleep.

Something inside him shook so hard he was surprised Idess didn't get jiggled right off him. This was the closest he'd ever been to a female. Oh, he'd fucked them, and he'd even cared for one he'd foolishly thought could be his. But never had any female fallen asleep on him. It was a surprising intimacy that gave him some hellacious warm fuzzies in a situation he had no right to feel good about at all.

And yet, he stroked her hair and tried to be still, because crazily, this was the most amazing thing that had ever happened to him.

Eight

⁓

Underworld General was the last place Sin wanted to be. But Lore was missing, and the fact that the chick who had interrupted Sin during her assassination attempt had tried to kill Sin with *his* dagger was a chilling sign that he was in trouble. The only upside was that the blade had tasted the female's blood, which meant it wanted more.

Unfortunately, the Gargantua dagger had one serious limitation; it could only be used to track a victim during the devil's hour in the time zone where the prey's blood had been shed. So, since Sin had time to kill, she searched for Lore in all of the obvious places. She'd gone to the assassin den. Nothing. She'd stopped by his house. Nada. She'd called and texted and emailed. Not a goddamned thing.

Her last resort was UGH, where he might be a patient . . . or where he might be getting all chummy with his brothers. *His* brothers, because she refused to acknowledge them.

And why the thought that he might be hanging out with them made her horribly uncomfortable—jealous, even—she had no idea.

She stepped out of the Harrowgate and into what must be the emergency department. A male Umber looked up from the triage desk, his steel gray lips peeled back from white teeth.

"What do you want?"

Apparently, people skills weren't necessary to work in a demon hospital. Sin approached him, limping from the wound she'd taken during the battle with the mystery chick. "Do you have a patient named Lore?"

The Umber sneered. "I'm not allowed to give out information on patients."

Both relief and dread flooded her. "So he *is* a patient."

"I didn't say that," the Umber said.

Sin slammed her fists down on the desk. "You ass."

"Is there a problem here?" The deep voice froze her to the black stone floor. It wasn't Lore's, but the forbidding tone was the same. This would be one of the brothers. Crap-o-rama.

Slowly, she turned. Found herself looking at a sinister medical symbol on a scrub top covering a broad chest. Swallowing dryly, she dragged her gaze up, and yup, this guy, with his short hair, I-own-this-hospital presence, and stern expression might not be the spitting image of Lore, but close enough. Plus, the *dermoire* that extended to his neck and connected to two rings around his throat—mate marks and maturity marks—sort of gave him away. Well, that, and his nametag. *Eidolon*.

Not good.

"The female is looking for Lore," the Umber said, and

inside, she cringed. This was the scenario she'd hoped to avoid.

Eidolon's expression remained stony, and she suddenly wondered what it would take to rile him up. "How do you know Lore?"

"That's none of your business."

"Guess you don't want to know if he's a patient." Eidolon swung around and headed toward a couple of curtained cubicles.

Cursing, Sin jogged to catch up. "I work with him."

Eidolon stopped and eyed her with suspicion. "He's not here."

"You couldn't have said that without all the drama?"

Eidolon didn't have a chance to reply, because the sliding emergency room doors opened, and two medics guided in a stretcher—a stretcher laden with her warg victim. *Holy shit.*

One of the medics straddled the warg, pumping compressions into his chest. Eidolon sprang into action.

"What do we have?" he asked, moving alongside the medics. Sin kept pace despite her limp, but hung back to play fly-on-the-wall.

The medic pushing the stretcher, his flashing fangs giving away his vampire status, said in a clipped voice, "Warg. Found unconscious and not breathing. Our attempts to resuscitate him were successful, but we lost him three blocks out."

He rattled off some vital statistics that Sin didn't understand as they wheeled the stretcher into one of the curtained rooms. More medical staff swarmed inside. Sin waited just outside, listening to more medical-speak that didn't sound good. Well, not good for the warg. Good for her.

After a few minutes, the medics exited. One took off through the doors, while the other, the blond vamp, paused outside to scratch notes on his clipboard.

Sin cleared her throat. "Hey, how is the warg?"

His eerie silver eyes shifted to hers, but he kept writing. "Dying. Why?"

"No reason." She rubbed her arms through the sleeves of her denim jacket and fidgeted under his unnerving gaze. "What's wrong with him? Was he in an accident? Is he sick with something?"

"You're kind of nosy."

You're kind of hot. She shrugged. "Just a concerned citizen." Yeah, concerned Eidolon would save the werewolf and she'd have to kill him again.

The vamp watched her for a moment, and the floor seemed to shift beneath her. He really was extraordinary. He was easily as tall as Lore, his shoulders as broad, but that was where the resemblance ended. Hot Vamp Medic had a lean, athletic build, chiseled cheekbones, and a full, sensual mouth that no doubt could latch on to a female's most sensitive spots and make her whimper.

He scanned her from head to toe. "You should get your leg looked at."

Frowning, she looked down at the spot of blood that had seeped through her jeans and the bandage she'd wrapped around her thigh. "It's no big—"

He didn't even wait for her to finish. He handed the clipboard to the Umber and exited through the doors he'd come through. He was a charmer, that one.

She'd have been irritated by his blatant dismissal if not for the fact that the warg she needed to die was being treated by her brother, who didn't know she existed. Christ, only she could get herself into this kind of mess.

This had never happened before—a victim of hers surviving even minutes after being infected by her touch—and a horrifying thought stabbed at her brain; what if he'd infected someone else? While her heart had turned to brimstone decades ago, and for the most part she couldn't care less about the lives and deaths of people she didn't even know, she didn't kill for fun. When she killed, it was deliberate and quick. Controlled. Killing was the only thing she had any command over, the only aspect of her life that wasn't chaotic, and she couldn't stand the thought that she might be responsible for deaths she couldn't prevent or make happen the way they should.

She paced, hanging back near the Harrowgate where the Umber wouldn't notice her but she could keep an eye on the room. It was weird, being in the hospital her brothers had built. She hadn't known what to expect, but disarray and unprofessionalism wasn't it. The staff was grumpy, and when a patient came in with a spear impaled in his gut, two doctors spent so much time fighting over who got to treat the guy that he collapsed while the doctors screamed at each other.

She'd seen more order in a bar brawl.

"What the hell is going on?" Eidolon stepped out of the warg's room, his gold-glowing eyes fixed on the guy bleeding out on the floor. His fury seemed to knock some sense into the arguing doctors, but as Eidolon rushed toward the patient, his expression told Sin that those physicians were soon going to wish their parents had practiced birth control.

But hey, the commotion made for a great distraction,

and Sin could turn any situation into one that benefited her.

While all attention was on the skewered-guy drama, Sin peeked into the warg's room. Relief flooded her at the sight of a sheet draped over a body. Now, if she could just gather her proof of death and get out of there so she could find Lore...

Of course, she couldn't very well get proof while the body was lying in the middle of the emergency department. She'd have to wait until they took him to the morgue. In the meantime, she needed privacy.

Making sure no one was watching, she slipped down one of the halls and into a room full of medical equipment, wicked-looking, odd restraints, and even odder homey touches, like a wooden dresser and shelves stocked with towels and slippers in various sizes and shapes.

Sin removed her jacket, sat on the edge of the bed, and waited. She didn't have to wait long. A vibration started deep in her body, growing steadily until it concentrated in her right arm. Her *dermoire* writhed, tightened, and finally, the skin between two symbols split, and a deep gash appeared in her biceps.

Even clenching her teeth so tightly her jaw popped, she couldn't contain a cry of pain. Blood spurted, but she didn't bother to stop it. No, this was a cleansing of sorts, something that happened after every kill, as though her body was purging itself of the guilt she couldn't allow herself to feel.

"What the fuck?" Eidolon rushed into the room, grabbed her wrist, and slapped his hand over the gash.

"Don't touch me!" She wheeled away from him, but he moved like Lore, with incredible speed and grace, and in a heartbeat he had her back on the bed, arm stretched out, with one palm putting pressure on her biceps.

His *dermoire* lit up. She kneed him in the junk, and with an "oof!" he doubled over, his grip loosening enough to allow her to leap away, scoop up her jacket, and dart toward the door.

He tackled her before she made it.

She smacked the floor hard, her breath exploding from her lungs. Eidolon rolled her, straddled her, and pinned her wrists together on her chest. Then he stared down at her with that furious, golden-eyed glare Lore had perfected.

"You want to explain those?" His gaze cut to the markings on her right arm. "And how you got around the Haven spell?"

"Haven spell? Get the fuck off me and I'll leave you alone."

He kept her wrists pinned with one hand and used the other to tear away her tank top's shoulder strap, revealing her *dermoire* all the way to her neck. "You had this applied. How? Magic?" He rubbed his thumb over one of the symbols. "Permanent ink? Tattoo?"

"Fuck you." Pain streaked up her arm from the tear in her biceps, which was gaping open from the awkward grip he had her arm in, and blood was pooling on the floor next to her.

She wriggled, but he held her tighter, squeezed her more firmly between his thighs even as he slapped his palm over the laceration and applied pressure. "The top symbol is my father's. Were you mated to him? To Khane?"

Mated? To a Seminus demon? Eew. Still, she put on her best honest expression. "Yes. Love those hot, sexalicious Seminus males."

He narrowed his eyes at her. "You're lying. Wrong arm for mate marks."

"If you already knew the answer, why'd you ask?"

He went on as though she hadn't spoken. "Unless...you could be bonded to Lore, since the markings are the same. With his human genes, the bond could have gone funky."

"Yep," she said, feeling nauseated at the mere thought of being bonded in any way other than birth to Lore. "We were wondering what happened with that."

His gaze cut sharply to hers, and in the long, tense silence, they stared at each other. It was weird, looking at the complete stranger who was her brother, as he tried to puzzle together both the obvious and the impossible.

Blood pumped from her wound in a warm rush between his fingers, and his *dermoire* lit up.

"No!" she snapped. "Don't heal it. It's mine to deal with."

Ignoring her, he slid his fingers into the wound. She rocked her head up and bit him in the biceps.

"Ow!" He jerked his hand away. "Damn you. At least let me stitch it."

"I've hit you, kneed you, bitten you...and all you can think about is fixing a scratch?"

"It's more than a scratch, and I *am* a doctor. So, go figure, I've got this crazy desire to help people." Warily, he released her. "You going to play nice so I can close that wound?" He scanned her body. "And the one on your leg?"

Shit. This had gotten way out of hand. She could promise to play nice and try to escape again, but she had a feeling she'd end up in the same situation she was currently in. And he wasn't going to let the *dermoire* thing go. The fire in his eyes made that clear enough.

Damn you, Lore. You just had to find these guys, didn't you?

"Fine," she growled. "But don't you dare use that stupid healing thingie Lore says you do. I want stitches. On my arm. You can zap the leg scratch."

"Stitches will leave a scar..." He trailed off as he took in the hundred other scars running the length of her arm. "Though I guess that's not a big deal for you."

"Duh."

He shook his head in exasperation, but he eased off her and offered her a hand up. She refused. Her arm hurt like hell, but she managed to get up and plant herself on the bed while he gathered a tray of supplies.

"So. You're mated to Lore. Since when?"

Her heart shot into her throat at the seemingly innocent question she knew was really a grilling. Low-level heat, but still. "It was recent. Still honeymooning, you know?" God, it actually grossed her out to say that.

"Really." He drew a chair and the tray around the bed in front of her. "And you say you're looking for him?"

"Yeah. I'm worried."

"Is he in pain?" His *dermoire* lit up, and he channeled an excruciating amount of power into her leg.

"I have no idea," she gritted out. "How the hell would I know?"

He leaned forward to look her in the eye, and she started to sweat, because he'd just turned up the heat a notch. "Because," he said, "if you were bonded, you'd feel his pain. You aren't mated to him. So why don't you tell me the truth?"

"And what would that be, Dr. Smartypants?"

"That you are somehow his sister." His voice went low. Dangerous. "Which means you're somehow mine."

Eidolon shut off his healing power and waited for the female's response, his mind working overtime to believe what it insisted made sense, despite the utter impossibility. A *sister*? How?

"There are no female Seminus demons," she said finally. "You should know that, brainiac."

His movements were jerky and brisk as he swabbed the area around her arm laceration and prepared to inject her with anesthetic. "I do know that. But unless this is a trick, the evidence is telling me otherwise."

"Well, aren't we the logical one?"

"I try."

He eyed her, noted that she had their family's dark hair, though hers was so black that it had a blue cast to it. She had their dark eyes, tan skin, and the markings on her arm were fucking perfect. Of course, any of those things could be manufactured. Only her size was odd—she was short, maybe Tayla's height, and though she was toned, she was petite, and in that way very opposite Eidolon and his brothers.

"Whatever." She rolled her eyes. "You're wrong. And don't put that shit in me. I can take the pain." She shoved his hand away as he attempted to inject the numbing medicine.

"Funny how you sound just like Wraith, Ms. I'm Not Related to You." Ignoring her Wraithlike string of insults, he paged a nurse, and while he waited, he prepared a suture kit and let what he'd learned sink in. Lore's markings were identical to hers...faded, with no personal symbol. Lore was a *cambion*, born of a human-Seminus mating, and those went screwy a lot, so even though it was unlikely that a female could be born of that kind of mating, it might not be impossible.

The door opened, and Chu-Hua, a Guai nurse who resembled an upright wild boar, stepped in. "Yes, doctor?"

He gestured to the female. "Take a blood sample. I want DNA results compared to mine ASAP."

The little female jerked away. "Oh, no. Stay the hell away from me."

"You got something to hide?"

"No."

He nodded to the nurse, but his patient hissed and backed away. He grasped her wrist. "We can do this the easy way or the hard way. I *strongly* recommend the easy way."

Her glare drilled holes right through him. "I hate you."

"I'm hurt." That earned him a middle-finger salute. He held her arm while Chu-Hua started the draw. "How is the patient?" he asked the nurse, referring to the one who'd been bleeding out while doctors Pon and Rivers went at it.

"He's being prepped for surgery," she said, dragging out the "y" in a grating piglike squeal.

"Keep me informed." He'd have dealt with the patient himself, but the elflike *blanchier* demon was one of the few species that didn't respond well to Eidolon's healing gift. "And make sure Rivers and Pon don't leave my office." On any other day, he'd have fired the doctors, but Eidolon suspected that whatever was making the rest of the staff snap was affecting the two physicians as well.

Chu-Hua left with the blood sample, leaving him alone with the female, whose glare hadn't eased up at all.

"What's your name?" He pinched the base of her laceration and started the first stitch.

"Ouch! Fuck. Where did you get your degree? Online?"

"I told you it was going to hurt. What's your name?"

"Sin."

"Short for?"

"How do you know it's short for anything?"

Because a human wouldn't name a child Sin. "Answer the question."

"Sinead."

"So...Loren and Sinead. Twins, I'm guessing?" It wasn't a longshot of a guess; their father had been the rape 'em and leave 'em kind, and Eidolon seriously doubted he'd impregnate the same female twice. When Sin didn't answer his question, he sighed. "The DNA test will confirm what I already know. So just admit it."

"Yes," she snapped. "Lore is my twin brother. You must have been at the very top of your online class."

He ignored the barb. Tayla had broken him in to a female's sharp tongue a long time ago. "Why hasn't Lore mentioned you?"

She snorted. "I told him not to tell you about me."

"Why keep it from us?"

"Why not?"

Gods, she was exasperating. She was like a female Wraith. "Are you going to answer the question?"

She sighed. "I have one pain in the ass brother already. I don't need more, okay?" There was a defiance and a wariness in her eyes that indicated there was more to the story than what she was telling him, but now wasn't the time to push.

Working carefully, he put the final stitches in place. "So if you didn't want to know us, why risk coming to the hospital?"

"I told you. To find Lore." She bit her lip, and he gave her a moment to decide if she wanted to say anything more. "He's sort of missing."

Yeah, Eidolon was achingly aware of that. But before he told her what he knew, he wanted as much information from her as possible. "He's after a friend of mine. You know that, right?"

For the first time, something other than anger flickered in her expression. Fear. "What did you do to him? I swear, if you hurt him—"

"I didn't do anything to him. Yet."

She swallowed audibly. "It's not Lore's fault. He has to do it. There are severe consequences to failing a mission."

"You sound like you know this from experience. Are you an assassin, too?"

"Another gold star for you."

"My online degree has served me well," he said dryly. "So who hired him?"

"Even if I knew, I couldn't tell you, nosy-ass." She swung her legs to the opposite side of the bed and leaped down. "Now, unless you plan to tackle me again, I'm going to go find my brother."

Eidolon blocked the door, fully intending to physically restrain her if he had to. "I just want to ask a few more questions. And maybe I can help find Lore."

She seemed to consider that, and though she narrowed her eyes at him, she nodded slowly.

"How did you get hurt?" he asked.

"That's none of your business." When he cursed, she huffed. "What? It's an answer."

Gods, she was starting to make Wraith look agreeable. "What's your gift?"

A plastic model of a set of lungs crashed to the floor, startling Eidolon and making Sin jump. "What the hell was that?"

"Ghost." Damn, he was getting sick of this shit. "Your gift?" he prompted.

Glancing at the shattered model as if it was going to launch at her, she rubbed her bandage, but when she realized what she was doing, she let her hand drop. "Gift isn't the word I'd choose for it."

"Ability, then. What is it? You don't wear a glove, so I'm guessing it's not the same as Lore's."

She laughed bitterly. "No, but it's still fucked up. Apparently, only you purebreds get the cool stuff."

"Apparently." He waited for her to answer his question, but she didn't, and he gnashed his teeth. "So...your ability? What is it?"

"I can cause disease at a touch."

"Disease?" he repeated, just to make sure he heard correctly.

"D-I-S-E-A-S-E. Disease. You should have learned all about them in one of your internet classes."

Deep breath in. Deep breath out. "What kind of disease?"

Turning away, she rubbed her injury again. "It's different in everyone. It's like I send a spark into someone, and the spark searches out the most horrible, personalized disease it can find to kill that individual."

Gods, Lore and Sin couldn't be more the opposite of Eidolon in terms of abilities. He healed; they killed. "And you do this, why?"

She rounded on him, jabbed her finger in his chest. "Don't you judge me, asshole. You're not exactly an angel, either. I do what I have to do. And if it makes your highly educated, superior self feel any better, I do it quickly. The werewolf was an accident."

"What werewolf?"

She jerked. "It's nothing. I have to go." Sin shoved at him, but he seized her arm and hauled her up so she was on her toes, off-balance, and couldn't possibly mistake how through with her games he was.

"The warg that came in," he growled. "His death was your doing, wasn't it?"

"Fuck off."

"Sin, dammit, answer me!"

"Yes, okay?" Her black eyes glinted with flecks of gold, a Seminus trait that couldn't be faked, and every last drop of doubt left him in a rush. "You happy now?"

"Not really," he muttered, releasing her. Gods, his mind was still having trouble processing all of this. Lore's existence had been unexpected, but a sister? A brother with a human mother was fucked up enough, but Eidolon couldn't even begin to imagine what could go wrong with a Seminus female. "I was hoping to help Lore deal with his gift...maybe I can help you with yours."

She laughed and put a few steps between them. "Help? Yeah, okay. If you really want to help you'll chop off the warg's head and bring it to me in a bag. That would be a big help."

He let out a disgusted breath. "You need proof of his death."

"There goes the brain surgeon again."

"You're not getting his head," he said tightly. "I won't let you desecrate his body."

"You have to!" Panic snuffed out the gold flecks in her eyes. "I need proof."

"Or what?" When she said nothing, he repeated himself, his voice cracking in the still air. *"Or what?"*

"Or I'm going to be sold to Neethul slave traders."

Eidolon inhaled sharply. As far as punishments went, it didn't get much worse.

"Hey!" Sin jabbed him in the biceps. "You stroking out or something? You're pale. And you're not being all superior. Something's wrong."

Oh, she was a riot. "Will anything other than his head be acceptable?"

"Sometimes a unique identifying feature will work, but you need a damned good reason for not having the head."

"Would your employer accept my word as a Justice Dealer and physician?" Granted, he was no longer an enforcer of demon law, but he had powerful connections and a fucking great game face.

She leveled a look of disbelief at him. "You're kidding, right?"

"I can make it look official. I'll include an autopsy report and a photo."

"I guess that's not a horrible idea." She slid him a puppy-dog look with a side of pout and batting eyelashes that must come standard on every sister, because Omira, the Judicia sister he'd grown up with, used to try the same thing. "You sure I can't have his head? Pretty please? It's not like he needs it."

"I'm sure. Come back tomorrow for the report." He paused. "About Lore..."

Sin froze as she reached for the door handle. "What?"

He told her about Lore and Idess, and everything that had gone down, though he left out the details about Kynan's Sentinel status.

"So this chick is protecting Kynan? Why?"

"I don't know," he lied.

Sin erupted with a creative flow of curses, and when she was finished, she asked, "What does she look like?" Sin asked.

"Like she'd look good on a mattress."

Sin jammed her fists on her hips. "That tells me nothing, and aren't you mated?"

"I'm also a male sex demon. I didn't go blind when I took a mate." He had, however, lost all desire to so much as touch another female. He only wanted Tayla. Wanted her constantly, and even now heat began to kindle at the mere thought of her. "Long, dark brown hair she keeps in a ponytail, light brown eyes. Tall. Right ear is pierced at the top."

"That bitch." Sin's voice went low and deadly, her body coiled like a predator about to strike, and he suddenly saw the assassin she was. "She attacked me, too. And she had Lore's Gargantua-bone dagger. I got it back."

Eidolon blinked at that. Those daggers were rarer than acid sprite mana and just as priceless. "Did it taste her blood?"

Sin's grin was downright evil. "Yes. Come 3:00 A.M., I'm hunting."

Eidolon had no doubt Sin would find Idess. He hadn't known his...*sister*...for long, but already he knew she'd inherited their family's single-minded determination. And stubbornness. "Sin, you can't kill the female when you find her."

"Oh, I plan to kill her. Like, a lot. After she tells me what she's done with Lore."

"She's an angel. You'll only get yourself killed."

"You might be surprised. But what happens when I do find Lore?" she asked quietly. "He's after your friend. You just going to stand by and let Lore have him? Or will I be rescuing him just so his own brothers can kill him?"

"Nothing is going to happen to him," Eidolon said, but he doubted she believed him, because he didn't believe it either.

Warmth surrounded Idess like a blanket. A heady, masculine spice tickled her nose. Wriggling, she burrowed closer to the scent and warmth. After all the years of loneliness and feeling as if she didn't belong—or deserve to belong anywhere—she finally felt at peace. She must be dreaming...except, she didn't dream. She had nightmares. Not that she was going to complain. She was going to enjoy this wonderful feeling while she could.

"Idess?" The husky voice floated down to her. "Angel?"

"Mmm."

"I gotta take a leak."

She jerked upright, blinking, trying to focus her eyes and her brain. It took several seconds to recognize her bedroom, her bed...her demon that was chained to said bed.

Stunned by the realization that she'd fallen asleep on him, she muttered into her palm, "Oh, I'm...sorry. Are you okay?" Her weight had to have put extra pressure on his shoulders and arms.

"Yeah." His voice was gruff. Maybe he'd fallen asleep, too. A sudden tenderness in her groin nixed the sleep theory, as arousal pulsed into her through their blood connection. *Grr.* She knew it had been a mistake to feed from him. "I just gotta take a piss."

Flustered by the powerful sexual need coursing through her, she scrambled awkwardly off him, wondering how they were going to manage this. Wondering how much longer she could keep him prisoner.

She checked her watch and let out a mild curse.

"What is it?" Lore asked.

"It's almost 3:00 A.M. in New York, which means that in about fifteen minutes, your girlfriend is probably going to be hunting me down with your Gargantua dagger."

"You stole it from me?"

He sounded so indignant. "I borrowed it. But she took it."

"And she knifed you?"

"Please. It was just a scratch."

The morning sun streaked through the window and fell across his body but cut off abruptly at his neck, leaving his face in shadow. His espresso eyes seemed even darker in the gray wash.

"What do you plan to do?"

A note of jealousy rang through her at the way his voice had gone low and dangerous at the mention of his girlfriend. His fear hit her as well, a psychic blast that gave her a headache.

"Nothing," she snapped irritably. "I'll flash around and make her chase me, but I won't kill her."

"Why not? She hurt you and killed your Primori. Why not take revenge?"

"I'm an angel. I'm above that kind of selfish pettiness."
Liar.

"So you're saying you've never let your emotions rule your actions? You've never done anything shitty to someone in your entire life? Not buying it." He jerked on his chains, and her heart jerked in response. "What are you going to do to her, Idess?" He tugged on his chains again, more violently, and sparks of gold pierced the coal in his eyes.

His concern rattled her, became her concern. No matter how desperate she was, she would never feed from him again. "Lore—"

"Tell me!"

"I already said I won't hurt her," she said, but his doubt screamed in her mind so loudly she wanted to cover her ears. "We try not to mess with Primori lives if we can avoid it."

His breath caught. "She's Primori?"

"No, you are," she blurted stupidly. So stupidly. Primori were never to be told what they were. The idea of being watched didn't sit well with many of them, and in the past, they'd found ways to hide themselves. She had to get away from Lore. Now, before she said something else that compromised her. Or Kynan. Or the entire universe, with the way she was going. "I'll be right back."

Ignoring his irate curses, she hurried to the garage and found another length of chain. He'd stopped swearing by the time she returned, and he remained silent, watching her with shrewd, intelligent eyes while she rigged the chains so he had some freedom to move around. Not much, but he could at least get to the bathroom five feet away.

She stood back as he came to his feet smoothly, if a little stiffly. Instead of moving directly to the bathroom, he stalked toward her. More accurately, he stalked *her*. And now that he was on his feet, he was much bigger than she'd remembered, a wall of muscle and male flesh that filled her vision so there was nothing else but Lore. Every step made her heart skip a beat, as if the heavy thud of each footfall shocked it out of rhythm.

Though she knew the chain would stop him, she couldn't help but take a step back.

The chain yanked him short two feet away. He stood there, dark eyes drilling into her and holding her as captive as he was.

"I'll get free," he growled. "And when I do, you're going to experience everything I have. I promise you that."

Swallowing dryly, she stepped forward, resisting the urge to flinch when he strained against the chains so he was no farther than an inch from her.

His gaze dropped to her mouth, surprising the wind out of her, and she suspected that if he could, he'd kiss her.

"You can't best me," she ground out, a little breathlessly.

"Yeah. I can."

Oh, he was arrogant and intimidating and way too sexy for his own good. And worse, he might be right. She was vulnerable to him in a way she'd never been vulnerable to anyone before. Especially now, with his blood coursing through her veins, and his every desire and emotion channeling into her, making her sympathize with him. Empathize. Want him.

"Maybe we don't have to best anyone," she said, hoping her voice didn't sound as choked with lust to him as it did to her. "We can help each other."

He smiled and lifted his gaze so their eyes were locked. "Agreed. You let me go, and I'll do whatever you want." He inhaled deeply, and his smile grew sinister. "And I know *exactly* what you want."

Her body tingled and her heart raced, pushing superheated blood through her veins. Yes, he knew exactly what she wanted. And it was something she could never have.

Nine

Wraith really hated family fucking meetings. Always had, always would. That he had a mate and kid now didn't mean he loved to sit in Eidolon's den and listen to his brothers chew him out for something.

Not that this would be an ass-chewing. Wraith had been a good boy—relatively, anyway—since Serena and his son had come into his life, and he wasn't about to jeopardize the happiness he'd found.

So if this meeting wasn't about him, he had a feeling it would be about Lore.

So fucking cool to finally not be the brother causing the trouble.

Mickey, Tayla's ferret, attacked him the moment he walked through the front door of Eidolon's Manhattan high-rise apartment. Wraith handed his infant son, Stewie, to Serena, just as the weasel scampered up his body and onto his shoulder, all chatter and nuzzling.

Serena laughed, a sound Wraith didn't ever think he'd tire of hearing. Sometimes, he wondered how he'd lived without it for so long. "You weren't kidding when you said he likes you."

"Yeah," he said, as he stroked a finger over the critter's narrow head, "bugs the shit out of Tayla, too. Cracks me up."

Serena lifted their son so he could see Mickey, and between the baby's toothless grin and the weasel's chatter, Wraith figured they'd end up the best of friends soon.

He left his mate and son in the living room with Tayla and Mickey, and as he was heading to E's den, Shade came in, a baby in each arm. Behind him, Runa brought in the third of the triplets. She was smiling, but Shade didn't look happy to be here. Obviously, the fight earlier was still too fresh. Which was odd, since Shade had never been one to nurse a grudge against E or Wraith—and Wraith had definitely deserved some continued resentment.

Wraith left him to get the kids settled and walked into E's den. As usual, his brother was sitting at his desk, nose buried in a medical text, his dog, Mange, at his feet.

E looked up. "Is Shade here, too?"

"Yeah." Wraith sank down on the leather sofa and sprawled out, kicking one foot up on the cushions.

Shade slammed into the room. "What's this about?" He didn't sit, just stood near the door, arms crossed over his chest, jaws working overtime on a piece of gum. "Because if it's about Lore, you're wasting your time."

"It's about Lore," E said softly. "But mostly it's about his sister."

Shade narrowed his eyes. "How does he have a sister? His mother was human, so any sister would be long dead or really fucking old."

"He does have a sister, and she's not going to be happy with us if anything happens to Lore."

"So what?"

Abruptly, Eidolon came to his feet. "Gods, Shade! How can you be so cavalier about Lore's fate?"

Shade's eyes sparked gold, and Wraith braced himself for Jerry Springer, round two. "I'm not. I'm just not as in love with him as you are. And I couldn't give a shit about the sister. I don't know her, and I don't want to."

"Well, here's the thing," Eidolon said. "I do know his sister. And you're both going to want to."

Wraith yawned. "I don't."

Eidolon shot him an annoyed look—as if Wraith hadn't seen one of those before. "Yes you do. Because she's not just Lore's sister. I think she's ours, too."

"Hell's bells," Shade muttered. "I must have hit you in the head harder than I thought."

"Her name is Sin," E continued. "She's Lore's fraternal twin. And she's a female Sem."

Whoa. Wraith sat up straight and wondered if he looked as stunned, confused, and skeptical as Shade did. "That's impossible."

"I know. But I met her. Unless she's using one hell of an illusion enchantment to change her appearance, she's not faking it. I took DNA samples to be sure. We'll know something tomorrow."

Shade paced, his long strides forcing a U-turn every five steps. "Bullshit. You're wrong. She put a spell on you or messed with your head." He halted and swung around. "Hell, you're so fucking desperate to save Lore, I wouldn't put it past you to invent this new sister."

"You think I've manufactured this?" Frost formed on E's words, and shit, things were going to go critical.

Wraith shoved to his feet. "Ah . . . look. E's got a hard-on for Lore, but he's not a liar." Gods, when had *he* become the voice of reason in the family?

Shade barked out a laugh. "So you think we should just roll over and let Lore kill Kynan so this *sister* doesn't get her little feelings hurt?"

"Fuck that," Wraith said. "Lore isn't touching Kynan. But it's a non-issue right now, since the angel took him. He could be dead."

"What a shame," Shade said in a taunting tone as he swung his head toward Eidolon in a blatant attempt to rile him . . . and it worked. E lunged.

Wraith caught him, and in one easy, fluid motion, shoved him against the wall. This was crazy. These two had never been at odds like this before. It wasn't like E to be so hot-tempered, and it wasn't like Shade to be so callous. Something was seriously wrong.

"We're not doing this," Wraith gritted out. "Not in a house full of kids. So you boys need to step off, or I'll lay you both flat." His threat pretty much flew in the face of what he'd just said about not fighting, but E and Shade were too busy snarling at each other to notice.

Shade put his fist through the wall. "No problem. House won't be full of kids, because we're out of here." He moved toward the door.

"Shade!" Eidolon's booming voice halted their brother in his tracks, though he didn't turn around. "If you *ever* accuse me of trying to pull off a deception like that again, you'll need more than Wraith to save you."

Shade's fists clenched at his sides, and for a long,

drawn-out moment, the tension vibrating the air danced on Wraith's skin. Finally, Shade stalked out, and the room seemed to breathe easier. At least, until E tried to follow.

"I don't think so." Wraith held him against the wall until the commotion outside and the slamming of the front door made it clear that Shade, Runa, and the little ones were gone. The moment he released E, his brother took a few laps around the room, dropping cuss-bombs with every step.

"What the fuck is wrong with him?" E asked.

"Him? You're both being assholes." Wraith folded his arms over his chest. "E?"

"Yeah?"

"Do you really think this Sin chick is legit?"

Eidolon stiffened. "You doubt me, too?"

Wraith chose his words carefully, not wanting to send E into orbit again. "It's just damned convenient. I know you're not fucking with us, but what if *she* is? What if this is a scam to help Lore kill Kynan?"

"I don't know, Wraith. I really don't."

Man, what a freak show. "What if it's true? What would it mean that there is a female Sem in the world?"

"Best guess?"

Wraith nodded.

"Chaos," Eidolon said grimly. "From what I've seen, this female is chaos on legs."

Three A.M. New York time took forever to arrive.

Sin had hung out at the assassin den for a while, had won six hundred Sheoulin gold marks in two games of pool, but ultimately, the wait had driven her aboveground and back to Lore's place. At least in his house, she could feel him, could hold on to the hope that he was still alive.

Finally, as the clock struck the devil's hour, the dagger in Sin's hand began to glow. The heat seeped into her palm and up her arm to her brain, as though it had plugged into its target's life force.

Idess was a great distance away, but thanks to the Harrowgates, thousands of miles translated to seconds of travel time. Which was good, since Sin only had sixty minutes to work with the dagger.

She stepped into the gate near Lore's shack. Closing her eyes, she let the dagger guide her hand over the lit maps of the world and Sheoul. When her fingers touched down, she opened her eyes once more.

The lines in the walls shifted, bringing Canada into detailed view. The dagger guided her hand to the northwest, to the Yukon Territory. Once again, the lines rearranged, focusing on the remote province. And then her finger came down near the center, and the Harrowgate opened up into a forest—and about three feet of snow.

Mother. Fuck. Did Canada not know it was May?

Idess must know she was being tracked, and she was going to make this as difficult as possible. Furious, Sin tapped the maps until she came out in Sheoul, at the gate near the assassin den. She hurried to her quarters, changed into her cold-weather gear, and hit the Harrowgate at a run. As she tapped the map to get back to Canada, she glanced at her watch.

Dammit! Half an hour wasted. She practically dove out of the Harrowgate, cursing up a storm in every language she knew. Not that she was fluent in any but English. She just knew a lot of cuss words.

Almost instantly, the cold ate her curses as her breath froze in her throat and nose. With every step, her boot broke through the thick crust of ice on top of the snow, slowing her down and pissing her off.

Sin was *so* going to torture Lore's location out of this bitch.

Hands shaking, she peeled back her parka sleeve and checked her watch. Time was nearly up. And then, ahead...a lone figure stood in a clearing, wearing nothing but jeans, boots, and a damned tank top. How nice that abductor chick was impervious to the cold, while Sin was about to freeze to death.

"Where is he?" she called out. "Where is my brother?"

Idess blinked. "Brother?" For some reason, she smiled. "No worries. He's fine."

"I don't believe you."

"I don't care."

In Sin's hand, the dagger vibrated, hungry for another taste of the female's blood. But as Sin moved forward, Idess moved back.

"Let Lore go," Sin growled.

"That's not possible."

"Then I'll kill you."

"It's not going to be easy."

"Nothing worthwhile ever is." Sin took another step forward. Idess took another back. "Damn you! Lore can't be held prisoner. He needs...he has needs."

"Yes," Idess said flatly. "I've discovered that."

"If you've let him suffer—"

"I haven't." She glanced down at her watch and smiled. "Looks like our time here is done. If you want your brother returned, you'll have a name for me next time we meet."

"A name?"

"The name of the person who hired you and Lore."

Sin sucked in a harsh breath and nearly choked on the icy air. "Can't," she wheezed. Jesus, even if she knew who hired them, to tell would break the assassin code and earn you a fate way worse than death.

Idess shrugged. "Then you won't see Lore again." She waggled her fingers and disappeared, leaving Sin half-frozen and furious in the middle of a godforsaken forest.

Idess had been gone almost twenty hours. *Twenty freaking hours.* She'd needed only an hour to evade Sin, and scenarios of what might have gone wrong kept tripping through Lore's head. Worry, helplessness, and hunger gnawed at him, and he'd had to take care of his physical needs with annoying frequency.

For some reason, his releases had been unsatisfying, and tension remained just below the surface of his skin, as if at any moment his skin could split, releasing his inner demon for a devastating rampage. His body had experienced Idess, and it was *her* touch it craved, which could be a serious fucking problem if his usual methods for rage control began to fail.

So yeah, twenty hours spent worrying, jerking off, and plotting an escape that involved seducing Idess into letting him go. It was the lamest escape plan in the history of lame escape plans. She was two thousand years old. No way was she falling for the old I Love You So You Can Trust Me ploy.

Which wasn't to say that he wasn't going to try. He just didn't have high hopes for it.

He did, however, have high hopes for his other plan. Because when he'd cuffed himself while under the bore worm's influence, his subconscious had been in self-preservation mode. He'd done a shitty-ass job, and with little else to do during the last twenty hours, he'd managed to work his left wrist out of the cuff, and if he could get Idess close enough, he could snare her.

But she needed to hurry back. In addition to his impending rage-out, his chest had begun to burn. Detharu was summoning him. Worse, the bond's pulse, which grew stronger and faster as his deadline approached, had just kicked up a notch.

He'd been here for almost two days. Almost two days closer to Sin's death. Assuming she was still alive, where did she think he was? She had to be worried. At least, as worried as Sin got about anything.

The sound of footsteps shocked his heart into a stuttered beat, and he quickly snapped his wrist back in the cuff, leaving it loosely closed. His gaze glued to the doorway, he held his breath as he waited to see whether Idess or Sin would walk through.

Idess. Strangely, he was as relieved to see her as he was suddenly afraid for Sin, and how fucked up was that?

Then she smiled, and his mouth dried up. That was a very wicked smile.

"So," she said. "The Seminus female? Seems she's your sister."

Control was at a premium right now, and it took every last drop of it to keep from lunging at Idess and demanding answers. "I'm aware of that. If you did anything to her—"

"I said I wouldn't." She waved her hand in a dismissive gesture. "I got her to follow me to the Canadian wilderness. I'll have to keep avoiding her...tonight I'm thinking I'll start in China, and then maybe bounce around a little. Do you think she'd like to see the Great Wall?"

Relieved that Sin was okay, Lore relaxed and put on a nonchalant smile. "Sin likes to travel."

"Good. So do I." She held up her hand, and bless her little angel heart, she had a bag of fast food. The scent of burgers and fries made his mouth water.

The sight of a long, creamy expanse of stomach between Idess's bunched-up tank top and low-slung jeans did, too. His stomach growled and his cock hardened as his body played tug-o-war with its two hungers.

"You hungry?"

"You can't even imagine."

Regret swirled in her eyes. "I really am sorry, Lore. I'm not practiced at holding anyone captive."

"Yeah, your rookie is definitely shining through," he said gruffly. He didn't know how to deal with a captor who was actually nice. If she'd beaten him or taunted him or even just said nothing at all, he'd be right in the zone. But Idess left him in a state of what-the-fuck-do-I-do-now, when he normally knew exactly what to do in any situation.

She also left him in a state of arousal, and he definitely knew what to do in *that* situation.

He had to get her naked. And chained up. And if the signals she'd given off during and after her feeding were any indication, she wouldn't mind. No, she'd been hot for him—that much had been certain.

She sank down next to him, and her hand came up to

cup his cheek. The gesture was so tender, so intimate, that once more, he wasn't sure how to react. His head felt like a damned Ping Pong ball.

"I'm sorry I was gone so long. Believe it or not, I'm trying to find a way out of this."

"Ah...keys?" he suggested. "That would get me out of this."

One corner of her mouth cocked up in a flirty little half-smile. "Nice try."

"So that's a no?"

"That's a no."

He glanced at the bag. "Could I get something to eat then?"

"I wasn't sure what you like, so I got a Coke, burgers, fries, tots, and a chicken sandwich." She gave him a puppy-dog-did-I-do-good look that made something inside him melt when nothing should be melting for this woman. His dick twitched, and okay, not everything was *melting*.

"At this point, I'd eat a fucking cactus," he muttered, and her shoulders slumped a little. And he actually felt bad about making *her* feel bad.

Welcome to Stockholm Syndrome.

She handed him the bag and waited as he wolfed down the chicken sandwich and fries. When his stomach stopped rebelling so loudly, he slowed down. "So. Tell me about yourself."

She blinked. "Me? There's nothing to tell."

"You're two thousand years old, and you're saying you have absolutely nothing to talk about?" He downed half the soda. "Tell me something about how you were born. Were your parents human?"

For a long time she sat there, long enough for him to eat

one of the two burgers. One delicate hand came up to worry her ponytail as she spoke. "I was born of an angel...I was switched out with my mortal parents' true infant daughter. They were slaves in a wealthy Roman household."

"So you grew up thinking you were human?"

"Yes."

He had, too, but deep down, he'd always felt different, and in the 20/20 hindsight, he could see the neon signs. Like the one where his mother screamed, "*You're the spawn of the devil!*" And, "*I should never have let that demon plant his seed in my womb.*" Sure, all the doctors in the sanitarium said his mother was insane, but her "delusions" never changed, and the friends who had been with her the night they'd "summoned Satan" had confirmed everything his mother said. They hadn't believed the dark-haired stranger with the tattoos on one arm was Satan himself, but they were sure he was either some sort of demon, or a con artist.

They were right on both counts.

"Was there ever anything that made you stand out?" he asked, mainly to get out of the past. "Did you feel different from everyone else?"

"Not all." She twisted one of the gold bands in her hair the way she'd twisted her palm around his cock. "I felt perfectly at home until my nineteenth birthday."

"So you lived a normal life? Married? Kids?"

"Not even close."

He wasn't a historian, but he'd thought that back in those days, when lifespans were short and girls married young, Idess would have been a rarity. It was probably rude to ask, but it was also rude to chain someone to a bed, so fuck it.

"Why not?"

"It's a long story."

He tugged on his chains. "It appears that I have nothing but time."

Idess shifted, but he had a feeling that no matter how comfortable she got next to him, she wasn't going to get comfortable with this subject. He'd definitely poked a bruise here.

"At the age of sixteen, I was given as a gift to the son of a nobleman."

"But wouldn't you have to be of noble birth or something to marry?"

"It wasn't to marry."

Her pained tone set his teeth on edge. "For sex? Like, a prostitute?"

"As a mistress. I was considered very beautiful," she said, without an ounce of pride. "My virginity was the gift. I was with him for two years, but when he took a wife, I was sent to a cruel friend of his. If I pleased him, I was to become either his mistress, or a toy to share with friends."

"Your master was a dick." Man, he wished he could go back in time and kick that guy's ass. Hard.

She laughed. "Before he could touch me, my brother Rami came for me, and the friend died a suitably horrible death in battle a few years later."

He purred with approval. "God, I love a bloodthirsty woman."

"Well, you *are* an assassin."

"I wasn't always." A note of defensiveness crept into his voice. "I'm more than a killer." Though, was that true? Even he doubted his own words. He'd been nothing but a killer since the day he got his *gift*. And when he'd gone to

work for Detharu, his killer status had only been secured.
He'd even earned the title of First Assassin. How special.
Yeah, he was real proud to be so good at offing people
that he'd won an award.

He was such a piece of shit.

"How are you more?" There was no condemnation
there. Only curiosity, and he couldn't answer. Her hand
came up to his chest, right over his slave mark, and a
sweet, balmy heat broke out over his skin. "Your master...he can summon you through this, yes?"

"Yes," he said hoarsely. He concentrated on bringing
his libido down, concentrated on the odd cooling sensation in her hand. It wasn't working. "He's been trying all
day."

Her hand froze, and her nails dug into his skin. The
luscious pleasure-pain made his breath catch. "What will
happen if you don't go?"

"The pain will gradually get worse, until I need to go
or suffer in agony."

She sucked in a startled breath. "How long?"

"Depends on how bad he wants to see me. And I'll tell
you right now that he's got a real burr up his ass about it."

She closed her eyes and bowed her head. Her ponytail
slid around, brushing his waist, and man, what he wouldn't
give to free her hair, let it shroud his body in silk as she
kissed her way down. "How bad is it? Right now, I mean."

"It burns," he said, and it wasn't a lie. He felt like he
had a hot iron on his chest. "But your hand...it's cool. It
feels good."

She lifted her head. "I can get you ice."

"Doesn't work." He covered her hand with his—his
right hand, partly because his left was in a precarious

position in the loose-fitting cuff, and partly because he *could* touch her with his *dermoire*-marked hand as long as it was still braceleted in the Bracken Cuffs. "But this is helping. I don't know why. Your touch is magic."

He was supposed to be seducing her. Supposed to be making her believe she was beautiful and perfect and sexy. Supposed to be doing all of that to get the fuck out of here. But suddenly, he wanted to do it because she *was* all those things. He brought her hand to his mouth. Though his chest began to burn again, it was worth the discomfort to be able to brush his lips across the soft skin of her knuckles. "You make me burn far more than anything my bond can do."

She made a small surprised sound, just a whisper of air, a catch of her breath. "If you're trying to seduce me, I told you it won't work." And yet, she was breathless, and he could scent her spicy arousal. When she shifted, the neckline of her top gaped, revealing deep cleavage that was at once too much flesh, and not enough.

"Oh, it'll work," he drawled. "It just won't get me free."

She bristled. "Then what is your plan? You have to have one. I would."

He rocked his head back against the wall and watched her through half-lidded eyes. "Come closer."

"So you can try to hurt me? I don't think so."

"No," he murmured. "So I can touch you. Everywhere."

She stared at him as if his words were a trick, but his incubus senses picked up the sound of her heart beating faster, her breaths coming in a rolling stutter, and he knew she was putting his audio to visual. "You're a pig," she said, with a lot less conviction than he knew she was capable of.

"You want me to turn into a raging monster?" Actually, he wasn't in much danger at the moment, but she wouldn't know that. He just... wanted her.

"You have plenty of slack in your chains. If you need release, you have a hand..." She cleared her throat. "The bathroom is right over th—"

"I need to touch," he growled. "I'm an incubus, Idess. I need contact. A female. You. This is torture." Sure, he was playing on her guilt, but he wasn't lying. Having her so close and being unable to do anything about it was killing him.

Her chin came up, all haughty. "You ask too much of me."

"Then, will you..." He took a deep breath. "Will you kiss me?"

Her lids flew up. "What? No. I can't."

"Is it against your angel rules?"

She swallowed hard enough for him to hear. "No, but—"

"Then give me that at least."

"I don't have much experience with kissing." Her gaze jerked away, and he felt the odd need to comfort her.

"Neither do I," he admitted.

"Liar," Idess whispered.

"Not about this," he whispered back.

Their gazes locked. Tension bloomed like a Sheoulin rose, dark, beautiful and, potentially, poisonous. And then, with agonizing slowness, she leaned forward and braced herself on his shoulders. The first, fleeting contact of her lips against his sent a buzz of lust through him. The second contact was bolder, lingering, and the buzz grew strong enough to send reverberations all the way to his toes.

She might not know what she was doing, but it didn't matter, because what she was doing was enough. More than enough. He lifted his face to meet hers, to intensify the kiss that was already building steam. When her tongue flicked timidly across his bottom lip, he jerked as if he'd been goosed and damned near forgot why he'd asked her to kiss him in the first place.

Steeling himself, he eased his wrist out of the cuff. Flexed his fingers. Wished he could touch her, could run with this kiss and see where it would lead.

Instead, he struck.

Ten

The ominous sound of metal clamping around Idess's wrist reached her ears a split second before Lore flipped her over and slammed her into the mattress.

"Remember when I said I'd get free and make you experience everything I had?" he growled.

"You bastard!" Still dazed from the kiss, she struck out with her free hand, but he caught her fist, tugged it up to his chained hand, and took it prisoner. Effortlessly, he pinned her with his heavy body and drove his fingers into her jeans pocket.

"*I'm* the bastard? You're the one who chained me up."

"You gave me no choice!"

"Yeah, yeah." He smiled, and she knew he'd found the key to the cuffs. "Killing Kynan is a no-no. Bad Lore, bad."

Snarling, she rocked her head up to catch him in his lying mouth, desperate to cause any kind of damage she could. If he freed himself . . . well, she didn't even want to think about what he could do to her. To Kynan. He reared back, and she caught only a glancing blow to his chin.

"Feisty," he mused. "I like it. Gimme more."

"Oh, I'll give you more." The Bracken Cuffs prevented her from morphing into her fallen angel father's form, but that didn't mean she was helpless. She brought her knee up hard, nailing him on the inner thigh. He sucked air and wrestled her leg back down before trapping both her legs between his.

Cursing, he lunged, and she heard the click of the key in the cuff lock. In an instant, he was free, and both her wrists were secured. He rolled off her and yanked on the chains, tugging them taut and pinning her to the bed with her arms stretched above her. She shouted in frustration, but he must have taken it as a cry of pain, because he loosened the chains before looping them around the bedposts, effectively keeping her from getting to her feet.

For the first time, she wished she could still sense his emotions, could use the knowledge to get her out of this. Instead, she'd wasted hours burning off the blood link at a distance, feeling what he felt while safely away from him. She liked to think she was strong, but every time the lust he felt pulsed through her, she'd fallen to her knees and prayed for the willpower to not go to him.

"You're going to pay for this!" She threw everything she had into an assault on the chains, screaming and pulling until she was sure her arms would pop out of their sockets.

Lore reached for her, but snatched his hand away at the last second. Foul words fell from his lips as he found one glove and his jacket on the floor. He tugged them on, and the next thing she knew, he was on top of her again, settling down as if her body was the most comfortable place in the world to be. His weight acted like a blanket, wrapping around her and calming her like a swaddled infant.

"There, now," he said softly. "The tables have been turned. The captor is now the captive, and all those other fun movie lines I never thought I'd say."

Idess's heart pounded against her rib cage as helplessness and fresh anxiety set in. "Let me go."

"Like you let me go when I asked?"

She swallowed. "Please. You can't kill Kynan. He's important."

"Yeah. Important to me."

"To the world."

"I think the world will survive without one human asshole."

Actually, it might not, but she'd found that demons rarely cared about the fate of humankind, so she switched tacks. "This isn't just about the world. I have a personal stake in his life."

He snorted. "What, you won't earn your wings if he dies?"

"That's exactly what will happen."

He rolled his eyes, but when she just stared, he stiffened. "You're serious."

"You can't even imagine." Tremors of panic swept from her toes to her scalp. Only a handful of Memitim had never Ascended, were doomed to either guard Primori forever or spend eternity as a human, being born again and again and never making it into Heaven. Some had even been snuffed out of existence. But as terrible as those punishments sounded, they weren't her primary motivation for not wanting to fail.

If she didn't succeed in protecting the most important human in existence, the very fate of all mankind, of billions of souls, would be affected when the ultimate battle between good and evil erupted on Earth.

Her betrayal of Rami had weighed on her for twelve hundred years, and every day she'd prayed for a chance to beg forgiveness. But if she betrayed the human race? There would be no absolution.

Something hot and wet dripped down her cheek. A tear. Geez, she hadn't cried in centuries. Not since the day Rami had Ascended. Before she knew it, the tear turned into a stream and suddenly she wasn't just sniffling or even crying. She'd gone into a full-on bawl that included great, shuddering sobs and gasps for air.

"Idess…calm down…Idess?" Lore's hands framed her face. "Hey. It's okay. Easy, Angel. Easy…"

She cried harder. She couldn't stop…it was as if she'd been storing tears for all these hundreds of years, and now, like a dormant volcano that had finally erupted, the flow wouldn't be stemmed.

Then Lore's lips were on hers, and he was kissing her. His mouth followed the trail of tears across her cheeks as his thumbs, one bare, one leather-clad, swept back and forth across skin that had grown as sensitive as if it were sunburned.

"Shh…" He tenderly kissed her ear. "It's all right."

"No," she moaned, because it was far from all right.

His hands stroked her cheeks, his bare thumb drifting lazily across her bottom lip. "I'm sorry," he murmured. "I'm not used to handling anything like this. I don't know what to do."

"I—" She cut off when the tip of his thumb slipped into her mouth. She didn't think. Didn't want to.

On impulse, she latched on to it and drew it deeper into her mouth. His eyes darkened and his mouth fell open so his piercing flashed and wow, if she'd thought she'd had power over him before, when he'd been at her mercy, chained, and needing release...it was nothing compared to now. The knowledge that she could affect him while *she* was restrained was a revelation.

Now she just had to figure out how, exactly, to use what she'd just learned.

Drawing on her very rusty seduction skills, she swirled her tongue around his knuckle and then nipped the pad. When he released a ragged breath, a zing of pure excitement shot through her in a powerful, almost sexual rush. Her breasts grew achy, her belly fluttered, and okay, there was no *almost* about it. Bringing a male pleasure was an aphrodisiac, for sure.

"I hate how much I want you." His voice was rough, as though he also hated that he'd made such a confession.

She squeezed her eyes closed. "Is it bad that I'm glad you hate it?"

"I'd think it was weird if you didn't." He pulled his thumb from her mouth and slid his hand along the curve of her neck. Her skin tingled under his palm, and her nipples tightened into hard little beads.

Why did he have to be so understanding? She wanted to rail at him, to fight him, but he captured her mouth with his in a surprisingly gentle kiss given how tense his body was, how rapid his breathing. His tongue teased the seam of her lips, tiny, wet flicks. She told herself that he wasn't affecting her, that she wasn't loosening up, that opening up to him was about seducing him.

But as she parted her lips, all she could think about was how good it felt to be touched like this, no matter what the circumstances.

With a moan, Lore thrust his tongue into her mouth to tangle with hers. The cool, smooth piercing against her tongue was an erotic contrast to the rough heat of the kiss. He shifted to ease his hand between them to her breast, and lower, his arousal came into contact with her core. Against her will, she arched against him, welcoming the pressure and friction and sudden hot wetness that flooded her.

She had enough play in the chains to thread her fingers through his hair, and the moment she did, he jerked as though he'd felt an electric shock.

"What's wrong?" she murmured against his lips.

Lifting his head, he blinked down at her. "Just…" He shook his head. "Nothing."

"Tell me." She had no idea why she wanted to know so badly, given that he'd just imprisoned her and made her cry.

He also made her burn.

But he said nothing, instead he buried his face in the curve of her neck and shoulder and kissed her there. Again, she arched up, and he began to grind against her, sparking a deep ache.

His hand roved down, between their bodies, and with a flick of his nimble fingers, he ripped open her jeans. Panic flared, and she stiffened.

"Lore…no. I can't."

His calloused palm slid into her panties to cup her

intimately, and she nearly swallowed her tongue. "Can't what?"

"H-have sex. Intercourse."

A soft curse whispered across her skin. But then one finger slid between her folds and his lips caressed her ear as he said, "Can you do this? Let me make you feel good?"

Yes. "No," she moaned, gasping when his fingertip brushed her clit.

"You're lying. I can feel it."

Yes, she was. Sort of. This didn't have anything to do with her vow of chastity. This was about her, and what being intimate in any way with this man would do to her.

"Don't," she said, but her body betrayed her, and she rocked into his touch.

"Don't what?" One finger slipped inside her core, and she nearly wept with pleasure. "Don't do this?"

She couldn't speak anymore. Even breathing had become an effort. Intercourse and self-gratification were forbidden, but what about gratification at the hands of others? Oh, no doubt it was prohibited, but even Rami had admitted that there was a murkiness in the vow, probably intentional, to allow for free will to get you into trouble.

And Lore was definitely trouble.

"Do you want to come?" Another finger joined the first, stretching her sensitive tissue and sending streams of almost overwhelming sensation straight to her brain. "Say it."

Her teeth were clenched too hard for her to speak. She squirmed, trying to get his thumb to the right place, trying to get it away from the right place—both, neither, because she didn't know what she wanted at this point.

He didn't let up, kept making little back-and-forth

sweeps across the tip of her clit that drove her out of her mind and to a place where her physical needs were beating down her thoughts.

"Say it," he murmured.

"No," she gasped.

"I want to watch." He dipped his head and brushed his lips over hers. "I want to see you come so badly, Idess. Let me."

He wanted this. Giving him what he wanted was part of the seduction, right? She was chained and helpless and she couldn't be blamed if she did whatever it took to get free and protect Kynan. Besides, Lore was Primori, and she couldn't betray the Memitim/Primori relationship by denying something her charge wanted.

The reasonings were pathetically weak, but it was all she had and she was *starving* for this and she barked out a desperate, "Yes!"

His smile was one of primal male triumph. His fingers began a furious, deep pumping rhythm, and his thumb circled and swept. It had been so long since she'd experienced this that it all felt new and wondrous, and she was absolutely certain that the best full-on sex she'd had hadn't been this good.

Lore added another finger, increased the pressure with his thumb, and her body went wild, thrashing as she detonated. Colors swirled behind her eyelids like a kaleidoscope, carrying her through the ecstasy as his hand worked its magic. He brought her down with gradually lighter strokes, until finally she could breathe—and see— again.

"Beautiful," he whispered. His half-lidded gaze was intent, awed, and so full of hunger that her body instantly sparked to life again. "God, you're—" He broke off with a wince. Tiny pinpoints of crimson peppered his dark eyes as he glanced at the bathroom.

"I...I have to—" He swallowed, and when he spoke again, his voice was so deep and gravelly that she felt it inside, almost as though that tone was meant to prepare a woman for penetration. "Need...privacy." He shoved to his hands and knees above her.

"No. Please. Stay." Shockingly, he halted. "I want...I want to watch." *I don't want to be alone.* Alone meant time to think. And regret.

A low growl of approval dredged up from his chest as he unzipped his pants.

Lore couldn't believe he was about to do this. He'd never had any sexual hangups—well, other than the fact that sex tended to kill his partners, but still. He'd never jerked off in front of anyone before. And though Idess's request had been a massive turn-on, his hand was shaking as he undid his fly.

So maybe he did have hangups.

"Shit," he growled. "I can't." He started to climb off the bed.

"Please?" Idess lay there, all sprawled out, relaxed, sated, the scent of sex coming off her and wreaking havoc on his libido.

He wanted to be inside her, not touching himself in a dark bathroom like some sort of pervert, while she was just feet away. But he also had no experience being so...sexual...in front of a female. Oh, he had arrogance in spades and overactive male instincts roaring through him, but he also wasn't sure stroking himself while a bound female watched was something he could do.

"You're embarrassed?" The surprise in her voice lashed at his already shredded control.

"I'm not a fucking virgin."

"You haven't been with many females, though, have you?"

Now *that* was just insulting. He'd been with some. He just hadn't been with any more than once. And those he had been with were all about instant gratification—get in and out with no playtime. No real touching.

No connection.

This...this would be a connection. He didn't know why or how, but it would. He just felt it. And feeling anything for this woman would be bad. That he *did* know.

"It's okay," she said softly. "You don't have to answer. And you don't have to stay if you don't want to."

The fact that she was being so nice to him, was so concerned about his feelings, pissed him off. He'd just turned the tables on her, chained her up, could do anything he wanted to her...Biting back a nasty curse, he adjusted his erection, even as the pressure built under his skin and in his balls. "Why? Why do you want to watch?"

"Because," she said in a husky voice, "you're beautiful, too."

His heart tripped over her words, and warmth spread through him. No one had ever complimented him like that, with such...reverence.

Ruthlessly shoving his reservations aside, he gripped his shaft with his bare hand. He heard her soft intake of breath, the little hitch that somehow turned him on more than anything ever had. His stomach tightened and he had trouble breathing, and holy shit, having her watch...a total turn-on he hadn't anticipated. Now that his power was no longer contained by the Bracken Cuffs, all he had to worry about was keeping his right arm away from her when he came.

"See?" Her voice was hoarse. "Not so hard, is it?"

"Oh, it's hard," he ground out, and her lips quirked in a smile.

"And big."

His cock pulsed as though happy with the compliment. Damned thing was too stupid to realize she was doing what he'd done—toss out niceties to get on the captor's good side. Not that what she'd said wasn't true.

"You say the nicest things."

Completely at ease now, he ran his bare hand up and down, loving how altering the speed or the length of the strokes made her eyelids grow heavy, or how, when he changed it up even more and twisted his fist around the head, her mouth would fall all the way open. And Jesus, when he rubbed the cap with the flat of his palm, she actually licked her lips.

Emboldened, he moved closer, teasing her with the sight of his cock. "You like this, don't you?" Her eyes flew up to his. "Tell me what you want me to do." When her mouth worked but nothing came out, he smiled and stopped stroking. "What's the matter? You embarrassed?"

Anger sparked in those amazing rum-colored depths, and along with it, the light of battle. Freaking hot.

"Stroke." The command might have been more effective if there hadn't been a slight quaver in her voice, but he did as she'd ordered. Slowly.

"How's that?"

"Faster."

Suppressing a groan, he increased the speed, but not by much.

"I said, faster. And...and do that twisty thing you do when your hand is at the top."

He would have laughed at the cute fierceness in her voice, if he wasn't too busy holding back his orgasm. Perspiration beaded on his forehead as he clenched his teeth and panted through the growing pressure.

"Stop," she said, and damn her, he barely had the control to obey. "Slide your hand down. To your...your balls." Splotches of pink colored her cheeks. She was powerful and sexy, yet the word "balls" made her blush.

Lore loved that.

He let his palm ride slowly down his shaft. By the time he reached his sac, his cock was aching. "Now what?"

"Rub them," she said breathlessly. "Pretend I—a female was doing it."

Closing his eyes, he cursed, because it was so easy to pretend it was her warm palm cupping him, rolling his balls gently between her fingers as she'd done before. She made him play for a minute, and just as he was about to beg her to let him do more, she said, "Now. Make yourself come." Her voice lowered dangerously. Seductively. "On me."

Surprise shot through him and the climax came on its heels, her words sparking a chain reaction that went nuclear. He barely had time to fall forward to brace himself on his right arm, keeping it well out of the range of her touch as he pumped his seed onto her hard, flat abs. His vision went completely offline as pleasure short-circuited a couple of his senses, including his hearing, because he heard Idess talking but had no idea what she was saying. He just wanted her to keep saying it, because her voice was an aphrodisiac, and his orgasm went on and on…

Finally, as his trembling arm threatened to collapse under his weight, it ended. His head swam and his breath felt like fire in his throat. He opened his eyes and met Idess's.

"I'm so jealous," she whispered, and he blinked.

"Of what?"

Her head fell back on the pillow, and she stared up at the ceiling with the saddest eyes he'd ever seen. "You're so alive, Lore. There's fire in you. A will to live, when all I want is to be done with this life."

An unfamiliar emotion clogged Lore's throat, cutting off his breath. A will to live? He couldn't care less about his own life. What he did care about was Sin, and making sure she never had to be owned again. Until that happened, he had to hang on. She was one of the reasons he'd hoped his brothers didn't turn out to be total shits, and that she'd get to know them. She needed someone to take care of her. Someone better than Lore.

"Don't be jealous of me," he croaked. "There is *nothing* about me you should envy. I'm a terrible person."

A smile trembled on her lips. "Your *choices* are terrible, but a terrible person wouldn't love your sister the way you do."

He didn't buy that, not by a long shot. But strangely, Idess was right about one thing. He was alive—at least, now he was. For the first time since going through the transition that had turned him into a cold killer, he felt a spark. The banter with Idess energized him. Their battles challenged him. The sex excited him. Sure, none of that had happened under ideal conditions, but he had to wonder what things would be like between them if they weren't going head to head over Kynan.

And if she wasn't chained up.

He stifled an insane laugh, because all of that was a dream, and he'd never been a dreamer. Besides, once Kynan was dead, Lore figured his brothers—or Idess—would make sure he never dreamed again.

Who in their right mind built a medical facility for demons? It was a question Rariel had asked since the day he'd heard about Underworld General, and as he searched for the Harrowgate's UGH symbol, he found he was actually curious about it.

UGH. He had to chuckle at the utter lack of forethought someone had displayed when he'd named the hospital. Moron.

This would be the sixth time he'd been there, though the first five times he hadn't even stepped out of the Harrowgate. He'd simply opened it up, let Roag out or in, and continued. Apparently, the curse Roag's brother had saddled him with had left the shriveled demon not only invisible to most, but without the ability to manipulate objects like the Harrowgate or doors, which made travel difficult.

Poor guy. Being betrayed by a sibling was the worst pain one could experience, and Rariel knew that firsthand.

He cast a sympathetic glance at Roag, who appeared to Rariel as a transparent specter, not nearly as solid as spirits were. And, unlike spirits, Roag's only communication with Rariel came telepathically.

"Are you ready?" Rariel asked.

Yes.

Rariel tapped the hospital glyph with anticipation. This time, he was going to deliver his traveler and hang out. Observe. Plot.

The gate opened, and he stepped out. The emergency room was bustling, but he doubted anyone else could see that.

Most of the people milling around were ghosts, and as Roag entered the hospital, those spirits went mad. Some fled, some cowered, some stood in place and wailed until Rariel wanted to clap his hands over his ears.

Rariel's invisible friend terrified the ghosts, and even the living beings in the emergency room became suddenly agitated.

A female vamp wearing scrubs approached him. "Do you need help?"

"No," Rariel said, as Roag literally ripped into one of the screaming ghosts. That was the fun thing about spirits. You could tear them apart, causing unimaginable pain, and yet, they didn't die. "I'm just here to watch."

"Suit yourself, creep." The vampire walked away, and he settled in beneath the Waiting Area sign. Distantly, he heard pitched, angry voices, and in another direction, something screamed. The spirits were still freaking out, wailing and beating the walls.

Nearby, between one plastic-covered couch and a sturdy stone table, two females gathered three infants closer to them. The pretty female with brown hair and striking champagne eyes let out a wolflike growl. The harder-looking female with red hair caressed the hilt of a blade in her hip scabbard, her green warrior's eyes alert.

The moment Roag spotted them, fury blasted off him in a concussion wave that affected everyone in the emergency department. Staff and patients missed steps, dropped equipment, hugged themselves as though cold.

Roag moved toward the little group, murder in his eyes. Ah, yes...the females were Sem mates, and the triplets were Sem cubs. This was the family of the very brothers Roag wanted destroyed. And interestingly, one of the infants seemed to see him. Roag smiled...at least, the twist of his lips looked like a smile. He shifted form into a big Sem with shoulder-length, dark hair.

The little one reached out his hand toward Roag. Roag circled the family, and the baby watched, squirming in its mother's arms as it tried to reach for Roag.

"Rade, take it easy," the female said, hefting the baby tighter against her.

Roag shot Rariel a grin, and Rariel's stomach twisted. He might be evil, a sick fuck in his own right, but torturing any species' young was not something he enjoyed.

But as Roag's thoughts melded with his, he relaxed. He wouldn't have to torture. Just kill.

Eleven

"Kynan, please. Stay at the hospital with me. You're safe here."

Kynan Morgan had a hard time denying his wife anything, but he had been a soldier in the Army and for The Aegis for most of his life, and it wasn't in his nature to hide from the enemy.

How often, though, was the enemy your best friends' brother?

He wrapped his arms around Gem, the soft rasp of her purple scrubs against his leather jacket a comforting sound. He loved holding her, couldn't believe that there had been a time when he'd foolishly wanted nothing to do with her.

"I'll be fine," he murmured into her hair. "I was battling demons even before I became all untouchable and immortal." And before he learned he had an angel in his family tree.

"I don't care." She gave a petulant shake of the head and stepped back, hands on hips. "You never had a trained killer after you before."

"I'll be surrounded by Guardians, Gem. Tayla will be with me the whole time you're on shift. Your sister would never let anything happen to me."

Gem tugged on one violet-streaked braid. "I know. But what if—"

"Shh." He pressed two fingers to her lips. "I promise I'll be okay. I have an angel watching over me, too."

She grasped his hand. "They should *all* be watching over you. It's stupid that they can't."

He thought so, too. Reaver had explained the situation back when Serena had been keeper of the amulet, Heofon, and even then Kynan had to call bullshit on the whole can't-interfere-with-human-will crap. At least his Primori status—whatever that was—had gotten around the no-interference rule a little.

He understood Gem's worry, though—the chain around his neck held the key to unimaginable destruction, and thanks to the events of last month, it wasn't as secret as it should be. It made him a target, and he couldn't help but wonder who could have known that Lore was the only non-angel who could kill him. Only a handful of people had been present at Kynan's resurrection and gifting of the necklace and immortality charm, and there was no way the Sem brothers would have talked, any more than the Guardians would have. Probably. Not everyone in The Aegis was happy about the fact that Tay and Ky were still Guardians, and they were both still dealing with the fallout.

Gem's green eyes became liquid as she kissed his knuckles. "Just be careful."

"Always." He had a baby on the way, one who would be born charmed—the first ever to receive the immortality gift in that manner—and he would make damned sure he was around to raise it. And to make more. Gem wanted a big family, and so did he.

But in order to have his big family, he had to deal with the threat to it.

Lore.

His gut knotted. He owed the Sem brothers big-time. They'd given him a job, a wife, a life. But he'd take out the brother they hadn't even gotten a chance to know in a heart-beat. Though he hadn't told Tayla, he had every member of the Sigil using their resources to scour the planet for the demon.

Eidolon had better pray that he found Lore before Kynan did.

"She's definitely our sister, Shade."

Eidolon stared at the DNA report as he spoke into the phone. This was crazy. Unreal. He'd had the test run twice to ensure accuracy and to confirm that no one had tampered with the report, even though in his heart he'd known since yesterday.

Sin sat on the bed in one of the patient rooms, feet swinging while she waited for him. Through the window to the room, she looked small and innocent as she stared at the anatomy posters on the wall. She'd come back as she'd said she would, though Eidolon had no doubt she wouldn't stay once she got the autopsy report on the warg she'd killed. She had no new helpful information on Lore, except that she'd had a tense confrontation with Idess, and Eidolon was starting to worry.

Making matters worse, he'd had to suspend four staff members for fighting, three for dereliction of duty, a patient had died today when a nurse had accidentally injected a lethal dose of medicine, and now the family of the dead Mamu was threatening bodily harm against all staff members. To top it all off, tension still pulsed between him and his brothers, particularly Shade.

All this time, he'd taken pride in the hospital he and his brothers had built from the ground up, and yeah, UG was an amazing accomplishment. But now its heart—its denizens—were sick, and he couldn't help but feel that it was his fault, that he'd neglected them somehow. And by suspending workers, he was treating individual symptoms instead of the underlying illness, but at this point, slapping on a bandage was his only option.

"E," Shade said, his voice drowned out by the sound of the ambulance engine, "this is freaky. Hope dear old dad doesn't have any more surprises in store for us. Half-goats, dog-boys…"

"I know." Eidolon glanced at Tayla, who had just joined him. "Look, I gotta go. Runa's waiting for you. Wraith will be here any second with an exorcist."

He hoped that getting rid of the ghosts would end the problems plaguing the hospital's staff, but even if it did, this was an example of his failure to consider all potential problems that might affect his workers. He should have been practicing preventive medicine instead of waiting until an emergency cropped up.

He should have seen this coming a long time ago, though he had to wonder why it was happening *now*.

"Good. I'll be there in five." Shade paused. "I'm bringing in another warg."

Eidolon's stomach slid to his feet. "Diseased?"

"Looks like. Same symptoms as the first two."

The first two. Who were dead. Apparently, the one Sin had diseased had transmitted his mysterious ailment to another, who had come in just hours after the first warg. If Shade's patient was sick with the same symptoms, they could be looking at a possible outbreak. Eidolon hadn't told Sin about the second warg, but a few minutes ago he'd taken more blood from her to analyze.

"Tell Runa to go to my office," Shade said. "I don't want her and the boys anywhere near this patient."

"You got it," E said, but Shade had already hung up.

Eidolon snapped his phone shut, called the triage desk with the message for Runa, and then stared at the DNA report again. "This is so fucked up."

Tayla stole a peek at the report. "What's fucked up? The Smurfette?"

"The what?"

"Smurfette." Tayla rolled her eyes. "You've never watched cartoons, have you?"

Wraith came around the corner, his leather duster flapping around his boots. He shot Tay a look drenched with sympathy. "E's way too starched to watch cartoons. That's so not happening to Stewie. He's already digging *The Simpsons*."

"He's three weeks old!" Tayla gaped at Wraith in outrage.

"Almost four."

Tayla huffed. "Good God. I can't believe *you* are raising

a child. Isn't there some sort of demon equivalent of Child Protective Services?"

"Hey." Wraith crossed his arms over his chest. "I have as much right to screw up a kid as anyone else. So what's going on, anyway?"

Eidolon really had no idea, since he'd never seen *The Simpsons*, and Stewie, Wraith's son, had been named after some hell child on another cartoon Eidolon hadn't seen. Fortunately, the kid also had a proper demon name, but Wraith and his mate, Serena, seemed to think he needed time to grow into Talon, so for now, Stewie it was. In any case, this conversation was either way over Eidolon's head, or way beneath him. He was going to go with the latter.

Tayla cursed under her breath. "I was just explaining to Eidolon that Sin is a Smurfette."

Wraith swung his big body around to study Sin with blue eyes that were very different from Shade's, E's, and Lore's. Sin's, too. "Nah. Smurfette is way hotter."

"What the fuck is a Smurfette?" Eidolon was seriously getting annoyed now.

"There's this cartoon called *The Smurfs*," Tayla explained, slowly, as though Eidolon were the child here. "They're these little blue people, and they're all male. But one day a female shows up. She shouldn't exist, but she does."

Eidolon considered that for a second. "How did she get there?"

"An evil wizard named Gargamel made her," Tayla said. "In a lab or something."

"So you're suggesting that an evil wizard made Sin?"

"Of course not, silly. I'm just saying she's a Smurfette. A lone female amongst males."

Eidolon frowned. "Did the Smurfette mate with the males?"

"Dude." Wraith grimaced. "It's a cartoon."

"Then why are we talking about this?" Eidolon asked, and Wraith and Tayla exchanged looks that said he was a hopeless case. "Wraith, did you find an exorcist?"

Wraith shoved his blond hair back from his face. "Yup. He's a weird one. Left him in the emergency department to get a feel for things."

"Good. I'll have him start work right away. If there's anything he needs, I want you to get it for him." As the hospital's procurer of nontraditional supplies unique to demon medicine, dealing with an exorcist's needs fell within Wraith's job description.

"No problem." Wraith jerked his chin at Sin. "Did she find Lore?"

Sudden tension took root at the mention of Lore's name. "No."

"Hope he's not dead," Wraith said, startling Eidolon. His brother stuck his hand in a coat pocket, probably feeling up a weapon. "If he needs killing, we should do the honors."

Okay, yeah. That was more like it. "Wraith—"

"What?" The challenge in Wraith's voice was what made Eidolon back down. Not that he was afraid of going toe-to-toe with his brother, but that was exactly what Wraith wanted, and Eidolon wasn't going to give him the satisfaction. There had been too much fighting between them lately.

"Nothing. Just make sure Kynan has a lot of backup. If one assassin has been sent after him, there could be more."

"Kynan hasn't been left without a Guardian since all this began," Tayla said. "In fact, it's my turn to stay with him. I need to go."

"Be careful."

"It's no fun if I do that." She kissed him and took off, and Eidolon took a much-needed moment to admire her swinging retreat.

Wraith stared after Tayla, but for different reasons. "What does The Aegis think of all this?"

"They don't know any more than we do," Eidolon replied, returning his gaze to his brother. "Kynan said they know a hit has been put out on him, so they're prepared to have to fight fallen angels, but they don't know who's behind the hire."

"You know," Wraith muttered, "life was a whole lot easier when we hated all humans and didn't give a shit what happened to the lot of them." He laughed. "Okay, I couldn't say that with a straight face. I still don't give a shit."

That wasn't entirely true—Wraith considered Kynan a friend and brother, and then there was the fact that he'd fallen in love with Serena while she was still human. And he had a human father-in-law who also happened to be a member of The Aegis's Sigil. Wraith wheeled around. "I'm going to see if Exorcist Dude needs anything, and then I'm going home to Serena and the hellspawn."

He jogged off, nearly colliding with Shade as their brother took a corner.

"Where's the fire?" Shade shouted after him, but Wraith kept going. Shaking his head, Shade stopped in front of Eidolon. "What's going on?"

"Sun's up."

Shade nodded in understanding. As a vampire now, Wraith's mate was all but trapped in their home during daylight hours, and Wraith didn't like leaving her unprotected. Not that she was completely helpless. He'd had an underground tunnel built from their cellar that led into a maze of caverns with exits near Harrowgates, and within a month, one would lead directly to the hospital.

"How's the warg?" E asked.

"Not good. Shakvhan is working on him, but he'll be lucky to make it another five minutes."

"Damn." Eidolon shoved his hand through his hair. "I'm going to set up an isolation room in case we get any more. And until further notice, I want all warg staff to avoid the emergency department and all warg patients."

"And I'll inform my warg medics that they're banned from responding to any calls that involve werewolves." Shadows came alive in Shade's nearly black eyes, writhing angrily. "This was the last thing we needed right now."

"The ghost problem should be fixed soon, so that'll be one thing off the plate."

"Good. This morning both ambulances had flat tires."

Eidolon growled in frustration. "And we nearly lost another patient because his respirator had been turned off."

"I hate ghosts—" Shade broke off at the sight of Sin, still sitting on the bed, now pawing through a medical text. He swallowed, and the shadows in his eyes settled. "Is that . . . her?"

Eidolon inclined his head. "She's been waiting a while. I need to grab her paperwork."

"Guess I should go say hi."

"Does this mean you're willing to give Lore a break?"

Shade glared. "I'll do what I have to do to protect Ky, whether you get that or not."

"Gods, Shade! It's not that I don't get it—"

Shade cut him off with a dismissive flick of his hand and started toward the room where Sin waited. E stopped him with a hand on his forearm.

"Shade. She's not...she's not what you're used to."

For a moment, Shade looked perplexed, but gradually, his expression shuttered. "She's not Skulk, you mean."

Shade had been extremely attached to all his Umber sisters, but as the only survivor of a slaughter that had killed the others, Skulk had been special to him. Now there was a hole inside Shade that E was afraid he'd try to fill with this new female, and Sin didn't seem to want anything to do with her newfound brothers.

"Just don't expect much."

Twelve

_____

Sin swung her feet back and forth over the edge of the bed like a little kid waiting for her parents in the principal's office. Not that she knew what that felt like. She and Lore had been educated at home by grandparents who placed more emphasis on physical labor than the three Rs.

And what the hell was taking Eidolon so long? She'd come in for the autopsy stuff, and he'd made her wait for—she glanced at her watch—a freaking hour. She practically had the entire volume of *Medical Parasitology* memorized, and...eww.

She didn't have time for this. She had a plan, and she needed to put it into action.

Deth still felt Lore's life force, which meant Idess hadn't been lying. Lore was alive. So instead of trying to injure the angel with the Gargantua dagger, she was going to mark her with an assassin's secret weapon. A tracer grenade, once detonated, contaminated everything within twenty yards with a substance that left an easily followed trail. There were limitations and catches that made them unstable, dangerous, and often unreliable in untrained hands, but Sin was an expert, and nothing had ever gone wrong with one of her grenades. No, the greatest challenge was locating the ingredients and assembling the thing.

After she finished, she'd have to cool her heels until the devil's hour, which was easier said than done. Unlike Lore, Sin had never been patient. Her brother would make a good sniper, could wait for days to get the one perfect, surgical shot; Sin would rather charge into a situation with all guns blazing, mow everyone down, and let God and Satan sort out the souls.

Tired of waiting, she hopped off the bed. She'd hunt Eidolon down if she had to. The door opened before she reached it, and a Seminus wearing a black paramedic uniform walked in. With his dark hair, stern expression, and broad shoulders, he looked like a cross between Eidolon and Lore.

"You must be another brother," she muttered.

"Shade."

"Great. Nice to meet you. Now, if you don't mind, I have to go."

He seemed a little taken aback, but his expression closed off as he blocked the door. "Eidolon will be here in a minute. He went to grab the report you're waiting for."

She blew out a frustrated breath. "I've been waiting for an hour already."

"He's had some emergencies to deal with, but he's going to get it now. Really."

"Fine." She crossed her arms over her chest and stared at him.

He stared back.

"Well?" she snapped. "You gonna stand there all day? Don't you have somewhere you have to be?"

"I just got off duty." He dug into his shirt pocket and pulled out a pack of gum. "I figured we should meet."

Sin gestured to the door. "'Kay. We've met. Buh-bye." Shade looked completely at a loss. "Why aren't you gone yet?"

"Why are you being like this?"

God, what was it with these guys? "Because I just want to be left alone, okay? Is that so difficult to understand?"

He cocked a brow. "No, actually. But maybe if you got to know us—"

"I don't want to!" She shoved him out of the way and swung open the door, needing to get away from the crushing pressure of sudden family. "Just stay away from me. I've lived over a hundred years without you, and I certainly don't need you now."

She didn't need anyone. She'd learned a long time ago that she couldn't rely on anyone but herself. Not even Lore. He'd left her when she'd needed him the most, and though she understood why he'd done it and she knew he was trying to make it up to her, some part of her just couldn't fully lower her defensive shields and let him back in all the way.

Trust, as her old master used to say, was evil and insidious. And he'd know. He'd taken her off the streets when she was vulnerable, made her trust him, and then he'd forced her to do...things. He'd taken advantage of her ability to kill and her need for sex, and he'd used them until her soul had shriveled.

Even before he'd come along, trust had made her believe that her mother would love her. She hadn't. It had made Sin think her grandparents would always be there for her. They'd died. It had made her believe Lore would take care of her. He'd abandoned her.

No one would abandon her ever again.

Except, that really wasn't true anymore, was it? She'd come close to letting Lore back in, closer than she'd thought possible. And now he was gone. Sure, it wasn't logical to blame him this time, any more than she should blame her grandparents for dying. But logic had never been her strong suit.

She stalked away from Shade, heart pounding and hoping he wouldn't chase her down. Problem was, she didn't know where she was going. She'd come via the Harrowgate, but she didn't remember the way and when she was freaked, her senses dulled. She couldn't sense the gate at all.

An exit loomed ahead, double sliding doors. Quickly, she slipped through them and found herself in an underground parking lot that didn't appear to have a way out. Didn't that just figure. After wandering around for a few minutes, she gave up, but there was no way she was going back inside the hospital. Not yet. She just needed a few minutes of peace and quiet, with no annoying brothers watching her every move.

The last two days' events had taken a toll on her, and although she could use a quart of Lore's homemade rotgut and a week-long nap, she figured the best she was going to get right now was a few minutes of hiding herself away. Exhausted, she sank down onto the pavement next to a black ambulance.

She wasn't there for more than thirty seconds when

she heard footsteps. Groaning, she buried her head in her hands.

"Fuck off, Shade—"

"Not Shade. Conall."

Startled, she snapped her head up, and no, the guy standing there was definitely not her brother. It was the extremely hot vampire paramedic she'd seen wheel in the warg she'd killed. The one with the funky silver eyes and sandy blond hair. Mr. Personality.

"You okay?" he asked gruffly.

"Ah...yeah."

"Then why are you skulking around my ambulance?"

"I wasn't skulking. I was resting."

"In a parking lot." He gave her a dry look. "On the ground."

She shoved to her feet. "Do all medical personnel take classes on how to be obnoxious? Because I thought maybe it was a brother thing, but I'm starting to think it's a medical thing."

"You've got one hell of a chip on your shoulder, don't you?" The vampire opened the back of the ambulance and tossed a nylon bag inside.

Sin frowned. "You don't even know me."

"And let me guess," he said, sounding utterly bored. "That's the way you like it."

"What, are you psychic or something?"

He laughed, a deep, melodious sound that rang through her. "I'm over a thousand years old. I've seen it all. You, sweetcheeks, are nothing new." At what must have been an outraged expression on her face, he laughed again. "Come on. Surely you can't think you are the only female out there who's had a rough life, had her heart walked on, been kept in a dungeon for three centuries, blah, blah, pick your trauma, and are now stomping around with all this pent-up anger you spill like acid on everyone who tries to get to know you." He narrowed his gaze at her. "How close am I?"

Sin's mouth worked, but nothing came out. She finally snapped it shut to avoid looking like a fish gasping on the bank of a river.

"That's what I thought." He made a shooing gesture with his hand. "Now, run along and go be caustic with someone who cares. Oh, wait, no one cares, do they? Because you won't let them—"

She struck out, wanting to break that perfect nose. He caught her wrist when her knuckles were half an inch from his face. He didn't blink, and the only part of his body that had moved—like lightning—had been his arm. Baring his fangs, he bent over her so their noses nearly touched. "Do not ever strike me. You have no idea what I am capable of."

"Ditto, dickwad." She should fire up her gift and give him some horrible vampire disease. Vamps might be dead, but that meant they succumbed even more quickly. She wasn't sure how that worked, but it did. Except... his hand was warm. His body was warm. He wasn't a vampire. At least, he wasn't a dead vampire.

"Go away." He released her with a shove. "I have better things to do than spar with a little girl in need of a good spanking."

Oh, she'd show him who was going to get spanked. As he turned away, dismissing her with nothing more than a curt shake of his head, she swept her leg out, catching him in the knees, and as he lost his balance, she spun, striking him in the back with her other foot. He went down, but she didn't even have time to smile at her victory, because he was up in a flash, and suddenly she was pinned to the side of the ambulance. Conall's face was a mask of cold fury, his eyes glazed over with frost. "With those markings, I'm guessing you're here on some business related to the Sem brothers, so that's why I'm not going to drain you right here, right now. But fuck with me again, and I'm going to get my first taste of Seminus blood." His forearm was across her throat, his other hand trapping her arm against her side, and his six-foot-six body was holding her so she couldn't move.

But she couldn't help but notice the long, lush lashes that framed his feral, intelligent eyes. And the harsh, masculine slope of his jaw. Then there was the promise of raw sex that oozed from every pore, a promise she had no doubt he could deliver on.

Something in her gut began to throb, moving lower the longer she stared at him. Shit. Her hormones were acting up, right on schedule. If she didn't get a daily dose of sex, she became extremely ill. It was possible, even, that she could die. She'd just never gone long enough to know whether that was actually the case.

This morning she'd been either too distracted or in too much of a hurry to climb into bed with one of the assassins she bunked with, and she was paying for that now, as her raging hormones were quite happy to let her know. But one thing she'd learned over the years was that her hormones didn't just affect her. They were also good for attracting males...and getting herself out of bad situations with them.

"You want to taste me?" she purred, and his head snapped back. Well, well.

His eyes narrowed. "What are you playing at?"

"Me?" she asked innocently. "Nothing."

His gaze swept her face before dropping lower, to her exposed throat. The hunger in his expression kicked her pulse into doubletime. And when he pushed back from her, just enough to let his gaze travel lower, to her breasts, her pulse rate tripled.

She wasn't sure what might have happened next, and she'd never know, because she heard heavy footsteps. When she turned her head, there was another huge male in a paramedic uniform standing near the rear of the truck. His expression was as black as his shaggy hair.

"Conall, man, what are you doing? Shift hasn't even started and you're already humping the females. E warned us about sex in public. Take it into the rig."

Sin snorted. "What makes you think there is going to be sex? I was about to kick this guy's ass." Conall had loosened his grip, allowing her to tear free and shove him away. His snort followed her as she pushed past the dark-haired medic and headed for the entrance to the hospital.

She might not want to see her brothers, but better them than a vampire with questionable life signs who, for some reason, made her feel alive when all she wanted was to remain dead.

———

Conall watched the female take off, her ass swaying temptingly in tight, well-worn jeans. A strategically placed rip pinched and gaped at the crease where her leg and her left ass cheek met, drawing his eyes like a magnet.

Luc watched too, his gaze hot. "She's..."

"Yeah."

Luc arched an eyebrow. "Didn't know there were female Sems."

"Me either. Think she's here for business? Like a Council member? Or do you think she's related to the brothers? Maybe she's their queen or something."

"Dunno." The hundred-year-old warg never said much, and when he did, he mostly grunted. "Ever done a succubus?"

"A couple." Conall generally avoided succubi, though. You never knew what they were after. Your seed, your soul, your life. Con kind of liked hanging on to the second two.

Luc crossed his arms over his chest and braced one shoulder against the ambulance. "Dare you to do her."

Conall's cock stirred. Well, it stirred *more*. "I've never done a Seminus demon." Conall was all about doing things he'd never done. And in a thousand years of life, he'd done a lot.

"I hope to hell not," Luc said. "Since until today you thought they were all males."

Con laughed, even though Luc wasn't trying to be funny. He liked the warg, which was a miracle considering he'd met Luc in a bar fight—had *fought* Luc in the bar fight. They'd both ended up in the demon-run hospital Con hadn't even known existed, and he'd been impressed—and bored—enough to sign on to become a medic. Now he and Luc sometimes worked together. Partners. Not friends—friendly rivals was more like it.

"I'll give you a hundred bucks if you nail her."

Con shot him a *fuck-you* look. "Five."

"Five hundred?" Luc snorted. "For a succubus? She'll probably jump *you*."

"If she's related to the Sem brothers, I'm not risking my balls for a hundred bucks."

Luc nodded. "Good point. Five hundred. With proof."

"Done."

Con grinned. This was going to be the easiest money he'd ever made.

Heat still flooding her body, Sin burst through the emergency room doors—and ran into Shade. God, these guys were like fucking Terminators. Or Borg. Resistance is futile and all that shit. It was clear she wasn't going to shake the Brothers From Hell, so she might as well get what she could from them. "Where's Eidolon?"

"Probably in his office," Shade said.

"I want what he promised me. Now. I'm tired of his stall tactics."

"Why would he stall?"

"Gee, I wonder. Maybe so I'd be forced to hang out here and get to know you guys?"

He sighed, as if she were a child to be humored. "Come on. I'll take you to his office."

"About time," she muttered. She followed him to an administrative area, where they walked through a maze of offices, some separated by cubicles where various male and female demons sat, and some more private—full rooms with doors and hall windows with blinds.

Eidolon was at his desk, and he stood when she and Shade entered his office. He held out a file, as though he'd been expecting her. "Here's your proof of death. If your boss has any questions, tell him to contact me."

"Took you long enough."

"You're welcome," he said dryly.

Shade turned to her. "What now?"

"I'm going to turn this in."

"Are you coming back?"

"I doubt it." She smiled. "Nice knowing you. Buh-bye."

"Leaving so soon?" The deep voice came from behind her, startling her. She spun, coming face-to-chest with a tall, blond male she assumed was the one brother she hadn't met. Wraith.

"Soon?" She stepped back so she wouldn't have to crane her neck to look at him. "I've been stuck here for way too long."

"I thought you went home," Shade said.

"Forgot my iPod in my office." His blue eyes flashed at Sin. "Where's Lore?"

"If I knew, he wouldn't be missing."

"He's probably dead." Wraith's tone was matter-of-fact, utterly cool, and Sin wanted to punch him.

"Wraith..." Eidolon's voice was quiet.

"It's okay, Eidolon," she said, still glaring at Wraith. "I can handle anything this guy can dish out." She started forward. "Get out of my way."

Wraith's broad shoulders filled the doorway...and he didn't move. "Easy there, Smurfette."

Smurfette? "Move."

"No."

She hit him. Put her knuckles right in his perfect nose. He didn't even flinch, and she got the impression he could have stopped her if he'd wanted to. Instead, he grinned, those wicked fangs gleaming. "You hit like a girl."

She gasped in outrage. "I. Said. *Move*. I'm going to find my brother."

He snorted. "If *I* can't find him, *you* don't stand a margarita's chance at an AA meeting."

"Y-you arrogant ass," she sputtered.

"It's not arrogance if you can back it up."

She was going to kill him. She really was. "You don't care, do you? You don't give a shit that the angel chick could be hurting him, doing horrible things to him." She spun to Shade and looked from him to Eidolon. "See? This is why I didn't want to get to know you, even though Lore kept saying we should give you a chance."

"Why would he say that?" Shade asked.

"I have no idea," she snapped.

Eidolon steepled his long fingers in front of him. "I think you do."

"And I think you can guess," she shot back. "How would you like to spend your life alone, stuck in some backwoods North Carolina hovel, thinking you didn't belong anywhere or with anyone?" She glared at each of them in turn. "When he found out about you, he thought that finally someone might *get* us. We might get some answers about what we are. But then—" *But then I told him to stay away from them.*

Oh, God. She'd been so freaked out, so concerned about herself that she'd kept him from the one chance he had to maybe relieve a little of his loneliness. And because of her, his brothers didn't know him, and they wouldn't be as willing to cut him some slack over the Kynan thing.

If any of these guys hurt Lore, it would be all her fault.

Nausea washed over her, and she broke out in a cold sweat. Shade frowned and reached for her. Her chest tightened with a claustrophobic sensation. "Hey, why don't you take a seat."

She wheeled away, swaying a little. "I have to go."

Wraith casually braced his shoulder against the door-jamb. "Not happening."

"I have to find Lore!" Sin slammed her palms into Wraith's chest. "Move!" Again. "I have to save him." Again, harder. The guy was a solid wall of muscle. "You have no idea what it's like to be held captive, tortured—"

His hands circled her wrists. He didn't hurt her, but his fingers might as well have been iron shackles for all they yielded to her struggles. "I know more about that than you can imagine." His voice was calm and quiet.

"Let her go, Wraith." That from Eidolon.

Wraith's gaze flickered to Shade, who must have nod-ded, because he released her and stepped aside. As she darted through the doorway, Eidolon called out, "If you find Lore, let us know."

"I'll do that," she called back. *When hell freezes over.*

Shade took off the moment Sin was gone, without so much as a good-bye. Wraith did the same, and Eidolon wondered when and if this was ever going to end.

Pinching the bridge of his nose to stave off a killer headache, he headed to the emergency department. A male of undetermined species who looked mostly human except for the stubby set of black horns at his temples stood near the triage desk, head bowed and fingers clutch-ing a long rope of beads . . . some sort of demonic religious artifact, probably.

That would be the exorcist.

Eidolon approached him. "How quickly can you have the hospital cleansed?"

The demon looked up, his hazel eyes swirling with what Eidolon would swear was fear. "It can't be cleansed."

"What do you mean, it can't be cleansed? Why not?"

The demon looked around wildly and lowered his voice as though afraid of being overheard. "Great evil has a hold on the spirits who are trapped here. I've never felt anything like it."

Perfect. A chickenshit exorcist. "What is this *great evil*? Is it another spirit?"

"No. That's why I can't perform an exorcism. Whatever is controlling the spirits is a demon, but I cannot tell you who."

"So who *can* track down this demon?"

"I know not. But it will not be me." He shivered. "Great evil. Hatred such as I've never felt." He scurried toward the Harrowgate. "I'll send you my bill."

"Thanks for nothing," Eidolon muttered.

Someone tapped his shoulder, and he turned to find Runa. Shade and the children were nowhere to be seen, and Runa must have anticipated his question, because she cocked her head toward the ER doors.

"Shade is putting the kids in the car." She shifted her weight and chewed her lower lip before blurting, "I hate what's happening between you guys."

"So do I, Runa. Shade is being impossible—"

Her fierce growl cut him off. "Don't blame all of this on him."

His headache was now a sledgehammer against his skull. "I'm trying to keep everyone safe. I'm not choosing Lore over Kynan, no matter what Shade thinks or what he's told you."

"What if it comes down to a choice?" Gem's voice

came at him from behind, and he swore silently. Nothing like an ambush to make a shitty day even shittier.

"It won't. We will find a way to keep Lore from having to kill Ky."

"I understand how hard this is for you." Gem's voice was strained, which given the circumstances, was completely understandable. "You have a new brother and sister you want to protect. But I'm telling you now that if anything happens to Kynan, not even Tayla can protect you from my wrath."

Thirteen

Lore didn't think he'd ever enjoyed a shower more. Granted, he hadn't been chained up for all that long, but he generally showered twice or more a day, and going without made him grumpy.

At least he couldn't hear Idess yelling at him anymore.

He'd cleaned her up and then beelined for the shower, ignoring her curses and threats and demands to let her go. She'd quieted down for a little while, but about half an hour into his shower she'd started up again, loud enough that he could hear her shouts of "Lore, damn you!" even over the thunder of water.

"I'll be right with you, Angel Food," he called out, and braced himself for her furious response.

She didn't disappoint, and though he couldn't hear exactly what she said, the tone made it pretty clear that it wasn't complimentary. She said something else, something that sounded like, "Heave a rock," and that actually made him laugh. No doubt she'd like to heave a rock right at his head.

And she probably would after he took out Kynan.

The thought sobered him. Sin's life was at stake, but so was Idess's future. He shouldn't care. Caring for her could lead to bad things. Like accidentally killing her, now that he wasn't wearing Bracken Cuffs. Or like considering not whacking Kynan.

Fuck. The not killing Kynan thing was already tripping through his brain. Not that he wouldn't do it. He would. But maybe he could put it off while Idess tried to find out who had ordered the hit.

Putting it off would be stupid. Procrastination always resulted in shit going wrong at the last minute. Always. But maybe he could—

Always.

But—

Always.

Dammit! Spewing the most vile curses he could think of, he shut off the water and toweled off. Sucked to have to dress in the same clothes, but it was better than nothing, and as he fastened his pants, Idess made an odd noise.

"Idess?" For a second, nothing. But in that second, her shower-washed words filtered through his head. "Heave a rock." He glanced at his watch. Three o'clock New York time.

Three o'clock. Not *heave a rock.*

Fuck!

"*Lore!*" Her pained shout drilled into his brain as he blew through the bathroom door so fast the thing tore off its hinges. The nightmare that greeted him drew him to a halt more effectively than if he'd hit a wall.

Idess…on the bed…a Gargantua dagger buried in her shoulder. Sin was standing in the bedroom doorway, preparing to let a throwing knife fly.

"No!" He dove to cover Idess. An instant, searing pain ripped into his neck, and he dropped like a stone onto the bed, twisting to avoid crushing her. Blood splattered down around him, and he lifted a shaking hand to his throat. He knew what he'd find.

Sin's throwing knife.

Her scream overtook the sudden pounding of his pulse in his ears. Sin wasn't a screamer. This was not good. His vision swam and his hearing faded in and out and the next thing he knew his sister was right there, tears streaming down her face.

She wasn't a crier, either.

This was way worse than not good.

"I'm sorry, Lore, oh, my God, I'm so sorry!"

"Hospital…Idess…too," he gasped, but his words drowned in a stream of blood.

"Okay. Okay. Just hold still." The fact that Sin so readily agreed meant that this was worse than he thought.

"Release me!" Idess's tone was a command that should have ruffled Sin's feathers. "I can flash him there."

Sin didn't hesitate. He heard the clank of chains, and then the next thing he knew, he was lying on the asphalt of Underworld General's parking lot.

Idess was crouched beside him, her hand on his shoulder. "I can't flash into the building," she said, with a tremor in her voice, "and you're too heavy to carry. I'll be right back."

He didn't have the strength to answer. The life she'd said he had was draining onto the asphalt. He probably

shouldn't have cared all that much, but while he didn't
deserve for his brothers to save him, he really hoped they
would.

Idess ran toward the sliding ER doors so fast that she
stumbled over her own feet twice. The pain in her shoulder was nothing compared to the agony that streaked up
her arm from Lore's *heraldi*. He was dying.

Crying out, she held the dagger jutting from her shoulder as she ran. Blood seeped between her fingers and
dripped to the ground, but she didn't care. She burst into
the hospital, and instantly, medical staff rushed toward
her, but she gestured wildly toward the parking lot.

"Outside. It's Eidolon's brother. Get him. Hurry!" She
didn't allow anyone near her until Lore was wheeled in
on a stretcher, a flurry of activity surrounding him. She
didn't understand much of the jargon the staff was using,
but their tones and short sentences told her it was bad.

Then again, all she needed to do was look at Lore's
ashen skin and glazed eyes as he was wheeled into a
trauma room to know that.

"We've paged Eidolon and Shade." A female nurse
guided Idess toward another room with a furry hand
on her elbow. "And his arm is wrapped to prevent any
accidents."

"Good. Is . . . wait." Idess halted. "Accidents? With his
arm?"

"As I said, we've wrapped it. There's no need to worry.
The entire staff has been made aware of his condition."

"And what condition is that?"

"You don't know?" The nurse's bushy eyebrows dove

into a deep frown. "Anyone who comes into contact with his right arm dies instantly."

Idess remembered his telling her not to touch his arm when she'd been cleaning him...was that why?

"Now, let's take care of you. That knife isn't going to come out on its own."

"No." Idess backed away from the Slogthu nurse whose underbite and patchy fur made her look like a scrawny bulldog. "I have to make sure Lore is going to be all right."

"He'd better be." Sin stepped out of the Harrowgate and marched toward her. "This is your fault."

"*Your* blade is in his throat," Idess pointed out. "Not mine. And I did bring him here for help."

Sin's fists curled into balls at her sides. "Just pray Lore makes it."

Sin sank down in a chair and stared blankly into the room where staff was frantically working on Lore. He lay motionless on the gurney, blood pooling on the floor beneath him. A technician was squeezing the contents of an IV bag into him through a line in his left arm. Another was forcing air into his lungs through a mask and bag.

Please, God, let him live. A useless prayer, no doubt, given that he was a demon, but helplessness and terror had her desperate to try anything. *Please don't let me lose another Primori.* Because that was her major concern. He was Primori, and if she lost him, she would never get into Heaven and earn her wings.

She was concerned *only* because he was her Primori.

The lie sat on her chest like an elephant, especially when one of the doctors stepped back to grab some sort of metal tool and she saw Lore's hand dangling over the edge of the gurney. It was the same one he'd used to touch her. To pleasure her. And now it hung limp and lifeless, streaked with blood.

Idess's chest constricted. *Please don't die.*

His *heraldi* screamed with pain, as if someone was trying to scoop it out with a dull spoon. The excruciating pangs made her own knife impalement seem like nothing more than an insect sting.

Don't die! She reached deep for the gift she shouldn't use, the one that had the power to heal—or kill—and she never knew which it would do. But Lore was going to die anyway, so she could try it and hope for a positive outcome—

Eidolon exploded out of the Harrowgate. Thank God. If anyone could save Lore, it would be him. His hair was mussed and his shirt untucked and only half-buttoned, and he barely glanced her way as he raced into the room. Immediately, his *dermoire* lit up, and he was barking out orders and calling for an operating room.

Eidolon wheeled Lore out of the room, slowing just long enough to say to Sin, "I'll keep you posted."

Fourteen

⌒

Sin couldn't wait. Couldn't sit around and do nothing but snarl at hospital staff while her brother lay dying on an operating table.

Bile backed up in Sin's throat, bitter and caustic, because what had happened to Lore wasn't entirely Idess's fault. But right now, Sin wasn't prepared to take any of the blame on herself. Now? Try never, if Lore died.

Venomous pricks of anger stung her skin. She didn't rage out like Lore did when he didn't have enough orgasms in a day, but she did get irritable and ill if she didn't take care of herself, and she had a tendency to fly off the handle with very little provocation. That certainly wouldn't help her brother, and could possibly make things worse if she pissed off the wrong staff member.

The warning signs were creeping up on her, from her stinging skin to muscles that felt stretched to the point of snapping if she didn't do something to loosen them up.

She could fuck something or kill something, and either way she'd get the release she needed.

She eyed Idess. Killing her would definitely trip Sin's relief valve. Too bad she couldn't do it, and not because of the Haven spell. Lore had taken a blade for the wench for some reason, and until Sin found out why, Idess got to keep her head.

So as Idess finally allowed doctors to treat her knife wound, Sin fled, trying to outrun her rage, her fear, her thoughts. She didn't know where she was going, but anywhere was better than being alone in her own head.

Maybe the hospital had a gym, where she could beat the hell out of a punching bag. Or a pub, where she could beat the hell out of her liver.

She ran faster. Blindly. She had to go *somewhere*.

Before she got there, she ran into Conall. Literally. He collided with her when he stepped out of a room that, when she peered inside, looked like a dentist's office. And sure enough, the sign on the door confirmed it. *Demon dentists?* Her brothers thought of everything, didn't they?

"Hey." Conall took her elbow and brought her to a halt. "You okay?"

"Stop it," she snapped. "Just stop it! I don't need their concern or yours or anyone's."

"Whoa." Conall held up his hands and stepped back. "Bite my head off."

She tried to dredge up a kernel of guilt for snapping at him, but she'd trained herself too well to feel that emotion. Well, that wasn't true. She felt it, but it mostly manifested as physical pain in her killing arm. And this guy was not worth a scar.

Under any other circumstance, however, he'd be worth

a healthy leer. Men in uniforms had never done it for her, but something about the way he filled out his paramedic BDUs did it for her far too well. From the black turtleneck beneath the black uniform shirt, to the well-fitting, multipocketed pants and huge combat boots, he was a solid wall of yum. Something told her he was as good at his job as he was at...everything.

"Why are you here?" she asked, not bothering to temper her irritation at all.

Conall cocked a brow. "I work here."

Well, duh. But he wasn't exactly upset to see her, as he'd been in the parking lot. "And?"

A sheepish grin lit his face, exposing sexy fangs. "And maybe I was hoping to find you."

She snarled. "I knew it. Eidolon probably asked you to keep an eye on me. Or get to know me or some shit." She jabbed him in his *very* muscular chest with a finger. "Well, fuck you and fuck him. And Shade. And Wraith. I don't want anything to do with you or them or this hospital, and I sure as hell don't want to get to know any of you."

"I don't want to get to know you." Conall's hand closed around hers, and an instant shock of lust sparked at the contact. "I want to fuck you."

"Oh." *Oh.* Well, that was more like it. Her blood heated, but at this point, that wouldn't take much. She was jonesing for sex, and the more she looked at Conall, the more antsy she became. This might just be the distraction she needed from her thoughts and fears about everything that could go wrong in an operating room. But Sin narrowed her eyes at him, because nothing around here seemed that simple. "You promise that's all you want?"

His gaze seared her as he boldly dragged it up and down her body. "I swear I want only to get into your pants."

What a relief. Finally, someone in this damned hospital who didn't want to get to know her or get into her heart or head. "Well, in that case…" She grabbed his hand and dragged him down the hall, figuring she could find a suitable room, but he yanked her to a halt outside a supply closet door.

"In here," he said, tugging her inside with him. "No one ever looks in here."

In a heartbeat he had her backed up to the wall, his mouth on hers and his thigh between her legs. His lips were soft but his kiss hard, and he tasted like brandy and exotic, dark coffee. Kissing was not her favorite act, but Conall wielded his tongue and fangs like erotic weapons that penetrated her defenses with remarkable ease.

He palmed her breast, and a moan escaped her. God, she never moaned, had always been silent in her passions. Her sexual needs controlled her, but she refused to give any of that control over to the males she slept with. Determined to take charge, she dropped her hand to Conall's fly and cupped his erection. Oh, my. This was going to be *good*.

Wetness flooded her sex as her blood heated even more. Conall was only making it worse by dragging his lips down her neck, nibbling and kissing as he kneaded her breasts and rocked his leg against her core.

"I've never done it in a storeroom." Her voice was rough and low, throbbing with the same arousal that was now working its way between her legs.

His smile tickled her collarbone. "These rooms see a lot of action. Though not so much now that the Sem brothers are mated." He froze. His gaze snapped up at her. "Wait. Who are they to you? Cousins? Friends?"

"Assholes."

"Yes, but how do you know them?"

She bucked in frustration. "They're my brothers. Can we get back to it?"

"Brothers?" He cursed. Backed up. "We're not doing this."

Sin's entire body cramped at the lost contact. Getting this worked up and breaking it off led to pain and misery, and no way was she letting this jerk tease her and leave her. "We *are* doing this." She fisted his collar and forced him back to her.

His hands came up to peel hers away. "No. We aren't. Those guys are hyperprotective. Once, an orderly tried to seduce Shade's sister, Skulk, and…let's just say that the guy still walks with a limp. I'm pretty sure he's missing his tongue, too. Don't know, because he doesn't talk anymore."

"Dammit." Sin tore off her top and ripped open her jeans. "They don't know me, don't like me, and they have no say in what I do." She shoved down her pants and thong and stepped out of them, loving the way Conall's eyes darkened from sterling silver to wrought iron despite his sudden paranoia.

Conall swallowed. A couple of times. "No."

At least the conviction had gone from his voice. Still, he backed toward the door. "Don't do it, vampire," she warned. "Or whatever you are."

"I have to." His hand came down on the doorknob.

"Open it, and I'll tell them you tried to rape me."

He hissed. "You wouldn't."

"Try me." Her body was aching. Hot. So hot she

couldn't even feel bad about the threat she'd just delivered. Foul curses fell from Con's made-to-please mouth. "You bitch."

"Hey, *you* approached *me*. Got me all worked up. You need to work on your follow-through."

"Oh," he began, in a husky tone, "I have no problem with follow-through. What I have a problem with is your brothers and what they'll do to my balls if they find out I fucked you like an animal in a damned closet."

"An animal?" The images of him taking her rough and hard filled her head and actually made her sweat a little. "Really?" She was proud of the way she didn't sound hopeful.

"What? You're the tender loving type?" He snorted. "Not buying it."

She'd never had tender, loving sex, so no, she wasn't that type. Even the nicest of her masters had never been overly gentle, and the sex partners she chose for herself never hurt her, but neither did they pretend that she was anything but a screw. And she didn't want them to, because they were nothing but a screw to her either.

"I'm definitely not that type," she said. "So let's do the animal thing. Or are you too chicken?"

A decidedly wolflike growl erupted in his chest. "Don't test me, female."

Her chin came up, and she said clearly and distinctly, "Chicken."

The growl intensified. "You are very lucky the moon tide hasn't stirred my blood yet."

"*Bawk. Bawk.*"

His control snapped like a two-hundred-pound mastiff tethered by kite string. He let out a howl and surged toward her, and oh, wow . . . the truth hit her just before his body did. Moon tide. Wolfy growl. Bloodsucking fangs, but warm-blooded.

He *was* a vampire, but he was also a warg. He was a dhampire, a rare cross between a vampire and a werewolf. So rare, in fact, that their existence was thought by many to be a myth.

Conall caught her by the shoulders, spun her, and put her against the wall so his chest was hot against her back and his erection was hard against the seam of her butt.

"I warned you," he rasped into her ear. "Know this; I'm not going to have sex with you because you taunted me with childish name-calling." She heard the unmistakable, soft rasp of a zipper, and then felt the searing heat of his cock on the bare skin of her ass. "I'm going to fuck you because you need a sound thrashing."

She gasped in outrage, and then gasped in pleasure as he sheathed himself inside her. Her core clenched around him, and she clenched her teeth. She wouldn't make another sound, wouldn't give him the satisfaction of knowing he could affect her in any way.

Again, habit. Habit born of humiliation, of the knowledge that she was a disgusting, horrible, evil creature that climaxed only when her partner did. Any partner. Under any circumstances. And if that wasn't the most fucked-up thing ever, she didn't know what was.

Conall's breath fanned her ear as he thrust into her, his rhythm wild and raw. Even his grip on her hips was fierce as his fingers dug in.

"Bite me." The command slipped out before she could take it back. She'd never allowed her vampire partners to bite her, but by the time she could gather the words to stop him, it was too late.

His fangs penetrated her throat, and sweet, blissful pain and ecstasy coursed through her. Conall let out an appreciative moan, and his thrusts became deeper, harder, bringing her to the brink of ecstasy she couldn't tip over until he came.

"Please," she whispered. "Now."

He disengaged his fangs and tongued the bite before saying in a voice thick with lust, "I want to satisfy you before I come." His hand reached around her, and he rasped one finger over her swollen clit.

"Can't…can't…until…" Oh, God, this was good. "Until you do."

His hand clamped down tighter on her hip. "Semen is a trigger for you?"

When she nodded, because the ability to speak had deserted her, he began a new, frenzied pumping that accompanied a roar of release. His hot seed splashed inside her, the fuel her fire required, and she joined him in a ferocious climax.

They collapsed together against the wall, his weight on hers just short of crushing. But it was a good weight, the kind she'd never taken the time to enjoy. She could only stand being touched like this for so long.

As soon as she caught her breath, she reached her threshold for intimate contact. "Get off me."

"Your gratitude astounds me," he said flatly, but he pushed away.

"I should be grateful that you fucked me?"

"You're a succubus, aren't you? You need it, right?

Some sort of biological imperative." He tucked his semi-hard cock back in his pants.

"Ah. So you lowered yourself to service me out of the goodness of your heart. How nice. Then yes, thank you for performing this distasteful deed. I will forever be in your debt."

He laughed. "I didn't say I didn't get anything out of it."

Asshole. "You got an orgasm and blood. I'd say you got more than I did."

"You got that right." He winked, and suspicion bloomed. She had a sudden feeling he'd gotten even more than a moment of pleasure and sustenance. "This remains between us, right?"

"As long as you don't piss me off," she said as she tugged on her pants. "You gonna piss me off?"

He gave her a wolfish grin. "Every chance I get." With that, he was gone, and once again, she was alone with her thoughts, and crazily, she felt more alone than ever.

Conall found Luc at the open rear of their rig, sitting on the step and chowing down on a very rare roast beef sandwich. So rare that blood dripped to the pavement. Con was tempted to look around for the cow it had come from, because surely it had to be close.

"Did Shade catch up with you?" Luc asked.

Shit. Did the Sem know Con had hooked up with his sister already? "No. Why?"

"Another warg was brought in on Medic Two's last run."

Medic Two was Shade's ambulance with his partner, a False Angel named Blaspheme. "Same as the other two?"

"Yep. Shade wants all warg medics to stand down from calls to all warg emergencies."

Conall swore. He hoped these cases were isolated, but he'd better inform the Warg Council as soon as possible. As a member of the Council, the lone representative for dhampires and the only councilmember employed by UG, he was duty-bound to alert them to potential trouble. Not that they'd pay heed to anything he said. In warg hierarchy, dhampires barely rated above turned wargs, and that was only because there were so few dhampires that they were no threat in any way to born wargs.

"So? What happened with Sin?" Luc cocked an eyebrow, and then the other when Conall pulled Sin's thong from his pocket and twirled it on one finger. "I'll be damned," he said. "You nailed her."

For some reason, the way Luc spoke so casually, as if Sin was some swan Conall had picked up at a vampire bar, grated on him. Probably because he respected the Sem brothers, and he couldn't quite dismiss their sister as a cheap suck-and-fuck, even though that was how he'd treated her.

"Yeah," he ground out, "I nailed her."

"Where?" Luc always wanted the dirty details.

"Stockroom." He held out his hand. "Pay up."

Luc snorted and reached for his wallet. "I really got taken on this one, didn't I?" He handed over four hundreds and five twenties.

"Yeah, well, you can have the last laugh once the Sem brothers catch up with me." Con ran his thumb over the bills. "Seems she's their sister."

"Dude." Luc stretched out the word and then whistled, low and long. "Nice knowing you."

Con could take care of himself, wasn't too worried despite what he'd said to Sin about keeping his balls, but he did like this job and didn't want to lose it. At least, not until he got bored with it. And he would. He always did. In a thousand years he hadn't not gotten bored with anything.

Or anyone.

"So," Luc said, "will it at least have been worth it? Being gutted by Shade, I mean. Was she good?"

His body heated as though remembering. And wanting again.

"Of course I was."

Fuck. Con spun around to find Sin standing there, hands on hips and fury in her expression. Like a kid caught stealing candy, he whipped the money behind his back.

She looked at him as if he was an idiot and grabbed his arm, bringing it around.

"It's not what you think," he said lamely, because it was exactly what she thought.

"Really? So that big asshole behind you didn't bet you five hundred bucks that you couldn't fuck me?"

"Ah…"

"That's what I thought. You dick. How stupid do you think I am? Your name really fits you, *Con*." She snatched the money from him, took two hundreds and three twenties, and thrust the remaining two hundred and forty dollars back into his hand. Then, smiling broadly, she punched him in the shoulder. "Next time you make a bet like that, don't cheat me out of my half. I owe you a ten."

She winked and left him, jaw-dropped and gaping, as she sauntered away.

Luc made a strangled sound. "Did that just happen? She wasn't mad because you made the bet—she was mad because you didn't give her half the money?"

"Yeah." Con grinned. "Yeah, it did. I think I may be in love."

"Man, don't even joke about that. Females like her are a piss-bucket full of trouble."

True. But females like that were also the kind that made life a challenge, and it had been a long time since Con had last been challenged.

Fifteen

———

Eidolon lost Lore twice on the operating table. And the most fucked-up thing about it was that both instances could have been prevented.

Someone or some*thing* had turned off the respirator, and then later, the lights at a crucial moment. These weren't equipment failures. Eidolon had seen the respirator switch flip to the off position with his own eyes. Wraith needed to get a new exorcist and fast.

He put the finishing touches on Lore's healing and told a nurse to have him taken to a recovery room. He'd be fine, but only because Eidolon had arrived when he had. Two minutes later, and Lore would have bled out right there in the emergency department.

After stripping off his bloodied gloves and gown, he stepped into the hall and was immediately enveloped by a crushing sense of hatred. The force of the animosity was so powerful that he staggered, and then he drew a sharp breath when he saw Shade leaning against the wall, expression as black and threatening as a storm cloud.

"Did he make it?"

"Don't sound so excited." Eidolon forced his watery legs to take him toward the waiting room.

"You'd better hope you made the right decision."

Eidolon swung around. He inhaled deeply, seeking composure, but the hate swirling in the air like a toxin filled his lungs and spread through his body. The poison affected him at the cellular level, tapping into his inner demon and bringing his temper to the surface.

"I know you aren't implying that I should have let Lore die. Because I've had it with this discussion, Shade. I'm done. He's our brother, and we don't let our brothers die."

"You're done? Yeah, okay. Me, too. You've made your choice, and so have I. So I guess there's nothing left to say." His voice degenerated into a rasp, and his eyes glistened. "Ever."

Shade's words, as sharp as a scalpel blade, sliced Eidolon in the heart, and his anger drained out of the laceration.

Gods, this had truly happened. Something had broken them. Crushing pain radiated outward from the center of Eidolon's chest with almost the same intensity as when a brother died, severing the connection that allowed all purebred Seminus brothers to sense each other's health and location. He was too stunned, too freaked out to speak. Even when Shade spun around and stalked off, Eidolon couldn't drum up words as the canyon between them widened.

And as Shade disappeared around a corner, E swore he heard the cackle of laughter.

Idess slipped out of the shadows cast by a gargoyle statue in one of UG's double-wide halls. Shade had just strode away, and Eidolon had gone in the opposite direction after slamming his fist into the wall. Neither one of them had seen her in the dark corner, where she'd been eavesdropping on their conversation. Her spying hadn't been intentional; she'd been restless waiting for news about Lore, and she'd tried to burn off her nervous energy by pacing the halls.

She was glad she had. It looked as if Shade had become a true danger to Lore, and that was a development she'd have to keep an eye on.

There was another danger lurking nearby, as well. A hooded figure had watched the two brothers argue, and though he'd stood right next to them, they hadn't noticed. But then, they wouldn't, if they weren't capable of seeing ghosts. Except that if the hooded creature was a ghost, he was the most unusual one Idess had ever come across. His form had been transparent rather than solid, appearing to her the way ghosts appeared to humans.

The evil in him was off the scale, his sinister vibe so malignant that she could feel it as prickles on her skin, and the closer he'd gotten to Shade and Eidolon, the redder their eyes got and the more vicious they'd been to each other.

After the brothers separated, the creature swiveled his head around to nail her with a bone-chilling stare. But there was no itch between her shoulder blades, and it occurred to her that she'd never experienced the demon-warning sensation in the hospital.

Or with Lore—the mansion incident could have been caused by other demons. Or with Sin. Or their brothers. And what did that mean?

Who are you?

"My name is Idess," she said, still a little shaky over the failure of her evil sensor.

The thing smiled, a hideous baring of teeth that stretched shiny, scarred lips. *Help me.*

She'd assist the human spirits however she could, but this thing...she shuddered. "I cannot."

Please. I was burned alive and cursed by my own family. I need only a small favor. There is something that can ease my suffering. Can you take me from this hospital?

Idess closed her eyes. This creature was evil, but he'd been hurt. By family. Her gut wrenched at that. Maybe what he was wasn't his fault. In any case, getting him away from the hospital could only be a good thing.

"Where do you want to go?"

A peaceful park.

Well, that didn't sound too bad. "We need to go through the parking lot." She led the demon ghost-thing outside the ER, gripped his shoulder, which, under her touch, was solid. He told her where to go, and she materialized with him in a residential neighborhood.

"This isn't a park—"

The creature laughed gleefully and darted away, disappearing into a copse of trees behind several houses.

Hoping she hadn't made a huge error in judgment, she returned to the parking lot and slipped back into the waiting room, where she'd spent most of the three hours Lore had been in surgery. The first hour had been the worst—staff had repaired her shoulder, but her arm, his *heraldi*, had been constantly on fire, twice with such intensity that she'd cried out and fallen to her knees.

Now she sank into a chair near Sin and sat in tense silence. After much fidgeting, Sin kicked her feet up on a chair and leaned back. "If Lore dies, I'll kill you."

"Maybe you didn't notice that I tried to save his life."

"If you hadn't kidnapped him in the first place, you wouldn't have had to."

"Did it escape your notice that I was the one chained up when you arrived?"

Grinning, Sin folded her hands over her abs. "He got one over on you, didn't he? Must have pissed you the hell off."

It had. Up until the point where he'd given her the most intense orgasm of her life. "Of course not. I let him restrain me."

"Right." Sin raked her gaze over Idess. "You so look like you're into bondage."

"How else do you explain his trying to keep you from killing me?"

Sin narrowed her eyes. "Cut the shit. What was going on? I know you're protecting Kynan, so why not just kill Lore?"

"That's a good question." Eidolon strode into the room, and Sin leaped to her feet. Idess fought the urge to do the same, even though she knew Lore was out of danger. "He's going to be fine, Sin." He sounded better than he had when he was with Shade, but he looked worse. From his wildly grooved hair that spoke of a lot of fingers raking through it, to the dark circles under his eyes and his rumpled clothes, he was a mess. "And you," he said to Idess. "What's going on?"

There was no point in lying. Lore knew the truth,

and maybe if she got on Sin and Eidolon's good sides—
assuming Sin had a good side—she'd get some help. Earn
some trust.

"I have to protect him," she said, meeting Eidolon's
gaze levelly. "He's Primori like Kynan."

"I don't understand this Primori thing," Sin said. "But
right now, I don't care. I need to see him." She started past
Eidolon, but he caught her by the arm, and Idess wondered if Sin's Seminus power killed as the nurse had said
Lore's did.

"Out of the question. He's recovering and needs rest."

"Fuck you." Sin jerked out of his grip. "I'm going to see
him."

"Sin." Eidolon's voice cracked like thunder in the small
room. "You can't."

Idess's heart stuttered. "This isn't about his recovery,
is it?"

"What's she talking about?" Sin demanded.

"They're going to keep him here," Idess said, speaking
to Sin but not taking her gaze off Eidolon. "Restrained.
And you can't see him because he's afraid you'll set him
free. Isn't that right, doctor?"

Sin settled into a fighting stance, fists clenched, body
leaning aggressively forward. "You bastard."

"I don't have a choice, Sin." Eidolon rubbed his eyes
with one hand, working his fingers and thumb so hard
Idess expected to see blood. "We'll work something out.
Just give me a day to talk to him. Think this through.
We'll come up with a plan that works for all of us."

Idess stood. "Let's give him twenty-four hours." She
squeezed Sin's shoulder and hoped she'd get the message.
Humor him.

"Fine," Sin growled. "But at the end of the day, you had better set him free." She wrenched away from Idess and slammed out of the room, leaving Idess alone with Eidolon, who stared at the door.

"This is a fucking nightmare," he muttered.

"You feel like you've betrayed your brothers."

He swung around to her. "I haven't betrayed anyone."

"That's not how Shade sees it." Out of nowhere, Idess pictured Rami and wondered if he knew what she'd done. Did he understand, or was he as furious as Shade?

"What do you know about that?"

"I overheard you arguing in the hall."

Eidolon's vile curse accompanied a violent adjustment of the stethoscope around his neck. "Shade doesn't get it. No one has to die."

"But you've still lost a brother." Emotion made her voice rough, and she recognized that same misery in the demon doctor's eyes. "I'm sorry. I know what it's like to fight to keep a brother, and then lose him anyway."

"Then you know why I have to keep Lore safe. Now more than ever."

Yes, she did. If Wraith sided with Shade, Lore would be all Eidolon had left. Losing him meant he'd gone through all this hell with his other brothers for nothing.

"Shade could come around," she said in a quiet voice. "There's still hope. What's the saying…time heals all wounds?"

Eidolon laughed bitterly. "Doctors heal wounds. Time? All that does is allow wounds to fester."

As he walked away, all Idess could do was pray he wasn't right, because if he was, she could only imagine what five hundred years of festering could have done to Rami.

⌒

Hangovers sucked.

Lore couldn't remember the last time he'd had one. He healed fast, which meant he rarely got them unless he'd overdone the drinking to the point of near-death. But he always remembered his binges, and as he peeled his eyes open he found that he had absolutely no memory of slamming shots or downing beers.

He jerked as one memory pierced his brain like a dull needle. Idess. Sin. Shit! With a panicked shout, he levered into a sit. He was at the hospital. But where—

"Hey."

He snapped his head around to Idess, who was standing at his bedside, looking as if she hadn't had a Gargantua-bone dagger impaled in her shoulder. "You're okay." His relief didn't even seem strange. They should be enemies, but something had changed, and unlike Sin, he knew when to stop fighting and roll with it.

"I'm fine. And you are, too. But it was close."

He swallowed, remembering the blade that had lodged in his throat. "Sin?"

"Eidolon won't allow her inside. I'm only allowed in because he thinks I'll behave." She smiled, but it was forced. Something was wrong. And when he lifted his hand and discovered he was secured to the bed, he knew what it was.

"Eidolon intends to keep me from going after Kynan, doesn't he?" From one set of chains into another. Unbelievable. "And that's why Sin can't see me, isn't it? He's afraid she'll free me."

"Yes," she said. "I think he's right to be concerned."

"Sin can be a handful," Lore muttered.

Idess raised a delicate eyebrow. "That's one way to put it."

Lore reached for her, only to be jerked short by the chain. "I'm sorry, angel." He blinked. Had he just used "angel" as a term of endearment and not a snarky insult? He blinked again. Yes. Yes, he had. Huh. "I shouldn't have left you alone in the bedroom. I didn't think—"

She shut him up with a kiss. It was just a peck, but it was enough to derail his thoughts and wreck his emotions. His sister had nearly killed her, but here she was, smiling warmly and kissing him and being just way too good to be true.

"Took a page from your book," she said, as she straightened. "It's an interesting maneuver, kissing someone to shut them up or calm them down." She paused. "I think I like it."

A weird possessive instinct made his gut burn, and he wanted to tell her not to use that particular trick with anyone else. Instead, he narrowed his eyes at her. "Something's off here. Sin wouldn't stand for being shut out. She'd have found a way in here."

"She's not raising a stink . . . because I swore to release you myself."

All kinds of red flags went up. "Why? So you can take me home and chain me to your bed again?"

She flushed, and damn it, he felt things below his waist start to stir because as much as it bit dick to be chained up, there were worse things than being chained to Idess's bed. Better her bed than a hospital one.

"Not unless you force me to."

"So you're saying you're just going to let me run around loose? Aren't you worried about your precious Kynan?"

"I am," she admitted. "But this hospital is a very dangerous place for you to be."

"Ah... it's a hospital."

"Full of brothers who want you dead."

Okay, so he knew they wouldn't be happy with his plan to kill their buddy, but dead? "If that were true, why did they save me?"

"Eidolon is the one who wants to keep you alive. He thinks that if you're contained, the other two will be placated enough to not kill you."

"But you don't believe that?"

She let out a long breath, as though dragging it out would put off whatever she was clearly reluctant to say. "I saw murder in Shade's eyes."

"I can handle Shade," he said. "But why are you willing to take a chance on releasing me?"

"Because I think it's time we started working together. Started trusting each other."

He laughed, but quickly sobered. "Good God, you're serious."

She nodded. "I have to protect Kynan, but I also have to protect you. It's clear that someone is trying to mess with my Primori. You and your sister are the keys. You help me get to the bottom of it, Kynan lives, and your brothers won't be a threat to you anymore. We're all winners."

Sure, it made sense to combine resources, but it also shoved them together when the last thing he needed was to be distracted by her. Because he doubted they'd find the contract holder, which meant he'd have to kill Kynan, and the closer he got to Idess, the harder that would be.

But if her plan worked, big *if*, Idess would earn her wings and Sin would live. And so would Kynan, the rat bastard.

"Okay, so what do you need from me, right this minute, to get these shackles off?"

"I need you to take me to your master."

"No can do. Unless you're branded, you can't get past the guards and into the den." Lore could kill the guards, but he wasn't about to risk Deth's wrath until Sin was safe. "Which means that the only way to get to Detharu is through the Guild, and trust me, you do *not* want to do that."

She drifted closer to him, and in painfully slow motion, she covered his slave-mark with her hand. Her touch was like a punch to the soul, and he had to clench his teeth and his fists to keep from trembling. "Why not?"

It was a full thirty seconds before he could answer without sounding as if he'd lost his testicles in an industrial accident. "Because they won't tell you anything. It doesn't matter how much you pay them or what you threaten them with. The only way they'd reveal something like that is if you made it very worthwhile, and even then...I wouldn't trust the information they give you. Assassins have a reputation for keeping secrets. If they didn't, they wouldn't be in business."

Though she lost a little color in her face, she managed a smile. "Well, then, I guess I'll give them something worthwhile. We're going, and you're going to take me." He would have protested, but she unsnapped the cuff on his left wrist, and he'd promise to take her all the way to Mars if she'd release the other arm, too. "Oh, and you might have mentioned your little death glitch."

"Death glitch?"

She gestured to his right arm, which was wrapped in thick layers of gauze and tape from his fingertips to his shoulder. "You know, how you could possibly kill me with a touch."

Busted. "Ah, yeah. That. Minor detail. And if you'll remember, I did tell you not to touch."

"Yes, but you said it was because your arm is sensitive."

"It is."

"We'll have to chat about it. Later." She handed him his Gargantua-bone dagger. "Right now we have to get you out of this hospital. Alive."

Sixteen

⸺

Getting Lore out of the hospital wasn't a problem. His room had been close to the emergency department, and while Sin created a very loud and obnoxious distraction near the Harrowgate, Idess and Lore had made a mad dash to the parking lot, where Idess flashed them out of there.

But contacting the Assassins' Guild was going to be a lot more difficult. Its headquarters was located in Sheoul, an extremely dangerous place for angels—especially pre-Ascended ones who were easier to kill and more vulnerable to corruption.

Making matters more hazardous, as a not-quite-angel, Idess couldn't flash into or out of Sheoul. She could only get there if her Primori was in mortal danger, forcing her to flash in, or if she traveled via Harrowgate. But naturally, there was a catch to that, too; she could only use a Harrowgate if she was with a demon, because no divine being could operate the controls.

So Lore would take her, but if he was killed or rendered unconscious while they were there, she couldn't get out. And if the Guild was under a *maltranseo* treaty, no divine being short of God himself could enter.

Idess and Lore had gone to his house first, so he could shower and change, and then, outfitted in black leather from head to toe—including his hands—he'd taken her through the Harrowgate to a wet, cavernous region of Sheoul, where the spongy ground growled and bled with every step. Some sort of pale light illuminated the place, but as far as she could tell, there was no source. All she knew for certain was that the light affected their shadows, making them move when Idess and Lore were standing still, or making them motionless when Idess or Lore moved.

Ignoring the mild itch in her shoulder blades, Idess summoned a scythe and held it tight as they picked their way between boulders and thorny vines that curled around their ankles if they came too near.

"You sure you want to do this?" Lore spoke loudly so she could hear over the sounds of the furious earth. "There isn't a being in Sheoul that wouldn't like to put an angel head on their mantel. Down here, you stand out like, well, an angel in hell. You're sort of . . . glowing with goodness. All you need now is a fucking halo to make sure even the dumbest demons know what you are."

"I can take care of myself, you know."

He waggled his brows. "I can take care of you better."

Oh, she knew firsthand how well he could take care of her. Her body warmed up at the unwanted memory of his magic fingers working between her legs. She cleared her throat. "Tell me what to expect at the Guild."

"You'll have to make a blood sacrifice." He tensed, the only warning before something scaly, with massive rows of teeth and about the size of a raccoon sprang at them from a rocky ledge. Lore caught it easily out of midair, narrowly avoiding its snapping jaws...and the thing fell dead to the ground.

Impressive. And a little scary.

"How did you do that?"

He flexed his hand, answering her without ever taking his watchful gaze off their surroundings. "It works even through the leather if I force it to."

"Oh." She stepped over the still-twitching dead creature, a little shaken to have seen Lore's power firsthand. She hadn't expected it to be so...fast. "So, uh...were you born with this issue?"

"Nope." He kept walking, his eyes constantly scanning for danger. "Came with my *dermoire* when I was twenty. First person I touched was Sin, and it didn't affect her. Second person dropped dead. I thought it was a heart attack or something. Not that I cared. I was crazed at the time."

"Crazed?"

He paused, head up, black eyes scanning, and the hairs on the back of her neck stood at attention. "Along with the *dermoire* came an uncontrollable lust and that fun rage." He started moving again, as if he'd never stopped.

"It all happened suddenly?"

"Yeah." His voice was gruff. "Sin and I shared our grandparents' house for a year after they died. One morning we both were struck with this massive pain. Went on for hours. When it was over we had new tats, and I was a raging monster." He kicked at a steaming, softball-sized stone. "I scared her pretty bad. Tore up the house. I guess

I took off, was gone for days. I don't remember much of it, except bits and pieces I wish I didn't remember."

She started to reach for him, but dropped her hand to her side at the last second, unsure if he'd appreciate a comforting gesture. "I'm sorry."

"Whatever. It was a long time ago."

Maybe, but it was obviously still painful. "What happened to Sin? I mean, if you went nuts, did she?"

"I don't know." He launched a morning star in a smooth motion that barely registered until a winged demon fell out of the air in front of them, the blade bull's-eyed in the center of its third eye. This place was going to give her a heart attack. He, on the other hand, was acting as if they were strolling through a park. "We've never talked about it."

Never talked about it? Idess and Rami had discussed everything. Nothing was off-limits for them. Granted, they'd spent centuries together, and Sin and Lore had only a fraction of that, but it still seemed odd, given how protective they were of each other.

She watched him fetch his weapon and wipe it clean on the creature's leathery skin. "What did she say when you finally went home?"

Tucking the star into a leather hip housing, he picked up the pace. "We're almost there."

"Lore," she said, catching up to him, "what did she say?"

He patted down his jacket and cursed. "I forgot my claw darts." Silence stretched as he kept walking. Finally, a long, drawn-out sigh came from him. "I betrayed and abandoned her. It's ugly, and I don't like going back there."

She grabbed his arm and forced him to stop. "Tell me you've apologized."

He frowned down at her. "What's it matter to you?"

"It's just . . . if you don't, you might never get the chance. And you'll regret it for the rest of your life."

"You sound like you know something about that," he murmured, but somehow she heard him over the growling earth and bone-chilling shrieks that came at them from all sides.

"I do."

His eyes were in constant motion, alert and seeking out potential threats, but he also seemed to be making a conscious effort to not look at her. "She knows I'm sorry."

"Are you sure about that?"

His frown deepened. "I'm paying for what I did every day of my life."

"That's not the same thing."

"Trust me, it is." Something screeched nearby, making her jump. "She knows."

"How?"

"God, you're persistent," he muttered. She crossed her arms over her chest and started to tap her foot, but when the ground protested with a bark, she froze and decided she might make Lore carry her the rest of the way. "I'm an assassin because of her, okay? She got herself into trouble with Detharu thirty years ago, and she came to me. We hadn't seen each other in about seventy-five years, which should tell you how desperate she was. He was planning to sell her into service at a blood gallery."

Idess's stomach turned over. *Oh, sweet Jesus.* She'd never been to what was a demon version of an opium den-slash-whorehouse, but she'd heard enough about them to understand Sin's fear. Some humans and demons participated willingly, but others were forced. They would be given drugs and then turned into the "pits," where blood-feeders like vampires could drink and get high while using the humans for sex. Each gallery had different rules governing the treatment of the humans, but even in the strict establishments, accidents and overdoses happened. In the worst places, the humans were disposable, rarely surviving more than a day, or even beyond one customer.

"What did you do?" she asked hoarsely.

"Tried to find a way out of the assassin bond. When we couldn't, I went to him and offered myself as an assassin in trade for her life. And now her life is on the line again."

"I don't understand."

"She's why I have to knock off Kynan." His voice became so deep and ominous that it vibrated. "If I do it, we both go free. If I don't, she dies."

Idess's hands went white-knuckled on her weapon and somehow she managed to speak past the swelling lump of panic in her throat. "Lore? If your master wasn't holding Sin's life over you, would you still want to kill Kynan?"

"*Want* to? Yeah." He laughed bitterly. "But would I? No."

"Why not?"

He looked off into the distance, his gaze going somewhere she couldn't follow. "Because my brothers might be assholes, but they'll be good for Sin. And I kinda hoped...I mean, they're immune to my touch...but whatever. Killing Kynan is going to polarize everyone. It already has."

Emotion joined the lump of panic that clogged Idess's throat, as he started walking again. Lore had wanted some kind of relationship with his brothers, and he might have had a chance if he hadn't been set against them...she stumbled to a halt. Lore turned around.

"What now? I've already told you more than I should have."

"It's not that," she said. "Listen...all along I've believed that the hits put out on my Primori were about me. But what if this isn't about me at all? What if it's about you?"

"Ah...why would it be about me?"

"Well, you or your brothers. I mean, what are the odds that *you* were chosen to kill Kynan? Don't you think it's quite the coincidence that he *happens* to be related by marriage to your brother? And look what the job is doing to you and them. It's tearing everyone apart. So what if this is about getting to you guys?"

Lore whistled through his teeth. "Wouldn't be the first time. I was originally hired to kill them by our own brother. But why sic Sin on one of your other Primori? The warg didn't have anything to do with me or my brothers."

"That is the one kink in my theory." She shook her head. "And wait, did you say you were hired to kill *your brothers*? *By* your brother?"

"Yup." He ran his gloved hand down his face. "Sick bastard wanted revenge on them so badly that he arranged for their deaths even in the event of his own death."

Idess considered that. "So he's dead then? He couldn't be the one who is behind this?"

"According to Shade, the guy is as good as dead." They started walking again.

She blew out a breath. "Okay, so there has to be another answer. Your involvement in something that's putting your brothers at odds is just too convenient."

He shrugged. "I'm sure we'll find out soon enough. The summoning area is just ahead."

"Wait." A screaming itch flared up between her shoulder blades. She wasn't sure if she should be happy that her evil-detection system was working, or worried because it was. "Something's wrong."

Lightning quick, Lore's hands were gripping blades. "The ground is silent."

"Angel flesh is sweeeeet."

Idess whirled around to see two demons of unknown species peel away from the stone ledges. Dark gray and about eight feet tall, they were thin, spindly, with pitted, crocodilelike snouts and sharp, pointed scales covering their bodies.

She heard a whisper of air, and then Lore's blade punched through one of the demon's chests. The thing laughed. The other one ripped a scale off its arm and launched it like a Frisbee. Idess threw herself to the ground, her breath hissing out of her at the sting as it grazed her cheek.

"Stay down!" Lore shouted, but if he thought she was going to cower while he fought, he was crazy.

Heart pounding, she leaped to her feet. Lore ducked a swipe from one of the creatures, its claws catching air. The second strike hit him in the face, and he catapulted backward, slamming into a rock ledge.

Enraged, Idess attacked, swinging her scythe at the closest creature and catching it by surprise. The blade lopped off its arm. Black sludge spewed from the wound and splatted on the shrieking ground. She swung again, but the second demon attacked, its jaws clamping down on Idess's shoulder. Pain surged, and as her concentration broke, the summoned weapon shimmered out of existence.

The demon released her with a screech and crumpled to the ground. Lore stood behind it, his eyes swirling gold and crimson, his gloved hand flexing. That death thing he did was beyond frightening.

"Down!" he shouted, and Idess ducked, narrowly avoiding a Frisbee scale as she summoned another scythe. Two more scales whistled through the air, and she heard a grunt as Lore took one.

A clawed hand came out of nowhere and knocked her feet out from under her. The air whooshed from her lungs and her ears rang as she fought to reorient herself. Another demon, a newcomer, lunged at her. She rolled, swept her weapon up in a violent arc. Flesh ripped as she split the thing in half from its crotch to its neck. Entrails and blood poured down in a gruesome rain.

Idess scrambled to her feet to avoid being crushed by the dying demon as it fell. Lore, bleeding from a nasty gash in his chest, was engaged with the armless creature, his blade swiping at it as he tried to get closer. The demon had caught on, and it moved in blurs of motion as it avoided Lore's killing arm.

Idess swung her scythe, but the blade struck only empty air. The thing danced around them, an odd, scratchy noise emanating from its chest.

"It's calling more," Lore panted. "We have to kill it. *Now.*"

Idess lunged, but once again, her scythe caught wind. Forcing herself to calm, she breathed deeply, studied her opponent the way Rami had taught her to do. Study the landscape. The air. Anything that could be used to her advantage.

The shadows . . . Idess frowned, and though she scarcely

had time to pause, she watched the shadows form and fade...and, yes! Their sequence made sense now—they moved *before* the demon did.

The demon's shadow flickered in range of her weapon. She swung with all her strength, and the creature's head plopped to the ground.

Panting, Lore bent over, braced his hands on his knees, but he looked up at Idess, a grin splitting his handsome face. "You're awesome, babe." He straightened and grabbed her hand. "Come on. We have to get out of here before more of those things come for us."

"You're injured—"

"So are you. Our injuries will be gone in a minute. Hurry."

She didn't understand, but now wasn't the time for twenty questions. They ran until they rounded a corner that opened up into a flat, steaming plain.

"This is the summoning area. It's called the killbox." He gestured to two brimstone pillars, around which opossumlike, eyeless creatures skittered. "Those are guardians. Anyone with deceptive thoughts is ripped apart. There's the altar. You'll need to offer your blood."

Gingerly, Idess picked up the dagger lying atop a blood-stained, flat stone. She put the sharp edge to her skin, but he gripped her wrist.

"I would do it myself if I could."

His stare was intense, full of a masculine promise that took her breath and made her heart race. And then, as though he hadn't just sworn to endure the pain for her when he had every reason to wish her harm, he released her and stood back, a silent sentinel, all power and muscle and confidence. Idess was more than capable of taking care of herself, but for the first time since Rami had left her, someone had her back, and it felt good. Lore was ready to protect her, even if it meant risking himself.

He'd been so wrong when he said he was a terrible person.

Her hand shook as she drew the blade across her wrist and let her blood drip onto the stone. Once a pool the size of a coffee cup rim had formed, a ring of light flashed all around the wet puddle.

"It's done." Gently, Lore put pressure against the cut with the palm of his hand. "I wish I had Eidolon's gift. I wish I could heal you."

"I wish you could, too." Only she wasn't talking about a mere cut. Her heart and soul hurt, and the only cure could be found in Heaven.

A wet slurping noise preceded a dark-skinned, humanoid female who emerged from the sleek archway like toothpaste from a tube. Suppressing a shudder, Idess pulled away from Lore. She hated Sheoul...the smells, the sounds, the denizens. Everything here was warped.

Steam swirled around the female's feet as she stopped before Idess. "Are you inquiring about a single killing? A mass killing? Is the victim human or demon? A quick death, or a painful one?"

Nice. "None of the above. I must meet with the Guild."

The demon's jaw dropped, revealing a forked, gray tongue. "You are either joking or are very, very stupid."

"*I will see the Guild.*"

"That is not possible."

"Then you bring the wrath of Azagoth down on your heads," Idess said with a shrug.

The demon's skin went ashen. The name Azagoth was

only whispered among demonkind. When a name was synonymous with death, no one spoke it out loud. "You lie."

Idess had been prepared for this. Taking a deep breath, she summoned every ounce of fury she'd ever felt, let it condense and build until she felt like a shaken bottle of champagne. When the pressure became an unbearable pounding behind her eyes, she let it out in a painful release.

All around her, the black-streaked ground trembled as her skin split and her body doubled in size, morphed, and erupted in glowing light. The demon wheeled away in terror and the things guarding the archway cowered. Within seconds, Idess was a winged, skeletal creature that no one, demon or human, could look upon without thinking of Death incarnate.

She was, in fact, a perfect cross between Azagoth's true form and an angel.

"You represent the Guild, and I represent Death." Her voice was a dark, deep rumble that put fissures in the sheer rock faces on either side of her. "Take me."

The female bowed, making the bone beads in her hair clatter. "I'll deliver your message." She disappeared into the gate, squeezing through once more. Idess returned to her preferred form, and turned to find Lore gaping at her. Oops.

"Ah . . . is there something you want to tell me?"

"Not really," she muttered, and amused herself by hissing at the creepy things milling around the arch and making them skitter away in terror.

"Idess? Who is Azagoth?"

Oh, hell. "You've never heard of him?"

"I've heard the name, but I figured he was some regional baddie warlord in Sheoul."

She snorted. "Hardly. He was once an angel. Back

before there was such a thing as death." She hissed at the creepy things again when they inched too close. "But then that idiot, Cain, killed Abel, and because humans could die, demons had to lose their immortality as well. Some species, anyway. So after that, human and demon souls were running around all willy-nilly and wreaking havoc. Angels were assigned to escort human souls to Heaven, but someone needed to be in charge of the other souls."

"So, what...this Azagoth guy volunteered?"

"Apparently," she replied, keeping an eye on the Crest Gel Archway. "Better an angel than a demon to handle the work. So, according to legend, Azagoth willingly fell. He created the holding tank, Sheoul-gra, and all the while, he tried to maintain his goodness, but eventually, he was corrupted. Maybe because he started feeding on demons, or maybe because dealing with demon souls and seeing everything they'd done in their lives chipped away his purity. In any case, he presides over souls his *griminions* escort to Sheoul-gra."

"*Griminions?* As in, the Grim Reaper's little helpers? Those *griminions*?"

"Yes. Azagoth is the being humans know as the Grim Reaper." She glanced at the portal, which began to shimmer. "He's also my father."

Lore made a strangled sound, but he didn't have a chance to say anything, because a seven-foot-tall male Neethul squeezed through the gate and came straight at them.

The Neethulum were a beautiful race, elven in appearance, which made them all the more terrifying. They were proof that evil was not always ugly. This one had emerald eyes and long white hair, with several jagged facial scars that marred his perfection.

"If you are lying about who you are," he said pleasantly, "you will be skinned and disemboweled while still alive and hung from the rafters until you die."

Lore casually peeled off his glove, exposing his killing hand, and his cold smile matched the Neethul's. Except that on Lore, it was sexy. Sexier than it should be, but she was rapidly realizing that Lore was a lot of things he shouldn't be.

"Follow. And know that you cannot summon weapons inside the Guild Hall." The Neethul led them to the portal, kicking one of the slithering demon things on his way through.

The gate flashed them to something that resembled a small, underground medieval village. Spiny hellrats scurried under the feet of various species of demons, some of whom appeared to be there against their will. Actual balls and chains dragged behind them, and near a hovel next to a black, steaming pool, an imp in stocks was being whipped.

"See?" Lore whispered. "We're healed."

Sure enough, Lore's injuries no longer bled, and when she touched her cheek, where the scale had sliced it, her skin wasn't even tender. Neat. But her back itched like crazy.

Lore took her hand in his left one and followed the Neethul into the largest of the buildings, a keeplike structure made of bone-colored stone that bled a black substance. Inside, everything was gray, from the hard-baked clay floor to the ceiling, from which hundreds of heads hung, some fresh, some so old they'd rotted to nothing but yellowed skulls.

Idess's stomach lurched as the Neethul led them through

rooms that seemed to have no purpose except to display the heads and a few other choice body parts, until they reached a long, dark hallway. At the end, a rolling vertical door opened into the largest room yet. In the center was a crude wooden trestle table, at which at least a hundred demons sat, some drinking from ale tankards, and others gnawing on bloody hunks of meat. The Neethul took a chair near the middle.

A lizardlike demon of unknown species stood at the far end. "Why do you request this audience?" he asked, his voice booming with an unnatural resonance, a trick of the room's architecture, Idess was sure.

"I come for information about one of your clients. I must speak with the master known as Detharu."

There was an explosion of talk, and the lizard-man gestured for silence. "Your request is ridiculous. You will therefore be killed."

"I will speak with Detharu, or you will face my father's wrath." She locked gazes with the demon.

Lizard-man's ominous growl vibrated the air. "I do not think you understand. No master can reveal the name of the one who entered into a contract with him."

"I didn't say I wanted a name." At this point, even a sketchy description would be better than nothing.

Conversation ensued, and finally, the demon turned back to her. "The price for even the smallest kernel of information will be great."

"And that price would be?" she ground out.

"You will become an assassin."

They couldn't be serious. The way Lore went taut beside her said they were. "I will not."

One eyeless male stood up, his pasty skin reminding

her of a grub. Or a maggot. His hands were encased in metal, with spikes at the knuckles. "One kill. Whoever we command. Just one. Agree or leave."

"Don't do it, Idess," Lore growled in a voice so low she doubted the others could hear.

Adrenaline coursed through her veins in a stinging rush. She couldn't do it. To kill like that... it would eliminate her as a candidate for Ascension. But she'd be eliminated if she lost Kynan, too.

"I cannot kill," she said. "But I could serve in some other way."

"Idess!" Lore squeezed her elbow. "*Don't.*"

They all looked to the white-skinned one. "Agreed."

Oh, God, what had she done?

He moved toward her, peeling off one of the gauntlets as he approached. When he was in front of her he smiled, a baring of tiny, sharp teeth. "For six months you will be mine."

A seismic rumble rolled up from Lore's chest. "Oh, no she won't." His arm hooked around her throat as he yanked her backward, and then there was an incredible pressure on her throat, and then... nothing.

The world went black.

⌒

Shit, shit, shit. Lore had really stepped in it this time. He sprinted through the Guild Hall, Idess in his arms, after knocking her cold with a modified sleeper hold. Deth's furious shouts followed him. The demon was going to torture the ever-living fuck out of him for this.

Spurred by footfalls behind him, he kicked the outer door so hard it splintered, vaulted through it, and hit the portal at a run. When he emerged in what felt like slow motion into the killbox, he didn't pause. And when his slave-bond lit up as if it was on fire, he breathed through the agony and ran harder, until he was safely shut into a Harrowgate. Panting and cursing, he tapped out the map until he arrived at the gate closest to his house.

Idess began to stir, and shit, she was going to kick his ass, too.

Freaking Grim Reaper's *daughter*.

Leave it to him to get messed up with Death's little girl. *Fuck*.

He exploded out of the Harrowgate and didn't stop until he reached his front door. It was unlocked, as always, and fortunately, Sin wasn't there waiting for him. The last thing he needed right now was her concern, lectures, or drama fits.

He laid Idess on the couch, but she'd awakened enough to squirm into a sit. "What... what happened?" She blinked up at him, her gaze a little glassy.

"I saved you from making a monster of a mistake."

She blinked again, and then came to her feet so fast he had to take a step back. "You *what*?"

"I take it you remember?"

"They were going to tell me who is trying to kill my Primori!" she shouted.

He held up his hands. "You wake up grumpy. You're not a morning person, are you?"

She gaped in outrage. "You... you—"

He palmed the nape of her neck, tugged her close, and kissed her. His assault tactics didn't work. Her squeal of outrage and fists against his shoulders were his first clue that this might not be the best approach to the situation. The knee to the groin was the second.

He'd been prepared for that, though, and he'd stepped back and twisted, avoiding what would have been a painful blow.

"You son of a bitch!"

"What?" he said, wiping his mouth with the back of his hand. "You were mad."

"I wasn't talking about the kiss."

He grinned. "Does that mean I can do it again?"

She stomped her foot. Actually stomped her foot in indignant fury. It probably shouldn't have been cute, but it was. "Lore, this is serious!"

"I *seriously* saved you from Detharu's service." Rubbing his seared chest, he moved toward the kitchen and had to bite down on a smile at her huff of frustration.

"I didn't need to be saved," Idess said, following him into the tiny kitchen space.

"Yeah, you did. You were in way over your pretty little angel head."

"I'm two thousand years old. I've been around the block, you know."

He laughed. "Really? Do you have any idea what he would have used you for? Go ahead and picture him naked. Because he uses his assassins for more than just killing."

"Oh...good Lord." Her hand flew up to her throat. "Has he...does he..."

"I've been lucky." He dug a glass out of a cupboard. "I think he's afraid of me. None of his assassins can harm him with intent, but because just touching my arm can kill...he's not taking any chances."

She looked down at her jeans and brushed away some

invisible lint. "Still, I would have worked out specifics with him—"

"He was going to brand you. When he reached for you, that's what he was going to do. You would have had a handprint on your chest to match mine and it would have been too late to negotiate."

Her mouth worked soundlessly. "Oh."

"A thank-you would be nice," he drawled, as he grabbed a jug of his rotgut out of the fridge. It wasn't even cold. Damned fridge had shit the bed again. But then, he'd had the Kelvinator since 1940, just like the oven he never used.

"You couldn't have warned me? You had to kidnap me instead?"

He laughed. "That, coming from *you*?" He splashed liquor into a glass and took a swig. "Want one?"

She hesitated, then shook her head. "Thanks, no."

"You hungry? I have sandwich makings. I think. If you like peanut butter. And bologna."

"As appetizing as that sounds, I'll have to pass. Thank you, I'm fine." She dragged her hand through her hair, tugging strands out of the ponytail, and sank back down on his couch. "Now what? I'm running out of ideas."

"I have one, but it's going to require Wraith. I need to contact the guys anyway, let them know that what's going on could be about them instead of you."

Lore's plan for Wraith would be a longshot, though—he had no idea how effective Wraith's mind-invasion thing would be on a being like Deth...assuming Lore could get the two of them together. And assuming Wraith didn't kill Lore before that could happen. First, though, he was going to have to go to Detharu and take his punishment for stealing Idess. His chest was burning like a mother, and the pain was only hours away from holy-shit-I'm-going-to-die-debilitating.

In rapid succession, he slammed four more shots of alcohol to numb himself. He'd have to take his other edge off, too, the sexual one, so he'd be less likely to rage out during his torture. "Look, I have to take off. I'm just going to, ah, shower up and head out."

"Where?"

"I need to see Sin," he lied.

"I'm going with you."

"No, you're not."

Idess let out an aggravated breath. "I'm not going to let you go alone."

"You're afraid I'll hunt Kynan." Guilt put shadows in her eyes, and he cursed. "I said I wouldn't." An unusually powerful blast of heat in his chest made him grit his teeth. "You don't trust me?"

"I want to, Lore. But this is important."

"You can't go. I'm going to the assassin den."

"No need." Sin's singsongy voice came through the screen door. "I'm here for a friendly visit."

Shit. "Now's not a good time, Sin."

She ignored him to plop down in the recliner. She was dressed like a street thug, in baggy pants with chains, a black hoodie, and sneakers. Even her hair was tucked up under a backward Yankees ballcap. "So. How'd it go at the Guild?"

"It didn't," Idess said. "Your brother felt the need to rescue me."

Sin cocked an eyebrow. "Rescue her?"

Lore slammed another shot. "Let's drop it, 'kay?"

"What did you do?" He should have known better than to expect Sin to leave anything alone.

"He knocked me out and threw me over his shoulder like some sort of caveman," Idess said, and yeah, that was pretty true. "He claims that if he hadn't, I'd have been branded like you two."

Sin's eyes widened, because she knew exactly what saving Idess had cost him. "Fuck," she muttered, and gestured to his bottle. "Gimme."

He passed it to her, and she swigged right from it. Dainty, his sister was not.

"I'm going to shower and go," he muttered, and started toward the bathroom.

"But Sin is here," Idess pointed out. "You have no reason to go to the den."

Black eyes sparking, Sin planted the jug between her thighs. "Oh, he didn't tell you?"

"Sin . . ."

She ignored his warning tone, but then, he didn't expect anything else. "He seriously pissed off Deth by taking you away like that. He's going to be tortured."

Idess felt sick to her stomach as Lore ushered Sin out the door with instructions to bring Wraith back to Lore's place. When he turned around, she stood, though not without effort. His couch must be a hundred years old, and if it had springs, they were dead. He truly didn't care about his comfort. Or maybe he couldn't afford nice things.

Or personal things, she noted with a frown. The walls were achingly bare. He had no knicknacks. Nothing that revealed anything about him—except what the *lack* of personal effects revealed about him; the house was set up so an intruder would learn nothing crucial about him or his sister. He could leave forever in a matter of minutes.

"Lore? Tell me what Sin said about you being tortured wasn't true."

He didn't look at her as he moved toward the bathroom. "It wasn't true."

"You're lying."

"You told me to."

"Damn you!" she snapped. "Stop!"

He halted, but he still didn't look at her. "It's all right, Idess. It's not like Deth hasn't done it before."

The way he said it, as if it was no big deal because he was used to it, broke her heart. How many beatings did it take before one grew numb to it? Way too many, she suspected.

"I won't let him do this." She took a deep, ragged breath. "I'll go to my father. I'll—"

"Stop." Lore rounded on her, but he didn't look angry. If she had to pick a look, she'd say he seemed startled by her vow to help him. "I have to do this. I knew what I was getting into, and I'll deal with it."

"But why? Why did you do it? After what I've done to you, you should enjoy seeing me enslaved."

"You really believe that?" He took a step toward her. "I'm risking Sin's life by putting off what I have to do to Kynan. I'm doing that for you. Not for Kynan or my brothers. I took a knife for you. I've kissed you over and over when I never kiss anyone. So why the hell would I want to see you suffer?"

Her mouth dropped open in shock, and her stomach fluttered. Some idiotic feminine instinct she didn't even know she had went tail-wagging stupid at his admission. "What are you saying?"

"I don't know." He swiped the jug of liquor off the coffee table, where Sin had left it. "Fuck. I have no idea. Forget I said anything."

Fat chance of that. She moved closer to him, not wanting to miss even the slightest nuances in his expression when she hit him with her sudden suspicion. "You don't kiss anyone because you're afraid of killing them, aren't you? Same with sex, right?"

He turned away again, and she grabbed his arm—the right one, protected by his thick leather coat. "Lore? Tell me."

"Yeah, okay? Do you have any idea what it's like to watch your partner drop dead because you got off? No," he said nastily, "I'm guessing you don't."

"But if you wear a sleeve and glove—"

"When I climax, my power punches right through it."

She thought about how he'd stroked himself to completion over her and realized that he'd pinned her legs between his and held himself away from her—to keep her from thrashing and accidentally touching his arm when he came.

"Have you ever been with a woman safely?"

He swallowed, and now probably wasn't the time to notice how sexy his throat was as the muscles worked beneath his tan skin, but *whoa.* "Just once. A long time ago."

"Did you love her?"

He snorted. "I didn't know her name. She blew me in an alley while I braced my arms above my head against a building."

"Oh." She could have gone all day without knowing that.

"You disgusted now? Because I am. Not because I paid some whore for sex, but because I was so fucking lonely that I risked killing her. I told you, I'm a selfish piece of shit."

It broke her heart to hear him say that, because she'd seen a lot of evidence to the contrary. "A selfish person wouldn't have signed up to be a slave to save his sister. A selfish person wouldn't have locked himself away from society in order to protect them. You're not selfish. You've slipped, like everyone else."

He threw the jug across the room, shattering it against the wall. "My slips kill people, Idess!"

She looked down at his scuffed hardwood floor, at the wetness spreading across it like spilled blood. "Have you ever loved anyone? Besides your sister, I mean." *Say no.*

"Why the hell are we talking about this?"

"I'm curious."

"Because this is such great pretorture talk."

The reminder dropped a bowling ball right into the pit of her stomach. "Please," she begged. "I have to do something to stop it. I'll go to my father and see if Deth can be given a heart attack or something."

"Seriously?" He cocked an eyebrow at her. "That's what your father does?"

"Sort of. I don't know how much pull I have with him. I haven't seen him in centuries."

She'd lived in Azagoth's realm for a hundred years, right after she was pulled from her human life. She'd been Rami's apprentice, learning the ways of the Memitim, how to flash and use her innate skills, learning the bazillions of rules. But once she was given Primori, she left the realm and hadn't been back.

Lore reached out and tucked a strand of her hair behind her ear. The gentle gesture was a lover's touch, and it triggered an ache deep inside. "I told you," he said quietly. "I knew what I was getting into."

Flecks of gold pierced the black of his irises, moving fluidly, like sunlight on a stream. "Why do your eyes do that?" She went on her toes to get closer, amazed by the beauty. "They were red when you were enraged, but they're gold now."

"They do that when I'm mildly annoyed." His gaze intensified, somehow growing both darker and more golden, and his earthy male scent filled her nostrils. "Or aroused."

"Which are you now?" she croaked. No sooner had the question passed her lips than her body answered with a warm, wet rush between her legs.

"Guess." His voice was deep and gravelly, and he spun around and headed for the bedroom.

"Where are you going?"

"I'm about to be tortured," he said, without looking back, "which will probably send me into a rage. If I don't let off some steam before I go...it could be bad."

"I can help," she blurted. Part of her longed to experience the intimacy again, and part of her just wanted to do something for him. To be useful. To make up for chaining him and nearly getting him killed.

He ground to a halt at the doorway. "I don't think that's such a good idea. In fact, it's a terrible idea."

"But you want it, don't you? You want me to be the one to ease you."

His big body shuddered. "God, yes." And there was that penetrating rumble that made her heart quiver in her chest. "It's better with you."

"Better how?" It was stupid to keep pressing, because the more she knew, the closer she got to him. Yet, some dark, wild side of her wanted that. Wanted to walk the line between love and hate and see which way she tipped.

"Are you asking to feed your ego, or are you genuinely curious about how you affect me?"

"Both, I think," she said honestly.

The long, deep breath he took told her she'd given him the right answer. "My release is more powerful. It's not that it feels better...I mean, it does...but I get more relief, more time before I need it again. Fuck, Idess...I can't."

"You didn't have a problem letting me help you before," she pointed out, though she did so breathlessly.

"I was chained with Bracken Cuffs the first time. I didn't need to worry about touching you. The second time, you were restrained, so I was in control." He rolled his broad shoulders, and the leather of his jacket strained at the seams. "I can't risk it."

"Not much can kill me." She walked around him so she could look him in the eyes. "I'm not worried."

"Then you're a fool."

Maintaining eye contact, she slid her palm down his arm to his gloved hand. His fingers curled around hers.

"Idess, this is stupid." But he stepped into her, so close she could feel the heat coming off him.

Haltingly, she placed her other hand on his waist, felt the very slight tensing in his body. "I know."

Seventeen

⌒

Idess's words ricocheted through Lore, sucker punching him right in the soul.

You're not selfish. You've slipped. Slipped. A *slip* could cost Idess her life.

Panic became shrink-wrap around his chest, and he released her. "No," he croaked. "No. I can't do this. Accidents happen."

And no way was Idess going to be an accident. Just a few days ago, he might not have cared. But now he cared way too much.

"Lore—"

"No!" Before she could argue, he shut himself in his room. To his surprise, she didn't barge in or even knock. She respected his privacy, and for some reason, her consideration sucker-punched him again.

Chest screaming with bond-pain and groin tight with the need she'd stirred, he paced, practically ran laps around his bedroom. He was hard and achy, but when he palmed his cock, God help him, it felt numb. His last couple of shower sessions had taken forever, but now? No matter how fast or hard he stroked, how hot the fantasy about Idess, he couldn't get there.

Just like a purebred Seminus. Fuck.

He had no idea what was going to happen once the torture began.

As if his body was trying to prepare him, a lightning bolt of pain struck him, spreading from the bond and into every extremity. Cursing, doubled over in agony, he slipped out his window and headed to the Harrowgate.

Lore hated leaving Idess, but he had a demon to face. At least he could take comfort in the fact that Idess couldn't flash into Sheoul. No way did he want her getting messed up in this.

The moment Lore entered the den, his bond-pain eased to a dull ache. Detharu was waiting in his chamber, looking really fucking pissed off. The foul stench of someone's terror soured the air, so thick Lore could taste it on the back of his tongue.

"Lore," Deth snarled. "My patience with you is at an end."

"I can see you aren't in the best of moods," Lore said, reversing course. "I'll come back later."

Deth's guards blocked the doorway, and Lore turned back, carefully schooling his expression to hide the fact that he knew he was in for a world of hurt.

"Where is the female?"

"I don't know."

"You're lying."

"And you're ugly. What's your point?"

Deth shot out of his seat. "You will bring her to me."

"Go fuck yourself."

"I am going to make you suffer," Deth snarled.

"Isn't that why I'm here?"

"Oh, yes." Anticipation glinted in the male's eyes as Deth shambled toward him. "Have you killed your mark yet?"

"I still have time." Lore studied his nails. "I'll get to it."

"Getting to it will be difficult, if you're locked in my pit for a month."

"You can't do that." Lore crossed his arms over his chest, still playing nonchalant. "I'm on a deadline."

"Then you should have thought about that before you spirited away the female."

A shiver of dread skittered up Lore's spine. "Look," he said calmly, even though inside he was sweating bullets, "I swear, as soon as I have Kynan's head, I'll submit myself for your punishment. Whatever you want."

Deth's steel-gloved fist nailed Lore in the jaw. Pain spiderwebbed up his face, into his skull, but he refused to show any reaction.

"You will not negotiate with me!" Deth roared. "I am going to punish you for taking the female. Right now."

Lore snorted. "Pussy stuff." Antagonizing Deth wasn't the smartest move, but pain was coming no matter what, so Lore might as well get in a few jabs of his own.

This time, Deth's blow struck him in the chest, those knuckle spikes puncturing, clawing like an eagle's talons and snatching the breath right out of Lore's lungs. Lore staggered back, but he managed a smile and a raspy, "Love the foreplay."

Deth snarled, blasting Lore with his fetid breath. "Does Sin also love it?"

The demon wanted to see fear, but Lore would never give him that satisfaction. "Dunno. Probably."

Deth got right in his face. Again with the rotten breath. "I cannot wait for you to fail your mission. I will make you watch as Sin is slaughtered. Her screams will be the music that fills this den for weeks."

Lore's skin grew tight, his muscles twitchy, and he was on the verge of erupting. A growl escaped as though through a relief valve. "I *will* kill you someday. I swear it."

Deth laughed. Flickering flames from the fire in the hearth and torches on the walls played with the shadows on his face, twisting his expression into something even more hideous. "How many times have I heard that?" He shoved his fist into Lore's gut and twisted so the spikes gored him viciously, ripping and tearing. "Now, will you bring the female to me?"

Pain wrenched through Lore, not all of it physical. He would never bring Idess here, and he would save Sin. Somehow, he'd protect them both.

"Fuck you," he spat, even as he fought to stay on his feet.

Deth hissed, and the trapdoor beneath Lore gave way. After a twenty-foot drop, he made a bone-breaking landing on the wet, cold floor in the dungeon. A Nightlash female stood next to a wall of torture implements, smiling at Lore as if he were a gift.

Foreplay was over. It was time for the main event.

The sound of torture was like the sound of someone coughing during a movie. Rariel found both to be extremely irritating.

"Add an extra lash for me," he said to Deth. Lore had

seriously screwed up something Rariel would have paid to see; Idess as an assassin slave. "And make sure his life will not be endangered by this."

Having Idess show up to protect Lore, now that he was Primori—and hadn't that been a nasty surprise—would definitely be a bad thing. She couldn't flash in here under normal circumstances, but Rariel didn't want to test her ability to do so if her Primori was facing death. Though it might be worth it to see her forced into slavery as an assassin...

Deth gave an indignant snort. "My torturer is a master, trained in all arts and all species' weaknesses. She would never accidentally kill one of her victims."

Like Rariel hadn't heard that before. "Just be careful. And I want his dagger. I have a special use for it."

Deth signaled a sentry, who disappeared.

"You will have him healed after this is over?"

"I don't like it," Deth growled, "but since he is on a deadline for your contract, I'll use my newly acquired Sem assassin to heal him."

"Good." Rariel smiled as the guard returned with Lore's Gargantua-bone dagger.

Now, it was time to fulfill an obligation to Roag and ruin—and *end*—some innocent lives.

By the time Idess flashed into UG's parking lot, she was in a full-blown panic. Lore had gotten away from her, and touching his *heraldi* didn't flash her to him. Which meant he was in Sheoul. Probably being tortured. Or maybe hiding out from her down there.

At the back of an ambulance, Eidolon was loading a

stretcher. When he saw her, he slammed the doors shut so hard they bounced open again. "Where is he?"

"I'm pretty sure he's at the assassin den."

"*Pretty sure?* Are you kidding me? You helped him escape, and now you've fucking lost him?"

"I just need help finding the den. Is Sin here?"

"Do I look like her keeper?" Eidolon dug his cell from his pocket and dialed. "Ky? Where are you? Yeah, okay. But you should know that Lore is unaccounted for—"

"He's not unaccounted for," Idess interrupted. "He's at the den." *Being tortured.*

Eidolon told Kynan to stay safe and flipped his phone closed. "Why can't you find him? He's your Primori, right? Shouldn't you have some sort of line to him?"

"Yes, but if he's in Sheoul, he's invisible to me."

"Is there any other way he'd be invisible?" When she didn't answer, his tone plummeted right into Sheoul with Lore. "Idess?"

She huffed. "It's possible that he could find someone to cast a shield spell on him. It's why we don't ever tell Primori what they are." She'd only broken about a million rules by now, but sometimes you had to cheat to win.

Rami would slap her if he heard that particular thought. He'd always been about playing by the book. She'd always been more concerned with winning, and when it came down to a battle between good and evil, rules went out the window.

Eidolon's curses blistered her ears.

"You know," she snapped, "I wouldn't force you to listen to a Bible reading, so I'd appreciate it if you'd show me the same courtesy and not curse me and my kind to hell."

Eidolon glared, but at least he didn't cuss at her anymore.

"Idess," he said with very forced calm, "I've had a really bad day, and I just watched a warg infant die of a disease I can't cure. So excuse me if I'm a little on edge because you lost the brother I swore I'd keep from killing one of my best friends."

"I get it," she said softly. "And I'm sorry. I needed Lore to help me get into the Assassins' Guild. If I can find out who hired him—"

"Did you?"

"Unfortunately, no. But I had a thought. Is it possible that all of this is about you instead of me or Kynan?"

"What, you think Lore was hired to kill Kynan just so my family would be torn apart?"

"Sounds a little thin, I realize. But it's one heck of a coincidence. Do you have any enemies who might want that to happen?"

"We're sex demons," he said wryly. "We pissed off a lot of males before we took mates. And Wraith has made a career out of making enemies."

That wasn't very helpful. "Lore mentioned another brother. One who hired him to kill you."

"Roag. He's gone."

"Gone? How?"

Eidolon shrugged. "*Maluncoeur* curse. He's doomed to an invisible existence, starving, thirsty, in pain...nothing he doesn't deserve."

Idess shuddered. Talk about eternal torment. Wait... "He's invisible? But he's still around?"

"I guess. But he can't hurt anyone."

But he could still lurk. Watch anything going on around him. *Oh...oh, no.* "Is it possible he's here?"

Eidolon's shoulders bunched with tension. "We left

him in Scotland, but he could have hitched rides in the Harrowgate with other demons."

"I think…" She inhaled a ragged breath. "I think he did exactly that. You know how I can see spirits? I've also seen a figure who appears transparent to me. He's sort of…"

"Burned?"

"Yes."

"Roag." Eidolon's eyes went crimson, and he buried his fist in the side of the ambulance, leaving a grapefruit-sized dent. "Son of a bitch!"

"Eidolon!" She grabbed his arm, and when he would have snatched it away from her, she jerked him around. "I took the creature out of the hospital. He's not here right now, unless he found a way back."

He went as still as a lamp post. "Where did you take him?"

"Phillips Court…some sort of apartment and housing complex—"

"Shade's old place. But why would he go there?" Eidolon was talking to himself rather than her, which was good, because she didn't know the answer. She did feel incredibly guilty, however. Finally, he shook his head. "I'll figure it out. You need to find Lore. I'll find Shade."

Sin so did not want to go back to the hospital. Her brothers were asses, and the whole place gave her the creeps.

The only positive thing that had happened lately was sex with Conall and outing him for making that bet. The two-sixty she'd gotten out of it would buy her a new pair of Fae-crafted stun darts.

Except... she wouldn't need them, would she? She was almost done with Deth, and then she could... what?

Something splashed painfully in her stomach, as if a stone had been skipped across a lake of acid. She hadn't thought that far ahead. Since the age of twenty, she'd never been free, unowned, and she had no idea what she was supposed to do with herself if she suddenly had no orders.

She stepped out of the Harrowgate and into the emergency department... and right into chaos. Shade and Eidolon were rolling around on the ground, throwing punches and, as far as she could tell, not holding anything back.

Conall and Luc were watching, each holding a handful of bills. Another bet. *Wonder how I can get in on that one.* Conall's molten silver gaze locked with hers, and she took a sudden, hot breath. He was every woman's fantasy, from his perfect body to his remarkable eyes to his dangerous masculinity. Nice girls would tremble before him, even as they entertained wicked, private fantasies. Bad girls would make those fantasies reality any time, anyplace.

Sin was a bad girl.

And her inner bad girl—well, her inner demon—was itching to do anything that might get in her brothers' faces.

Fucking one of their paramedics might just be the ticket. Plus, as she'd already learned, sex with Conall wasn't exactly a hardship.

The battle raged as she crunched all the delicious possibilities in her mind, until suddenly, Shade rolled away from Eidolon, clutching his stomach, his mouth open in a silent gasp. Sin instinctively stepped forward to help, and was surprised when Eidolon did the same. They'd been fighting as though they hated each other, were bloody and bruised, but the fear in Eidolon's expression left no doubt that they were not enemies.

"Shade?" Eidolon was on his knees next to his brother, his *dermoire* glowing. "What is it? Dammit, Shade, talk to me!"

Shade shoved to his knees. "Fuck," he breathed. "*Runa*. She's... she's... in trouble." He struggled to his feet and lurched toward the Harrowgate. "E. Send Tay to my place. The house. Fucking hurry!"

Eidolon wasted no time in fishing his cell phone from his pocket as Shade disappeared into the gate.

Sin had no idea what had just happened, but a sinking feeling told her this was just the beginning of something horrible.

Eighteen

The female named Runa sprawled in a rapidly spreading pool of blood, Lore's knife impaled in her gut. She'd tried shifting into a warg, but Rariel had been prepared, and he'd jabbed her in the neck with a silver pin.

Don't kill her, Roag said. *I want her to live. To suffer for the rest of her life, forever hearing her children's screams and knowing they died in excruciating pain.*

Rariel had to hand it to the demon—he was sneaky as shit, tricking Idess into flashing him to Shade's old apartment. From there, he'd hoofed it over here and slipped inside when Runa opened the door.

Rariel kneeled next to her and adjusted the ski mask he wore to conceal his identity. The bitch had wrenched it askew in her struggles. "I'm going to kill your cubs now."

He gently smoothed his knuckles over her face in an odd, impulsive need to comfort her despite what he was saying. He despised that about himself, the little glints of goodness that hadn't yet been corrupted by the evil surrounding him. Fortunately, they didn't last long or happen often.

"You'll hear their cries," he continued, "but you can do nothing about it. I'll take one of them, and you will tell Shade that I will trade him for Kynan. If you don't hand over the human within twenty-four hours...use your imagination."

She let out an agonized cry and tried to claw her way toward the stairs. He admired her pluck, for all the good it would do her.

Leaving her to bleed, Rariel followed the sound of wailing babies. They were at the top of the stairs, three of them, in a nursery decorated in deep blues and greens. Though toys littered the floor and animal murals covered the walls, the room was in no way set up like a frilly human nursery. Still, from the two rocking chairs to the daybed where it was obvious one or both parents had lain with the infants, the room was a testament to the love Runa and Shade shared for their offspring.

Regret turned Rariel's stomach inside out, but after a single, shaky breath, he got over himself and lifted the loudest child out of his crib.

The thing bit him. Maybe wringing his little neck wouldn't be so hard after all.

"*Runa!*" Shade's shout carried up the stairs, and so did the pounding of feet. Shit.

Go, Roag said. *I'll slip into the Harrowgate with them. I want to watch Shade's misery.*

"Have fun." Rariel cast one last glance at the two infants in the cribs, and flashed out of there with the third.

So he hadn't killed the babies, but he'd still get what he wanted: Kynan. Dead. Amulet. In hand.

Idess. Disgraced.

Victory was so close he could taste it. As he materialized in his central Sheoul hideout, he smiled down at the glaring baby, and thought maybe he'd allow Deth a taste, too.

Of the child.

Needing to stretch her legs and feeling the itch of help-lessness, Sin went to grab some coffee. Not that she knew where the cafeteria was. Funny how she found the very closet where she'd knocked boots with Conall, though.

Warmth flooded her body at the memory, and she actually trailed her fingers over the door as she passed.

Idiot.

And where the hell was the cafeteria? Lost in the maze of hospital halls, she followed the signs back to the emergency department, where the staff was concentrated around one curtained cubicle.

Craning her neck, Sin could make out the top of Eidolon's head. Nimbly, she climbed up on one of the waiting-area chairs so she could get a better view. And then she wished she couldn't see a damned thing.

Shade and Eidolon were in the tiny room, where a bloody female lay motionless on the bed. Shade looked as if he was going to break down at any second. The female must be Runa, his mate.

Eidolon and Shade were both channeling power into her, Eidolon cursing and Shade pleading. Twice Shade's *dermoire* flared so bright Sin had to squint. Both times, Eidolon reached across Runa to lay a hand on his brother.

"Easy, bro," Eidolon murmured the second time. "Downshift a gear. You're going to burn yourself out."

Shade trembled as his markings dimmed, though they still glowed brighter than Eidolon's.

"Please, Runa." Shade's voice broke. "Come back to me, baby."

Sin stood frozen, unable to look away from the female fighting for her life and the two males who were so fiercely trying to make it happen.

"Yo, Sin."

She spun around to the owner of the voice, nearly falling off the chair. A red-haired female who bore the Seminus mate marks on her left hand stood next to her, but Sin couldn't tell to which of the other brothers she belonged, given that her leather jacket and high collar covered the rest of the *dermoire*. But she held a squirming infant in each arm, and as Sin stepped down from the chair, the other female shoved a baby at her.

"Here. Hold your nephew."

Too startled to refuse, Sin held out her hands, and the next thing she knew, her hands were full of rugrat. She sniffed it. Didn't smell like baby powder or crap. Bonus.

"Are you Tayla?" Sin vaguely remembered Lore mentioning that Eidolon's mate was a Guardian, and this woman was wearing a weapons harness beneath her jacket and a scabbard at her hip. Sin totally respected that.

"Yeah." Tayla absently rocked the infant in her arms as she watched Shade and Eidolon work on Runa. Some of the staff had dispersed to handle an incoming trauma, leaving the scene open for Sin and Tayla to see everything going on.

Sin emulated the Guardian's rocking motion. Tried to, anyway. For some reason her baby jiggled a lot more than Tayla's did. "What happened to Runa?"

"I don't know," Tayla said. "I got to Shade's place right after he did. Runa was unconscious and Rade was gone."

"Rade?"

Fury turned Tayla's green eyes into a forest on fire. "One of the triplets."

Sin peered down at the squirming baby she held, unable to imagine someone stealing something so small and innocent. "Do you know who did it? Or why?"

"No. But if anything happens to him…" She trailed off, and Sin filled in the blanks. The kidnapper was so dead. Probably was whether or not the child was hurt.

"Sh-Shade?" Runa's voice was reedy and weak, but both Eidolon and Shade appeared relieved to have heard it at all.

"Thank gods," Shade whispered. "What is it, *lirsha*?" He gently stroked her cheek with his fingertips. His throat worked repeatedly on hard swallows, and Sin got the impression he was trying to hold back tears.

Runa blinked, her gaze unfocused, but Sin saw the moment everything came back to her with horrifying clarity. Shade's mate screamed and levered up so fast no one had a chance to push her back down.

"*Rade*! Where is he?"

"Runa, calm down—"

"*Where*?" She fisted Shade's shirt and dragged him down to her. "He has him. Oh, my God, he has him! Have to find him…" Sobbing, Runa struggled to get out of bed, but Eidolon injected something into her IV line. Almost instantly, she grew dazed, her eyes unfocused, and Shade was able to ease her back onto the bed.

"Runa? What happened? Who has our son?"

"I can feel him…but he's so far away…"

"He's alive then. Thank gods." Shade squeezed her shoulder gently. "Runa, tell me what happened."

"I tried to fight . . . so hard . . ." Tears streamed down her face as she lay there, staring blankly up at the ceiling. "He said . . . he said we have to hand over Kynan within twenty-four hours. Or . . . or . . ."

Shade gathered her against him and used his big body to buffer her powerful sobs. In Sin's arms, the baby sobbed.

Misery like Shade had never known tore through him, his own considerable pain magnified by Runa's. She was strong, and her physical pain was bearable, but her emotional agony was a hot blade through the soul.

We have to hand over Kynan within twenty-four hours. Or else.

Only one person wanted Kynan that badly. The weird sense of malevolence that had overtaken the hospital lately seemed to seep inside Shade through the laceration in his soul, adding fuel to the rage and hatred that bubbled like molten metal in his heart. Gently, he lowered Runa, now knocked out from whatever E had dosed her with. He barely held himself together as he snatched up the dagger that had been impaled in his mate's body and stalked toward Sin.

She held her ground as he approached, even though he knew his eyes had gone red and she could probably feel the anger radiating off of him.

"Shade—" E palmed his shoulder, but Shade shrugged him off and planted himself in front of Sin. Wraith burst out of the Harrowgate.

Hilt-first, Shade thrust the dagger at his sister. "Who does this belong to?"

Sin drew a startled breath. "Where did you get it?"

"Answer the question."

Her eyes flashed with annoyance, but she smelled of anxiety.

"*Sin!*" His bark made her jump and made little Stryke stop crying.

"It's Lore's." Somehow, she made her answer sound like a challenge.

He might have respected that, had this been any other situation. As it was, a dark, icy void formed in his chest. Despite everything that had happened, most of the time he hadn't truly hoped for Lore's death. For some reason, when he was away from the hospital and Eidolon, he could actually settle down and think rationally. And ironically, Runa had championed Lore. It wasn't that she wanted Kynan to die; she just wanted Shade to not give up on any of his brothers.

It was too late for that.

"Where is he?"

Stepping back, Sin actually tucked Stryke closer to her chest, as though Shade might be a danger to his own son. "You can't think he had anything to do with your mate's injuries or your son's disappearance."

"Where. Is. He?"

"Listen to me—"

"*Where?*"

"He's being tortured right now, okay?" She met his gaze levelly and with defiance. "He couldn't have done it because he's being tortured."

"Did you witness it?"

"No, but, he wouldn't have done this," she snapped. "And there's no way in hell he'd have left the dagger behind."

"And why is that?"

"Because I gave it to him. He'd never have given it up willingly. Never."

Shade didn't give a shit about sentimental value, and right now, he didn't give a shit what Sin thought she knew about her brother, either. "Go to him," Shade growled. "Go to him and tell him I want to see him. Now."

Sin handed over Stryke. "I will. And I'll expect you to grovel at his feet and ask forgiveness when I prove you wrong." She glanced at Wraith as though she had something to say to him, but after a brief shake of the head, she took off, disappearing into the Harrowgate.

The moment she was gone, Shade hugged Stryke close and rounded on E, whose face was sallow, his gaze haunted.

"This is your fault," he snarled. "You son of a bitch, that bastard nearly killed Runa, and he has my son because you refused to do what was necessary." Shade's hands shook with the need to strike out, but instead he tightened his grip on his son. "If I didn't need you to take care of Runa, I'd tear you apart right now."

"You need to back off, Shade," Tayla said, her voice low and calm, so as not to frighten the babies, but the underlying warning was clear. "Before you say something you'll regret."

"There are a lot of things I regret," he said, never taking his eyes off Eidolon, "but trust me, nothing I say here will be one of them." He turned to Wraith, who looked as pissed as if his own child had been taken. "I can't leave Runa or the babies, and I don't trust Sin to do anything but tell Lore to run. Find him, Wraith. Find him, kill him, and bring back my son."

Nineteen

⌒

Sin sprinted down the assassin den's narrow halls, her weapons clanking against her hip, her breasts, the small of her back. She had to find Lore. Had to see for herself that he wasn't responsible for what had happened to Runa and the baby.

Not that she had any doubt. Lore would never harm a child. He'd been hired or ordered to kill them before, and refused... actions that had resulted in days of bleeding at the hands of Deth's special torturers. The ones he called Peelers.

Sin shuddered and silently cursed Deth and his unholy minions.

But what if Lore had taken the child as leverage, with no plans to harm it—just to frighten Shade into giving up Kynan? She couldn't imagine his being so ruthless as to hurt Runa like that, and he certainly wouldn't be sloppy enough to leave his dagger behind, but...

Oh, God.

Her sprint turned into an uncontrolled mad dash. She ran wildly through the den, bouncing off walls and knocking over Sunil, a tiger shifter with an unusually docile nature. He didn't even curse at her when she sent him sprawling. Lycus, however, did. The male warg had always despised her, and his nasty promise of retribution clocked hang time in the icy air as she ran.

Ahead, the door to Deth's chamber opened, and in the pale orange light streaming from the opening, a dark figure threw a large shadow. Encased in black robes, he swept down the hall, away from Sin, but not before she caught a glimpse of something squirming in his hands.

A tiny, pale foot draped over the crook of his arm. "Rade," she whispered.

Heart pounding, she sprinted toward the demon. "Hey! Stop!" The male cast her a hateful glare over his shoulder, picked up his pace, rounded a corner...and vanished.

Shit! Furious, and on the verge of freaking out, she hauled ass to Detharu's chamber, where her master was near the hearth, naked and observing as a new female Drekevac assassin was being held down by two guards and forcibly fitted for a tongue piercing. Deth's eyes were bright, his cock swollen, and Sin knew the female on her knees was in for a rude introduction to the world of the Detharu brotherhood.

"Yo. Deth. Where's Lore?"

"Below. He's free to go."

She blinked. "Can he be moved?"

"He will be healed."

Thank God. She cleared her throat. "The male who just left. Who is he?"

"Rariel?" Deth reached out to stroke the female's spiny head as her jaw was forced open. "Why?"

"Just curious."

"You're a pain in the ass." He cut a sharp wave of his hand. "Be gone."

His tone left no room for argument—he'd already been much more helpful than she'd expected, probably because he was distracted by his new acquisition. That, and all his blood had run south and left him stupid.

"Just one more thing...the infant. Was it his?"

Deth's head swiveled around as if it was on a ball bearing, and she knew she'd gone too far. "One more word, and you will join Ystla on her knees."

The female cried out as the piercing punched through her tongue. Sin had escaped that fate years ago, thanks to a loophole in her contract—a loophole Deth had since found a way around. Sin definitely didn't want him to take advantage of his underhanded maneuverings now.

"And remind your brother that time is running out for him to deliver the human's head."

She nodded just deeply enough to satisfy his need for bowing and scraping, and headed for the staircase that would lead to the dungeon below.

"Lore?"

Lore groaned at the sound of Sin's voice, groaned more as she cut him down from the beam he'd been hanging from. "Where's Idess?" he croaked. His throat was as raw as if he'd been screaming for days, and his jaws ached from avoiding doing just that. "Where?"

"Where you left her, I'd assume." Sin eased him to his

knees in the pool of his own blood and held a cup of water to his parched lips.

Yes…that's right. He'd left her at his house. She'd wanted to be with him, and he'd turned her down. He'd risked rage instead of stripping her to the skin and taking her as he should have.

Can't have her. She'll die.

But he needed her. The rage was running through his blood like motor oil, thickening and becoming more and more contaminated the longer it kept circulating.

"She's going to be pissed at me." He fell forward to his hands and knees as the room spun. His thoughts spun, too, all running together until he wasn't sure what were memories and what were fantasies. "She's how I got through this, Sin. I kept thinking about her. I can't have her, but I kept thinking about her and I know she's mad and fuck I'm babbling."

"Little bit." She nudged his lips with the cup. "Don't worry about that right now. We're leaving."

"Deth's not finished with me." The torturer hadn't worked her way to Lore's front side yet, and there was still an entire rack of tools that hadn't been used. Nope, Lore had several hours of pliers-in-fun-places still to come.

"Deth said you can go."

"Why?" He gulped the cool water gratefully, but spat out a mouthful when a horrible thought came to him. "What kind of deal did you make with him?"

"None."

Pain made him grumpy, and he swatted the cup away to get her attention. "What are you not telling me?"

The fact that Sin didn't scold him for his uncharacteristic display of temper told him that this was going to be bad. Suddenly every one of the lacerations on his back felt as if it had its very own heartbeat.

"Shade's mate was nearly killed, and his son taken." Sin's voice was grave. "You've been framed for it."

"Dammit." The rage in his blood turned to sludge, and his muscles started to twitch as though wanting to punch through his skin. "*Goddammit!*" Closing his eyes, he breathed deeply and wondered how he was going to get out of this mess. "Did you tell Wraith I need to talk to him? If he can get inside Deth's head—"

"Uh . . . did you miss how I said you were framed? I'm thinking you should avoid your brothers right now. At least until we get proof that you aren't responsible."

"I need them more than ever, Sin." And wow, he never thought he'd say that.

"No, you don't. I think I know who did it."

Lore whipped his head around to stare at his sister. "Who?"

"Dude named Rariel. I saw him come out of Deth's chamber with Rade."

"Long black hair? Robes?"

"Yep."

Son of a bitch. He'd known that asshole had been up to something. "You need to tell our brothers."

"They won't believe me. They'll think I'm lying to save you."

She was probably right. "Do you think you can find him?" His sister was one of the best trackers in the den.

"You bet. I'll meet you at your place in an hour. I should have a lead by then." She smiled grimly. "In the meantime, sharpen your weapons."

His muscles rippled hotly again, and he gnashed his

teeth, breathed through them as he held back the darkness that wanted to get out and swallow a whole lot of people.

The door to the pit creaked open, and an unfamiliar blond Seminus entered. "I'm Tavin. Detharu sent me to heal you."

This was a first, but Lore wasn't going to complain. "Just don't touch my *dermoire*," he said to the Sem. He didn't know if it would kill the guy or not—Lore's brothers and sister were immune, but he didn't know if it was because they were siblings or because they were Seminus demons, and he didn't want to test that right now.

"If you can knock me out while you're healing me, do," Lore gritted out. "Otherwise, we're looking at a shitload of trouble."

"You're close, aren't you?" Sin asked quietly, and Lore nodded.

Tavin cocked a blond eyebrow. "What's he close to?"

"Gutting you with his teeth. And that's just for starters." Sin stood. "Put him out, or you won't have a chance to wish you had."

Lore woke, completely healed and lying on the ground outside the Harrowgate near his house. Someone had even cleaned him off and dressed him. Probably Sin. She'd nursed him through a lot of beatings.

The rage still burned in him, but whatever Tavin had done during the healing had eased it a little. The fact that he was no longer in pain helped a lot, too.

He hoped he could keep a handle on his Incredible Hulk until he talked to Idess to figure out who the hell would have framed him, and why. Her theory that this whole thing was about him and not her was starting to seem more plausible.

He had to find this Rariel guy and get Rade back. Crazily enough, it wasn't even because the kid was his nephew. It was just the right thing to do. He laughed at that as he approached his house. Idess was rubbing off on him, infecting him with her do-gooder angel vibes or something.

He entered his shack through the back door, and before he'd made it five steps, Idess was in his face. "Damn you! How dare you sneak away like that! I've been looking all over for you. And—" She paused in her tirade to look him over. "You didn't get tortured. You're okay." She flew into his arms, startling the hell out of him and knocking him back a step. "Thank the Lord, you're okay. The guilt was killing me."

"Yeah," he said, hoping she didn't notice that he'd had to speak around a lump in his throat. Or that he now had a raging boner. "I'm okay."

She pulled back. "So where did you go?"

"To the den." Gently, he set her away from him and eased around her. He'd grossly underestimated his body's response to her, and even now it vibrated with the need to throw her down and take her hard and fast. It was partly about the rage, and partly about the fact that it was just…Idess. He wanted her, and there was no denying it. Wanted her so badly that when he'd been strung up in Deth's torture chamber, he'd entertained crazy ideas while in the haze of pain.

He wanted to bond with her so she'd be his forever. He wanted to come inside her over and over, so that his semen would act like a drug, becoming something she craved as her orgasms became stronger and longer-lasting. But he wasn't a purebred Sem, so could any of that happen?

Even if it could, she was an angel. They couldn't be

together. Not permanently. No doubt the big guy upstairs frowned on demon-angel relationships, and even if not, she'd be Ascending soon. Leaving him.

But all of that was a moot point anyway. His stupid death gift ruled out a relationship of any kind, and if that wasn't enough, they had the elephant named Kynan in the room.

Grinding his molars in frustration, he made a beeline for his booze, and stopped short at the layout on the table. Pasta with chicken and an olive-packed red sauce. Garlic bread twists. Colorful steamed vegetables. His stomach growled like a south Sheoul tar pit.

"I thought you might be hungry when you got back." Her hands came down gently on his shoulders, and the lump in his throat grew bigger. "Because if you were tortured..."

His heart clenched. She'd been worried about him, and she'd worked off her nervous energy by cooking. Her fingers began a deep massage into his shoulders as he bit into a bread stick and groaned. And she was a fantastic cook, too. He could barely make a sandwich.

She was mate material, pure and simple. The fantasies that had kept him sane during the torture came back to him in stark detail, and the rage that had been building inside him was replaced by a primal urge to mate. To make her his.

"An angel who cooks." His voice was rough with the effort he was expending to not jump on her. "Who knew you had it in you?"

She moved away from him to turn off the TV, which was blaring news about the neverending trouble in the Middle East. "I've never really cooked for anyone but myself, but I think I do okay."

That was the understatement of the century, and the bread turned to lead in his gut. She was so perfect, so decent, and so wrong for him, and while it was nice to fantasize about having her, these little slices of a white-picket-fence life were temporary.

"Hey," Idess's voice was a soft prompt from the living room. "Did I say something wrong?"

"Yes." He swore. "I mean, no. You didn't do anything wrong." *You did everything right, damn you.* "Cookie, we have a huge new problem." Food forgotten, bodily urges temporarily overridden, he turned to her. She stood there, hands clasped in front of her, watching him with concern. He wished she'd stop doing that, because he didn't want it, didn't deserve it.

"What now?" She'd changed clothes at some point while he was gone, was now wearing a pair of khaki BDU pants, combat boots, and a black, button-down blouse tied just below her breasts, revealing that flat belly he wanted to kiss every time he saw it.

She looked sweet and sexy and once again, he threw wood like a teenager who'd just picked up his first nudie mag.

He casually adjusted his erection and got back on track. "Shade's mate was attacked, and one of his sons kidnapped. Rade's being held as ransom for Kynan."

Every drop of color drained from her face. "Shade's mate? Where?"

"I don't know. Why?"

She hooked her thumbs in her pockets and looked down at the floor. "First... do you know who attacked her and took the child?"

"Sin saw Rade with some demon named Rariel."

Frowning, Idess looked up again. "Rariel?"

Hope sparked. "Do you know him?"

"No...but that sounds like an angel name. He might be fallen."

It was Lore's turn to frown. "If he's a fallen angel, why wouldn't he go after Kynan himself?"

"I don't know," Idess said, "but the reason I asked about Shade is that I may have another piece of the puzzle. Your brother, Roag, haunts the hospital."

Lore froze. "How do you know?"

"I've seen him. Angels are capable of seeing those who exist in dimensions your limited eyesight can't pick up. I helped him out of the hospital," she said thickly. "I didn't know who he was, and apparently, I took him to Shade's old apartment. I searched for him after Eidolon told me, but..." She shook her head. "What if he had something to do with the attack?"

Shock made Lore's mind sluggish as it played back the last few days from the beginning. The Rariel guy had been hanging with Deth...and he had Rade, wanting to trade for Ky. But if he was a fallen angel, why would he set up Lore to take the fall? Wait...

"Angel."

"Yes?"

"Not you." Lore smiled a little at that, but sobered quickly. "Bear with me, here. I met Rariel when Roag hired me. They know each other. If Rariel is a fallen angel—"

"He could see Roag like I can," she breathed.

"Exactly. What if they're working together so Roag can get his revenge on our brothers? Rariel could have contracted me to kill Kynan as well as set me up as Rade's kidnapper. Roag gets what he wants, and Rariel gets Kynan's special necklace." He frowned. "What's with that, anyway?"

"Necklace? I don't know." She was lying, and she

changed the subject before he could call her on it. "But why would Rariel also hire Sin to kill my other Primori?"

Yeah, that was still a missing piece of puzzle, but right now, his primary concern was getting Rade back.

"Sin's trying to get a bead on Rariel. She'll be here in an hour. But if he hurts that child..." It would be Lore's fault. Idess squeezed his hand, and fire shot up his arm. He hissed and backed away so fast he bumped into the wall. "Don't!"

She followed him, worry putting delicate lines in her forehead. "Lore? Hey, are you okay?"

"No," he ground out. "I'm not okay."

Something dark and primal vibrated through Lore, as though all of the lust that had built up over the last couple of days was tired of waiting. It wanted out. And it wanted Idess.

She reached for him. "I want to help you—"

He moved without thinking, his body heading down the backstretch before his brain even got out of the gate, and the next thing he knew, he was on her, sandwiching her between the wall and his body. He gripped her hip with his bare hand and the nape of her neck with his gloved one as he dipped his head so his lips brushed her ear.

"Help me? You know what would help me? Stripping you naked so I can dive between your legs and lick you until you scream."

"Oh, Lore." She brought her hands up to his waist and whispered against his cheek, "I wouldn't fight you."

It was totally the wrong thing to say. A groan rattled in his chest as he ground his erection against her. "You need to fight me, angel. Because I wouldn't stop there." He inhaled deeply, taking in her naturally spicy scent that was now mingled with an even more savory scent of arousal. "Before you caught your breath, I'd be inside you, fucking you until I filled you with so much of me that you'd feel me for weeks."

Her whimper of need put a crack in his restraint. Some deep, elemental urge came over him, and he sank his teeth into the gentle curve between her shoulder and neck to hold her as he thrust against her, wishing they were skin on skin. Idess cried out, but she arched into him to meet each roll of his hips.

"Lore…" Her breasts rubbed against his chest and her fingers bit into his waist and he was going to tear off her clothes with his teeth.

Mindless with need, he skimmed his gloved hand up her rib cage. Her heat practically melted the leather, and then he found her breasts, and…and dammit, he couldn't do this.

With a roar, he tore away from her. His cock throbbed and his balls ached, and in his veins, lava flowed instead of blood. She reached for him, and he rounded on her with a demonic growl. "Touch me, and the last of my control will shatter, Idess. I *will* have you. And angel or not, you won't survive it."

Inside, the demon half of him howled with pain and grief. It wanted Idess like it had never wanted anyone else. It demanded her. The human half screamed at him to run.

The part of him that was wholly male wanted to mark her as his and never let her go. The thought made him break out in an icy sweat, because if he didn't get away from her, the only thing he'd be marking would be her grave.

Twenty

⁓

Every cell in Idess's body was on fire. It was as if they were rubbing together, the friction creating maddening heat that nearly had her flashing home just so she could take a cold shower. Which was what she was pretty sure Lore was doing.

Either that, or he was...

The images of what he might be doing assaulted her brain and added to the inferno burning in her body. She saw him stroking himself the way he had when she'd been chained to her bed, and she went utterly wet between her legs.

Before you caught your breath, I'd be inside you, fucking you until I filled you with so much of me that you'd feel me for weeks.

More images. More heat. More liquid arousal.

She couldn't have intercourse, but she could join him in the shower. Right now. Replace his hand with hers. His hand with her mouth. And he'd let her. He'd been on the brink, but his fear of what might happen if she touched his *dermoire* had driven him back. But she knew his touch wouldn't kill her. Few demons could. Fallen angels, though . . . that was another story.

The thud of something hitting the living room window yanked her out of her thoughts. When she peeked outside, her heart stuttered. A mourning dove lay on the deck, his little wings fluttering and legs kicking.

"Hey, little one," she murmured, as she gently scooped it into her hands. Blood bubbled from one nostril, and its beak opened and closed on silent gasps. Its aura wasn't gray yet—she still had time.

Closing her eyes, Idess summoned her mother's powers, tapping deep into her well of healing and life. Power filled her, and though she didn't open her eyes, she knew her body was glowing with a vibrant, white light. In her hand, the bird trembled.

So did she. She had no way of knowing if she'd be healing the bird or killing it, but either way, its pain would end.

She opened her eyes. The blood was gone from the bird's beak, and it cocked its head to look at her with what she swore was gratitude. And then it flew away, disappearing into the canopy of trees.

"That was amazing." Lore's voice was impossibly deep, raw, and right behind her.

Startled, Idess whirled around. He stood just outside the doorway, the towel slung low around his hips doing nothing to hide the enormous erection beneath. His ripped fighter's body gleamed in the sunlight, and water dripped off the hard planes of his face and streamed over the slabs of chest muscle, leaving glistening tracks on his tanned skin. She had the strangest urge to lap up every drop, working her way up from his toes.

"It was nothing," she said, hoping he didn't notice how winded she sounded.

"It wasn't nothing to that bird." He shifted his weight, and the towel slipped a fraction of an inch lower. Another centimeter and he could probably be arrested in this state for indecent exposure. Or *decent* exposure. "Can all Memitim do that?"

She jerked her gaze up to his, and she nearly bit her tongue at the desperation haunting his eyes. Clearly, he hadn't done what she'd thought he'd done in the shower. "Lore? Are you okay?"

"Answer!" he barked. His hands flexed at his sides, and his *dermoire* writhed angrily.

She should be furious at his command, but she suspected that at this point, his control over his behavior was tentative, at best. "It depends on what kind of angel our mother is. My mother is *vivificus*, a restorer of life."

He ran a trembling hand through his wet hair, leaving deep grooves. "I want to know more. But..."

She took a step toward him, but a warning growl froze her in place. "You're on edge."

Strikes of gold lightning splashed down in the black pools of his eyes. "I'm being set up so my brothers will slaughter me, I have to kill Kynan or my sister will die, but if I do kill him, you lose your wings, some evil asshole is doing God knows what to my nephew, and I'm in agony and on the verge of rage because of you. So yeah, I'm a little on edge."

Agony? Rage? "Because of me?"

His chest heaved with the force of his panting breaths—
the kind of breaths one took when one was trying to control pain or anger. He'd done the same before, while in the
throes of rage, and even now, glints of red joined the gold
in his eyes.

"Why—" she licked her suddenly dry lips, and his
laser gaze fixed on them "—why aren't you taking care of
yourself?"

"I...can't." His cheeks flushed, as though he were
ashamed. "I need you."

"I don't understand. You said—"

"You did something to me." He stalked closer, and it
became a struggle to breathe, not because she was afraid,
but because alongside the fury in his gaze, there was a
smoky possessiveness that was aimed directly at her. "You
made me need you. Crave you." He reached out with his
right hand. At the last second, he snatched it back, and
cursing nastily, he stumbled backward.

"Lore!" She caught his left wrist. His entire body
jerked. "You won't hurt me. Just let me touch it—"

"*What?*" He leaped backward so fast he hit the side of
the house. "Stay away from me!"

"And then what?" she shouted. "You rage out because
you're too stubborn to let me touch you?"

"I'll kill you!" he roared back. "Don't you get it? I will
put you in the fucking ground, and I can't live with that!"

She threw up her arms in frustration. "Then what do
you want from me? You want me to get on my knees and
blow you while you do a repeat of the incident with the
prostitute whose name you didn't even know? Is that what
you want?" God help her, she'd do it, wanted to put her
mouth on him and taste his passion, but not until he got an

earful. "Because I can invest in a quality set of knee pads. We'll probably be doing that for years, since I'm your Memitim and I have to keep you alive, so let's get to it, okay?" She patted the side of the house, her palm making a sound as hollow as his voice against the wood. "How do you want it? Hands here? Yeah, that'll work."

"Please...I'm sorry." A sound of anguish bubbled up from deep in his chest. His entire body was trembling, and his clenched teeth were bared. His panting breaths hissed through them, and she had a feeling he was beyond being able to speak anymore. But then, somehow, he managed a raspy, "Chain...me."

Her heart bled. She didn't understand why or how his condition had changed so he couldn't take care of his needs himself, but he didn't understand it, either, and he was the one who was suffering. She was only making it worse.

"I'll chain you," she lied. "Just stay there, okay?" Casually, she moved to his left, so as not to spook him...and then she flashed to the other side and grabbed his arm, right over the odd swirl on his wrist that looked like a twisted sundial.

"*No!*" Lore threw himself away from her, but she held on, nearly getting her shoulder dislocated. He bucked and spun like a rodeo bull.

"Lore!" Her teeth clanged together so hard her skull vibrated. "Stop!"

The fact that she was touching him and not dead sank in, and he froze as suddenly as he'd exploded into action.

"See?" She could barely hear her voice through the ringing in her ears. "Nothing happened." Except that something *was* happening. A strange energy buzzed beneath her palm. It focused and moved up her arm, tracing lines from her fingers to her shoulder, and she drew a sharp breath when she realized that the energy was settling into her skin in the same pattern as his *dermoire*.

Seductive power filled her entire body, a heady, sexual force that sent tingles into all her erogenous zones. It was as though *every* inch of skin was an erogenous zone, and she wanted to rub on Lore like a big, purring cat.

"Idess," he croaked.

She melted against him, needing to feel his body on hers. His arm came around her, and oh, it felt good to be held like that. "I told you it wouldn't kill me."

His voice scraped gravel. "It did something to you."

"Mmm. I can feel your *dermoire* on my skin. Like it's mine."

He studied her arm, but there was nothing there. "When I was chained, you touched my arm. Did it feel like this?"

"Sort of." She nuzzled his chest, loving how his smooth skin felt against her cheek. "But a lot milder."

"Because of the Bracken Cuffs." His voice was low and rough, but much less so than before.

"You're affected, too."

"Your touch took the edge off, but..."

He pulled back just enough to reveal that the towel had fallen off at some point, and his thick, full erection was still demanding attention. The earthy male scent she associated with him swirled in the air, and with every breath, her body reacted and primed. Her nipples grew tight, her sex hot and wet, her breasts swollen and sensitive.

"Touch me," she whispered. "No holding back anymore."

He hesitated until she took his right hand and centered

it on her chest. For a long, desperate moment, he did nothing. And then, in a very tentative motion, he cupped her
cheek, the pressure so feather-light she barely felt it. His
fingers, the same ones that were capable of killing, were
gentle as he stroked her skin, and his gaze was soft, full of
wonder.

"I've never—" His voice cracked, and he cleared his
throat. "I've never felt a woman like this."

"I've never been touched like this." It was an admission she shouldn't have made, one that left her vulnerable,
but right now she couldn't care.

Once she was sure he wouldn't bolt, she covered his
hand with hers and guided it down her throat, over her
collarbone, and to her breast.

When the heel of his palm skimmed her nipple, they
both groaned.

Through her shirt, he rolled the sensitive bud between
two fingers, once, twice. His heated gaze snapped up to
capture hers, and that fast, the smolder was over and the
flames burst out of control. In a mighty surge, he ripped
off her shirt and backed her up against the side of the
house, his erection prodding the bare skin of her belly.

He nuzzled her throat, nipping and kissing. "Now," he
said against her skin. "I'm going to have you now."

"Yes," she gasped. "No. Not all the way."

Stiffening, he pulled back, and the sorrow in his eyes
nearly brought tears to hers. "I scare you. I'm so sorry,
angel."

She pressed two fingers to his lips. "It's not that. I've
taken a vow of celibacy."

His eyebrows shot up, and then a very naughty smile
turned up his mouth. "I'm dying to be inside you," he said,

"but we can make do with our hands." He licked a hot path along the length of her jugular. "And our tongues."

Lore couldn't freaking believe this. He was touching Idess in a way he'd never touched any female. Even better, when she'd put her hand on him, she'd somehow drained some of the raging need out of him. Oh, he still needed her, but the rage had been diluted, allowing him a measure of control.

God, this was unreal. Surreal. And altogether *too* real. His bare hand was on her skin, caressing her breast. And her palm was rubbing up and down his arm, leaving incredible tingling wakes on his *dermoire*.

More. He needed more of this miracle named Idess.

With no finesse whatsoever, he tore open her pants and yanked them down, along with her silky white panties. He helped her step out of them . . . and then he stayed there. On his knees.

Oh, damn. The junction between her legs . . . beautiful. Breathtaking. Bare. His mouth actually watered as his palms drifted upward, from her ankles to her thighs. When he couldn't stand it anymore, he leaned in to kiss the sweet, satin skin on her inner thigh. Her yelp drifted down to him, and she jerked, but he sank his teeth into her leg, not hard enough to hurt, but enough to hold her where she was.

This was the second time he'd bitten her. He had no idea where the urge was coming from, but it was powerful, animalistic, and he was running with it.

"Lore," she gasped. "I've never . . . maybe we should just . . . you know, use our hands . . ."

Hell, no. Now that he had her like this, the way he'd been fantasizing, he was so going to eat her up. He slipped his tongue between his teeth and made wet circles on her skin. She trembled, and he knew how she felt, because inside he was shaking like a leaf.

Gently, he released his bite hold, but before she could escape, he kissed her soft skin and then dragged his tongue up her inner thigh. He stopped just short of home, kissing, licking, rubbing his cheek on her.

As he played, she got into it more and more, thrusting her fingers through his hair and gently guiding him. Not that he let her. He was going to tease the hell out of this, for as long as they could both stand it.

He nuzzled the outer hills of her flawless sex, and her musky arousal went straight to his cock. His hips rocked upward as though trying to reach her and that tight place he craved. *Down, boy.*

He gently nipped her inner thigh and settled down on his hip. "Straddle me, angel. Get closer. I need to taste you." His experience doing this was ... well, he didn't have any. But he was half sex demon, and those instincts were roaring to the surface, giving him a desire and a confidence he couldn't explain.

She hesitated only for as long as it took her to exhale before she spread her legs more and moved in so that beautiful slit was at mouth level. Tilting his face up, he closed his lips over her. Her breath hitched, and he heard the slap of her palms against the house as she braced herself.

Lore wanted this like he'd wanted very little before, but he didn't rush. He let his tongue sweep back and forth lightly over her swollen sex, savoring her growing anticipation.

"You're a tease," she said, angling her hips to bring her even closer, but he turned away, not giving her what she wanted.

This was his show. She'd ruined him for self-gratification, and though the implications of that were troubling, right now wasn't the time to worry about it. He was going to torture her a little and make her beg.

Though he was definitely getting the better deal out of this situation. Didn't matter how good her orgasm would be, he would be the one to find satisfaction.

He rubbed his face on her thighs, sometimes brushing his lips over her core. Each time, she jerked, and each time, he made her sweat. Finally, when his heart started knocking on his rib cage as though urging him on, he touched his mouth to her naked, hot flesh.

More slowly than he thought he would ever be capable of, he slipped his tongue into her slick valley. She whimpered at the contact, and then went silent as he speared her core. Easing his fingers upward, he penetrated her while he sucked and licked every inch of her pink flesh. Working with a ruthless singlemindedness, he learned her responses and targeted every erogenous zone.

He gave, but he also took, and as his tongue delved in her cream, he swallowed her like a decadent dessert. She was soft and smooth and rich, and fuck, he could do this for days straight.

"Oh, yes," she moaned. "Right...there."

She was close. So he stopped what he'd been doing and dragged his tongue through her cleft. Her cry of frustration made him smile. While she came down off the ledge, he kissed her lightly, always shifting sensation so she couldn't catch it for too long where she needed it.

He wanted to hear her cry his name in her passion. Wanted to know that he'd gotten to her and that she knew *he* was the engineer of her pleasure.

The slow dance of his tongue drove her crazy, had her shifting her hips to chase the pleasure. "Lore, *make me come*."

"Beg."

"Damn you." The words were harsh but the tone was one of extreme arousal and delicious agony.

"Spread yourself for me, Idess."

With a small sound of relief, she slid her palm down her belly and parted her hot flesh. He blew a stream of air over her, and she shuddered. He flicked the tip of his tongue over her clit, and her shudders turned to convulsions of ecstasy. Just as she began to peak, he drew back once more.

"Beg."

"Lore," she sobbed. "Please, Lore. *Please*!"

Victory swept through him. He captured her core with his lips and sucked gently, swirling his tongue at the same time. Her release hit her with so much force that her pleasure actually rocked through him as though they were connected. Her scream—his name—vibrated the patio and her legs shook, and then she was sliding down to her knees in front of him as though they would no longer support her weight.

It took an eternity for Idess to catch her breath. She felt boneless, weak, yet at the same time, a new energy churned inside her. She couldn't describe it, but it came with butterflies in her stomach and warmth in her veins.

The rasp of Lore's breathing filled her ears as she clung

to him. Satiation shifted as a different instinct took over, and she took his hard length in her hand. She squeezed gently as she pushed herself away from his chest. He was watching her with curiosity, but at the same time, need flickered in those dark eyes, a reminder that this wasn't entirely about orgasms just for fun. His very life depended on what she could give him.

Anticipation made her heart race as she began to stroke. His hiss of pleasure joined the rustle of leaves and calls of the birds in the trees.

"Idess," he croaked, "I'm not ... not going to last long. I need it too badly." Closing his eyes, he sucked in a ragged breath and threw his head back. "In fact ... ah, *fuck* ..."

The sun caressed his face as he began to jerk, his big body surging and straining. His come splashed on her hand, and she used it as lubrication to speed up her strokes. A dark rumble of approval issued from his throat, then he was in the throes of orgasm again, this time eyes open and fixed on her with possessive hunger. He growled something that sounded like *mine*, before throwing back his head again and riding out the series of intense spasms.

"Now *that* was amazing," she murmured, when he finally gripped her wrist—with his left hand, she noticed—to stop her.

"Amazing? Try *embarrassing*. I lasted all of two seconds."

She laughed. "Not as embarrassing as things will be if we get caught by your sister out here."

"True." He reached for the towel, and as he was wrapping it around his waist, the dove cooed. "Did that thing watch us the whole time? The little pervert."

"I'm sure he wasn't watching," she said, as she tugged on her pants. "He's just grateful."

Still, Lore glared up at the trees. "So if you and other angels can save lives, why is it that people die?"

"Dying is the natural order of things."

"Okay…but I mean, you hear stories of miracles, of angels saving lives. Why just those few people? Why are they deserving and others aren't? Why does the drunk driver live and the innocent victims die?"

Idess watched the sunlight caress his handsome, angular features like a lover, as though not even nature could resist the temptation of a demon made for sex. "What makes you think that being saved from death means one is deserving?"

"Yeah," he drawled, as he cocked one knee up and draped his arm over it, "that's a crazy question."

She loved it when he got playful, even if his playful was pretty much just sarcasm. "The drunk driver is not given a gift by surviving. He's given more hell on Earth. He's either being punished, or his soul has something more to learn while earthbound. He might even be Primori whose actions lead to new laws or to activism that ultimately saves more lives. But the victims? Their souls are already perfected and ready for their reward."

"At the risk of sounding like a moron…huh?"

She laughed. "Life on Earth truly means little to angels, because we're concerned with the soul, not the body. The soul is the true essence of a person or animal. Life on the other side, in Heaven, is the *true* existence. In fact, those in Heaven see those who are earthbound as the ghosts. The way humans see spirits, as transparent beings, is how those in Heaven see us from there." She waved her hand.

"All of this? It's hell in comparison. But humans don't know that until they 'die.' What you call dying is, to us, birth."

"Then why would angels rescue anyone in those miraculous saves? Why not just let everyone die and go to Heaven?"

Idess had asked those same questions many centuries ago, and though Rami had tried to explain, it took centuries to truly understand. "Because there *is* a purpose to life on earth. Most of the 'miracles' you hear about are Primori who were saved by their Memitim. A child falls from a twenty-story building and survives without a scratch. A woman is found alive beneath the rubble of a building two weeks after hope was lost. A man is hanged and his rope breaks before he is strangled. All Memitim saves. Mine, actually."

Idly, he reached out with his right hand and drew circles on her knee, hesitantly at first, but he smiled at what most wouldn't consider even a simple pleasure. "But is that always the case? You saved the dove. What if he was supposed to die?"

"Then nothing I could have done would have made a difference. When I channel my power into a human or animal, either they are healed or their soul is released. It's kind of like draining them. I drain the life out of them, or I drain the death out of them. Either way, I prevent suffering and restore life…on the earthly plane or in the heavenly one."

"So why didn't you do that with me when I had a knife impaled in my throat?"

"Because I never know which result I'll get. I could have used it on you, only to send your soul away. I couldn't risk it." His loss could have cost her Ascension, but more than that, she would have lost *him*. If his soul was demon, he'd have been gone forever.

Her stomach turned inside out, but strangely, it wasn't because his soul might not be human. No, what had just sickened her was the reality that she'd come to care for him so much that she'd do anything to not lose him. She wanted him to stay with her.

Those same feelings had led to her betrayal of Rami.

Lore seemed to sense her anxiety, and she could have kissed him when he changed the subject. "You've never really talked about your mother. Have you met her?"

"We have no contact until we Ascend, and even then...I don't know." Didn't really matter, she supposed. To Idess, her mother was the human who had raised her with as much love as she had to give.

A breeze kicked up, rustling the leaves, and Lore turned his face into it, closing his eyes as he spoke. "So...how is it that the Grim Reaper and an angel get it on? Is there some sort of pickup bar where they meet and flirt and get drunk and take each other home, or what?"

Idess laughed at that particular image. "I'm not sure about the details, but Rami told me that a handful of angels volunteered to be birth mothers, just as Azagoth volunteered to fall for the good of the world. He can't leave his realm, though, so they go to him."

"How many baby mamas are there?"

"According to Rami, there are seventy-two. He was a scholar of human religions, and he was always convinced that many traditions and beliefs are loosely based in fact."

"Like the seventy-two-virgin thing for Muslim martyrs?"

"Exactly. That number came from somewhere, and

Rami believes it is based on Memitim mothers. He also believes that 'virgin' is actually a mistranslation and should read 'angels.'" She snorted. "As if any man would get seventy-two angels as a reward."

"How about one angel?" Lore's voice was husky and thick, a caress that made her shiver with appreciation.

"I'm not technically an angel yet," she said, "so I don't think I count."

He touched her face. "You're looking forward to going, aren't you?"

The question dove right to her gut and stirred it up even more, because for the first time since learning what she was and what her reward for good service would be, she was actually wavering.

"I can't wait to get out of here." Really. She couldn't. As she'd told Lore, Earth was hell. There was suffering and pain and cruelty.

And hot men like Lore.

Hurt flashed in his eyes, and he shoved to his feet. "Yeah, sucks here. Nothing worth wanting to hang around for."

"Lore, I didn't mean—"

"S'okay. We'd better get ready to go hunting. Sin will be here any minute."

She stood and reached for him. "Lore."

Ignoring her, he strode into the house, leaving her feeling more wretched than she'd been since the day she betrayed Rami.

By the time Lore dressed and outfitted himself with weapons, it was time for Sin to show. And Idess was back.

She'd flashed from his deck after he'd left her out there, obviously to go home and change, because now she was wearing jeans, sexy, calf-high boots, and a funky, multicolor Versace sweatshirt.

Let's see you wear that *in Heaven.* Yeah, he was a little bitter, though he had no idea why. What had he expected when he'd asked her a question he didn't want the answer to? A declaration of everlasting love and a willingness to give up everything to stay with him? Just because they'd masturbated each other a couple of times? Just because she was the only female on the planet not related to him who could touch his arm and not keel over?

Geez, Idess could have at least made it sound like leaving him on earth would mean a minute or two of sniffles.

Right, because she'll be so upset to say good-bye to a demon who practically demanded that she get on her knees and be a whore for him.

Fuck. With an extra-firm shove of his trench knife into its belt sheath, he made the mental slide into assassin mode. He couldn't afford emo whining when he was hunting.

But he really did feel like a piece of shit for how he'd treated her earlier, so he downshifted just a little. "I wouldn't have taken you for a lover of designer fashion," he said gruffly.

"I'm not. But I try to buy local when I can." She lifted one leg to show off her boot. "Italian leather. Love it."

He did, too. The way it hugged her calves. Made her legs go on forever. He let out an appreciative whistle as he dragged his gaze up. "Where do you get your money, anyway?"

She shrugged. "I think about it, and it's there."

"Must be nice." Nice to not have to kill people for it.

So much for assassin mode. God, Idess was hell on his discipline.

She nodded vehemently. "It is."

The front door crashed open. Whirling, Lore put himself in front of Idess, a dagger in one hand and a pistol in the other.

"Hey, there, brother," Wraith said, in a deceptively calm drawl. Deceptive, because the demon's body language—his clenched fists, coiled body, and red-flecked gold eyes—said he was ready to cause some damage. And oh, great, Kynan was with him, looking even more pissed off than Wraith.

Instantly, Idess came around to put herself between Lore and Kynan. Not happening. All of Lore's protective instincts came to bear, and with a snarl, he pushed her behind him again. She might not want to stay with him, but until she got her damned wings, she was his, and no one was going to fuck with her.

She poofed right back to where she'd been, damn her.

"Kynan, you shouldn't be here," she said, standing in the middle of the living room, hands on hips.

"No?" He glared at Lore. "I'm what he wants, right? So here I am. Give Wraith the baby."

"I don't have Shade's kid."

Wraith bared his fangs. "You'd better, because if you've left him with anyone other than Mary fucking Poppins, there won't be enough left of you to fill a juice glass."

"You deaf? I don't have him." Lore holstered his weapons before he killed his brother. Sure, he wanted to kill Kynan, but he'd do that with his bare hand.

"He's telling the truth." Not backing down at all, Idess folded her arms over her chest. "I've been with him."

Wraith snarled. "Even when he was being tortured? Because he looks pretty damned good for a tortured man."

"I was healed, you idiot."

"Call me that again." Grinning, Wraith flexed his fingers. "Seriously."

Lore stepped forward. "Idiot."

Kynan came at him. Lore angled his right side away, not ready to kill the bastard yet, and the move cost him. Cost him a fist to the face. Pain burst behind his eyes, and he wheeled around, too angry to think, and caught the human with his right hand—which got him a jab to the ribs. What the fuck? Why hadn't the guy dropped dead?

... *I drain the death out of them.* Idess's words popped into his mind just before the right hook that laid him out.

Lore came to his feet before Kynan could kick him, and Jesus, Wraith was grinning, and Idess was watching with her arms crossed, foot tapping, and just looking annoyed. Obviously, without his power, Lore was no mortal threat to Kynan. And Kynan was out to cause pain, not death.

Making it all even more fun was the fact that no matter how hard Lore tried to cripple Kynan, something always went wrong. He couldn't land a single punch or kick. Kynan was merciless, using Lore's failures against him.

Lore took a nice beating before finally Idess flashed between them and heaved them apart with her incredible strength.

"Enough!"

Panting, he and Kynan glared at each other. Wraith stepped forward. "If you two are done—"

"We're not," they said simultaneously.

"For now, you are," he growled. "We have a kid to

find." He yanked Lore to him. Lore took a swing, lost his balance, and stumbled without ever striking his brother. "I'm charmed, dickhead. Just like Kynan. You can't hurt me. And apparently you can't kill Ky with your touch. Guess we don't have to worry about you anymore."

"That's not true," Idess said. "I believe it's temporary. His ability to kill should return soon."

Lore hoped that would be before the deadline. His assassin-bond throbbed, marking time that was clipping along in fast-forward.

"How did that happen?" Wraith asked.

"I drained him."

Wraith arched an eyebrow at her. "I'll bet you did."

She rolled her eyes. "Not like that." Might have been believable, too, if she hadn't pinked up, because she *had* drained him like that.

Wraith gave a dubious snort, and Idess shook her head. "I still can't believe that *you* saved the world."

"I know, right?" Wraith turned back to Lore. "So where's Rade?"

"I told you. I don't have him. But we have a lead. Possible fallen angel named Rariel. Sin's hunting him right now." Lore checked his watch, and his heart tripped. She was five minutes late. Sin was *never* late without calling.

Lore expected Wraith to scoff, to call him a liar, to hit him. Anything but nod. "You can prove it."

It wasn't a question, and Lore scowled. "Not really."

"Yes," he said, "you can." Suddenly, Wraith was behind him, his thick arm wrapped around Lore's neck, and Lore was . . . well, he wasn't sure where he was. His memories flipped through his mind like a shuffled deck of cards, and then he was standing in his house again, a little dizzy, and Wraith was several feet away.

"Fuck me," Wraith muttered. "He's telling the truth."

"What the hell just happened?" Lore shouted.

Kynan smirked. "You just got a taste of Wraith's mind-fuck."

Ah. Lore hadn't expected Wraith's gift for getting inside heads to be so intrusive and unsettling. "You dick."

"Seriously?" Wraith asked. "That's all you got? Dick? Idiot? Your sister pops better insults than you do."

"She's your sister, too," Lore pointed out, more to gauge Wraith's reaction than anything.

Wraith grinned. "E says she's like a female version of me. Cool."

"No, *not* cool," Lore growled. "So now you know I didn't snatch the kid, you're going to haul ass out of my face, right?"

"Slow down there, Mario," Wraith said. "You're still planning to kill Kynan."

Idess crossed to Lore. "No, he's not."

Inside Lore's chest, something shriveled a little at her defense of him, because he would still do what he had to in order to save his sister. Yes, Idess would lose her wings and have to stay on earth. But she wouldn't die. And...she'd be able to stay with him.

"I was in Lore's head, Halo. I know what he was thinking." Wraith's eyes went wide with sudden knowledge. "Sin will die if you don't. Ah, fuck."

Kynan scowled at Wraith. "Are you serious?"

Lore nodded. "Do you think I'm stupid enough to kill you for shits and grins? Not that it wouldn't be fun," he added.

Kynan snorted. "Do you think it's this Rariel guy who wants me dead?"

"Him . . . and Roag."

"Yeah," Wraith said. "E mentioned that. Shade thinks you're working together."

"Just when I thought Shade couldn't think any worse of me," Lore muttered.

"We've got to find Rariel," Kynan said, fucking king of State the Obvious.

A cell phone buzzed, and Wraith dug into his pocket. "'Sup, E?" Wraith listened for a second, and hung up with a strained curse. "We gotta go, Ky. It's Gem."

Kynan lost all the color in his face. "What's wrong? Is it the baby?"

Baby?

"She was attacked," Wraith said. "She was attacked *inside* the hospital."

Twenty-one

Idess flashed Lore to UG's parking lot. They ran inside, where at least two dozen spirits were in a frenzy, attacking the walls, wailing, and cowering in corners. Eidolon was standing at the triage desk, and the second he saw Lore, his eyes went crimson and he made like a charging tiger.

"No!" Idess rushed forward and slammed her palms into his chest. "Lore didn't attack Shade's mate, and he doesn't have the baby. Wraith will be here in a moment. He'll confirm it."

Speak of the demon, the Harrowgate shimmered, and Wraith darted out of it, right behind Kynan. Kynan, as a human, shouldn't have been able to travel through the Harrowgates unless he was unconscious, but his charmed status protected him from certain death.

"What happened? Where's Gem?"

"Exam one," Eidolon said. "She was found unconscious and bleeding from a head wound in the staff lounge."

"Did the Haven spell go down?" Wraith asked.

"Nope."

Idess sucked in a breath. "It was the ghosts."

"Mother. Fuck." Wraith snarled. "This is the one place that should be safe from the sonofabitch who attacked Runa, and we have fucking ghosts to worry about. Are Serena and Stewie still here?"

Eidolon nodded. "They're with Tay in my office."

"I'm taking them home. Not letting them out of my sight." He jerked his thumb at Lore. "Big bro here wasn't responsible for Runa and Rade. Some asswipe named Rariel is."

Eidolon let out a long breath. "You'll need to tell Shade. He won't listen to me."

"Where is he?"

"He's at the cave with Runa and the boys. It's too risky to have them here when we have diseased wargs coming in."

Diseased wargs?

"He should be safe then. I'm outta here." Wraith took off down the hall at a jog, running right through one of the spirits, who cried out loud enough for Idess to wince.

Eidolon scrubbed a hand over his face and turned to Lore. "Where have you been?"

"Oh, hey, don't worry about apologizing for thinking I attacked my sister-in-law and stole my nephew or anything."

A muscle in Eidolon's jaw twitched, and Idess had a feeling he was trying to keep his temper in check.

"Your dagger was buried in her gut, and the message given to her was to turn over Kynan. What were we supposed to think? You *are* trying to kill the guy. For money."

"For his sister," Idess said tightly. She was tired of

these guys' blaming Lore, hating him, fighting him. "Sin will die if Lore doesn't do it."

"Fuck." Eidolon's dark eyes, so like Lore's, cut to his brother. "How do you plan to get out of it?" The doctor's voice was cool, professional, and just flat enough to give away how hard he was trying to hide his concern for his siblings' situations.

"We need to find Rariel. He's got to be behind the contract. Kill him, and the contract is void."

"And what about the ghosts?" Eidolon asked. "This is all too much of a coincidence to think it isn't related."

Idess tore her attention away from two spirits near the Harrowgate who were clawing at the posts, their desperate attempts to get the gate to work heartbreaking. "It's Roag. He's terrifying the spirits." She scanned the room, and sure enough, at the junction of two hallways, the dark phantom lurked, still wrapped in a cloak, menace emanating from him in a roiling cloud.

As Idess moved toward the demon, the Harrowgate flashed, and suddenly, a new sensation washed over her. Familiar. But warped, like a favorite song playing on the wrong speed. Her skin wanted to crawl right off her.

"Does the Harrowgate do that a lot? Flash, but nothing comes out?"

"Lately, yeah," Eidolon said. "It's weird."

The familiarity washed over her again, and tears sprang to her eyes. Lore grabbed her. "Idess? Cookie? What's wrong?"

"I don't... I can't explain it. It feels like Rami. And pain."

"Oh, dear sister," came an all-too-familiar voice behind her. "How I love causing you pain."

Lore caught Idess as she collapsed. She'd gone as white as the ghosts she'd talked about, and though she struggled weakly to stand on her own again, she didn't take her eyes off Rariel.

But...*dear sister*?

Lore kept Idess close, holding her tight against him. "Where is Rade?"

At the infant's name, Eidolon stiffened. "This is the fuck who took my nephew?"

"No," Idess whispered. "It can't be. Rami...no."

"Rami?" Lore gritted out. "As in, the brother who Ascended?"

"She told you about me?" Smiling, the male jammed his hands into the pockets of his jeans. "I'm flattered."

In Lore's arms, Idess trembled. "How is this possible?"

"Obviously, baby sister, I fell. Because of you."

"How? Why?" She shrugged off Lore's grip but remained next to him.

"Dumb bitch," he hissed, and Lore had to hold himself back from braining the fucker, Haven spell or no. "You betrayed me. You *ruined* me."

Staff members began to close in, all looking expectantly at Eidolon as though waiting for an order.

"What I did," Idess said, "was terrible. I'll do whatever you want to make up for it. Just don't hurt the child."

Both Lore and Eidolon simultaneously growled, "Where is he?"

"The whelp is...safe. Relatively." Rami rolled his shoulders, making his muscles bunch tight beneath his black tee. "Your sister, however..."

The air exploded from Lore's lungs in a painful rush. "What did you do to her?"

Rami bared his teeth. "Fun with razor wire. Now I have a cave to visit." He paused, offering a fake frown at Eidolon, whose expression had iced over. "Oh, you thought I didn't know about Shade's cave or how to get there? Roag is a treasure chest of information."

Lore launched at the fallen angel. Rami snapped his fingers in drama queen fashion, and Lore's hand closed on empty air. "How can he flash out of here?"

"He can't!" Idess raced toward the Harrowgate. "But he can go invisible—" The gate closed, and she skidded to a stop. "He's gone. Son of a bitch, he's gone."

Eidolon fumbled for his cell phone. His fingers shook as he mashed the buttons. "Come on, Shade. Answer. Answer…" He waited, and then, "Shade! Get out of there. Don't hang up…*fuck*!" He dialed again, pacing madly and cursing. Then, with a vicious snarl, he hurled his phone against the wall. Bits of plastic and electronic guts exploded into the air.

"We have to go to them," Lore said.

"I know." Eidolon ducked behind the triage desk and hit a button. "Medics to the ER, Code Green."

Almost instantly, two male paramedics jogged through a door near the parking lot exit, bags slung over their shoulders. The blond male with silver eyes stopped in front of Eidolon, who gestured for them to follow.

Tears shimmered in Idess's eyes. "This isn't your fault," Lore said as he brushed his lips over hers. He took her hand in his gloved one and entered the gate with Eidolon and the medics. The gate opened up in a steamy jungle, and Eidolon took off at a sprint down a sun-dappled trail.

They followed at a dead run. Branches slapped at their

faces and roots and vines seemed to reach up out of the ground to grab them, but they didn't slow down, kept running until they reached a waterfall set into a huge rock face. Eidolon slipped around it, reached into a hole, and a huge section of the wall rumbled and moved aside.

"Shade!" Eidolon's panicked shout joined the blood-curdling sounds of battle coming from inside the cave.

They charged through a strangely modern kitchen to a huge bedroom, where Shade was grappling with Rami. Rami's blows rained down hard and fast, while Shade's powerful punches seemed to be a minor inconvenience for the fallen angel. Blood—most of it Shade's, as far as Lore could tell—coated the floor and smeared the walls. In one corner, a huge, toffee-furred warg crouched protectively over an infant. Nearby, Sin was a motionless lump of blood and bruises.

He'd seen her like that before, and his head rocked back as the memory bitch-slapped his brain.

Lore didn't recognize the woman he'd slammed into the wall. She lay on the floor, bleeding and curled in on herself. Bloodlust roared through his veins, inflaming his already burning skin. His arm was on fire, the strange new marks glowing.

Kill.

The woman on the floor had the same marks. She whimpered.

Kill.

Cold sweat broke out over his body, but it didn't stop the burn. The female whimpered again.

Run.

Lore staggered backward, punch-drunk with memories. Through the fog of the fading vision, he saw Eidolon and the medics launch into battle, ripping Shade away from the fallen angel and lending some fresh muscle to the fight. Outnumbered, Rami snarled and poofed out of there. It all seemed so distant, when the memory of the day he'd gained his tats and gifts still clung to the walls of his mind.

Sin. He'd not remembered any of it. Until now. God, he'd failed her. Over and over, and he'd never be able to make it up to her. He sank to his knees next to her, taking the painful crack to his kneecaps as an inadequate penance. Idess and the blond medic joined him.

In the background, his brothers were speaking in harsh words and soft murmurs…and then Runa, now in her human form, was kneeling beside Sin.

Lore gripped his sister's shoulder. Her arms were tucked awkwardly beneath her, and she was strangely hunched up. Moaning, she shifted. Beneath her, cradled against her stomach, was the second baby.

Tears streamed down Runa's cheeks as she gathered the infant to her chest. "Thank you," she sobbed. "You saved his life."

"Yeah." Sin's sarcastic voice was a pained whisper. "I'm a hero." She eased onto her side, and Lore's gut twisted at the sight of her bloody wrists, which were bound with razor wire cutting deeply into her flesh. He resisted the urge to rub his own wrists in sympathy.

The medic cursed, and Sin's surprised gaze flickered to him. "Con," she murmured. "Couldn't stay away, huh?"

Con grunted and moved his gloved hands over Sin's body with practiced confidence. "What hurts?"

"Razor wire is not so comfortable," she rasped.

"Just hold still. I need Doc E's help to remove it."

Lore cursed. "Sin, I'm sorry—"

"Shut up," she said, but there was no anger in her voice. "I fucked up and let that angel scum catch me off-guard. He brought me here so I could watch my nephews die." Wincing, she shifted. "Beneath me. The dagger."

Carefully, Lore eased his hand under her, came away with his Gargantua dagger...which was covered with blood. "Is this—"

"Yeah." She offered a shaky smile. "I stabbed the fucker. Now go get him." Her smile faded. "Bro, you're running out of time."

She wasn't talking about Rariel, and he knew it. His slave-bond throbbed with such a rapid beat that the pain was almost constant now. Either Rariel died, or Kynan would have to, and he had barely twenty-four hours to make someone's death happen.

"I know, Sin. I've got it handled." Lore locked gazes with Con. "Take care of her."

"Don't worry."

Lore stood. The other medic and Eidolon were working on Shade as he leaned against a Saint Andrew's cross—and that was when Lore noticed all the...interesting...accoutrements lining the walls. Furry cuffs, soft leather flogs and masks...and yep, this was way TMI. He couldn't quite picture dainty Runa, who sat quietly on the bed, watching Shade with worried eyes and holding their sons tight, holding a flog.

"How's Sin?" Eidolon didn't look up from the massive bleeder in Shade's thigh.

"Vitals are good," Con replied. "Injuries are mostly contusions and shallow lacerations, but she's got razor wire embedded in her wrists. Capillary refill is satisfactory."

Eidolon gave a sharp nod. "The blades probably missed the major vessels."

Relieved that Sin wasn't in immediate danger, Lore turned to Idess, but she'd disappeared. He found her in the living room-slash-home theater, head bowed, arms wrapped around herself.

"Hey," he said, pulling her into his arms. God, she felt good against him. Like she belonged. Like as long as they stayed like that, everything would be okay.

"My brother." She heaved a great, shuddering sob. "How could this have happened? How could I have let this happen?"

Lore's heart cracked wide open. "It's not your fault, angel. He's not the guy you once knew. He's enraged and insane—" He broke off as the image of Sin bleeding on the floor of their grandparents' home came back to him. His voice became a husky rasp. "Everyone's okay. We got here in time."

She shook her head so hard her ponytail slapped his arm. "But, Rade. Oh, Lore . . . if he hurts Rade—"

"He won't," Lore swore. "We'll nail his ass to the wall. My dagger tasted his blood. You can flash us to him."

"Good," she whispered. "That's good."

The crack of boots on the floor announced two arrivals. Keeping Idess tucked protectively against him, Lore turned.

Eidolon snatched a satellite phone from the end table near the couch. Shade stood a few feet from Lore, still covered in blood and his gaze dark. "So this Rariel guy took Rade." It wasn't a question, and when Lore nodded, Shade swallowed. "I thought *you* had him."

"You were wrong."

More swallowing. And, no apology. "But you *were* hired to kill Ky."

"Hired" wasn't the right word. "Forced" was closer, but right now wasn't the time to split hellrat hairs. "Yes."

Shade's hands formed fists, and Lore set Idess aside and braced himself for a blow. "E said if you don't do it, Sin will die." He spoke in a hushed tone, for which Lore was grateful.

"Yeah."

"We can't let either happen." Shade's tone was dead. Flat. But at least he had seen the truth of the situation and wanted to help save their sister.

"That's why Idess and I are going to kill Rariel." Next to him, Idess went taut as a garrote wire, and shit, she had better be on board with killing the bastard. "You said his name is Rami. Why is he calling himself Rariel?"

"We're given new names upon Ascension." She hung her head, and her shoulders slumped. "I still can't believe this."

Shade grabbed a black biker jacket off a hook buried in the cave wall. "I'm going with you."

"You can't," Idess said. "I can only flash one person to his location."

"Hell's fucking bells." Shade's nasty curse echoed through the chamber. "I want to know how he found the cave." He threw down his jacket, knocking a gold rattle off the couch. Almost reverently, he picked up the toy, which was engraved with the name "Rade."

Eidolon replaced the sat phone in its cradle. "Roag." He hesitated before adding quietly, "It's what I was trying to tell you just before Runa was attacked, and then a little while ago when I called."

Tension winged through the air, and Lore held his

breath, unsure if Shade was going to strike out at Eidolon for Shade's own stubborn refusal to listen to Eidolon's warning.

The storm passed when Shade snarled. "That burned-up, slimy skullfucker." He clutched the rattle so hard Lore expected it to snap. But at least he hadn't turned on E. "He's as good as dead, and he's still fucking with us."

"Who is fucking with us?" Runa stood at the entrance to the living room. Her caramel hair hung in limp ropes around her pale face, but Lore suspected she was nowhere near as fragile as she appeared.

Shade went to her. "It's not important. You need to take care of the boys, and I'll handle this."

"The hell you will!" She jabbed him in the shoulder. "My son is in danger, and I want to know everything."

"Runa—"

"*Everything.*"

Shade sighed. "E says it's Roag. He has something to do with all of this."

Runa lost what little color she'd had, but her voice was steady and deadly as she ground out, "I want him dead. Painfully dead."

Idess crossed the room, and when she stood before Runa, she took the female's hand. "I will make this right for you," she swore softly. "I swear to you all, I will somehow make this right."

"Idess," Lore said, "I told you. This isn't your fault."

"But it is. My brother wants revenge on me, and somehow he's managed to draw all of you into it."

"If this is all true," Eidolon began, "I'd like to know how Roag and Rariel hooked up."

"I don't know how they managed to hook up after Roag

was cursed," Lore said, "but they knew each other before that. Rariel was there when Roag hired me to kill you."

That earned him a glower from everyone but Idess. "Hey. I said I was sorry." Actually, he didn't think he had, but maybe they wouldn't remember. It was probably time to go before they did. He checked his watch. They had an hour before they'd have to hunt down Rami.

"Idess, we gotta go. The devil's hour is coming, and we need to prepare."

She turned to Eidolon. "Can you send Kynan or Tayla to Lore's place with some weapons treated in *qeres*?"

"You got it."

"*Qeres?*" Lore asked. "Some sort of antiangel poison?"

She nodded. "It's what affected me so badly when Tayla shot me. It'll incapacitate Rami just as effectively."

"I don't want him incapacitated," Shade barked. "I want him dead."

Closing her eyes, Idess swallowed. Before she could say anything in defense of Rami that Shade and Runa might not appreciate, Lore grabbed her hand. "Come on, Cookie. Flash me to my house. We have a battle to prepare for."

Idess was still numb when they reached Lore's place. They stood in the middle of the living room, and when Lore attempted to pull her into his arms, she tore away, unable to stomach kindness after what she'd done.

"Hey. This is not your—"

"Stop saying that! You don't know. You don't understand what I did!"

"Then tell me," he said mildly. "Tell me what you

could have done that's so horrible that he got booted out of Heaven and went batnuts insane."

"This is serious, Lore. I betrayed him. And now he's earthbound and out to hurt me and everyone I'm involved with." She looked down, too ashamed to even look at Lore.

"Hey." He caught her chin and forced her to meet his gaze. "Even if you're right, the thing with Roag is definitely not your fault. The demon was off his rocker before any of this happened. He was just waiting for someone to help him get his revenge."

A knock at the door announced Tayla and Kynan's arrival. They entered, and for once, Kynan didn't look as if he wanted to kill Lore. Tayla carried a crossbow, and Kynan had a broadsword. He handed it to Lore hilt-first.

"The sword and two crossbow bolts have been coated with *qeres*," Kynan said. "I wish we had more, but The Aegis has a very limited supply."

"Why is that?" Lore asked.

"The recipe has been lost. What little we have is *all* we have."

"So use it wisely." Tayla handed the crossbow to Idess. "You sure we can't go?"

"Positive." In a lot of ways, Idess was glad for that. Fewer people for her brother to hurt. Fewer witnesses to her shame. "I can only flash with one person."

"Then take me," Kynan said. "It's me he wants. Trade me for Rade. I can handle myself once you get Rade out of there."

Idess sighed. "I can't risk you like that. And ultimately, he wants you dead, but not by his hand. His goal is to ruin me, which will only happen if you're killed by someone other than him."

"Damn," he breathed.

She nodded at the appropriateness of the curse. "Does The Aegis know what's going on?"

"The Sigil knows I'm in danger—" Kynan glowered at Lore "—but we're considering this a fallen-angel threat. Because if this asshole is dead, I don't have to worry about you, right?"

"You should still worry," Lore muttered, and Idess cleared her throat. He gave her a sheepish look. "Yeah, yeah. Once the contract is void, you have nothing to fear from me."

Kynan snorted. "I was never afraid."

"Bullshit. You've been on the verge of pissing yourself."

Idess half-expected their *heraldi* to start burning, so when Kynan laughed, she thought she was hearing things. "If I didn't hate you so much, I think I could actually like you."

"I'd probably like it better if you kept hating me."

Kynan's lopsided grin was a traffic-stopper. "You're just mad because I got the girl."

"No," Lore said, shifting his gaze to Idess with such hot possession that her breath clogged in her throat, "I got the one I want."

Heart pounding and face heating, she cleared her throat. "If you two are finished, we should get ready for what we have to do." She wasn't going to say, "Kill Rami," because she prayed it wouldn't come to that. Maybe she could bargain with him. Or save him somehow. Because destroying him could very well destroy her. "How is Gem, by the way?"

"Like I always said, she's got a hard head," Kynan said,

the affection in his gravelly voice unmistakable. "Apparently, when she bent over to pick up something on the floor, the coffee maker fell off the counter and beaned her."

It hadn't "fallen," Idess was sure. One of the ghosts had pushed it, probably at Roag's direction.

"We'd better go," Tayla said. "I want to check in with Shade and Runa. Oh, and E said to tell you that Sin is fine. She's at UG getting checked out."

"No doubt she's loving that," Lore said wryly.

"Well, I heard a lot of cussing in the background..." Tayla shrugged. "You guys be careful. And please, get Rade back."

"We will," Lore swore. "If it's the last thing I do, I will deliver that child to Shade."

Tayla nodded, and then she and Kynan were out of there.

"This is going to be dangerous," Idess said. "Even with the *qeres* weapons, Rami has an advantage, Lore. As a fallen angel, he's drawing on the power of Sheoul. I'm not a true angel, and I'm much weaker than he is."

"Is that why you were affected so badly by the crossbow bolt?"

"Exactly." She absently rubbed her sternum. "But really, you get a hole the size of a fist blasted through you, and see how you fare."

"I'll pass." He pulled off his gloves and tossed them to the kitchen table. "You poofed right after that. What if he does the same?"

"He won't. I have a trick up my sleeve."

His jacket went next, leaving his arms mouth-wateringly bare in his short-sleeved T-shirt. "Which is?"

"Powdered Benedictine monk wine."

"Monk...wine?" He paused in the middle of unbuckling the leather weapons harness strapped across his chest. "As in, wine made by monks?"

She nodded. "Wine made in a secret chamber at Buckfast Abbey in England is blessed by monks and dried. Once powdered, it can be used as a temporary antidematerialization weapon against fallen angels." And angels, which was why it was kept under lock and key. If it were to fall into the wrong hands, it could be used to immobilize God's army of angels during the Final Battle.

"How temporary?"

"It'll give us only a few minutes."

"That sucks, but it's better than nothing." Lore laid out his harness and systematically checked each weapon. If they weren't going after her brother, she'd actually think his efficiency and confidence when handling the weapons was incredibly sexy. "So where do you think he'll be?"

"Sheoul. The Forbidden Abyssal." Her voice was stronger than she felt on the inside.

Lore's foul curse scorched the very air. "That's the *nice* name for it. Do you know where it is? *What* it is?"

"I've heard of it." Who *hadn't* heard of it?

"It's known as the Butchers' Playground." His voice was grim. "It's said that nothing is off-limits there. There are no rules except that nothing can die quickly."

It was also one of the few places in Sheoul that angels couldn't enter at all. Some claimed that Satan himself liked to hang out there. No doubt it was a great vacation spot for someone like him.

"That's why I know he'll be there. He was never one for half-measures, and if he's gone evil, he's gone *evil*."

"Dammit," Lore muttered. "Since it's in Sheoul, you can't flash us there, and if the rumors are true, the nearest Harrowgate is days away. This could throw a King Kong–sized wrench into things. Twenty-four hours, and game over for me, angel."

Idess glanced at the clock on the wall. They had forty-five minutes. And even if Rami wasn't in the Playground, if they didn't find him within an hour, they'd be screwed for another twenty-three.

Which put them dangerously close to Lore's deadline.

She looked at the demon standing in front of her, a demon who had more honor and love in his heart than many of the humans she'd kept safe over the centuries. Fate had dealt him a bad hand, and he'd been paying for it for over a hundred and thirty years.

Fate had also made him Primori, which meant she had to protect him. He couldn't face Rami in the Playground alone.

And he wouldn't. If this was a test, she would pass—but she'd have to cheat to do it. She could go with him, but only if she was no longer an angel.

"Lore?"

"Yeah?"

Licking her lips, she placed her palm on his chest, right over his assassin mark, and then dragged her hand down. Slowly. By the time she reached the waistband of his jeans, his nostrils were flaring, as though taking in the scent of the arousal that had sparked in her the moment she touched him.

"Make love to me."

Twenty-two

"Idess..." Her name came out in a strangled rush of air.

"Please."

Taking a step back was the hardest thing he'd ever done. "Now isn't the time." What was he saying? Any time was *the time*. Especially since they could both die and this might be the last chance for having sex with anyone.

"It's the perfect time."

"Guess the Butchers' Playground thing isn't a big deal if you're looking death in the face, huh?"

"Guess not."

"But...your vow. What happens if you break it?"

She stepped into him again. "Some sort of penance. Nothing I can't handle."

Common sense told him the penalty for an angel's breaking a vow of celibacy wasn't going to be minor, and he couldn't allow her to suffer no matter how badly he ached for her. But when he tried to back away, she gripped his hips and pressed the entire long, sexy length of her body against him. Still, he might have had a chance against her...until she awkwardly palmed his crotch.

Tenderness flooded him. She wanted him but didn't know how to initiate sex. Not that he was so great at that either. Neither one of them was technically a virgin, but emotionally? He so was.

He'd fucked. He'd been sucked. But he'd never made love to anyone.

He looked down at her, into her guileless eyes that even now gleamed with a sort of hopeless honesty. She'd resigned herself to something—probably their death—and she was prepared to face it.

Her strength humbled him. Devastated him. Made him want to make her his no matter what the cost.

"Mine," he growled, as he swept her up into his arms and strode to the bedroom. He had no idea what kind of caveman instinct had come over him, but it had hijacked him and was now in control and the only thing he could do was let it fly on autopilot. And it wasn't as though Idess was fighting him.

Her chest heaved with panting breaths, her skin was flushed with arousal, and the outline of her nipples against her top left tiny peaks that begged for his touch. His tongue. Right through the fabric.

Mine.

Unable to bear the feel of clothes against his skin for one more second, he laid her on the bed and peeled off his T-shirt, but before he could unbutton his pants, she was on her knees on the mattress, slapping his hands out of the way.

"I get to do this."

Far be it for him to argue. Plus, it was really hot, the way the pink tip of her tongue slipped between her lips as she worked his zipper. His cock sprang free, didn't even have time to enjoy the shock of the cool air before her hot hand closed around it.

He dragged a ragged breath into his laboring lungs. "Idess..."

Her mouth closed over the head of his cock and he damned near swallowed his tongue. She applied suction that made his eyes roll back in his head, and then she released him with a soft pop.

"I have *so* been wanting to do that," she said, in a morning-rough murmur that grabbed him right between the legs more tightly than her hand ever could.

She looked up at him with a sleepy, seductive gaze, and damn, this was something right out of a skin flick. With a slinky smile, she took him into the warm, wet depths of her mouth again. Oh, damn, this was amazing. So amazing that his knees went rubbery as she sucked him. When she paid special attention to swirling her tongue in the slit, catching the crystal beads that formed there, he had to bite his cheek to keep from shouting.

One hand caressed his balls, her thumb stroking the seam between them. She blew a cool draft of air over his damp shaft, and he shivered with pleasure. She was an evil tease, but he wouldn't have it any other way.

Slowly, she dragged the flat of her tongue down his length, all the way to his balls. His muscles tensed, his come building like steam in his sac, made hotter when she sucked his testicles into her mouth and bounced them on her tongue.

"Idess," he groaned.

He felt her lips stretch into a smile, and she began a wicked hum that sent a shock of stimulation from his groin to his skull. His head swam and his skin tightened. His hearing became more acute, his sense of smell sharper. Colors were brighter, his emotions more intense.

Her mouth slid back up his cock, her teeth scraping gently and nibbling as she went. How had she learned this magic?

She took him deep, so deep he felt the back of her throat... and then she swallowed. Jesus, she swallowed him, creating a maelstrom of sensation at the tip of his cock as her finger and thumb ringed the base and pumped up and down, and the other hand squeezed his balls.

"Stop, oh, shit... stop..." He couldn't hold on, couldn't resist the sensations turning him inside out. He drove his hands into her hair, but as the climax edged closer, riding on a razor edge, he jerked his right hand away. He knew it wouldn't affect her, but a hundred years of paranoia wasn't going to be extinguished overnight.

Without breaking her rhythm, she took his hand and returned it to her scalp. For the first time, he truly realized how special she was. He could let go... she *wanted* him to let go. To be free. To be with her.

She sucked upward as her hand rolled his sac. His *dermoire* writhed, the power burning from his shoulder to his hand, but Idess was safe. Unaffected. The knowledge and freedom condensed all his emotions, all sensations, concentrating them so fully he couldn't believe his feet were still on the ground. His come boiled up his shaft, shot in a fiery stream. Surging, losing control, he pumped into her mouth. She took everything and kept licking and sucking until he was so sensitive he had to push her away.

Her smile as she looked up at him was one of satisfaction and affection. Desire burned there, too, and a heartbeat later she was shedding her pants.

"It's true," she said huskily.

"What is?"

She shot him a sultry grin as she lay back on the mattress and drove her hand inside her panties. He nearly came again. "The stories about your breed's semen. It's an aphrodisiac. Milder than I'd have guessed, but...mmm...this is amazing..."

"My human half probably affects the potency—" He broke off as she kicked her head back and began to pleasure herself. "Then again, maybe not."

"Do you want to watch? You know, watch me come?"

"Fuck, yeah..." He had to clear his throat because he was about to choke on his lust.

"Right...now...oh, yes..." Her body came off the freaking bed as she climaxed, and if this wasn't the hottest thing he'd ever seen, he didn't know what was.

Diving onto the bed, he gripped her thighs and spread them. The scent of her feminine arousal made his head swim and his mouth water and he wasn't waiting another second. He closed his mouth over her sex, over the silk that covered it, and licked her, right through the fabric.

Whimpers of pleasure accompanied frantic rolls of her hips as she ground against his mouth. She came hard, twice, before his impatience had him tearing away her underwear and plunging his tongue inside her. Sweet honey filled his mouth and clogged his brain. The taste of her was a drug, and he was instantly addicted, would need this every day. Twice a day. Morning and night. Maybe noon, too.

Her orgasms came one after another, piling up until he

lost count and until she tugged on his hair to drag him up to her. Dazed and sated like a big, well-fed cat, she watched him prowl up her body, and then she welcomed him between her legs.

His cock was rock hard as the blunt tip probed her entrance, but he wasn't ready yet. He wanted this to be special. Wanted to savor every moment.

Kissing her, he peeled off her sweatshirt. He did it slowly, taking his time, fumbling a little because his fingers trembled. Her hands were still tangled in his hair, her tongue tangling with his as her desperation rose another notch.

"Make love to me," she said against his mouth, arching her pelvis in an attempt to impale herself on his shaft.

"Nothing can stop me." He kissed a trail down her jaw to her creamy throat. She was a gift, and he was going to unwrap her slowly. His breath was hot as he unsnapped her flimsy lace bra. He didn't want to stop kissing her even to remove the last of her clothing, but he wanted her naked. Skin on skin with nothing between them ever again.

His cell phone rang. Sin's tone. He ignored it. He had to get inside Idess. No one was getting between him and what was his. As if she sensed his desperation, she wrapped her arms around his neck and her legs around his hips so tightly he didn't think he could break free if he wanted to.

Rumbling with pleasure, he sank into her soft, willing body. Idess gasped, clung to him fiercely, and whispered sweet, hot commands into his ear.

Electric strikes stormed through him as he began to thrust. He and Idess were joined by more than their bodies, and now he understood why his brothers had taken mates. The difference between fucking a random female and making love to someone with your entire body and heart could only be measured by something akin to the Richter scale.

Making love to Idess shook him to the core and razed every one of his walls. She was a ten-point-oh for sure, and as long as she kept rocking his world, he was ready and willing to take the damage.

Idess had never known anything so perfect. Lore was kissing her as he thrust into her, taking her to new, soul-shattering heights, and she finally understood the beauty of giving one's self to another.

Her life since Rami had been about punishing herself, engaging in self-imposed penance while she waited for a reward she wasn't sure she deserved.

She finally had that reward, though not in the way she'd expected.

"Idess." Lore's voice was wonderfully husky.

He thrust as deep as he could go, and she arched up, her body clenching and holding him there. In her passion, she scored his back with her nails, and he hissed in pleasure.

"*Yes.* Oh, damn..." He shifted, palmed her butt and brought her up hard against him. Dropping his forehead to hers, he looked into her eyes as he pounded into her in a wild, raw flurry.

The friction blazed, smoked, and then pleasure was rocketing her into the clouds. Lore released with a shout she barely heard through the thrum of her heartbeat in her ears. It seemed to go on forever, and as her senses tumbled over her, they melted together with so many emotions she wasn't sure how to separate them.

This was all so incredibly right. Closing her eyes, she

held Lore when he collapsed on top of her. His weight was crushing, but she'd never been happier to have her breath squashed out of her.

"Sorry," he muttered against her throat. "I don't have the energy to roll off." She laughed—tried to laugh, anyway, and he groaned and rolled, tucking her close. "What's so funny?"

Blessed air filled her lungs, and the laugh finally got out. "You. Big bad demon reduced to a lump of exhaustion by a mere female."

His hand stroked her arm. "There's nothing *mere* about you. You've given me a run from the beginning."

She smiled against his chest, loving how, for the first time in centuries, she could finally be herself again, could break the restraints that had kept her so contained. She wanted to go wild, to dance in a club, swim naked in the ocean, drink a margarita, and then try a whole lot of exotic sexual things with Lore. "We're quite the pair, aren't we?"

A long, drawn-out silence ticked by. At first, Idess basked in it, content and sated. But gradually, she became aware of a growing tension.

"It's time to go, isn't it?"

"Yeah." He squeezed her so hard her joints popped. "How much longer do you have? On Earth, I mean."

"I honestly don't know."

His entire body went statue still. "I don't want to lose you. I know that makes me sound like a pussy, but I don't." His throat worked on a hard swallow. "I even..." He shook his head. "Never mind."

"What?" She propped herself up on one elbow so she could look at him. "You can tell me."

He threw an arm over his eyes. "You're going to hate me."

"No, I won't." She peeled his arm away. "Spill."

Swallowing again, he stared up at the ceiling fan as it spun lazy circles over the bed. "I actually thought that if I killed Kynan, it wouldn't be so bad, because you'd have to stay longer."

Ice filled her chest cavity, leaving no room for her heart to beat. "You would do that? Wreck my future?" She had no right to be appalled, given that she'd done the same thing to Rami, but as the ice and pain spread through her, she truly began to understand how betrayed and hurt her brother must feel.

Lore sat up in a quick, fluid motion that startled her. "Hell, no. It was a desperate, random thought. I'm a selfish asshole, but I could never do something so unforgivable to you." She cried out, but he misunderstood, and he framed her face with his warm palms and brushed his lips over hers. "I'm not lying, Idess. I swear to you, I would never take something as important as your wings away. *I would die first.*"

Tears burned her eyes. Horrible, acid tears that she deserved. She'd known that what she did to Rami was unforgivable, but hearing Lore—a *demon*—say how awful it was with so much passion, oh, sweet, sweet Lord, she deserved whatever Rami did to her.

"Idess? I'm sorry. I shouldn't have told you—"

"It's not that." She really wanted to throw up. "You don't have to worry about me getting my wings. I'm not going to get them." She didn't deserve them anyway, had been fooling herself for centuries, thinking that she'd get into Heaven.

A scowl tugged his dark brows down. "What are you not telling me?"

"We only have one shot at finding Rami before your deadline. Angels aren't allowed in the Playground, so I broke my vow and made sure I'm ruined. I can flash into Sheoul now."

"Ruined?" He scrambled to his knees and gripped her shoulders as if he was going to shake her. "Oh, fuck. Do *not* tell me that I ruined you by making love to you."

"It was my choice. It was the only way we'd get to Rami. It was the only way for you and Kynan to be saved. Until I'm officially summoned, I still have my powers. Just not angel status."

"Damn it," he whispered. "I knew I shouldn't have made love to you. You're so much better than I am. I've tainted you—"

She stopped him with a finger pressed to his sinful lips. "You aren't listening to me. And no, I'm not better than you are. Don't you see, Lore? You've punished yourself for being what you are. For loving your sister so much that you did what you thought was best, even though you saw it as a betrayal. You've given everything to your sister, and it's time to take something for yourself. Take me. I can be with you now." He didn't need to know that "now" probably meant no more than a few hours before she was called before the Memitim Council . . . and likely destroyed.

He swallowed hard. "Do you realize what you just said, angel? Turn it back on yourself."

Sluggish realization wove its way through her. She'd been punishing herself over Rami for centuries, putting all her energy into her guilt. Doing the same thing she'd just accused Lore of. But her betrayal had been far, far more damaging to her sibling.

She gulped miserably. "It's not the same."

"How can you tell me to take something for myself, to forgive myself, when you don't walk the walk?"

He was right, and she nearly choked on her own hypocrisy. "I'll take something for myself then. After we deal with Rami."

"Prove it. Bond with me," he blurted. "Swear to be my mate."

Her heart slammed against her ribs. She hadn't seen *that* coming. She'd been thinking more along the lines of a tropical cruise or a bigger house. Swallowing dryly, she glanced at his bedside clock because she couldn't look at Lore, too afraid he'd mistake the doubt in her face for rejection of *him*, when the truth was, she still wasn't sure she deserved to take anything so wonderful.

"We have to go." Her voice cracked, and the doubt seeped out through it.

"I know." He gripped her chin and brought her face back around. "I want this, Idess. I keep telling you that I'm selfish, and this only proves it. I can't bond with anyone as long as I'm bonded to Deth, but as soon as we defeat your brother, I'll be free. We'll come back here, and I'll make you mine. Forever. Don't say no."

Maybe she didn't deserve this, but he did. And she couldn't deny him anything. "Yes," she whispered. "I'll bond with you." She smiled, hoping he didn't notice the tremor on her lips, because they definitely did not have forever.

Two-fifty-nine A.M. Venezuela time.

Lore breathed deeply and handed Idess the dagger.

"You ready to do this?"

"Not at all." She clutched the little bag of powdered

monk wine tighter. She'd flashed in and out of the abbey with no problems, and she'd admitted to him that she'd been glad to test her powers. Rami had told her that ruined Memitim retained their abilities until their official summoning to the Council, but she'd been nervous about it, nevertheless.

"*Can* you do this?"

She averted her gaze, and fear spiked through him. He got that they were going to kill her beloved brother. But if they didn't kill him, the contract with Deth would still stand, and Lore would once again be caught in an impossible situation with Kynan and Sin.

Though...if Idess had *ruined herself* by sleeping with Lore, would she still be required to guard Kynan?

Fuck. He still couldn't believe she'd done it—damned herself like that, when for two thousand years, all she'd dreamed of was earning her wings. And now she couldn't.

Because of him.

He would have to make it up to her somehow, even if he could only make sure that she spent the rest of her life happy. He'd spoil her and make love to her and treat her like a damned queen.

They just had to kill her brother first.

"Idess?"

"Yes," she whispered. "Yes. I can do it." She tightened her grip on the crossbow, grabbed his hand that held the dagger and suddenly, they were in a cavern deep inside Sheoul. The walls were lined by live demons crucified on twisted crosses, some being eaten alive by various hell-creatures.

Rami stood just three feet away from Lore and Idess, jaw-dropped and gaping.

"How—"

Idess released Lore and hurled the wine powder in Rami's face. The fallen angel screamed and clawed at his eyes. Taking advantage of Rami's misery, Lore buried his sword in the angel's gut, and Idess cried out at the gruesome sight of her brother being impaled. Steam hissed from the wound, a wet, grotesque sound that was joined by the slide of bone on steel as Rami stumbled backward and off the blade.

Chasing the momentum, Lore swung, a blow that would have decapitated the angel if it had landed. But the bastard wheeled away in a blur, and the tip of the sword only nicked his throat.

He backed against a wall, teeth bared, clutching his gut and glaring at Idess, who had him in her crossbow's sights. "You *bitch*."

"Rami, please. Listen to me. I'm sorry. What I did was stupid. Selfish. I know that—"

"You *know* that? Your self-serving exploit kept me on this hellhole of a planet for two extra centuries!" he bellowed. "And then it got me kicked out of Heaven, you cocksucking whore!"

The crossbow started to shake. Lore inched closer to Idess when all he wanted to do was shove the sword up her brother's ass. Her voice shook as hard as her weapon did. "What I did was unforgivable. But it affected you on Earth, not in Heaven."

"You have no idea." Rami circled them, his movements as sinuous as a snake's despite the hole in his gut. "I learned of your betrayal days after my Ascension. Did you know, sister, that once bitterness takes root in an angel, it grows like a weed? Grows until the soul becomes shriveled and polluted with hate, which is not welcome in Heaven. It *is* your fault I was expelled."

"No." Idess wanted to cover her ears, to block the ugly truth. "No!"

"Shut the fuck up!" Lore swung the *qeres*-coated sword, but Rami wheeled away again, and Lore caught only a glancing blow to Rami's shoulder. Still, the wound smoked and hissed, and Idess knew very well how much it hurt.

"So protective and possessive." Rami snared a two-pronged pitchfork tool from a barrel and stabbed one of the scaly rat things that had been gnawing on the foot of a crucified demon. "Like an animal," he said, as he watched the helpless creature squirm in agony on the tines. "Because that's all demons are, Idess. Lowlifes. Lower even than the animals humans feed on."

She might have agreed not long ago, but over the course of two thousand years she'd seen animals with more heart than some humans, and recently, she'd witnessed demons with more compassion.

Easing forward, she concentrated on keeping her voice soft and soothing. "Rami, you used to tell me that there was always balance in the world. If that's true, and you know it is, then not all demons are bad. Like the one you took. Rade is innocent. You have to give him to us."

Rami scoffed. "Innocent? He's an insect. Have you never stepped on a cockroach?"

"Oh, Rami." Despair sliced at her heart. "What have you become?"

"What I am is because of *you*!" he thundered.

"We can make it better. We can go to Father—"

"*Better?*" He laughed, but there was no joy in the

sound. "Do you know what will make it better? Your complete and utter ruination. I wanted all your Primori to die so you would never Ascend. I wanted you to fail. To feel the humiliation I felt when I learned what you had done to me."

Lore hurled a morning star, and though Rami twirled out of the way, it caught him in the shoulder. Rami ripped the weapon out of his flesh and threw it to the ground. "I'm disappointed in you, assassin. Roag swore you were competent, despite the fact that you failed him. Now I'll have to slaughter Kynan myself. And once I have the amulet, I'll bargain my way back into Heaven."

"You're insane," Idess gasped. "They'll never accept you."

"Then Satan will," he purred. "He will want that necklace, and he'll give me anything I want. You know the saying, it's better to rule in hell than serve in Heaven."

Lore snorted. "I have never met bigger assholes than fallen angels. Why work with Roag, though?" Lore's hand slipped beneath his jacket, and Idess figured he was going for another weapon. "What concern is it of yours if my brothers are punished?"

"Surely you understand binding contracts." Behind him, one of the impaled demons screeched, and Rami closed his eyes as if savoring the sound, and his voice was almost trancelike when he answered. "I had one with Roag. He used his black market and underground contacts to discover who Idess's Primori were, and in return, I was to give him anything he wanted. When he disappeared, I thought I was off the hook."

"Because you believed he was dead." In a movement so

fast Idess didn't see it until it was over, Lore sent a throwing knife at Rami's head.

"Yes." Rami slid to the left, and the blade whooshed harmlessly past his ear. His eyes were still closed. "But as it turns out, my contract is still valid. The terms are harsh. If I don't succeed in destroying your brothers' lives and breaking them apart, I will...disintegrate."

"That would be too bad," Lore drawled.

Idess's mind churned into high gear. "Roag was how you knew Kynan was charmed," she mused. "He'd been eavesdropping on his brothers." Kynan had received his charm well after Rami fell, so he couldn't have known about the human's Marked Sentinel status. She gripped the crossbow securely and raised her voice, because ultimately, none of this mattered, and they didn't have much time before the wine powder wore off and Rami could flash out of there. "Where is the child? I need to return him to his family."

"You don't need to do anything but suffer." Rami's eyes popped open, and from them came an unholy, blinding glow. In a blast of heat and blood, he exploded out of his beautiful skin and into a black, wraithlike creature dripping with shredded flesh. The very air screamed with fury, and the crucified demons shriveled like crushed paper. Their souls escaped their bodies and scrambled around the room, more terrified now than they had been when they were hanging from the walls.

An inky wind howled from inside a dark cavern at the rear of the chamber. The ground beneath Idess's feet bucked and rumbled. The wind snaked out of the opening in a billowing cloud of rank smoke and swirled around them, its roar blending with the sounds of the demon souls' agonized shrieks. Idess covered her ears, but within seconds, the gruesome noises stopped. The souls had vanished.

Dear God, Rami had destroyed them. He had the power to *destroy* souls. Just like their father.

"Now," he snarled, "I'm going to make you watch your lover die slowly." He lunged, slammed his fist into Lore's throat. The impact knocked the sword out of Lore's grip and drove him into the wall. His skull cracked against the stone, and he did a slow slide into a heap on the floor.

"Lore!" Idess sprinted toward him, but Rami beat her there. He plunged the sword down, stopping when the tip bit into Lore's neck. Blood ran in a slow rivulet down his throat.

"Did you feed from him when you fucked him?" Rami asked. "Can you feel his terror? Will you feel his pain?" He licked his lips as though anticipating the taste of Lore's death. Lore glowered in defiance as Idess raised the crossbow.

"Don't do it!" She stepped closer, wishing her knees weren't trembling and her voice didn't do the same. "I *will* kill you."

Rami laughed. "I've already won. You fucked away your purity and can't Ascend. *I. Win.*"

With a wink, he drew back the sword and plunged it forward in one easy motion. Crying out, Idess pulled the trigger.

Rami yelped as the bolt ripped through his rib cage just below his armpit and exited on the other side. The forward momentum of Rami's jab propelled the sword forward. In horrifyingly slow motion, Idess watched as Lore tried to block the blade. The sound of metal meeting flesh rang out as the sword bit into his forearm. Blood sprayed, but Lore didn't falter as he leaped to his feet and plowed his fist into Rami's face.

Rami wheeled away from Lore's attack, still clutching the sword. Twin rivers of red ran down his sides. His glazed, shocked eyes shifted to Idess. "You...shot me." His disbelieving voice was raw, gurgling, like the wounds in his ribs.

She jammed another bolt into the chamber. "I'll do it again, Rami. Tell me where Rade is."

A smile twisted his lips, the only warning before he swung the sword. Lore fell back under the assault, and pain flared in Idess's heart as she fired another round. The bolt punched into Rami's spine, dead center between his shoulder blades. His howl of agony was like acid in her ears, and she let out a sob as she watched him stagger into Lore.

"Bitch," he rasped. His hand snaked out with more speed than he should have been capable of, given his injuries, and he caught Lore around the throat.

Lore snarled, and with brutal efficiency, drove his fist through the bolt hole in Rami's side. Rami screamed, jerked as though he was being electrocuted, and crumpled to the ground. Twitching, he lay on his back, eyes wide and breathing labored, as Lore wrenched the sword from his hand.

Dear Lord, she knew Rami was corrupt, was no longer the warm, caring brother she'd loved, but as he lay broken and bleeding, his eyes liquid with pain, she saw only the brother who had comforted her when her human parents had died, the brother who had battled demons at her side.

"Rami, please. There's still time to do the right thing." She sank to her knees beside him. "There's good inside you. I know there is. Where's the infant? Tell us what you've done with him."

Slowly, Rami stretched out a hand toward Idess. His entire body quivered as he gripped her fingers. Tears streamed down Idess's face, and she sobbed when he coughed, spraying blood like a geyser. For a moment, Lore thought Idess had actually gotten through to the guy. But when the wheezing fit ended, Rami's cold gaze met Lore's, and his smile sent chills down Lore's spine.

"The . . . demon child—" he sucked in a gurgling breath "—made your boss a fine meal."

Pure, unadulterated hatred obliterated every thought in Lore's brain and replaced them with only one. *Kill.* With a roar, Lore brought the blade down on the angel's neck. His head separated from his body and rolled toward Lore's boots. But even as the blood poured like a river from Rami's shoulders, it formed sinewy ropes that gripped the head and tugged it toward the body.

Idess drew a blade from the sheath at the small of her back. "You are truly gone, my brother," she whispered.

Though her hand shook, she didn't hesitate as she slashed her wrist and held her bleeding arm so her blood mixed with Rami's. Hissing steam blasted upward, and a heartbeat later, the ex-angel's body went up in a puff of smoke and ash.

Tears streamed from Idess's eyes as she came to her feet above the pile of charred remains, holding her wrist as blood seeped between her fingers.

She didn't have to say anything. Lore swept her into his arms and held her as she collapsed into sobs.

Twenty-three

Idess didn't waste much time crying. She'd destroyed her brother, and somehow she'd have to deal with that, but both she and Lore were bleeding badly, and they had to tell two parents that their son was dead.

"We have to go," she croaked, and Lore nodded.

She flashed them to the hospital parking lot. Together they entered UG, and inside, found Eidolon cleaning up one of the multiple messes scattered around the emergency department; smashed equipment, overturned chairs, pills scattered on the floor. The spirits had been active.

Eidolon jogged toward Lore and Idess, slowing before he reached them, his devastated expression telling Idess that he'd read theirs.

"I'm sorry," Lore rasped.

For a long moment, she thought Eidolon was going to break down. He swallowed repeatedly, his eyes bloodshot and liquid. But when Lore's blood began to drip to the floor, he shifted into doctor mode.

"Come with me." He left them no choice but to follow him into an exam room, where he gestured to Idess to sit on the bed, and for Lore to take a seat. "I assume the bastard is dead," he said, as he gloved up.

"Very." Lore tucked his injured arm protectively against his body. "Take care of Idess first."

Before she could protest, Eidolon took her wrist. "Keep pressure on your wound," he said to Lore. Idess clenched her teeth as he began the painful process of healing her cut, and when he was done, he gently wiped away the blood and covered the mostly healed gash with a gauze pad and tape.

Eidolon sank into a chair across from his brother. "Did you get...the remains?"

Idess closed her eyes and offered a prayer for the small boy her brother had killed.

"I'm going to get them the second I'm done here." Lore said grimly.

Very gently, Eidolon rested Lore's arm on his thigh. "You did a number on this," he muttered. "Sword?"

"Wow," Lore said, as Idess moved to him and took his good hand in hers. "You're good."

"I see a lot of this," Eidolon said wryly. "Usually on Wraith. You ready?"

"Yeah." Gazing up at her, Lore squeezed her hand. "Yeah, I am."

Something in her chest lurched. Lore usually suffered alone and didn't rely on anyone, and he probably preferred it that way. But he was taking strength and comfort from her.

Eidolon's *dermoire* lit up, and when Eidolon was done, he wiped away the blood.

Idess sank down next to Lore just as the doctor's pager went off. He checked it, cursed soundly.

"What is it?" Lore asked.

"Wargs," he said. "There are two incoming via ambulance, and three coming through the Harrowgate." Eidolon closed his eyes and blew out a long breath. "This makes eight in a matter of days. We have an epidemic on our hands." He opened his eyes and gave Lore a look that chilled Idess to the bone. "Does Sin have any healing abilities at all? Any reversal powers?"

"No, why?" But Idess had a feeling she knew, and she saw in Lore's face that he did, too. "Oh, God. Sin. She started it, didn't she?"

"Yeah."

Lore cursed. "We can't catch a break around here, can we?"

Eidolon adjusted his stethoscope around his neck. "I'd like to say that this is unusual, but the last couple of years have been nothing but chaos. And it's only going to get worse if we can't get rid of Roag and his merry band of ghosts."

Stupid bastard! You can't get rid of me. You made me!

Idess wrenched her head around to the doorway, where Roag was lurking, hood shoved back to reveal a hideous, deformed face. His skin was a mass of dark scar tissue stretched tight over bone that was, in places, visible. Insanity gleamed in his dead eyes.

"Actually," Idess said quietly, "I think I can do something about that."

You can help me? Please. This curse... it is agony you can't comprehend. I did nothing to deserve it.

"You hired your brother to kill his own brothers," she said to him. "*Your* brothers."

"Ah... Idess?" Lore's voice came from behind her, but she held up her hand to stop both him and Eidolon.

"Did you hear me, Roag? You wanted your own brothers dead."

Because they burned me alive! He tore off his cloak, and she nearly gasped at the shriveled, twisted wreck that was his body. *And now I hurt. I starve. I thirst. Nothing relieves me. Please, help me.* His lips peeled back in the most evil grin she'd ever seen. *Slaughter my brothers and their families so their blood runs like a river through the streets. Gut them. Rend their limbs from their bodies and their eyes from their sockets!*

His laughter pierced her like a lance carved of ice. "You want help? Really?" She grabbed Roag by the arm. Though he wasn't solid to her, his energy clung to her like static electricity. "I can put you out of your misery. Absolutely. I don't have the power to destroy souls, but I know someone who does."

She dragged him out of the hospital and into the parking lot. Dimly, she heard Lore and Eidolon calling her name, but she kept going. Her brother had torn this family apart, and she couldn't do anything about that, but she certainly could do something about this.

Inhaling deeply, Idess flashed to the realm where her father resided, where only his children and his *griminions* were allowed. She appeared on the steps of an ancient

Greek temple, a great ebony building flanked by black pillars and set amongst other black structures. Once, she'd run her hand over a wall, only to have it come away covered with a sootlike substance. Where her hand had been, dirty white marble peeked through the oily grit.

The massive buildings and pillars and statues had once been pristine white. Now they groaned under the weight of taint and corruption. The entire realm was a giant replica of Athens, but in the dark. Athens, in her nightmares.

Still maintaining a grip on Roag, whose struggles were mere whispers against her skin, she climbed the steps and entered through the double doors big enough to allow King Kong passage. Inside, polished ebony floors stretched endlessly. Grim, dark statues of demons and humans in pain lined the walls, and in the center of the great room, a fountain ran red into a dark pool at the base.

She dragged Roag down a mazelike corridor, making dozens of lefts and rights, and finally, two of her brothers, one of whom she vaguely recognized, opened the huge iron door at the end.

Idess was nearly blinded by the bright lights blasting through the opening. The entire realm was set in a backdrop of gloom, but Azagoth liked his color, and, she noted with a wince, he apparently liked his Beatles music.

He turned to her from where he was standing before an archway, where *griminions* paraded by, leading the souls of dead demons. The moment he turned, the *griminions* halted in their tracks, unwilling to move forward to their final destination, Sheoul-gra, until their boss had seen and approved every soul brought before him.

Azagoth was the epitome of male beauty. Appearing to be in his early thirties, he was tall, with black hair, chiseled cheekbones, and a strong, square jaw. He wore a button-down emerald shirt that matched his eyes, and black, slim-fitting pants that emphasized long legs. In his hand, he had a cup of Starbucks coffee.

"Daughter," he said, his smile one that would make any human woman swoon but that only looked cold to Idess. "It's been centuries." He cast a glance at Roag, who, once inside the room, had become solid. "And you brought a guest."

"Where am I?" Roag shouted. "What have you done, you stupid cunt?"

Idess released Roag and wondered how many showers she'd have to take before her skin stopped crawling from the feel of his touch. He careened around the room, but when it became clear that there was no way out, he rushed her. He swiped at her, but his clawlike hand passed harmlessly through her body.

"As you can see, you have no power here." Azagoth casually crossed his arms over his chest. "Or anywhere."

Roag's eyes bulged as he stared at his hand. "Am I...dead?"

"Unfortunately not," Idess said.

"Why am I here?" The demon rounded on Azagoth. "Who are you?"

Oh, this promised to be good.

Her father had a flair for the dramatic, and he allowed a few moments of tense silence to tick by before saying, "I'm the being you know as the Grim Reaper."

Roag made a strangled noise. "Wh-what do you want with me?"

"I don't know. Daughter?" Azagoth moved to his desk, a modern oak monstrosity next to a fireplace that was lit, but didn't give off heat. His chamber was freezing. He took a seat, kicked his feet up on his desk, and waited for her to say something.

"Father," she said, prepping herself for the formal speech he preferred, "I humbly request that you put an end to this vile creature. I would have done so myself on the earthly realm, but he is cursed to formlessness, and has no body to kill."

Azagoth put down his coffee. "Truly? Interesting curse."

"Interesting?" Roag screeched. "It is suffering of the cruelest kind!"

"Please," Idess scoffed. "Hearing you whine about cruelty, given what you've done in your life, makes me sick."

Roag sneered at her. "So you brought me here to kill me. Do you think that scares me? Do you think I'm pissing my pants? Death is welcome."

No doubt death was much preferable to the fate he was suffering. After death, he'd be taken to Sheoul-gra, where he'd hang out with other demons until he was reborn.

"Father, I don't want him dead." She stepped forward, shoving Roag aside. "I want him destroyed."

Roag's gasp echoed through the room, and in the tunnel, even the *griminions* shuddered. "You can't do that," he rasped. "You have no right!"

Azagoth steepled his fingers over his chest and pinned her to the wall with his cold gaze. "What you ask is rarely done. In all my time, I have destroyed only a handful of souls, and not without consequence. So why, dear daughter, should I risk Satan's wrath for this one demon?"

She glanced at Roag, who stood near the tunnel archway. His eyes gleamed hellfire crimson, and malevolence emanated so strongly from him that the demon soul nearest him kept trying to inch away, only to be held steady by his *griminion* escort.

"He is evil such as I've never felt, Father. He has cavorted with fallen angels, including my brother, your son, Rami, also known as Rariel. Given his history and strength of evil, I fear that Roag's time in Sheoul-gra will be short, and that he's strong enough to be reborn with his memories intact. He will never stop seeking revenge, and a soul like that will only serve Satan and bring him more power."

Shadows flitted in Azagoth's eyes, and dread flitted in her stomach. "Speaking of Rami...I no longer feel his life force."

She nodded. "I destroyed him, Father."

The shadows danced faster, grew darker. "Where did you kill him?"

"Sheoul. The Forbidden Abyssal."

"Your service to humanity has cost you." Slowly, Azagoth came to his feet and went to Roag. The shriveled demon trembled as her father's hand clamped down on the demon's throat.

Roag's eyes squeezed closed. "Please...no..."

"I know who you are," Azagoth whispered. "I saw every soul you tortured and killed when they passed through my archway. I felt their suffering. My daughter is right about you, and even had she not asked me to end your existence permanently, I would have done so. You see, God demands equal and opposite. Tit for tat. And evil as great as yours has no pure, good match in the human world. You unbalance the universe. So you shall disappear."

With that, he squeezed. Roag's eyes flew open, and

his silent scream rang like a shrill whistle through Idess's mind as his body began a violent tremor. Fire flew from her father's fingertips and spread down Roag's already burned body until only ash in the form of a demon remained.

And then there was nothing. No ash, no soul, no evil.

For some reason, the Blue Oyster Cult song "Don't Fear The Reaper" rang through her head as he turned to her. "Was there anything else?"

The pleasant way he'd asked that made her want to reply with, "A side of fries, please." Instead, she bowed. "Thank you, Father, but no."

"Idess." His voice was soft, but urgent. "It's coming for you. The light. And whatever you do, *do not run.*"

⌒

Lore strode into Deth's chamber, mind focused on one single goal. He *would* take back Rade's remains. Eidolon had sworn not to tell Shade and Runa anything until Lore got back to UG, though Lore wasn't sure how much easier the news would be with a body to go along with it.

Either way, two parents were going to be destroyed.

He swore when he saw his sister standing before their boss. Dammit. He had no doubt that he'd have to bargain with Deth for Rade's remains, and he also didn't doubt that Sin would only complicate matters.

"For your sake, I hope you have completed your task." Deth's right hand was hanging over the side of his chair, and as Lore approached, the reason why became clear.

Deth had the new Seminus, Tavin, chained to the base of the throne and was petting him. The incubus was crouching, naked and bruised, head hung so his chin-length hair concealed his face. But when he glanced up, his eyes glowed gold with hatred and defiance—and, as he locked his gaze on Sin, lust as well. Deth, that sonofa-bitch, had denied the male females, something that would drive him insane, and, if let go too long, would result in his death.

Lore wanted to rip Deth's heart out and feed it to the Ramreels.

"I didn't kill Kynan," Lore said. "I killed the contract holder. Rariel is a stain. The contract is void."

For a moment, Lore thought Deth was going to stroke out. His piggy eyes popped wide and his skin flushed, and it was funny as hell. "I don't believe you. This is a trick."

Lore shrugged. "Check the contract."

Deth gestured at one of the Ramreels, who manipulated a lever in the stone wall. With a grind of rock, a panel peeled back, revealing another panel containing glowing stones set into the wall. The Ramreel palmed one of the stones and brought it to Deth.

Lore's master held the glowing green orb in one hand and passed his other hand over it. The thing morphed into a parchment, which Deth stared at for only a moment before it crumbled in his hands and fell like sand to the floor.

"Told you," Lore said.

"We're free, then?" Sin bounced on her toes, unable to contain her excitement.

Deth snarled. "This is an outrage! You tricked me."

"I got around the terms of the contract, you son of a bitch. Now release us."

Deth bounded from his throne and paced frantically, his teeth clicking in a grotesque display of annoyance, and Lore knew he was trying to find some loophole that would allow him to keep them in service.

"Now," Lore gritted out.

Deth hissed. "I have not received payment from Rariel. I will not lose my two best assassins until I have been paid in full."

"Not my problem," Lore said.

Curses fell from Deth's lips. He kept pacing, stalling.

"Deth, *now*!"

Deth whirled around, his armor clanking. "The boy," he said. "The child Rariel brought to me. He is related to you, no?"

The blood in Lore's veins congealed even as his heartbeat kicked into overdrive. It sounded as if Rade was still alive.

Stay cool. Stay calm. "No."

Deth's eyes narrowed. He snapped his fingers, and the nearest Ramreel disappeared through a side exit and returned with Rade, his body lying limp and motionless in the demon's arms.

"*What have you done to him?*" So much for calm.

Deth smiled. "I don't know how to care for an infant. There has been no reason to keep him alive. He was meant to be a meal, not a pet, after all."

Sin moved toward Rade, whose sunken chest rose almost imperceptibly.

"As you can see, he hasn't perished yet. But if you want him, you will agree to my new terms."

Sin sucked air between clenched teeth. "You fuck," she ground out.

Lore forced his own jaws to unclench. "What do you want?"

"I want one of you to remain with me. Forever."

Outrage nearly knocked Lore off his feet. "*Never.*"

"Then the child will be sent to the kitchens." Deth gestured to the Ramreel.

"No! Just...wait." By now, Lore's Incredible Hulk should have been knocking at the door, and though he was so furious his voice shook, he didn't get the jacked-up sense that he was going to explode out of his skin and into a monster. Idess's touch seemed to have soothed the savage beast. Idess, who had lured him out of his life of loneliness and death, and replaced it with warmth and light.

And Deth had just yanked all of that out from under him. Lore couldn't bond with her now. Hell, he didn't think they could be together at all. How was he supposed to come home to her at night and tell her about his day?

Hey, angel, I got to strangle someone today. Took him a while to die, because he had a fat neck and I couldn't use my death gift because you drained me. And tomorrow, Deth wants me to break some female's legs because she cheated on her mate. I think I'll turn that job down and take the two days of torture instead.

Oh, yeah. Good times ahead.

Lore took his sister's hand and guided her to a quiet corner, where Deth couldn't eavesdrop.

"That sick bastard," she snapped. "I'll kill him, Lore. I'll give him herpes and syphilis and Khileshi cockfire, and he'll die slowly and in pain—"

"Listen to me," Lore interrupted. "I want you to have that chance, but you have to be freed in order to do it." Not that killing Deth would be easy, if possible at all. "I'll submit to him for service. You go free. I just need you to take Rade to UG once it's done."

"What? No!" She gripped his jacket with both hands, went up on her toes, and got in his face. "You are handling the kid and your brothers. If one of us has to stay, it'll be me."

Gently, he peeled her hands off his coat and held them against her chest. "Sin, you have to do this. I owe you. I owe you a lot. I want you to have your freedom."

She shifted awkwardly, from one foot to another. Her eyes glistened, for the second time, since they were children. Even then, she hadn't been one to cry. "You don't owe me anything. It's because of me that you're here in the first place. You need to set yourself free."

Frustration drilled into his skull. She was making this more difficult than it needed to be. "You're here because of me, too. If I hadn't left you all those years ago, if I'd done what I could to protect you, you wouldn't have been forced to sell your services to survive."

"We're not talking about that," she said sharply. "It's the past, and it's over."

It would never be over for her, and he knew it. "My point is, you've never been free. You need it. You need to have a normal life. You can have that now."

She snorted bitterly. "Normal? You think I can be normal in any way? Hello, Lore, I'm a fucking freak of nature." She waved her right hand in front of him, as if he didn't know how much pain their *dermoires* had caused.

"Yeah…" He hesitated, not wanting to walk down a path that ended at Sin's door. Then Tavin yelped—struck hard in the face by Detharu, reminding Lore that some shit situations couldn't be avoided. "What do you know about diseased werewolves?"

The color siphoned from her face, confirming his

suspicion. "You need to see Eidolon. He's facing some sort of warg plague."

She exhaled a curse. "Yeah. Okay. Later. We need to settle this first." She shot Deth a dark look. "Look, I know you want to do this, but I can't accept."

"You don't have a choice." Lore wheeled around. "Deth, free her. I'll stay."

"No!" She shoved him aside and strode toward the demon. "I don't want to be free."

"Dammit, Sin, it's a life sentence!"

She skidded to a stop and turned around slowly, as if the words "life sentence" had finally sunk in. She swallowed a couple of times before shaking her head. "Doesn't matter. Truth is, I like it here. I'm good at what I do. It's all I *can* do. And you have Idess now. A chance to be happy. You need to take it." She rounded on Detharu. "Free him."

"Don't listen to her," Lore warned. "I want to stay."

The demon steepled his fingers and watched them with fierce interest. He was enjoying this way too much. At his feet, Tavin was watching Sin intently, his panting, agonized breaths filling the silence. Lore felt for the guy, but if he got loose, Lore would kill him. No way would Lore allow Tavin to do to Sin what his nature would force him to do.

"If she doesn't want to be freed," Deth said finally, "I won't force her."

"Then I won't go, either." Lore planted his feet and crossed his arms over his chest.

Sin cursed in a couple of different languages. "You're an idiot. Stop being so stubborn."

Lore clenched his hands to keep from wrapping them around her neck and shaking some sense into her.

"Enough!" Deth shouted. "Lore, it was your contract. Therefore, you are freed."

Before Lore could protest, Deth lurched out of his chair and slammed his palm on Lore's chest. The air blasted from Lore's lungs, and suddenly he felt a hundred pounds lighter.

Though the feeling was amazing, it was also horrible, because Sin was still Deth's bitch. Forever. "You bastard," he rasped.

Deth waved his hand in dismissal. "You no longer belong here."

Neither does Sin. Lunging, Lore fired up his gift. Tried to, anyway. It didn't even spark, but Lore could take Deth out with his bare hands—

"Stop!" Deth snatched Rade from the Ramreel and curled his fingers around the infant's throat. "I will kill it. Back out of the chamber, or the whelp dies."

Panting, cursing, Lore focused every ounce of hatred into his glare as he backed toward the door. Once he was standing in the hall, two guards jabbed machetes into his ribs while another brought Rade to him.

Deth dragged one hideous finger down Sin's throat in a slow, sensuous trail, a taunt that nearly had Lore going after the bastard again. "Get out of my sight and don't return unless you intend to sign a new contract."

Go, Sin mouthed. *I'll be fine.*

Walking away was the hardest thing Lore had ever done, and as he did, he couldn't help but feel as if, once again, he'd failed his twin.

Twenty-four

For some reason, Lore's *heraldi* no longer worked. Idess stood outside her father's temple, repeatedly brushing her finger over the circular welt.

Nothing.

Already unsettled by her father's talk of the light coming for her, she took several slow breaths to tamp down the encroaching panic as she touched the pad of her finger to Kynan's mark.

Still nothing.

Oh, no. This was bad. Very, very bad. Quickly, she flashed to Lore's house, but he wasn't inside. She darted outside to the deck. No sign of him, but the hairs on the back of her neck stood up. All around her, the air went calm and the forest animals went silent. Crouching in a defensive position, she eased around, expecting… what? The sensation she felt wasn't evil. In fact, her skin began to tingle pleasantly.

And then, blasting before her, in a strike of silent lightning, was a vertical column of light. It poured from the heavens in a shimmering cascade, calling to her. The tug went all the way to her soul, like a big, mushy embrace.

A tranquil, beautiful warmth settled over her as she drifted toward it. So lovely. So inviting.

Come home.

The musical voice sang not just in her head, but in her entire body.

It is time.

No. She stumbled to a halt, fingers outstretched and nearly touching the stream of light. She'd dreamed of this day, and now that it was here, she only wanted to run. This should have been the happiest day of her life, but this wasn't a summons to Ascend. This was a call to answer for her actions. She'd lost a Primori and slept with a demon.

The stream of light glided toward her. She moved to the side, but it followed. No way was she going. She'd seen what had happened to Rami and Roag when their very existence was snuffed. They were gone forever. And what if her fate was worse? Doomed to loneliness and guarding Primori for all time?

And what of Lore? Losing Rami all those centuries ago had left her grieving, bleeding from wounds that never healed.

What she felt for Lore was a thousand times stronger. Living without him would kill her.

The light moved closer. With a cry, she flashed to her house in Italy. The light followed her, piercing her roof and shining down in the middle of her living room. She flashed again, this time to the top of Mount Ararat.

The light was there.

Panic blurred the edges of her vision as she flashed

to Pompeii. Stonehenge. The Great Wall of China. And everywhere, the light followed. A sob of desperation escaped her as she squeezed her eyes closed tight and flashed to the parking lot at Underworld General. Shaking like a nervous Chihuahua, she peeled open her eyes and turned in a slow circle. *No light.*

Which, now that she thought about it, made sense, since the human ghosts had been trapped in the demon-built hospital because the heavenly light didn't penetrate.

The sudden rumble of a vehicle engine sounded like a dragon's growl in the underground space. A black ambulance eased out of its stall and rolled toward the far wall, which began to shimmer like a Harrowgate. Of course . . . that would be the opening through which vehicles came.

Sure enough, it seemed as though the entire wall became glass, allowing the ambulance to pass through and into the human-built parking garage on the other side.

A parking garage where a focused beam of light lurked. Waiting for her.

The vehicle gate closed, leaving a solid wall once more.

The fact that she could no longer see the light didn't comfort her, because it was still there. It would always be there, and her father's words came back to haunt her.

Do not run.

Lore went straight to UG. The second he stepped out of the Harrowgate, Eidolon was there. His shock and joy at seeing that Rade was alive was followed immediately by concern at his condition.

"Damn," he whispered, as he took the child. "What was done to him?"

"Nothing," Lore said. "I don't think he was fed or taken care of at all."

"He's definitely hypothermic." Eidolon told a nurse to call Shade and instructed another to fetch heated blankets as he rushed the boy to one of the trauma rooms, his *dermoire* glowing. Eidolon assessed the baby, who had pinked up a little and was already looking better after an infusion of whatever Eidolon had done to him with his power.

"Can I do anything?" Lore offered his left index finger to the infant, and Rade's tiny hand curled around it.

"What you're doing is perfect." Eidolon very carefully started an IV, and by the time he was finished, a physician assistant had arrived with blankets.

Lore helped swaddle Rade, and once he was completely mummified, Lore sat on the bed and held the boy to his chest, figuring the extra heat couldn't hurt, and Eidolon didn't tell him otherwise.

"Is he going to be okay?"

Eidolon smiled. "Once his body temperature is up and he nurses, he should be fine. He's a tough little guy."

Lore peered down at the baby, who lay calmly in his arms, staring up at him with big, brown eyes. A twinge of longing was like a pinch to the gut. Could Idess have children? Did she want them?

Shade had told Lore that human-Sem offspring were sterile, but if Idess wanted kids, Lore would move the sun to make sure she had them. "Has Idess come back?"

"Haven't seen her." Eidolon checked Rade's temperature with an ear thermometer thingie. "Looking good. I'm going to go check on Shade."

Lore wasn't sure how long he sat there alone with Rade, rocking him and talking to him in an idiotic, hushed baby-talk voice, before Shade and Runa arrived with their other two sons. They rushed into the room, and right behind them were Tayla and Eidolon, followed by Wraith and Serena.

It had been almost a month since he'd last seen Wraith's mate, when she'd been lying in a bed, only hours away from death. Now the gorgeous, tall blond was holding a very young baby.

Standing, Lore handed Rade to Runa, who was crying so hard he couldn't understand anything she said to him. He did his best invisible impression as he backed away from the crowd, only to halt when he bumped into a solid body. He knew who it was before he even turned around.

Kynan. Gem stood beside him, holding his hand.

For a long moment, they all stared. And then Gem hugged him. Wrapped herself around him the way he would have killed to have her do just a month ago. Now all he wanted was for Idess to do the same thing. *Where was she?*

"Thank you." Gem pulled away and stepped back to Kynan. "You saved Rade, and I don't think any of us can thank you enough."

It was Sin who deserved the thanks, but he wasn't going to ruin the happy reunion by announcing Sin's sacrifice. Instead, he got in a jab at his former rival. "I saved Kynan, too, you know."

"Yeah," Kynan drawled, "but we'll just try not to dwell on that."

"Oh, I intend to rub it in. A lot." Lore laughed at Kynan's curse. "Congratulations on the new spawn, by the way."

"Well," Gem said, "that was better than what Wraith said." She lowered her voice and did an imitation of Wraith. "Way cool about the fuck-trophy."

Kynan rolled his eyes. "The demon does have a way with words." He took Gem's hand and clapped Lore on the back. "Thanks, man."

The party in Rade's room hit its stride when Ky and Gem went inside. Lore's brothers all looked so happy, their mates grinning and holding each other tightly. It was a scene right out of a damned movie or something, complete with laughter, reminiscing, and a few good-natured insults.

Lore so didn't belong here.

He needed to find Idess anyway. He peeled off toward the Harrowgate just as the ER doors slid open. Idess darted inside and right into his arms.

Lore scooped her up, squeezing her hard in a silent promise that he'd never let her go. "Where have you been? Are you okay? Where's Roag?"

"Later." She took his mouth in a desperate kiss that pushed all his startup buttons. "Did you..."

"Yeah. Rade was alive." He let her feet touch the ground again. "He's going to be okay."

"I'm so glad." She sounded relieved, but there was an odd, underlying tone he couldn't identify.

Frowning, he tucked a flyaway strand of hair behind her ear. "What is it? What are you not telling me?"

Her hand came up to his cheek, her touch tender. "Nothing. It's just been a long day."

Rami. God, he was such an ass. The guy might have been a monster, but he had still been her brother, and she'd loved him for two thousand years. Expecting her to be okay with killing him mere hours after finding out what he'd become was just stupid.

"I'm sorry. I didn't think."

The sound of a clearing throat had Lore growling at the

interruption. But when he turned to see all of his brothers—and Kynan—standing there, the viciousness turned to confusion.

"Ah...yeah?"

Shade stepped forward. "Runa and I are in your debt." He breathed deeply, cast his gaze at the ceiling. "I don't know what the fuck has been wrong with me these last few days. I wanted you dead, I turned on my brother, and I don't know why."

"I do," Idess said, and five sets of eyes focused on her. "It was Roag. He wasn't just inciting the ghosts. His very essence was affecting all of you. When he was near, you were all more angry. More aggressive. It was what he wanted."

"Where is he?" That from Wraith.

"He's been destroyed."

Kynan's dark eyebrows shot up. "He's dead? For real? Not just invisible?"

"He's not dead. His soul was annihilated. Erased. He cannot be reborn."

"Holy shit," Shade said. "How?"

"Let's just say that my father is a very powerful man."

"That's a little understated, don't you think?" Lore draped his arm over her shoulder and tugged her into him where she belonged. "You know, seeing how he's the Grim fucking Reaper."

Man, you could have heard the ghosts tiptoeing by in the silence. At least until Wraith shot Lore a look of sympathy. "*Duuuude.*"

"No shit," Kynan chimed in.

"Well, whatever you and your father did," Eidolon said, "we're all very grateful."

Idess's gaze dropped to the floor. "It's the least I could

do." She cast a glance at the ER doors as if she expected the Prince of Darkness himself to pop through them at any moment. "I think I can do something about your ghost problem, too."

"Now that Roag is gone, shouldn't they settle down?" Eidolon asked.

"A little. But they don't belong here. They're trapped, and they're going to grow bitter. The ones who have been here the longest already are. It just took Roag to show them how to wreak havoc. Now they need someone to guide them to, ah... the light."

For some reason, she tripped over the last part of her sentence.

"And you can do that?"

"Yes, but there will be more. You'll need someone to purge your hospital on a regular basis."

"Are you volunteering for the job? Because I'm thinking I'll have a hard time finding another angel to handle it."

Idess stiffened. It was a subtle motion that probably only Lore noticed. But yeah, something was definitely wrong here.

"I can't," she said softly. "I'm sorry."

Lore expected his brothers to argue or try to convince her, but Eidolon merely nodded. "If you change your mind, I'd love to have you."

Shade gestured to Rade's room. "I'm taking Runa and the boys home. I don't like having them here with the plague going on." He squeezed Lore's shoulder. "Thanks again. And welcome to the family." Very slowly, he turned to Eidolon. Their gazes locked, and everything around them stilled. Then, Shade embraced E in a silent but powerful apology. When they broke apart, Shade's eyes were wet.

Wraith and Kynan left with Shade, and once they
were gone, Lore wrapped himself around Idess, because
she wasn't going anywhere for a while. "Speaking of the
plague, what's going on with that?"

There was a long, tense silence, and Lore wondered if
Eidolon was silently cursing Sin's existence or maybe he was
still soaking up Shade's apology—something Lore guessed
was a rarity. "Hell if I know. There doesn't seem to be any
pattern of how it's spreading or what segment of the warg
population it's affecting. Bodies are piling up in my morgue,
and the Warg Council is breathing down my neck."

"You have a morgue?" Idess asked.

"A morgue with no ME. He was a freaking warg."

Lore considered that. "Can I take a look?"

"At my dead medical examiner?"

"The morgue."

"Whatever gets your rocks off." Eidolon started down
one of the halls. "This way."

They followed him to an elevator big enough to hold a
Gargantua. They took it down, which was the only option,
and it opened up into a chilly area the size of a gymna-
sium. Drawers used to store bodies made up one wall,
their sizes varying from human to four times that large.

"What does your medical examiner do?" Idess asked.

Eidolon's fingers trailed over an autopsy table like a
lover's, which made sense; this hospital was his baby, and
he was proud as shit of it. "Since most demons aren't concerned with justice that requires detailed proof and scien-
tific evidence, our guy mostly just determines identity and
a general cause of death. Mystical or natural, accident or
homicide, type of weapon used...that kind of thing."

Lore tugged off his glove, opened one of the drawers,

and laid his bare hand on the stiff female inside. "This one died of natural causes. At least, she died of nonmystical causes."

E frowned. "How do you know?"

"Because my resurrection power only triggers if the person died of natural causes. I can only bring someone back if the death takes place a few minutes earlier, but that same power tells me how someone died." He glanced around the room. "Where are the diseased werewolves?"

Eidolon took Lore to a stainless-steel door. He tugged it open, and inside was a refrigerator a gourmet chef would give a nut for. If it wasn't storing two dozen bodies.

Lore palmed a male's forehead. The telltale sting of a supernatural death shot up his arm. "The disease is definitely not of natural origin," he said, "but that doesn't mean Sin is responsible."

"She admitted to killing the first victim," Eidolon said. "Apparently, she was interrupted before she could deliver a full dose of whatever she does. The warg ran to a packmate, who died a few hours after patient zero. The entire pack is wiped now, and the disease has spread to Europe."

"Oh, hell." Lore scrubbed his hand over his face. "What are you going to do?"

"I need Sin here. She's the key to all of this."

"That's not going to be easy—"

"Tough shit," Eidolon bit out. "She caused it, so she can damned well be at my disposal."

Lore shook his head. "It's not that. She's going to be busy." He leaned against Idess, needing her strength. "She committed to a lifetime of slavery in order to get Rade back."

Idess gasped, and Eidolon sucked in a harsh breath. "We've got to get her out of that."

Lore had tried that before, and had ended up serving for thirty years. "I'm open to suggestions."

Cursing, Eidolon closed the fridge door gently, as though he didn't want to disturb the dead. "You two have had a rough couple of days. Get some rest. The ghosts can wait. Let's meet soon and talk about what we can do to get Sin out of her situation." He took off, leaving Lore and Idess alone in pretty much the last place Lore wanted to be right now.

Right now, he wanted to be inside her, working off the day's events in bed, where there would be no assassin masters, no fallen angels, no evil brothers, no werewolf diseases. There would be only Lore and Idess, and lots of bare skin.

Lust flared in his belly, and she must have known exactly what he was thinking, because her liquid caramel eyes gleamed with heat, and her face flushed. "What do you say we take the doctor's advice and head back to my place to get some...rest?"

"I can't," she whispered. "I'm so sorry, but I can't go with you."

"Then your place. We don't have to go to mine."

"No, Lore. I can't go anywhere with you." She took a deep, shuddering breath. Lore stopped breathing completely. "Ever."

The confusion and devastation in Lore's expression nearly made Idess's knees give out.

"What is it?" Lore gripped her shoulders. "Dammit, what's wrong? You're scaring me."

"Can we go someplace else to talk about this? Someplace where there aren't a bunch of dead people staring at us?" Which included ghosts, because several had followed them down here even though they had a tendency to avoid places that reminded them they were dead.

They took the elevator back up, and Lore led her to an empty patient room. Regret and pain fluttered in Idess's chest as she sank down on the bed. He prowled the room like a panther.

"Tell me what's wrong." His words came out as a gruff command, but she didn't take offense. Anxiety was the driving force behind his tone, and she knew it.

"I don't know how."

"There's nothing you can say that will make me angry or upset with you. You know that, right? Why don't we just leave. Get out of this place. Go to some nice tropical island and drink rum and Cokes and roll around on the beach? Forget all this. God knows we could use a vacation."

Tears stung her eyes. "I can't leave here, Lore. Well, I can, but only to go to Sheoul." She hugged herself, suddenly chilled. "I've been summoned, and if I go topside, I'll be taken."

"Taken?"

"To Heaven."

He went rigid, and his voice broke. "But you said you were ruined. That we had sex and—"

"I was wrong." Her lie pounded as loudly as the pulse in her ears. She couldn't tell him the truth, couldn't let him mourn. She loved him too much for that.

"The right thing to say is congratulations, isn't it? I'm supposed to say I'm happy for you, right?" He bowed his head, and his voice faltered. "What kind of asshole am

I that I'm not happy? What kind of selfish prick wants to grab you and beg you not to go?"

"Oh, Lore…" She leaped off the bed and held him so tight the air whooshed from his lungs. "I want to stay with you."

"Is there…is there a way? I know I shouldn't ask. I know I should be all noble and shit…but I'm not. I'm a selfish bastard, and…fuck. Just, fuck."

In an attempt to stay calm, she ran her hands up and down his back, as if doing so grounded her and kept her from breaking into a million pieces. "I could hide out in the hospital for the rest of my life. That's my only option."

His big body shuddered. "Part of me would rather have you do that than leave me. But the other part of me can't let you live like that. You're too good for me, for that kind of life…God, Idess, when do you have to go?"

"Soon." There was no point in dragging this out. If she did, it would only get harder and she might actually be tempted to ask Eidolon if she could rent out a room.

His chest heaved and his arms tightened around her. "What can I do to stop you? Or help you? Hell, I don't know what I want."

"I know what I want," she whispered. "Make love to me. One more time."

"Anything, angel." Lore swept Idess up and carried her to the bed. Silently but quickly, he locked the door and stripped, first himself, and then her. He was gentle as he stretched out beside her, and his hands shook as he framed her face and kissed her. Tender lips caressed hers, slowly at first, and as the heat between them built, his kisses became more urgent. His hand trailed from her throat to her breast, and she hissed at the heady feel of his callused fingers petting her sensitive flesh with such finesse.

Moaning, she threw one leg over his hip, forcing him to slide between her thighs. His hard arousal rubbed against her sex, drawing a moan from him, too. And when he began to rock into her, sliding his shaft through her slick moisture and stroking her clit with every pump of his hips, they both gasped.

"I don't want this to end," he murmured against her lips. "Maybe we can do this forever. My brothers can bring us food, and we can just stay here like this."

Tempting, so very tempting. She twined her hand in his and squeezed. "I need you inside me. Please. Now."

He pushed up on one arm, the muscles bunching beneath his writhing *dermoire*. His gaze slammed into hers. "I love you. Never forget that. Never forget…me."

He loved her. Emotion bubbled up in her throat, leaving her voice completely wrecked. "Never," she rasped.

In a powerful surge, he entered her. They both cried out, and then he was thrusting, long, slow glides that went deep and then so shallow he nearly came free of her. But it wasn't enough. She needed more of him inside her. She wanted to feel his emotions. For the first time, feeding was a desire, not a chore.

Swiping her tongue over her canines, she willed them to extend, and they did with a vengeance, punching painfully out of her gums.

"That is so sexy." As if his body agreed, he pumped faster.

"Yeah?"

He tilted his head to the side, exposing his bronzed neck. "Yeah."

Tangling her fingers in his hair, she pulled him down. His scent filled her nostrils, and her core went molten. A masculine purr erupted from him, and she knew he'd felt it, too.

She dragged her tongue along his jugular, once, twice, three times, because she would never tire of tasting him and she wanted this to last. Wanted to remember everything about him. His taste, his scent, even the way he breathed.

"Jesus, Idess. I could come from that."

"Mmm." She licked him again, smiling at the way he sucked a breath between his teeth. "Can't have that." Mouth watering, she sank her fangs into him.

Her mouth filled with his silky, dark essence, and her body filled with power. The weird sensation she'd felt before, the one that felt as if someone was drawing his *dermoire* pattern on her skin with a pen, started up again. And every emotion he had punched into her...love, joy, despair. But mostly lust, and her body answered.

Between her legs, an erotic storm gathered, building like thunderheads in the spring. Lore's body seemed to have a mind of its own as long as her teeth were in him, as if he felt her need and could only respond to it. Relieve it.

"Ah, yes...Idess...I...can't...stop..."

As if she wanted him to! She wanted more. Harder. Faster. She wanted to be sore and aching, so that every step she took on the Other Side would remind her of him.

Bond with me.

He'd mentioned wanting to do that before they'd gone to battle with Rami.

Bond with me.

Oh, she wanted that. But when the Memitim Council destroyed her, he'd know when he felt the bond break.

"Bond with me!"

With a start, she realized he was speaking out loud. His words weren't in her head. Lightning from the strengthening tempest ripped through her, turning her blood to fuel and setting her body on fire. She was drunk with Lore's very essence, and his command to bond became a compulsion she couldn't fight.

"Your blood," he panted. "Give it to me."

Disengaging her fangs, she sealed the wound with her tongue. High on the overload of physical and emotional sensation, she bit into her wrist and pressed it to his mouth. Greedily, he latched on as he tightened the knot of his right hand and her left.

Burning, pulsing energy washed over her. The sharp blast of her orgasm shattered her. And her soul crashed into his, twisting and spinning until there was only ecstasy.

When it was over, he collapsed on top of her, though he braced his upper body on his elbows to keep from completely crushing her.

For a long time, they just lay there, panting and sweating. She barely had the strength to lift her wrist to her mouth to seal the punctures she'd made. Tingles ran up her other arm. Frowning, she rolled her head to the side.

"Lore?"

"Mmm?"

"My arm."

He lifted his head from where he'd buried his face in the crook of her shoulder. "Shit," he breathed. "We really did it. My *dermoire* is setting into your skin."

"How did you know what to do?"

"Dunno." His fingers trailed over the shadowy pattern that pulsed just beneath her skin, and she sucked air. Wow. Erogenous zone. Big-time. "Instinct, I guess. It just…took over." He went taut, and she felt his fear right in her heart. "We shouldn't have done it. What if your angel buddies see it? Being bonded to a demon has to be some sort of disqualifier for the job."

No, breaking her vow of chastity with a demon had already done that. "It's fine." She smiled reassuringly, because the doubt in his eyes said he wasn't buying it. "But I should go."

"No." He shook his head. "Just a little longer."

She touched his face, committing every angle, every curve, every pore to memory. "It's time."

More than three dozen spirits waited for Idess at the emergency room doors. They rushed her, but she did her best to ignore them as she walked hand in hand with Lore, who had been silent since they left the room. His eyes were swollen with unshed tears, and his jaw was tight, as though he was afraid to open his mouth, lest sobs fall out.

She knew exactly how he felt, and not just because of the bond.

Her steps were leaden as they walked through the parking lot, the herd of ghosts on their tail. When they reached the far wall, he finally spoke.

"What's going to happen?"

"I need the gate to open."

He nodded and shouted at the medic who had accompanied them to Shade's cave. "Yo! Con! I need you to open the vehicle entrance."

The medic climbed into the ambulance, and he must have hit a switch, because the wall shimmered and disappeared as it had before. Outside, the column of light waited. And beyond it, on a different level, was a bluish, less-focused glow. It was the one waiting for the human souls. They stood there, confused... apparently unable to see the light from inside the lot.

"Come with me." She led them to the gate, careful not to get too close to her own light. Not yet. "Go now." All but one of them filed out the door and straight into the glow, which swallowed them up in little flashes.

A boy of perhaps ten human years remained behind. *I'm afraid.*

Swallowing the lump in her throat, she went down on her knees before him. "I am, too."

Really?

"Yes, but only because it's something new. But it's also something wonderful. Do you miss your family?" At his sullen nod, she took his hand. "They'll be on the other side of that light, waiting for you."

My parents? And sister?

"I don't know about that, but trust me, generations of family are waiting to greet you."

He bowed his head. *I don't think so. I did something bad. I played with matches.*

"Is that how you died?"

And my sister.

"Oh, sweetheart, don't you worry. Your family loves you. There is eternal forgiveness in the light." She turned to the glow, where several adults and a young girl stood, all smiling. "See? They're waiting."

Tension mounted as he stared into the light, his chin quivering and tears rolling down his face. He kept shifting his feet, stamping them like a colt that was about to bolt. Finally, with a giant sob, he ran, straight into their arms. As he turned to wave to her, the spirit light faded.

Hers remained.

When she turned to Lore, his eyes were as large as the boy's had been. "Idess. My . . . God."

"You saw?"

He nodded numbly. "Must be the bond or something, but yeah. Wow. That was . . . beautiful."

She laced her fingers with his. "It's my turn."

"I know. Eternal forgiveness, right?" His smile trembled, but he was trying to be strong for her.

Eternal forgiveness. She hadn't lied to the boy. She felt it in her heart and soul, and for the first time since the light had come for her, she wasn't afraid.

Slowly, he dipped his head and touched his lips to hers. "I love you," he murmured. "I love you so much."

"Be good," she said, even as her heart split wide open. She wasn't afraid, but she was in pain.

Before she could change her mind, she pulled away from him and walked into the light.

She didn't look back.

Lore watched her leave, and the moment she disappeared and the gate slammed shut so it was nothing but dark, cold rock, he dropped to his knees and screamed.

Screamed until medics came. Then Eidolon. Then there was a prick in his biceps, and mercifully, the world went black.

Twenty-five

⁓

Lore was going to kill Deth. Okay, sure, he said that all the time. But after two days of doing nothing but sit in his hovel and drink, Lore realized he didn't have anything better to do anyway. And if Lore died during the attempt, so be it. He couldn't care less about himself, because the best part of him was gone.

The bond with Idess had broken. Which meant she was dead.

You fucked away your purity and can't Ascend. You'll probably be destroyed.

Rami's words had been clanging around in his skull since the moment she'd disappeared into the light. She'd lied about being summoned to get her wings, damn her. Lore had been stupid enough to believe it, and now she was dead. So yeah, if he died, too, so what. And if he survived, Sin would no longer be at the mercy of that evil bastard. Idess had helped him forgive himself for what he'd done to Sin, but that didn't mean he wasn't going to keep trying to make it up to her.

Lore just hoped his sister was all right. She hadn't contacted him, nor had she answered his texts or returned his calls. If Deth had hurt her . . .

Soul-searing anger joined the black hole of grief that no amount of white lightning could fill.

You shouldn't have left Sin behind again. You shouldn't have let Idess go. They're both dead because of you.

He took a swig of alcohol, relishing the raw burn in his gullet. If he couldn't scour away the grief, at least he could savor the pain. He raised the bottle into the air.

"To you, Deth. One of us will be dead by morning."

Lore hit the demon bars at midnight. He knew exactly who he was looking for, and sure enough, he found the tiger shifter, Sunil, at a poker table, doing his best to scam a vampire, a Sora, and an orange, horned thing of unknown species.

"Hey, man, can I talk to you?"

Sunil threw down his cards. "I'm out anyway." He followed Lore to a corner table. "Heard you're free. Congratulations."

"Yeah. How's Sin?"

"Haven't seen her."

A chill throbbed through Lore's veins. "What do you mean, you haven't seen her? How did you know I'm free?"

"The new Sem told me. He came to me for some healing after Deth was through with him." Sunil shook his head, making his long, tawny bangs swish across his eyes like wiper blades. "The bastard waited until Tavin was crazed with lust, and then he brought in a whore. Turned Tav loose and watched the show. I don't know what happened to the female, but damn, Tav's broken. Afterward, Deth kicked him to me to patch up."

That sick son of a bitch. Lore would take revenge for Tavin as well as for Sin. "Can you get me into the den?"

Sunil knocked back a swig of his beer. "Fuck that." He wiped his mouth with the back of his hand. "I like my head on my shoulders, thank you very much."

"Sin could be in trouble."

"You know I like your sister, man. But I can't risk my life for her. I have kids to feed."

"I know, and I wouldn't ask if this wasn't important. I plan to re-up with Deth," he lied.

"Then go through the normal channels."

He couldn't do that, because Deth would meet him in the Guild Hall, which was under a Haven spell similar to the one protecting Underworld General.

"I need to see Sin first."

"Dammit, Sem—"

"Please." Shit, Lore hated begging. But he sucked it up and added, "I'll do anything."

Sunil cursed. Long and hard. Finally, he growled, "I'll get you through the barrier. You're responsible for getting yourself inside Deth's keep. And if we're caught, I'll save my own skin and say you forced me."

Lore grinned. "I wouldn't expect anything else."

Deth was as good as dead. All Lore had to do now was pay a visit to Eidolon.

Lore had earned a fierce ass-chewing from Brother Doctor.

"I've left you a dozen messages," Eidolon said, as he spread his palm on Lore's bare chest.

"Didn't feel like answering."

"How have you been?"

This was exactly why Lore had avoided Eidolon. He didn't want to talk about any of this. Didn't want to talk about it, think about it, didn't want to be here, because he'd made love to Idess for the last time in this very hospital.

"I lost my mate," Lore rasped. "How do you think I've been?"

"I'm sorry. If anything happened to Tayla..."

"You'd die. I know." Lore took in a ragged breath. "Thanks, by the way. You know, for knocking me out the other day." Whatever his brother had shot him up with had put him on his ass for a good twelve hours.

But when he'd awakened in a hospital bed, Idess was still gone, and he'd gone into a fresh meltdown.

Eidolon nodded. "You shouldn't have taken off so soon."

"'Cuz I so wanted to hang out here and watch everyone pity me." He looked down at Eidolon's hand. "A little to the right. The scar has to look real if I'm going to get past Deth's goon squad."

Eidolon adjusted his palm. "You sure you want to do this? If you wait, we can work out a plan to get Sin out of there—"

"Can't wait. I need something to do." He didn't see any way for his brothers to help get Sin out of Deth's contract anyway. This was their best shot.

"We could keep you busy."

Lore snorted. "Doing what? Polishing the floors? Emptying the garbage? I'm good at killing people, not healing them."

"We haven't replaced our ME," Eidolon said with a shrug, and Lore stared.

"You have got to be fucking kidding me."

"It's perfect for you. You don't have to worry about killing anyone."

Lore shifted Eidolon's pinky a hair to the left. "You should be doing standup."

"I'm serious, Lore. We could use you."

"Yeah, whatever. Tell you what. If Deth doesn't kill me, you can do whatever you want with me." He figured he wasn't coming back, so hey, this would be just yet another promise to a sibling that he couldn't keep.

Eidolon pressed his hand more firmly over Lore's heart. "This is going to hurt."

"Again, whatever." There was nothing left in there to injure.

Eidolon's *dermoire* lit up, and instant, searing pain tore through Lore's chest. Who cared. He lost track of how long it went on, but when it was done, he had a hand-shaped scar on his chest. It wasn't an exact replica of Deth's, but it should be good enough to get him past Deth's minions.

"Good luck," E said. "You sure we can't help? Wraith can get inside anything."

"I can't risk an alarm being raised before I get to Deth and Sin. He'll kill her and get out before I ever hit the throne chamber."

"If you change your mind, call."

"You bet." He reached out, shook Eidolon's hand. "Thank you. For everything."

E nodded. "If anything happens to you, we won't stop looking for a way to rescue Sin."

"I'm counting on it."

Lore met up with Sunil at the demon bar, and together they headed to Sheoul. For the first time in thirty years,

Lore couldn't see the entrance to Deth's keep. Sunil took Lore by the sleeve and guided him through an invisible—to Lore—barrier. Ahead, beyond a narrow walkway of frozen earth, boulders, and vicious booby traps, was the arched entryway to the den, where two of Deth's henchmen kept watch.

This would be the first test.

Sunil revealed his mark to the guards, and after sliding Lore a good-luck glance, he disappeared inside.

"Well, Sem?" one of the guards snarled through tusks.

Lore lifted his shirt, revealing the palm-shaped mark they expected. For the space of a long, drawn-out breath, the guard stared, and Lore's pulse jackhammered through his veins.

"Mark is fresh. Re-upped your contract, eh?"

Lore shrugged. "Discovered all I'm good at is killing." Discovered Eidolon was good at making cosmetic scars, too.

The other guard cocked his thumb at the entrance. "Go."

Relief made Lore's knees weak, but he strode into the keep like he belonged. Like he wasn't going to tear Deth's fucking head off. He moved down the hall, boots thudding on the floor in time to his heartbeat. Ahead, the double doors to Deth's chamber were closed.

Inside, there would be two Ramreels. Smiling, Lore whipped two blades from the weapons harness under his jacket. He didn't even slow down when he reached the doors. He threw them open, and before the Ramreels could blink, he'd buried his blades in their throats.

Furious, Deth lurched out of his bone chair. Beside him, chained naked to the base of the throne, was Sin. What had that evil fuck done to her?

"Lore, no!" The concern in her plea only fueled the fires of his anger, which was rapidly turning inferno hot.

He dipped his hand into one pocket for a cutting tool and tossed it to Sin as Deth summoned more guards. An arrow pierced Lore's shoulder from behind, and pain popped along every single nerve ending. The familiar haze came down over his vision, and for the first time in memory, he was glad for the rage.

There was nothing but weightlessness in the light. There was no sense of time, no hot or cold, nothing but a sense of peace. Then, suddenly, Idess was standing inside a white-marbled gazebo in the middle of the most beautiful world she'd ever seen. It was like marshmallow clouds raining diamonds all over fields of emerald grass and ruby roses.

Even her imagination couldn't have spun this up.

Nice to visit, but I wouldn't want to live here. No, she wanted steamy North Carolina forests, McDonalds, and demon men who dressed in leather.

Standing to her left were four angels, two females and two males, all wearing what Idess guessed were ceremonial robes. In crimson. Interesting color choice. In their hands, they held golden scythes.

Obviously, this was the Memitim Council. And none of them looked happy.

Idess dropped to one knee in a deep bow, and realized she was wearing a robe that matched theirs. It pooled around her bare feet like blood.

"Stand." A male voice compelled her to her feet. "Do you know why you have been brought here?"

"For judgment," she replied. "For failing my test."

The auburn-haired female shook her head. "You did not fail."

Idess frowned. "But Lore. I had relations with him." *I'm bonded to him.* Actually, she couldn't feel him. She cast a covert glance at her hand, where the markings still colored her skin. So maybe they were still bonded, but their link had been dropped like a call on a crappy cell phone network?

"He was not your test."

Idess tugged her robe more snugly around her. "I don't understand. Even if he wasn't my test, is it not forbidden to know any male so intimately? Let alone a demon male?"

"Exceptions are made when the outcome is positive."

Now she was really confused. "Outcome?"

"Your selflessness was your test. After your betrayal of your brother, we had to make sure you'd grown. And you have. By giving up that which was most important to you—your Ascension—for the greater good, you proved your worth. You knew what intercourse with the half-breed would cost you, yet you did it to gain entrance to Rariel's lair. By slaying him, you voided the contract on Kynan's life and ensured his safety."

"Way to go, Idess." Reaver's rumbling voice came from behind her. He was propped against a pillar, arms and ankles casually crossed. "Thought I'd pop by to watch you get your wings."

"Wings?" Her voice was barely audible, even to her ears. So many feelings mixed together…joy, ecstasy…and panic. She'd wanted this for two thousand years. Had spent entire days dreaming about it. Imagining this very moment.

She'd give it all up in a heartbeat if she could go back to Earth.

"Wings," the blond male Memitim said. "You will be assigned new duties, for Ascended Memitim are not guardians. We are judges."

Rami had once told her that guardian angels abandoned evil humans, leaving Memitim to judge them in death. Great. Fine. But she no longer wanted that job.

"But…is there to be no punishment for betraying Rami in the first place? If not for me, he wouldn't have Fallen."

The blond male snorted. "He failed his test. We never should have allowed him in."

Stunned, Idess gaped at the angels. "He didn't fail. He didn't sleep with the woman."

"He did," the male said. "Why do you think he ran from the summons light for so long?"

"To be with me…" She trailed off, feeling like a fool under the Memitim's looks of pity. *He'd lied.*

"He came to us with a stain on his soul." The auburn female glared at the blond male, and Idess knew he'd played a role in this somehow. "Rami begged us to stay, rather than return to Earth, and because he'd failed his test out of love, we gave him another chance. But his own guilt is what blackened his soul. When he found out what you'd done, it simply accelerated what was fated to be anyway."

All those years, Idess had punished herself…and for nothing.

"Come forward," the auburn-haired female continued. "You have earned your reward."

Idess froze to the floor, which might as well be ice instead of marble. "I can't."

The blond male moved toward her. "You cannot be refusing to Ascend."

"I want to stay on Earth."

"You want to be with Lore," Reaver said.

She didn't deny it. "Please. I know I'll be human. Mortal. But I love him."

"If you're mortal," Reaver said gravely, "his gift could kill you. You know that, right?"

"I'm willing to take that chance."

"What if Lore isn't willing to chance it?"

She shrugged. "I won't know until I get there."

"Be sure about this," the black-haired female said. "What is done cannot be undone."

"That's not entirely true," Reaver blurted. "You know, the done-undone thing. I'm proof of that."

The carrot-topped male who had been silent shot Reaver an annoyed look. "Stay out of this, battle angel. Don't you have demons to smite?"

"Totally. There's an exorcism planned in Melbourne today. But I have an hour to kill, and this is way cooler than X-Box."

"You make me very glad I Ascended before the age of electronics and ridiculous slang," the blond male said.

"I'm sure your age of Black Death and witch-burnings was much more fun," Reaver said dryly.

The auburn female held up her hand. "Enough." She approached Idess, her expression concerned. "You are certain?"

"Yes," she breathed, "oh, yes."

"You cannot remain as Memitim, but your service has earned you more than a mortal existence. If your reason to stay on Earth is to be with Lore, then we will bond you to him so that his power will not kill you, you can travel via Harrowgates with him, and your lifespan will be his. As a half-breed, he has centuries of life ahead of him. When he dies, so shall you, and assuming that you don't fall prey to evil, you will both be granted entrance into Heaven."

Heaven? "So...his soul *is* human." Idess could hardly breathe at that news. They would be together. Forever. "Do it," she said. "Make it happen."

"There is a price. A duty, if you will."

"Anything. Just hurry!"

"So be it." The female waved her hand, and instantly, the link to Lore was back.

With a vengeance.

Idess's knees buckled. Reaver caught her before her knees struck the floor. Darkness and rage slammed into her brain, as well as misery and sorrow.

"Lore," she gasped. Automatically, she brushed her finger over her wrist, but his *heraldi* was gone.

"You are no longer Memitim, and he is no longer Primori," the female said.

"I have to go to him." She caught glimpses of him...no, not him...but of what he was seeing. Blood. Weapons. Detharu. "He's at the den. I have to go. Send me there!"

"We can't get you inside—"

"Then outside! Now!"

The raven-haired female shook her head. "You are human now, and no match for demons in Sheoul."

"I don't care! I remember how to fight. Just send me!"

Reaver gripped her shoulders and spoke to the Council. "I got this." When Idess looked up at him, he grinned and waggled his brows. "Battle angel. Let's go kick some demon ass."

Twenty-six

⁓

They materialized in Sheoul, just outside a giant door that was guarded by two drooling Ramreels. The beasts didn't even have time to draw their machetes before Reaver went Terminator on the demons. He didn't fight them; he *demolished* them.

When they were nothing but steaming piles of quivering flesh on the ground, he brushed off his hands and pushed the door open. "I can't enter without an executive order. Good luck."

"Thank you, Reaver."

With a nod, he was gone.

Idess's bare feet slapped the floor of Deth's den as she ran, the crimson robe flapping at her legs and ankles. Dread rumbled through her, plowing into the overwhelming fury and pain the link brought from Lore.

Oh, please no. Idess exploded through the doors . . . and

skidded to a stop. Her heart slammed into her rib cage and remained there, plastered to the bone and not beating.

Lore was raging, was a bloody mess as he battled several demons. Sin was on the ground, struggling against the fierce hold of three Ramreels. Their bleeding wounds and the weapons scattered around Sin spoke of her valiant attempt to kill them before they'd taken her down.

Deth stood at his throne, snarling like a rabid dog. "You!" he hissed at her. "We had a deal!"

She swung, but her newly human body lacked the strength she was accustomed to, and Deth easily captured her. He yanked her against him, his hand jamming into her chest, and fire melted her robe and seared her skin. She screamed . . . and so did Lore. In her peripheral vision, she saw him lunge for Deth, only to be slammed to the floor by a Ramreel.

"Kill him!" Deth commanded, and as the link to Lore faded, the fresh bond on her chest flared with heat. "Kill Lore." Deth's voice was reedy with panic and fury. "Do it now!"

Killing wasn't in the terms they'd negotiated at the Guild, but the need to comply tugged at Idess anyway. Against her will, her feet shuffled toward Lore.

No. Clenching her teeth, she battled Deth's compulsion. Sweat popped out on her brow, and her nails dug deep into her palms. As she ground to a halt, her resistance to Deth's command became an agonizing sting of nettles under her skin.

Sin's curses and the harsh sounds of battle rang in her ears. Lore was fighting with everything he had, from a Ramreel's machete, to his teeth. His eyes glowed crimson, embers of hate inside his skull.

"You bitch!" Deth screamed, as Lore took down one of the Ramreels and started after the assassin master. "*I said kill him!*"

Her bond became a white-hot brand that bored all the way to her spine. Woodenly, she retrieved a machete off the floor. The Ramreels had somehow pinned Lore's killing arm beneath him. He was vulnerable.

Kill him!

Idess swung. The loss of her Memitim strength made the weapon seem heavier and her movements slower, but she took off the nearest demon's head.

Freed, Lore launched at Deth, striking him full in the chest. The demon master flew into the wall, his armor buckling like a crushed tin can. The Ramreels came at Idess, mouths dripping foam.

Oh, what she wouldn't give for a feather-light Memitim scythe right now. Heart pounding in her throat, she leaped and spun, swinging the heavy blade with practiced skill. The demons scattered, but she managed to slice one of them open across his abdomen. The other fell back with a severed hand.

She went for Deth, but Lore was already there, hacking at the larger demon, the wet thuds of metal striking flesh echoing through the chamber. The assassin master's massive wounds didn't stop him from slamming his gauntleted fist into Lore, who rocked backward with a pained hiss.

Idess whacked him with her blade, and he howled with fury and pain. She struck again. And again. The armless Ramreel barreled into her from behind, and she stumbled, momentarily taken off her game.

Her entire body screamed for vengeance. Spinning,

she sliced him open as she had the other one. He hit the ground with a thud, hands futilely trying to hold his guts.

Idess gathered every last bit of strength and swung at Deth. Her machete tore through his chest.

Deth's eyes shot wide with disbelief, and then clouded over with death as his body crumpled. Before he hit the ground, Lore's blade cut through his neck in a grisly whisper. The demon's head struck the floor a split second before his body.

Behind her, she heard another thud; Sin's Ramreel had gone down. She stood over his body, naked and panting, a bloody blade in her hand.

An ungodly snarl cut through the silence. Slowly, afraid of what she'd see, Idess turned back to Lore. He loomed in the shadows, larger than life, blood running in rivulets down his leather jacket and pants, lava flows on basalt.

"*Kill.*" The word itself was chilling enough, but it was the way he said it, the feral tone of his voice, that turned Idess's blood to slush.

Detharu's death had done nothing to calm Lore's rage. Fury contorted his expression, and his eyes were crimson lasers that targeted her for annihilation.

"Lore," she whispered, her voice raw and aching. "Lore, it's me."

He came at her. Sin screamed at him, with no effect. He tackled Idess, coming down on top of her and shoving the tip of his blade into her throat.

"Lore!" Idess gripped his hand, using every ounce of strength she had to keep him from stabbing her. "It's Idess."

Sin ran toward them, and Lore's head swiveled around. He hissed at her, tensing to attack.

"Sin! Stop!" Idess swallowed, wincing at the bite of metal in her neck. "Stay back."

Sin obeyed, but her black eyes were wild with fear.

Idess tapped her foot against Lore's leg, bringing his attention back to her. "Hey. Look at me. You can fight this." Tenderly, she ran her foot up his calf in a soothing caress. "I know you don't want to hurt me."

The pressure on her throat let up, just a little. A warm trickle ran down her neck from the cut he'd made.

"Good," she breathed. "That's good. I love you, you know that, right?" Slowly, so she wouldn't spook him, she cocked her knees up, creating a cradle for his body between her thighs. He was hard, as she expected—his rages had a sexual side effect and vice versa.

Lore's nostrils flared, and a muscle in his jaw ticked as he stared at her. It might have been her imagination, but it seemed as though the insane glow in his eyes had dimmed. Then, a low growl erupted in his chest and his head wrenched back to his sister.

"Sin," Idess said, keeping her voice mellow—soothe the savage beast and all that. "Leave. Please. Just... wait outside the door."

"But—"

The violent snap of Lore's teeth shut her up. Keeping her gaze on Lore, Sin backed out the door, closing it behind her. With Sin gone, Lore's attention turned fully to Idess. His eyes had gone back to the intense burning coal color, but he'd let up even more on the blade.

"You won't hurt me," she repeated, and though she believed it, a small part of her cowered in terror. As a human now, she was vulnerable, and this might have been a really stupid thing to do. "You were so afraid you would, but I know better." Praying she was doing the right thing, she tilted her head to the side, exposing her neck even more. "Kiss me there. Put your mouth where the blade is."

His gaze dropped to her throat, and he licked his lips with a startlingly sensual swipe of his tongue. Her senses wobbled a little, a completely inappropriate reaction given the circumstances, but that was how he affected her, and she wasn't going to feel shame for it.

"That's it," she murmured. "Kiss me. Love me. Right here in this chamber, where your life has been hell. You can turn it all around." She arched into him, and this time the noise he made was a tortured moan.

"Love me, Lore."

The blade fell away, and she breathed a sigh of relief as he lowered his head and dragged his lips from her collarbone to her jaw.

"Idess?" His voice was resonant and deep, totally foreign. "*Idess?* Is it really you?"

"It's me, Lore."

He blinked. "Am I dead?"

"No, but not for lack of trying."

Suddenly, he gathered her in his arms and held her so tight she could barely breathe. "You're real," he choked out. "I can feel you. Inside and out." He buried his face against her neck and rocked her. Wetness rolled down her skin, and she knew he was weeping.

Her big, strong demon was weeping for her. Shaken to the core, she joined him, and as her tears rolled down her cheeks, his emotions seeped into her, the bond they shared tying them together once again. The burn in her chest from Deth's mark eased, becoming merely tender, and then it was gone altogether.

"How did this happen?" he asked finally, sitting back and covertly wiping his eyes. "Did you get your wings?"

"I passed. I got you instead. And mortality. Modified."

He jerked as though he'd been stung. "You gave up being an angel? Idess, you need to go back!"

"Shh. I gave up punishing myself. It's time for me to take what I want, and what I want is you." She palmed his cheek, careful not to touch any of his wounds. "We're bonded so that our lifespans are connected. We'll be together in this life and the next one. And I can use the Harrowgates with you." Something flitted past, and she frowned. "And apparently, I can still see ghosts." *There is a price. A duty, if you will.*

He rested his forehead against hers. "Damn," he breathed. "Are you sure that's what you want?"

"Of course it is. Unless you don't?"

"Angel, now that you're back, I'm never letting you go."

There was an insistent pounding on the door, followed by Sin's muffled shout. "Hey! Are you guys okay?"

Lore pushed to his feet as Sin burst through the door.

She still brandished a sword, but she'd found clothes, a coarse burlap robe made for someone twice her size. Stark relief put a glow on her face and a smile on her lips as she ran to Lore and wrapped him in a big embrace. "Thank God you're okay." She slid Idess a glance. "And that you didn't kill my new boss."

"Excuse me?" Idess came to her feet, hoping the new altitude would clear her ears.

"Ah, yeah...'" Lore crossed to Deth and wrenched a ring off his finger. "Whoever strikes the killing blow on an assassin master takes over. That's why they maintain such high security."

"But you're the one who chopped his head off."

"After you struck the death blow. What I did was for fun." Lore shrugged. "His ring is yours. You also have to quarter his body and have the pieces sent to his four greatest enemies, and mount his head over the Guild entrance for ninety-two days." He said it like normal people would say, "You also need to bring potato salad to the picnic."

Suddenly, being human and normal—sort of—sounded really great. "So, if I take the job, can I just free all the assassins and be done with it?"

Sin glared at Deth with such malice that Idess figured he was lucky he was dead. "No. Their contracts are binding and must be fulfilled. If they break the terms, you can alter the contracts, but that's it."

"Can I give the job to you?"

"Seriously?" Sin's dark eyes flared, and then narrowed. "Why don't you want it? It's a great gig."

"I'm sort of human now." She scanned all the dead bodies, the death and destruction. "And running an assassin organization isn't exactly my dream job."

Shrugging, Sin held out her hand. "Okay."

"Okay?" Lore laughed and flipped the ring into the air at her. "That was easy."

"I told you this was all I know," she said, and a flicker of sadness crossed Lore's face. "So I might as well be the boss." She slipped the ring onto her index finger. "Hey, I know everything about everyone's contracts!" Grinning, she looked at Idess. "Yours is fulfilled."

"But he ordered me to kill Lore, and I didn't do it."

"Since I'm the new owner of the contract, I say that Deth's demise counts toward the kill he ordered you to make."

Happiness leaped through Idess, and she crushed Sin in a hug. Sin went stiff as a board, but she gave Idess an awkward pat on the back before shoving away and putting a few feet of distance between them, clearly uncomfortable with affection.

"Well, what now?" Idess asked Lore.

"Now," he said, with a lustful stare, "we head home."

His hunger slammed into her through the mate bond, intensifying her own until she was burning up on the inside. "My place or yours?" she breathed.

"Whatever's closest," he said roughly, and she was definitely on board with that suggestion.

Sin rolled her eyes. "Get outta here already."

Lore grinned. "Couldn't keep me here. If I never have to see this shithole again... well, you get the picture." He sobered then, as if maybe what he'd said wasn't true. With a jerky movement, he slipped his hand under his jacket and withdrew his Gargantua-bone dagger. "Sin, this is yours now."

"But I gave that to you."

"And no gift has ever meant more," Lore said quietly. "But I don't need it anymore. You do."

"But—"

"Tell you what," he said, cutting her off. "You can give it back to me once you're free of this life."

The fierce glint in Sin's eyes said she'd never be free of it, something Lore had to have noticed, but his expression didn't waver. He held the weapon out, and after a moment, Sin took it.

"Thank you." Sin cleared her throat of the emotional hitch in it, and suddenly, she was the carefree, breezy assassin again. "You're the best brother ever."

"Speaking of brothers," he said, in a very big-brother tone, "you need to see Eidolon right away."

"So do I," Idess said. "Now that I'm back, I can play full-time ghost exterminator after all."

Lore laughed. "He wants me to play with his dead patients."

"Are you going to?" Sin asked, and there was an underlying concern in her voice that Idess didn't understand.

"Sin—"

"It's okay." She offered a shaky smile. "I want you to work there. Get to know them." She slid the dagger into her belt with a firm shove. "Now, I have a business to run. See ya."

Idess wrapped her arm around Lore's waist, and melted into him when he tugged her close. "Will she be all right?"

"Yeah," he breathed as Sin left the room. "She's a survivor."

Idess couldn't help but wonder if that was truly enough. She'd been a survivor for two thousand years, but all that meant was that she'd existed. Now, as she hugged Lore to her, she knew that she was *living*.

Twenty-seven

Sin tapped on Eidolon's office door, even though it was open. Scowling, he looked up from a stack of paperwork, but his severe expression softened when he saw her.

"Sin. Come in."

She hesitated. All the trouble she'd caused, piled on top of the fact that Eidolon was one of the most intimidating males she'd ever met, made her a little insecure, when she'd never been that way. Ever.

He was just so...different. Lore, Shade, and Wraith radiated danger with varying degrees of humor and moodiness. She'd been around danger all her life and could deal with it. Was comfortable with it. But with Eidolon it was impossible to tell where his thoughts were, and it seemed like the calmer he got, the angrier he was. Plus, he had a logical, intelligent side she couldn't relate to at all.

Nope, chaos and street-smarts were what guided her.

He said nothing when she didn't enter right away,

merely sat there with that shuttered expression and eyes that revealed nothing. Finally, she walked over to his desk.

"Have you learned anything?"

"About why you're a...what is it called...Smurfette? Or about the plague?"

"Plague," she said softly. She didn't give a crap about the reasons behind her existence. She was alive, and that was all that mattered.

"I've got nothing," Eidolon admitted. "Your blood hasn't revealed any clues. And this disease is like nothing I've ever seen. This is a hellfuck of Sheoulic proportions."

Oh, goodie, she'd caused a hellfuck of a plague. Lore always said that when she did something, she did it well. She'd worn his words like a badge of honor, but she just couldn't find the pride in what she'd done this time.

"Usually everyone I infect develops something unique...no one dies from the same thing. Have the wargs you've seen had different symptoms?"

Eidolon leaned back in his chair. "Everything has been identical to the first victim, from the signs and symptoms, to the way their capillaries dissolved, leading to internal bleeding and ultimately, cardiac arrest. Whatever you did to the first warg has been passed to the wargs he came into contact with, though the mode of transmission is still unknown."

She frowned. "Conall came into contact with him, so why hasn't he gotten sick?"

"I'm guessing his vampire half is giving him immunity or resistance."

"Maybe there's something in his blood that can help create a vaccine?"

A small smile tipped up one corner of Eidolon's mouth. "You're wasting your talents as an assassin. You should be working here."

That was a joke and a half. "I kill, brother. *That's* where my talents lie."

"It doesn't have to be that way," he said, in a voice that dripped with moral superiority and judgment.

"You don't know anything about me or my situation," she snapped. "So don't you dare tell me what doesn't have to be."

Though his expression didn't give anything away, he tapped his fingers wildly on his desktop. "You're overreacting a little—"

"Overreacting? Bite me, asshole. The next time you start a plague that threatens to take out an entire species, you see how you react." She slammed her palms on his desk. He didn't even flinch, just kept up that maddening calm. "All I know how to do is fuck and kill, and now I've diseased not just one warg, but possibly an entire population. So tell me how I'm supposed to react."

"Is this true?" The deep, booming voice had both Sin and Eidolon wrenching their heads around to the doorway, where Conall and another, older male stood.

Neither looked happy.

Eidolon glanced at his watch. "Valko. You're early."

The red-haired male snarled and stalked into the office, his glare murderous, and Sin had a sinking feeling that he was a warg. "*Is this true?*" He jabbed a finger at her. "Is she the cause of the disease that is wiping out our people?"

Eidolon turned to her. "Sin, why don't you come back later?" It wasn't a request.

Swallowing dryly, she nodded, but when she tried to leave, the warg blocked her. "I don't think so."

Eidolon exploded out of his chair, eyes gold, teeth bared. So her brother wasn't always the cool, collected guy he probably liked to think he was. Good to know.

"Let her go. *Now.*" His voice was a lethal drawl, and in that moment, she knew she'd seriously underestimated Eidolon. He was as dangerous as any of her brothers—maybe the most dangerous, because with him, you didn't see the ax until it was at your throat.

There was a torturous silence, which struck Sin as odd, because the tension crackling in the air should have made noise. Eventually...like, when her lungs were about to explode from her held breath, the warg stepped aside. Unfortunately, that meant she had to face Conall now. He'd remained in the hallway, and as she scooted past him, he grabbed her elbow.

Eidolon's growl followed, but she raised her hand to cut him off. "It's okay," she said, but she knew he was going to keep an eye on things.

Conall's eyes flashed silver daggers. "What have you done?"

"Didn't you hear? I've started a plague that looks like it'll wipe out the whole sorry lot of you."

"Why?"

He made it sound as if she'd done it on purpose. Fine. She could play his game. "For fun. Why else?"

A muscle in his jaw ticked, and she could hear the scrape of enamel on enamel. All that grinding was probably terrible for his fangs. "Did you infect me?"

"You're very indignant for a guy who bet five hundred bucks that he could get in my pants."

He seized her by the shoulders and shook her. "Answer me!"

She smiled sweetly. "If I had, you'd already be dead. And if you don't remove your hands, that's exactly what will happen."

His expression darkened even more, and she resisted the urge to shiver as he leaned in so his fangs scratched an earlobe. "Pray no one I know dies."

"I would be careful about threatening me," she said, jerking out of his grip.

"Why? Because your brothers will come after me?"

"No. Because I will."

With that, she stalked off, head high, but inside, her stomach was churning. She couldn't shake the feeling that she'd just made an enemy out of the wrong man.

Conall watched Sin walk away, his gut roiling with a mix of emotions. Anger, lust, disappointment. He'd wanted her—hell, he still did—but she was clearly much more than a female who had fascinated him with her confidence and humor.

She was a cold-blooded killer.

He waited until she'd taken a corner and disappeared before entering E's office, where the doctor was still standing, his body coiled as though he'd been ready to tear Conall's head off. It took a full thirty seconds for Eidolon to turn his attention back to Valko, who was practically boiling with rage.

"I want that female's head," he snapped, and Conall winced, because clearly, the senior Warg Council member had no idea Sin was Eidolon's sister.

"Touch her," Eidolon said in a disturbingly reasonable voice, "and I'll make sure you're dead by the next morning."

Conall brought his hand down on Valko's shoulder. "Check up. We'll deal with her later." He gave his fellow Council member a squeeze, a silent message that right now, antagonizing Eidolon was not a bright idea.

Valko tensed, but the male wasn't stupid, and he inclined his head in a brief nod. "I want to know what you plan to do about this plague."

Dammit. Conall had warned the warg to not treat Eidolon as if the doctor was his servant, but there he went, and the demon's eyes glazed over with ice.

"I'm doing all I can—"

"It's not enough," Valko barked. "Wargs are dying. The disease has spread to three continents and fifteen countries—"

"Maybe you could do better?" Eidolon suggested. "No doubt your medical training is superior to mine."

Conall would have laughed if the situation hadn't been so dire.

Valko tensed even more, becoming a steel rod. "Apologies," he gritted out. "But I'm sure you can understand my concern."

"Of course I can." Eidolon took a seat. "But there's only so much I can do. The disease spreads so fast that putting out a call for quarantine hasn't been effective, and I haven't had any luck isolating mode of transmission. Direct contact seems to be a definite, but I don't know if the pathogen is also airborne or transmitted by indirect contact. And as far as I can tell, no one who has come into contact with the infected victims has been immune."

"Except me," Conall said.

"Yes, but likely it's your vampire blood that's allowing for immunity. We're experimenting with the possibility of using your natural antibodies to work up an immunization, but even if that's possible, it could take years to come up with something usable in pure wargs."

Conall cursed. This thing was moving so fast that he didn't think his species had years. "What can we do to help?"

Eidolon blew out a breath. "Spread the word about this. I suggest that packs stay isolated for now. Keep away from other wargs. And if you hear about anyone not contracting the disease after contact with an infected warg, I need to know about it. Immediately."

"You got it."

Valko wanted to say something about Sin; Conall knew it. But in an uncharacteristic display of restraint, he thanked Eidolon and strode out of the office. When Conall followed, the doctor cleared his throat.

"Hold up, dhampire."

Shit. Conall swung back around. "What's up?"

"What's going on between you and my sister?"

I fucked her, and man, it was good. "Nothing."

Doubt put lines around Eidolon's eyes, but he nodded. "Keep it that way."

Conall didn't say anything. He merely joined Valko in the hall. They walked in silence to the Harrowgate, and once the gate closed on them, Valko punched the symbols that would get them to Warg Council headquarters in Moscow.

When they stepped out, Valko took Conall by the arm. "I want to know everything there is to know about that female who brought this down on us. Whether Eidolon finds a cure or not, she *will* pay for what she's done. And I want you to see to it."

As soon as Conall and Valko were gone, Eidolon propped his elbows on his desk and buried his face in his hands. This had gotten out of control and beyond his ability to handle by himself.

Unfortunately, pretty much every demon doctor he knew of worked at UGH, and those who didn't were surgeons or general practitioners. He needed infectious-disease specialists working on this problem.

And, actually, they were. He'd been watching the news, keeping up on the latest medical alerts, and the disease had caught the attention of human doctors.

Anatomically, wargs were no different than humans, and physicians wouldn't pick up on the fact that the people they were treating turned into bloodthirsty beasts three nights out of the month. So yes, they were seeing a few cases of this mysterious new disease, but they would never in a million years figure out what connected them.

Still, anything they learned in their research would help Eidolon.

Just not quickly enough.

As much as he hated to do it, it was time to call in the troops.

He picked up the phone and dialed Kynan. "Hey, man, it's E. I need you to get me in touch with your Army buddy, Arik." Arik was also Runa's brother, but Eidolon didn't want to bother her right now, and besides, Kynan had worked with the guy for years and knew more about the military's secret paranormal unit than anyone.

Eidolon could hear Kynan suck air. "Jesus . . . E, I don't think getting involved with the R-XR would be a good idea."

Eidolon didn't either. "I don't have a choice. This were-wolf disease has to be stopped, but I don't have the resources to do that."

"And you're hoping the Army will help?"

"They do operate USAMRIID, and you can't tell me that the R-XR doesn't have contacts within the organiza-tion. You know damned good and well that half the para-normal unit's function is to find underworld substances and biological elements to use in warfare. They'd defi-nitely be working with someone inside the Army's Insti-tute of Infectious Disease."

Kynan's curse blistered the airwaves. "Yeah. Okay. I'll contact Arik."

Eidolon hung up, wondering if he'd done the right thing. He had no doubt that the military could help. He just hoped the price would be something he could pay.

Twenty-eight

⌐

"Beat you there." Idess darted out of the Harrowgate and raced toward her house. Lore's curse followed her, accompanied by heavy footsteps that were closing the distance between them.

"Idess." His shout held a predatory, ominous warning. "When I catch you, I'm taking you where we land."

And that was supposed to be a threat? "When? *If*," she called out.

Laughing, she picked up the pace, dodging tree branches and leaping over tree roots that wove veins into the worn path to her villa. She risked a glance over her shoulder and screamed in delight. He was nearly upon her. Intense hunger burned in his dark eyes, and she suddenly felt what it must be like to be a rabbit running from a wolf.

Somehow she scrounged up one last burst of speed, enough to make it to her front door. He caught her there, pinning her against the wood with his big body. At some point he'd lost the glove he still wore, even though she regularly drained his death power to give him temporary bits of freedom.

One hand cupped her breast and the other gripped her hip and her entire body hummed with anticipation.

"I warned you." His voice was breathless from the run and with need, the latter of which she could sense all the way to her soul.

She lifted her leg to put her aching sex in contact with his erection, and he hissed in a breath. "Right here against the door?"

"Yes." His sizzling gaze challenged her as his fingers found her jeans buttons. But she wasn't going to stop him. In fact, she nearly wept with relief at the soft yet urgent rasp of his knuckles brushing her skin as he tore open her fly. "You should wear skirts."

"With no panties?"

A wicked smile tipped up his mouth, robbing her of her ability to speak. "*With* panties. That way I can rip them off with my teeth."

The words, the images, were dizzying.

"And if I'm in too much of a hurry to take them off," he said, as he drove his hand down the front of her pants, "I can move them aside." Which he proved by tugging the silk to the side and pushing two fingers into her core.

She cried out at the wonderful invasion. "Lore..."

He braced his forearm against the door next to her head and leaned in as his fingers began a slow glide in and out. She expected him to kiss her, but instead he watched her, his breaths labored, his eyes half-lidded. Under his admiring gaze she felt like a beautiful treasure.

"I'll never get tired of looking at you," he whispered. "I want to watch you come every day. Ten times a day. A hundred."

"You say the most wonderful things," she panted. "You are never getting rid of me now." It had been a week since they'd left the assassin den forever, and she had said the same thing every day since.

"Good." He made a sinful twist with his fingers, and she arched into his hand, hanging right on the edge. "Damn, Idess. You're drenched, so wet, and all for me."

"For you," she agreed.

"Mine," he growled.

"Yours."

His fingers raked a sensitive spot deep inside that ignited her, sent flame racing through her until even her breath burned in her throat. Every pulse of her climax sang with pure, rich notes as her body churned to life.

Lore brought her down with light, gentle strokes over her center, never once taking his eyes off her. Before he'd come along, she hadn't believed that being watched during such a private, intimate moment would be so sexy, but the way his gaze grew hotter, his expression more intense, and his body harder...yes, this was something she enjoyed and wanted to repeat often. Her mind started flipping through future scenarios, more things she could do while he watched, and the fire sparked again.

"Inside," he rasped. "Now."

"What happened to against the door?" she said saucily.

"I want you so bad I'll break it." He nipped her throat before turning her around and giving her a playful slap on the bottom. "Bed. I need your bed."

She opened the door and paused at the threshold. "*Our* bed now."

Stark masculine pride and possession took over his expression. She shivered with appreciation as he swept her into his arms and carried her to the bedroom. With a gentleness she didn't expect, he placed her on the bed they'd both been chained to. Still were, in a way, and she wouldn't change a thing.

She trailed one finger along the whorls of his *dermoire*, and he marveled at the blessed sensation, didn't know if he'd ever get used to feeling something he'd stopped praying for decades ago. "You said once that you weren't always a killer. That you were more than that. You were right."

"At the time I said it, I was lying."

"And now that you aren't an assassin? Do you still think it's a lie?"

"No," he said, as he trailed kisses along her shoulder. "I'm a man with a future and a family. Because of you. My old life is over, and I can't thank you enough for that."

She grinned. "I feel the exact same way." Her hand drifted to his waist, and then lower, until he was gasping in pleasure. "For us, the end is just the beginning."

"Larissa Ione has gone straight to the top with this series."
—FallenAngelReviews.com

Please turn this page
for a preview of
the next thrilling romance in

Larissa Ione's Demonica Series

Sin Undone

Available in mass market
in September 2010

One

⌒

Sin had been summoned.

Here she was, the freaking head of an assassin den, master of over two dozen highly skilled killers, and she'd been summoned like some lowlife imp to an audience with her brother. The great demon doctor.

She'd already given him her blood, her DNA, her pee, her spinal fluid...whatever samples the doctor wanted for his research, she'd handed over. Sin was, after all, responsible for the disease that was wiping out the werewolf race.

What a claim to fame.

Sin muttered to herself as she traversed the dark hallways of Underworld General on the way to Eidolon's office. Wraith, the only one of her four brothers with blond hair and blue eyes, stood in the doorway as though he'd been waiting for her.

"Well, if it isn't Typhoid Mary."

She shot him the bird and pushed past him to enter the office, missing a step when she saw not only Eidolon, MD, but Conall, SOB.

Great. When she'd last seen the vampire-werewolf last month, they'd parted on shitty terms. Granted, she'd led him to believe she'd intentionally started the plague that was killing his people, but if he hadn't been such an ass, she might have told him the truth.

Not that the truth was much better.

"Sin." Eidolon remained at his desk, his dark eyes bloodshot and framed by dark circles. "Sit."

The command ruffled her feathers, but she hooked a chair with her foot, yanked it as far from Conall as possible, and planted her ass. "What now? I don't have any blood left, and if you think you're getting a stool sample, you can—"

"I don't need a stool sample," Eidolon interrupted. "I need your help."

She felt Con's silver eyes drilling into her, and to her annoyance, her body flushed with warmth as though remembering another drilling he'd done to her. That was *so* not happening again. She'd die before letting him so much as touch her. "What kind of help?"

"Thanks to Harrowgates and the ability to travel instantaneously, the virus has made its way to every continent except Antarctica. The death toll is climbing. The disease has a 100 percent mortality rate, a practically nonexistent incubation period, and no victim has lived longer than seventy-two hours after infection. Basically, by the time a patient arrives, we don't have a lot of time for treatment."

Jesus. It was worse than she'd thought. "Haven't you made any progress at all?"

"A little." Eidolon leaned back in his chair. "And we've discovered a half-dozen wargs who were exposed but didn't contract the infection. The R-XR is trying to determine what makes them immune."

The U.S. Army's paranormal unit was involved now? And Eidolon was working with them? She'd known that her sister-in-law, Runa, used to be a member, and that Runa's brother still was, but holy crap—it just didn't feel right for the government to be getting involved in any way with Underworld General.

"So I'm here, why?" she asked. "You in need of assassination services, or what?" She'd thrown that out just to get a
reaction from her uptight, always-in-control brother, but to her
surprise, it was Con who made the noise.

"You're here because wargs are dying, and it's your fault,"
he growled.

She wrenched her head around to peg him with a glare. Which
might have been a good plan, if he hadn't looked so damned good
in his black paramedic uniform, which set off his deeply tanned
skin and sun-streaked blond hair so beautifully. Toss in those
sterling eyes, and there was no glaring at him. Only admiring.

"Why are you even here?" she snapped, more irritable with
her reaction to him than anything. "I didn't think the disease
affected dhampires."

"I'm on the Warg Council. I'm keeping them informed."

"Well, good for you."

Eidolon cleared his throat imperiously. "Actually, you're
both here for a reason. Sin, it's time that we work with your gift.
We've got to determine a way to use it to treat the disease."

"My *gift* kills. It doesn't cure." Her *gift* was something she'd
really like to give right back to her Seminus father. Too bad he
was dead.

"Yeah, well, technically, you shouldn't exist, so I'm not
ready to write off the impossible."

Oh, she loved the reminders about how she was a freak of
nature, the only female Seminus demon to ever have been born.
"So what's your plan?"

"Can you use your gift to determine what kind of disease
resides inside a body? If you touch someone who is ill, can you
tell what he or she is sick with?"

"Sort of. I can feel the arrangement of the virus or bac-
teria or whatever. And once I learn it, I can replicate that specific
disease." She shot Conall a smirk. "Khileshi cockfire is a favorite."

Wraith laughed. Conall paled. Eidolon looked at her as if she was responsible for every case of the excruciating venereal disease he'd ever treated.

"As disturbing as that is," Eidolon said, "it's exactly what I wanted to hear."

There was a tap at the door, and Lore strode past Wraith, who was still playing doorjamb sentinel. Lore held a folder in his leather-gloved hand, and Sin didn't think she'd ever get used to seeing her twin brother in scrubs. "I read the R-XR's initial report on the immune wargs, and something stuck out. The wargs who didn't catch SF after being exposed were born wargs. So I examined the bodies in our morgue. I know not every warg that's been infected has come through the hospital, but every one who has? *Turned* warg."

Sin frowned. "SF?"

"Sin Fever," Wraith chimed in with a little too much enjoyment. *Sin Fever?* They'd named the fucking disease after her? Bastards.

E seemed oblivious to everything as he flipped excitedly through the folder. "Just when I thought we'd never find a link between the victims. I'll call the R-XR and let them know. Excellent work, Lore."

"So, what was it you wanted with me?" she asked.

Eidolon looked up from the paperwork, and the circles under his eyes seemed to have lightened a little. "About that...see, that's why I called Con to this meeting."

Bracing his muscular forearms on his knees, Con leaned forward in his chair. When he spoke, his fangs flashed as fiercely as his eyes. "What are you saying?"

"You know you were exposed to SF when you brought in patient zero." When Con nodded, Eidolon continued. "It's in your blood. Your body isn't attacking it, nor is it attacking you. But when we introduced Sin's blood to the mix in the lab, your white blood cells and hers joined forces to attack the virus. It's a major find, and we're working on developing a possible vaccine, but as I told you before, it could take months, if not years."

Sin's skin prickled with foreboding. Eidolon was dancing around something. "Skip the buildup and backstory. Bottom line. What do you want from us?"

"I need Con to feed from you," he said softly. "And I need it to happen now."

⌒

I need Con to feed from you.

Eidolon's words kept ringing in Con's ears. To Sin's credit, she wasn't ranting and raving. But then, with the *hell no* burning in her black eyes, she didn't need to. Lore looked as if he wanted to take a piece out of Con. Wraith just looked amused.

Con shoved to his feet. "As much as I'd like to help you out, Doc, I can't do what you're asking." Sure, he'd tasted Sin's blood before—and it had been damned good—but that was exactly why he couldn't do it again.

"I get that she's not your favorite person—"

"He said he can't do it," Lore growled. "Let it go, E."

Eidolon shook his head. "Unfortunately, there's no *let it go* option. This might be our only shot at a fast solution."

"I don't understand." At some point, Sin had produced a throwing knife and was now flipping it between her fingers, and Con had a feeling the speed directly related to her level of agitation. The sucker was flipping *fast*. "What do you mean, a solution?"

Eidolon tapped his finger on one of the papers on his desk, where he'd scrawled a lengthy column of numbers. "I can't inject the amount of your blood we need to destroy the virus into Conall without killing him. He needs to ingest it. As a dhampire, he has a double-chambered stomach to deliver blood almost directly into the bloodstream. So if my calculations are correct, a normal feeding will allow him to take in enough blood to start attacking the virus. Once that's done—"

"I can use my gift to learn the composition of his blood and replicate it inside someone who is diseased," Sin said.

"Exactly." Eidolon grinned. "Told you that you should be working here instead of as an assassin."

"Bite me," she snapped.

Eidolon gestured to Conall. "That'll be his job."

"No," Con said grimly. "It won't. It's not that I don't want to help. But there has to be another way."

"I agree." Sin came to her feet, her blue-black hair swishing angrily around her waist. "I don't let anyone fang me."

You let me, you little liar. Hot little liar. Man, Con wanted to call her out on that, but at least two of her brothers in the room were a little on the overprotective side, and the other didn't need an excuse to kill things.

"Look," Eidolon said. "If there was any other way, I'd find it. But there's not. And there's something else to consider."

Con didn't like his tone. Not at all. "What else?"

"You." Eidolon paused as though searching his brain for the right words, and Con's gut hollowed out. "The virus is inside you, alive and replicating like crazy. It wants out."

"Oh, Jesus," Con rasped. "I'm a fucking carrier. I could have infected people."

"Unfortunately, yes. The disease seems to be transmitted via both direct and indirect contact, as well as by air, but as an asymptomatic carrier, you might transmit it differently. We need to run tests to be sure, but since Luc hasn't come down with the virus, it's not likely that you're breathing it out or passing it on by casual touch. But you need to avoid intimate contact."

Oh, holy fuck. How many females had Con fed from and slept with in the last month? His mind raced as he counted and eliminated those who weren't werewolves. Only one had been a warg...but had she been born that way, or turned?

Con had a call to make. "Hold on, Doc." He dug his cell from his pocket, dialed, and tried to keep his pulse rate at a reasonable level. Yasashiku, a member of the Warg Council, answered on the second ring.

"Con. You're missing the meeting. Valko's about to pop a vein. Where are you?"

"I'm at work. I'll be there as soon as I can." Moving toward a corner, he lowered his voice. "Have you heard from Latisha lately?"

The sudden silence made the pulse in Con's ears pound even louder. "You didn't hear?"

"Hear what?" *Don't say it. Don't. Fucking. Say it.*

"She caught the virus," Yas said, his faint Japanese accent thickening with emotion. "She was...she died last night."

Con didn't even reply. Numbly, he closed the phone. He'd done his share of killing in his thousand years of life, some of it justified, some not. But there was something truly obscene about killing someone with pleasure.

Sure, there was no proof that he had given the virus to the ginger-haired warg. No proof at all, but the timing was right, given the timeframe from onset to death.

Crimson washed over his vision as both nausea that he'd killed an innocent female, and anger that the person ultimately responsible was right there in the room with him, collided. This had to end.

Especially since all of the risk would be Sin's.

"Con?" Wraith's deep voice was a mere buzz amongst the other noise in Con's head. "Dude. You okay? You look like you're about to take a header."

"Then I guess I'd better feed." Conall's voice was as cold as the center of his chest as he swung around to Sin. "And it looks like you're lunch."

THE DISH

Where authors give you the inside scoop!

♥ ♥ ♥ ♥ ♥ ♥ ♥ ♥ ♥ ♥ ♥ ♥ ♥ ♥ ♥ ♥

From the desk of Larissa Ione

Dear Reader,

"Family" is a word that means something different to everyone. Your family might consist of those who were born into it, or it might be made up of the people (or pets) you choose to bring into the fold. Your family members might be tight, or they might be estranged. Maybe they fight a lot, or maybe they get along beautifully. Often, family dynamics exist in a delicate balance.

So what happens when something happens to throw off that balance?

In ECSTASY UNVEILED, the fourth book in the Demonica series, I explore that question when the assassin hero, Lore, is forced to go up against his newfound brothers in a dangerous game of life or death.

In previous books, the conflicts each hero faced brought the demon brothers together to battle an enemy. In ECSTASY UNVEILED, the conflict is more internal, their bond is put to the test, and they become their own worst enemies.

Can love and trust overcome suspicion, tragedy, and an old enemy bent on tearing them apart?

When Idess, an angel bent on thwarting Lore's mission to kill someone close to his brothers, begins to fall for the coldhearted assassin, family ties are tested, betrayals are revealed, and a dark shadow falls over Underworld General Hospital.

Fortunately, "family" can also be a source of hope, and with Idess's help, Lore may yet find the family he gave up hoping for so long ago.

For more about the Demonica world and the families that make it come alive, please visit my Web site at www.LarissaIone.com to check out deleted book scenes, sign up for the newsletter, and enjoy free reads.

Happy Reading!

Larissa Ione

♥ ♥ ♥ ♥ ♥ ♥ ♥ ♥ ♥ ♥ ♥ ♥ ♥ ♥ ♥

From the desk of Laurel McKee

Dear Reader,

When I found out I had just a few days to come up with something for The Dish, I froze! There were just so many things I *could* write about that I couldn't decide. Should I talk about the rich history of late eighteenth-century Ireland? The beautiful Georgian architecture of Dublin? The gorgeous fashions? Irish music? The inspirations behind the characters? Or maybe a cautionary tale of my one attempt at Irish step dancing (there were head injuries—that's all I will say about that!).

I confessed my dilemma to my mom, who suggested we throw an Irish party with lots of Irish food and some Chieftains CDs, and then I could write about it (though there would be no dancing).

"Great!" I said. A party is always good. "But what are some Irish recipes?"

"Er—there's your grandmother's soda bread recipe," she said after some thought. "And, um, I don't know. Something with potatoes? Fish and chips? Blood pudding?"

"And Guinness," my brother added. "Every Irish party needs Guinness. And maybe Jameson."

I happily agreed. Fish and chips, soda bread, Guinness, Irish music, and you have a party! Blood pudding, though, can stay off the menu.

It was lots of fun to have what we called a "halfway to St. Patrick's Day" party. I just wish my characters, the Blacknall sisters and their handsome heroes, could have joined us. And if you'd like to try the soda bread recipe (which is supereasy—even I, officially the "Worst Cook in the World," can make it), here it is:

4 cups flour
1½ tsp. salt
1 tsp. soda
2 cups buttermilk

Preheat oven to 375 degrees.
Grease a round pan. Mix the ingredients
  thoroughly before kneading into a ball.

Cut a cross in the top, and bake for 50–60
  minutes.
Serve with fresh butter and a Guinness!

And for some background on the history and
characters of COUNTESS OF SCANDAL and the
Daughters of Erin series, be sure to visit my Web site
at http://laurelmckee.net.

Enjoy!

Laurel McKee

♥ ♥ ♥ ♥ ♥ ♥ ♥ ♥ ♥ ♥ ♥ ♥ ♥ ♥ ♥ ♥

From the desk of Lilli Feisty

Dear Reader,

For those of you who have read my previous book,
Bound to Please, you may have noticed I have a bit
of a thing for music and musicians. My latest novel,
DARE TO SURRENDER, is not about a musician,
but it's still related to music. It's about a woman whose
emotional release is to dance. She won't dance in
public; she's much too shy for that. But she dances by
herself. A lot.

And it's not just any sort of dancing; she prefers to
belly dance. She's quite good at it, better than she

thinks. In fact, Joy is better at a lot of things than she gives herself credit for, and it was great fun helping her realize that. Because don't we all have our hang-ups? And working our way through them can be quite an exhilarating release.

If you read DARE TO SURRENDER, I'll tell you right now that there are a lot of similarities between the heroine, Joy Montgomery, and myself. She's a redhead. She's not necessarily comfortable with her curvy figure. She's totally disorganized. Her handbag is the size of a small suitcase.

There's more. She works in an art gallery—I owned one. She's very spontaneous, to the point of getting herself in crazy binds because of it. I do that. A lot. She drives an old Mercedes. So do I.

So you can see we have a lot it common. Except the dancing in public thing. To put it simply, I love to dance. Am I any good at it? Probably not. But I simply can't help myself. If I'm out, and I hear a good beat, I'm lured to the dance floor. In fact, I tend to dance at any opportunity, however inappropriate. It was quite pathetic, but just the other day, I was reprimanded at the grocery store for doing the Wang Chung in the frozen food aisle.

However, let me tell you, belly dancing is not as easy as it looks. To be good, you have to be able to move separate parts of your body at varying speeds and rhythms. For some people (me), it's not easy. But that's irrelevant—it's fun, and once you let yourself go, it really doesn't matter how good you are. You feel the music take over your body and you want to shimmy. To undulate. To dance! I think belly dance is one of the sexiest, most feminine, mesmerizing forms of dance there is.

Some people assume belly dance was created for the sole purpose of entertaining men. In fact, this is not true. It was invented by women, for women. I think that's why it's such a sexy form of dance. When you belly dance, you're celebrating being a female. You use your hips, your arms, your waist. And, of course, your belly. And you don't need to worry if your belly is a bit round because it's about having fun and using your body to express yourself. And let's not forget the costumes. Belly dancing costumes are pretty darn gorgeous.

So this is Joy's hobby. And it's mine too. The only difference is that Joy is too shy to do so in public so she only practices in her own bedroom. (Also Joy is way better at it.) Of course, when she meets Ash Hunter, he slowly begins to chip away at Joy's inhibitions. But does he get her to dance in public?

Well, I won't give away the ending. But I will say, by the end of their story, Joy is ready to take the dare to surrender everything, even if it means embracing every facet of her femininity.

I hope you enjoy their story.

XXOO,

Lilli Feisty